THE
TWINS
ON THE
TRAIN

BOOKS BY SUZANNE GOLDRING

My Name is Eva

Burning Island

The Girl Without a Name

The Shut-Away Sisters

The Girl with the Scarlet Ribbon

The Woman Outside the Walls

The Girl Who Never Came Back

SUZANNE GOLDRING

THE
TWINS
ON THE
TRAIN

bookouture

Published by Bookouture in 2024

An imprint of Storyfire Ltd.
Carmelite House
50 Victoria Embankment
London EC4Y 0DZ

www.bookouture.com

Storyfire Ltd's authorised representative in the EEA is Hachette Ireland
8 Castlecourt Centre
Castleknock Road
Castleknock
Dublin 15 D15 YF6A
Ireland

ISBN: 978-1-83525-619-0
eBook ISBN: 978-1-83525-618-3

In memory of Rachel Goldring
a lifelong Quaker

It is necessary only for the good man to do nothing for evil to triumph.

EDMUND BURKE (1729-97), *THE OXFORD DICTIONARY OF QUOTATIONS, FOURTH EDITION*

This is the second time in our history that there has come back from Germany to Downing Street peace with honour. I believe it is peace for our time.

NEVILLE CHAMBERLAIN, BRITISH PRIME MINISTER 1937-40, SPEECH FROM 10 DOWNING STREET, 30 SEPTEMBER 1938

PROLOGUE

ESTHER, 2023

Esther peers through half-closed eyes as she watches the young woman threading her way around the care home's lounge. A smile here, a light touch on the hand there, feigning intense interest in each of the elderly residents. She bends right over them, kneels down beside their chairs sometimes to look into their blotched, wrinkled faces, persuading them to reveal their memories, both remembered and imagined.

Esther's pretending to be asleep. She's avoided talking to this volunteer so far, but she's bound to get picked on one day. Life story coordinator, that's her grand title. Some of the home's residents love talking to her, showing her their family photos, telling her how their parents met, where their grandparents lived and describing a family tree filled with aunts, uncles and cousins, but not Esther.

Of course, the home means well, and so does this woman. What is her name? Becky, Betty, or something like that? A do-gooder with time on her hands probably. Other people here might appreciate it, but Esther doesn't want to talk to her, doesn't want to tell her the story she doesn't know the end to.

Maybe she could keep pretending to be asleep. That

worked last time, but the woman stayed so long, Esther nearly missed out on the chocolate biscuits served with their milky morning coffee. Only plain digestives left by the time she opened her eyes.

Or perhaps this time she'll give the woman a shock. Give her something she'd never expected to hear. Tell her the truth, tell her how much Esther doesn't know about the start of her life. Yes, I'll let this Becky-or-Betty woman ask the questions, encourage her to talk, then surprise her.

Esther rehearses what she'll say in her head. She'll say, I'd like to tell you my life story, but I suspect I don't know the half of it. I don't blame you kind people who come here to help us oldies talk about our memories, it's good for a lot of them. But the trouble is, I know hardly anything about the beginning of my life.

You could try talking to my brother Josef as well; his daughter always brings him in to see me on a Thursday afternoon. But he doesn't know any more than I do. Anyway, he's starting to forget the little he ever knew in the first place. I may be doddery on my legs, but my brain's sharp as a pin. It's not that I've forgotten anything about my life, it's just that there's lots I've never known and never will.

Josef and I have been told that we're twins, and we know when we were born, but we don't know much more than that. All I do know is that we've both had a good life. We were well educated, we've had good jobs, been married and we have families. Josef has two sons and a daughter and six grandchildren. I've got four daughters and twelve grandchildren, plus a newborn great-grandson. Steven, they're calling him. I'd like to think that might be a family name but, you see, I have simply no idea who came before us. Aunts, uncles, cousins, parents, all gone. We never knew them, never knew we had them.

But you can see we've done our best to replace those who were lost, though we can never do enough to make up for the thousands, the hundreds of thousands, the millions who lost their lives. We were the lucky ones, Josef and I. We were saved.

I've tried to make myself learn about what must have happened. It's all terrible of course, but without knowing all the names of our family members it's meaningless. We just don't know. Were they sent away on the pretext of being given work? Were they all crammed into a filthy ghetto that shrank around them bit by bit with each new consignment of terrified people? Did they die of thirst on a hot summer's day, roasting in a cattle truck, or were they herded into a gas chamber as soon as they left the train?

The more I ask myself these questions, the more I look at what was done, the more I shy away from wanting to know. I can only know our story, mine and Josef's, and give thanks every day that our mother, Rosa, took that risk, giving us away to a total stranger. We were saved, we were given a chance to live.

Yes, that'll give this Becky-Betty a bit of a shock. It'll be a bit different to the stories the rest of them are telling her, their boring tales about their safe, ordinary lives. She'll be surprised to come across one of us. One of the train children. So many of us were saved, thanks to Dora, a young woman who risked her life and her marriage for us. So, I'll start by telling this helpful volunteer all about her and tell the story Dora told to us so many times.

ONE

THE ARMS OF A STRANGER

BERLIN, MAY 1939

Dora couldn't stop herself comparing the time on her watch to that of the station clock. The train had been due to leave at ten in the morning and it was already nearly half past that. As far as she could tell, all the seats were now taken and there were no more children waiting on the platform. Their parents waited though. They waited to see their children depart, knowing this might be the last time they saw them, but hoping they would soon return, well fed and grown stronger and taller from the care they were going to receive from their foster-families in Britain.

Dora had accompanied several similar groups of children since the Kindertransport was first authorised in December 1938. But tensions were rising and this might even be the last such journey she would undertake. Every time she and Brenda travelled back to Berlin to escort another group, they wondered if this might be their final trip. Germany's invasion of Czecho-slovakia in March and news of Britain's rearmament the following month had not reassured them at all.

Stepping aboard, Dora could hear the excited chatter of the train's labelled occupants above the clamour of the busy station.

All were identified by a luggage tag strung round their necks. A few had trembling lips and faces wet with tears, but most were stoical, believing this was going to be a great adventure and that it wouldn't be for long. Some knew they would be received by open arms belonging to familiar faces; aunts and uncles who had left Germany over the last few years, to make new lives in a new country. Others didn't know where they were destined for but trusted in their parents' advice that they were in safe hands and that it was 'only until this is all over'.

She turned to count the children in her carriage, all wearing their winter coats despite the warmth of this sunny early summer's day, because they were only allowed to take one case each and their mothers were sending them away with clothes for the seasons to come. All clutched bags and parcels of food for the journey. Little though there was to spare, their parents had ensured their children would not go hungry during their travels. Dora thought of her own dry bread and waxy cheese, and hoped she wouldn't have to dip into her meagre rations to feed any extra-hungry child. On previous journeys like this, once they had crossed the border into Holland the trains had always been greeted warmly by Dutch farmers' wives. Hot chocolate and fresh milk to drink, newly baked loaves and bars of chocolate to share had been distributed among the carriages, leading the children to believe they had left a land of little to spare and entered a land of plenty.

Dora could feel the train begin to shudder, as if it was tensing itself for the start of a race. Clouds of steam and smoke wafted along the platform. She was just about to pull the carriage door shut and close the window when she saw a young woman weaving her way through the huddles of anxious relatives holding hands and waiting to wave farewell to their young ones. A small girl, about seven years old, trotted close to her side. The woman rushed towards the train bearing a large wicker hamper. Before Dora could say anything, she shoved the basket into Dora's hands, saying, 'Bitte, nimm sie.' Then she grabbed the girl's hand and ran away through the close-packed crowds of worried parents before Dora could ask what was happening.

It seemed strange, but strange things kept happening with these journeys. Perhaps the woman had been able to collect extra provisions for the children already on the train, Dora thought, as she laid the basket down in the corridor and closed the door securely. Though what she meant by saying *take them*, Dora couldn't be sure. The basket was certainly heavy in her arms as she shuffled back to her seat in the compartment, where she had left her valise to reserve her place.

She wondered for a fleeting second whether she should leave opening the hamper until she knew for certain that extra food would definitely be needed. After all, the children already had adequate provisions, but if they saw something they liked better in the basket it might make them feel dissatisfied or inclined to waste their carefully provided packages. But then, if it was filled with fresh produce it might be better to consume that early on in their journey.

Dora remembered one Christmas when her mother had ordered a hamper from Fortnum & Mason, the royal grocer's on Piccadilly. It had contained not only tins of shortbread and chocolate, wine and port, but also a waxed wheel of cheese and a golden-crumbed ham wrapped in muslin.

Dora could not resist taking a look. She asked the boy sitting next to her to lift her case up into the luggage rack, which he did by standing on her seat somewhat precariously. She set the heavy basket down in her place, knelt down and undid the two buckled straps fastening the woven lid, then lifted it open with a creak of wicker and leather.

She stared in utterly shocked silence at the contents. There was no cheese, no ham, nor wines. There were certainly no biscuits, savoury or sweet. The only edible things in the basket were two bottles of milk with rubber teats. Baby bottles. For sleeping soundly in the depths of the basket were two tiny babies, swaddled in shawls and cushioned with wads of clean, folded napkins.

Dora dashed back to the carriage window and frantically scanned the platform for any sign of the young woman. Poor desperate mother, so afraid of what was coming that she was prepared to hand her newborn babies to a total stranger. Who was she? How would Dora ever be able to reunite her with her children?

There must be some information in the basket, she thought. And where was the documentation that would ensure she could take these little ones past the scrutiny of the German guards? Two soldiers were usually assigned to each transport and this time they had already given the children and their luggage a perfunctory check. With luck they might spend the rest of the journey sleeping and playing cards in the goods van, as they often did. But sometimes the trains stopped before they ever reached the Dutch border and more soldiers boarded to check papers and even ransack the children's suitcases all over again, to their immense distress.

Dora turned back to the basket, which had already attracted the attention of the young passengers seated nearby. They were peering inside and a little girl gently pulled the shawl away from one of the peaceful faces. A bubble of milk dampened the lips of one baby and it pursed its rosy mouth in its sleep.

'Shush,' Dora said, putting a finger to her lips. 'We must try not to wake them.' She felt around the sides of the hamper and her fingers touched paper. Thank goodness, there was an envelope, hopefully containing everything that would ensure a safe journey for these infants.

But it didn't contain travel documents or tickets. There were just two photographs, one of a solemn-looking man and

woman, the other a picture of a dark-haired baby, and a letter
headed with a Berlin address:

112 Rosen Strasse, Scheunenviertel

To whom it may concern

*Please take care of my two-week old twins. They were born on
2 May 1939. I have named the girl Esther and the boy Josef.
Their family name is Goldberg, which was also the name of our
tailoring and dressmaking business until we were forced to
close. My husband was arrested several months ago, before I
gave birth. I believe he has been sent to Dachau and I despair
of his return. If I should also be arrested or if I should fall ill,
my babies would be sent to a Jewish orphanage and so I fear for
their lives. These are dangerous times, so I beg you to take them
away to safety. Please write to me at the above address so I will
know they have reached England and let me know where I can
find them once we can be assured of our future. I fed my children myself this morning, so they should sleep for a couple of
hours. They are both freshly changed and I have packed their
basket with clean napkins. I hope I have provided enough milk
and linen for the journey.*

I wish you a safe journey. Leich l'shalom.

Rosa Goldberg

As Dora read these words, her heart felt heavy with this
woman's pain. What a dreadful decision for any parent to have
to make. But for a new mother, breasts swollen with milk, womb
still bleeding, even more so. She could imagine how in a couple
of hours, when the babies woke and cried to be fed, the mother's
breasts would swell and leak, as if they viscerally sensed that

message appealing to them from a distance, even as the train rattled along miles of track towards the border.

'We must take great care of these little ones,' she said, looking around the compartment at the solemn children watching her. 'But we must keep it a secret until we are in Holland.' All the heads nodded in serious agreement as they and Dora heard the whistle outside, signalling that the train could depart.

They felt the first shudder of the great iron wheels turning and soon they were sliding past the platform and out into the countryside around the city. Dora breathed a sigh of relief and prayed that the train would not stop until they were safely across the border and were welcomed by the smiles and plump arms of Dutch farmers and their wives.

She clasped her hands around the basket, holding it steady on her lap. How could it have come to this, that a young mother was prepared to throw her newborns into the hands of someone whose name and position she didn't even know? She must have heard of the good work being done by the Quakers with the help of Jewish agencies and that would have given her some confidence that her little ones would be safe. But she could not possibly know who would feed the babies, who would change them, bathe them and care for them until they could be reunited with their mother.

Dora's fear almost engulfed her. How was she going to keep these babies safe and ensure they survived this journey? Her trembling limbs shook in time with the rumbling of the iron wheels on the track.

As the train gathered speed, she thought back over the past five years and wondered how they could not have seen the storm coming. Despite all she knew about the dangers in Germany, she could never have predicted a day when a new mother would rather give her tiny babies away than keep them by her side.

TWO
PASSIONATE TIMES
GERMANY, MAY 1934

Even years later, when Dora tried to explain how she had known that terrible times were brewing in Germany, she couldn't quite think when she had first felt the threatening clouds. Like many British visitors, she and her family were very fond of the country, its forests and lakes and its beautiful cities and towns. She even had a dear penfriend, whose letters and visits had helped her to become fluent in the language. But it was in 1934, when she went to see the Oberammergau Passion Play in Bavaria at the tender age of twenty, that she first saw how the mood of the country was changing.

Dora knew that the play about the life of Jesus was world-famous and had been staged since the seventeenth century. But she hadn't realised quite how many tourists, as well as Germans, would flock to the village in southern Germany for this partic-ular performance. This year the production was going to be even more special. It was the 300th anniversary of the very first enactment and the open-air auditorium had been expanded to accommodate 5,000 spectators. And this was also the first time the play had been staged since Hitler had come to power in January the previous year. Everyone knew that he was going to be attending and whether people were excited to see him or the play, or maybe both, Dora was startled to see how many members of the Hitler Youth and the so-called Brownshirts were among the crowds, as well as large numbers of officers. Everywhere she looked, there were clusters of grey-green and brown uniforms, worn by strapping young men who were surrounded by awestruck civilians.

Dora had been persuaded to attend the play with her cousin Verity, whose grandmother, the Dowager Lady Ponsonby, thought it would make a marvellous twenty-first birthday present for her favourite granddaughter. 'You might meet a charming German or Austrian count there,' she said. 'They're so correct and polite. I'd be delighted to see you bearing a title, my dear, even if it was a foreign one.'

Verity's father, Lord Ponsonby, had approved of the trip too, but then he also approved of the man leading the British Union of Fascists who seemed so keen to emulate the ideals of their German counterparts. 'Sensible chap, Mosley, like this Hitler fella,' Sir Peregrine said when he was recounting Oswald Mosley's visit to the family's Yorkshire pile, Featherstonehaugh House, pronounced 'Furstoner', an eccentric pronunciation that flummoxed many a new house guest invited for the shooting and fishing in season.

But Dora's father took a more cautious view. When he heard of their planned trip to Oberammergau he took her aside and said, 'Keep your eyes open, my dear. Don't be fooled into thinking all is well. There's a strong suspicion that these new Nazi types are taking advantage of this village's charming tradition. They'll use it to their advantage to slander the Jewish population still further.'

Dora didn't fully understand this remark of his at the time, but as the play progressed there was more than one scene in which the audience accused Jewish Germans of the death of Jesus. When Pontius Pilate asked the centurions who had arrested Christ to state his crime, before the head guard could even answer the crowd roared, 'He says he is King of the Jews! And they're the ones who killed him!'

As she concentrated on the drama, set against the vast backdrop of the sky and mountains around this quaint Bavarian village, she felt increasingly uneasy. It was picturesque and charming, yet also unsettling. All the roles were played by a cast of villagers, supported by goats, horses and donkeys. The simple home-made costumes with cloaks and sandals evoked familiar artistic scenes of biblical times, but Dora was also constantly reminded of the underlying message this year's performance was striving to convey. This was no innocent, harmless pantomime, this was now shameless political propaganda.

When Judas Iscariot made his appearance, he was dressed in yellow. 'Look at him,' she heard audience members muttering. 'He's wearing the colour that has always marked out the Jews.' Dora instantly felt a prickle of distaste crawl down her neck at those words. And when the actor in the leading role, tied to the cross in the final, dreadful scene, uttered the phrase, 'Father, why hast thou forsaken me?' thousands of voices shouted, 'The Jews have forsaken you! They're the ones to blame!' It was as if nearly all the members of the audience had learnt their lines as well as the actors.

Afterwards, still shaken by the emotional acting and the highly charged response of the enormous crowd, the girls began walking back to their lodgings, in a colourful wooden Bavarian house that reminded Dora of a cuckoo clock she had once seen in a neighbour's home. She half expected the master and mistress of the house to take turns to pop out of the front door to greet them on the hour. The day they arrived, strong young men clad in white shirts and leather breeches had heaved the girls' cases from their coach, their tanned limbs displaying firm muscles. All wore lederhosen with embroidered braces and the women of the house were dressed in skirts and blouses decorated with folk art motifs that probably hadn't changed in centuries.

Dora had at first been charmed by the traditional houses, the friendliness of their hosts and the cleanliness of their accommodation. Feather mattresses and feather quilts dressed their beds, causing Verity to say, 'How quaint! But then I haven't seen many sheep, so maybe they don't have woollen blankets here.'

The repetition of sausages and cheese with black bread, at both their breakfast and their midday meal, also didn't please Verity, who said, 'Surely it wouldn't hurt them to give us some white rolls?'

Dora chided her intolerant cousin, using her childhood nickname. 'Vee, I'm perfectly happy to eat whatever they usually have here. It was the same whenever I visited my penfriend. And everyone looks remarkably healthy on this diet.'

But late in the evening after the play was over, when they were walking through the cheering crowds, passing inns where men and women were sitting with huge tankards of foaming German beer, Dora felt that the initial gloss of the occasion was wearing off fast. Already intoxicated by the mood of the play, the drinkers were clinking their steins, beer spilling over tables and bodies, belting out rousing drinking songs with gusto. Uniformed men of various kinds were gathered everywhere, young and old, and she felt uneasy at seeing such a large military force infiltrating this historic village. Then she remembered her father's warning and truly understood its meaning. 'Keep your eyes open,' he'd said.

'What did you think of it, Vee?' Her cousin was glowing and smiling and waving to the drinkers they passed, but particularly to the smart blond officers dressed in black and silver uniforms, who saluted her and clicked their heels.

'Wasn't it all simply magnificent?' she said, fluttering her fingers at yet another tall, handsome officer. 'And as for Hitler, I thought he was just wonderful. So forceful and charismatic. Everyone adores him.'

Dora recalled the fawning crowds admiring him, kept at bay by his entourage. She hadn't found him impressive, in his ordinary brown suit and tie. But she'd noticed the fervent reaction of the audience, the constant saluting, the shouts of 'Heil Hitler'.

'The performance wasn't quite what I'd been expecting,' she said. 'It implied that the Jews will forever be considered guilty of Christ's death.'

'Well, so what? They are guilty, aren't they? I've heard people saying that Hitler says the play convincingly portrays the menace of Jewry.' Verity waved again and a very good-looking, young, uniformed man strode across from his companions. He gave a deep bow in front of her and kissed her hand. Verity giggled and for once, to her credit, she blushed.

'Gnädige Fraulein,' he said and bowed again.

Dora pulled her cousin's arm and hissed, 'We don't know these people. We haven't been properly introduced. For goodness' sake, we must go back to our lodgings. It's nearly eleven o'clock.'

'Oh, but they all look so handsome. Couldn't we stay and talk for just a little while? We'll be perfectly safe here. Everyone is simply lovely.' Verity looked over her shoulder at her admirer as Dora pulled her away and quickened her pace.

'Stop it, Vee. You're drawing attention to yourself. Well, to both of us, come to that.'

'Oh, very well, spoilsport. You're no fun at all. I shan't take you with me tomorrow if you carry on being so mean.' Verity shook off her cousin's firm grip on her arm.

'What are you saying, where are you going? I thought we agreed we'd stay here in the village. There's still lots to see and I don't mind at all visiting one of the cafés during the daytime. I just think it's getting rather late now and a lot of people have been drinking enormous amounts of beer. Our fathers wouldn't approve.' Dora hoped this last remark would remind Verity how she should behave.

'Oh, well, I suppose I did say we'd stick together, so if you promise not to be such an old stick-in-the-mud, I'll let you come with me.'

'Where to? What have you got planned?'

'We're going to see one of the great innovations of this new government. Daddy said we'd be astonished at what they're achieving here. He says Hitler is working absolute wonders in this country and we would do well to copy some of his ideas.'

Dora stopped walking and turned to look at her cousin. 'So, what are we doing? Are you going to tell me, or aren't you?'

Verity smiled, her eyes shining. 'We are going to have a private escorted tour of one of the projects that will make this country strong and powerful. It will be so exciting. We are being taken to see Dachau by two charming officers.'

THREE
MODEL PRISONER
DACHAU, MAY 1934

The next morning, Verity was glowing with delight at the prospect of their guided tour with two handsome young men. 'Daddy says that a country that lost a war has to really pull its socks up. And look how well Germany is doing now.' The girls were being driven by the uniformed officers in a gleaming black Mercedes-Benz with polished seats from the humble simplicity of Oberammergau towards Dachau, which was near Munich. The scent of car wax and leather was overladen by the cologne worn by one of the well-groomed young men.

Dora wasn't looking forward to the tour one bit, but didn't feel she could abandon Vee. They had embarked on this trip to Germany on the understanding that they would stick together. She had gathered that they were being taken to see a model prison, which she wouldn't have expected to be recommended as a desirable destination for visitors to the country. But Verity said other English tourists who had already seen the play were saying Dachau was quite marvellous and everyone could learn from its example.

Dora tried to tell herself that all countries had to have prisons and this would be no worse, maybe better even, than any in Britain. Aunt Vera, her father's sister, had often talked about her voluntary work in English women's prisons and how she had been proud of teaching several inmates to read, which would help them get better-paid jobs at the end of their sentences.

And after all, Dora told herself, people fall by the wayside everywhere and can be rehabilitated and lead better lives in the future. But she rather thought that her cousin's motivation for the visit was more the presence of their handsome blond escorts. Their driver and his companion told them the prisoners were 're-educated through work'. Heinrich had a gleaming smile that had made a deep impression on Verity, and Friedrich tried to enamour Dora, but she stared resolutely out of the window at the fresh green countryside, where milk cows grazed lush grass in the sparkling sunshine.

When they arrived at their destination, the men opened the car doors and escorted the girls to the camp entrance, set within a wide stone arch. The heavy, barred iron gates contained a smaller door, through which they stepped into the well-swept prison grounds. All seemed very orderly as they were greeted by an official, who started the tour by leading the group to a workshop where a number of men in prison uniform were concentrating hard on their task, bent over lathes at benches. Wood shavings littered the floor and the air was filled with the smell of sawdust littering the workplace. Shafts of sunlight pierced the windows, capturing motes of dust dancing in the air as the men planed and shaped the wood.

'The workers here are involved in preparing timber for our construction programme,' their guide said. 'We are planning many more buildings here at Dachau. We have plans for considerable expansion.' He waved a proud hand across his solemn workforce, who glanced briefly at the visitors, then lowered their heads again to focus on their task.

'Oh, that's a shame,' Verity said, 'I was rather hoping they'd be making those adorable dark wooden carvings we've seen everywhere. Black Forest carvings, I think they're called. They look just like something out of a fairy tale, like *Hansel and Gretel*. I'm longing to take a pair of gorgeous little carved bear bookends home with me for Granny, as a thank-you for this marvellous trip.'

'Schwarzwälder Schnitzereien,' Heinrich said, with an approving nod. 'I know the best place to buy such wooden carvings. We are very proud of our traditional crafts in Bavaria and they are very popular with our many visitors from other countries.'

Dora had no such thoughts as she scanned the workshop, wondering what had brought these men here. They appeared to be clean, well fed and industrious. The prisoners were all intent on their work and there was no noise apart from the buzz of the lathes and Verity's chatter. Perhaps this was a model prison after all.

The group emerged into warm sunshine and were shown a clean barracks with bunks and straw mattresses, where they were told the prisoners were housed. A neatly folded blanket lay at the end of each bed.

As they strolled the freshly swept and weeded paths around the buildings, their guide pointed out another block, saying that was the accommodation for Schutzstaffel officers who were training to become prison guards. 'Dachau is a great success and is the model for many other sites we shall have elsewhere. Our young men will learn the best way to implement our system in similar installations across the country.'

'This site was once a munitions factory,' Friedrich said, 'but we have no need for munitions now that our country is at peace.' He pointed to a workforce in the distance from which they could hear the faint thuds and bangs of construction. 'The men over there are demolishing the remains of the old factory buildings, where they will then build more barracks and workshops.'

'Dachau has only been open for just over a year,' their guide said. 'There is still much work to be done but we are pleased with our progress so far and particularly with the improved behaviour of our residents. We are confident that our achievements here will be a great help to our country's future.'

'What crimes have your prisoners committed?' Dora asked. 'If you don't mind me asking.'

She caught a glance flit between their guide and the two officers escorting them.

'This kind of organisation is best suited to disruptive elements,' Heinrich said. 'Common criminals, those who steal and commit the worst crimes, are imprisoned elsewhere. And unfortunately, some may not be suitable for rehabilitation.'

Dora caught his meaning. Britain exercised the death penalty, as well as harsh corporal punishment. Neither met with her approval, but she knew it was not unusual even in civilised countries.

'But here we believe in Arbeit Macht Frei,' Friedrich said. 'Good honest work will encourage the inmates to think about their responsibilities and correct their attitudes. They will leave here as reformed citizens.'

'Gosh, that is so sensible,' Verity said. 'Just like being given lines and detention in school, don't you remember, Dora?' She giggled. 'No, of course you don't. You were always such a perfect little Goody Two-shoes. I seemed to get them all the time. Such a terrible bore.'

Just then a scream pierced the air, followed by shouts and what sounded like a shot. Their guide's head jerked round towards the construction workers on the far side of the site. 'Forgive me,' he said. 'I must go and check on them. Sometimes accidents occur, despite all our precautions.'

He marched towards the demolition site on the far side of the prison.

'I hope you have gained a good impression of our work here,' Heinrich said, steering them back towards the entrance and the waiting car.

'And I hope you have seen enough of our system to feel it was worth the journey,' Friedrich said.

'Oh, it's been absolutely fascinating. I'm so impressed, but I don't know what on earth we're going to do for the rest of the day,' Verity said. 'After that marvellous performance yesterday, I'll feel totally miz and rather let down if we don't have any more excitement to look forward to.'

'Then perhaps you will allow us to take you into Munich,' Heinrich said. 'We would be honoured to take you to the Carlton Tea Room for afternoon tea. It would be our pleasure. The café is a great favourite with our Führer and he takes tea there nearly every day.'

'Oh, yes please,' Verity gushed, her eyes bright with excitement. 'Do you think we might even see him there? That would be simply wonderful.'

Her words made both the officers laugh as they assured her that they might not be in luck today, but that Hitler was a frequent visitor there.

Dora couldn't think of anything worse, but stayed quiet. She'd been hoping this association with the two Nazi officers could end quickly, but that seemed unlikely now. Perhaps she could claim tiredness after the long hours they had spent at the passion play the day before.

FOUR
TIME FOR TEA
MUNICH, MAY 1934

The Carlton Tea Room was situated on Briennerstrasse in an elegant quarter of Munich and was clearly very popular. When the party entered the high-ceilinged room, every table was occupied apart from one. The maître'd bowed to the two officers and assured them he would be delighted to seat them if they didn't mind waiting for a moment.

Dora noticed him scurry hastily to a corner table to speak to the family sitting there, who left immediately. She hoped they had enjoyed their tea, even if their time had been cut short, but thought she spotted half-eaten portions of cake remaining on the plates before they were cleared away.

When the group took their places at the freshly laid table, they had a good view of the entire restaurant. The high walls were studded with mirrors and bracketed wall lights, giving the whole place a warm glow. Scents of cinnamon, vanilla and baking teased the senses with a promise of the delights to come.

Studying the menu, Verity asked Heinrich to help her choose. 'They have such a lot of lovely cakes. What does Herr Hitler order when he is here?'

'The Führer's favourite is Apfelkuchen. I have it on good

authority that a fresh apple cake is also baked for him every day in his apartment nearby.'

'Gosh, every day? Surely he doesn't eat it all himself? He looks very fit and slender.'

Heinrich smiled and nodded. 'He is a fine example of restraint to us all.'

Dora didn't want to order apple cake, which her mother often baked. She wanted to taste something new. The menu listed cakes she had never heard of before and, although she asked Friedrich to explain them to her, he was struggling to find the English words for the different culinary processes.

'This one,' he said, pointing to a cake called Agnes Bernauer, 'has kaffe crème and hard, sweet egg. And this one is crêpes with cream.'

Neither sounded very likely to Dora, but then Heinrich added, 'But they will bring them to us on a trolley. You will be able to see for yourself and then choose.'

The first cake with the hard, sweet egg turned out to be thin layers of coffee meringue sandwiched with coffee-flavoured cream and the second, called Prinzregententorte, did look rather like a pile of crêpes but was actually made with the thinnest of sponges, about eight layers of them, filled with more cream. In the end, after admiring all the beautiful cakes on display, both girls and the two officers chose Schwarzwäldekirschtorte, as Heinrich said it was a speciality of the region.

The large portion of chocolate cake was filled with cherries that had been soaked in kirsch and was served with whipped cream. 'Schlagsahne,' Friedrich said helpfully, when he asked for an extra serving for the table.

Dora let a forkful of the delicious concoction melt in her mouth, thinking this treat was making the afternoon almost bearable. Verity didn't want to eat the delicate curls of chocolate that decorated the top. Dora was tempted to scoop them onto her plate, but thought that might look unladylike.

She had nearly finished her cake and was about to scoop up the last remaining piece when a hush fell across the whole establishment. Four men were being led towards the vacant table in the centre of the restaurant. Three were in dark uniforms and one wore a plain brown mackintosh over a brown suit.

Dora noticed how still the customers all were, watching this arrival. Their mouths, in many cases, were open; teacups hovered near gaping lips and forks had frozen in mid-air.

Verity nudged her. 'That's him,' she whispered. 'Oh my goodness, it's Herr Hitler. Oh, my word, I can't eat another mouthful. I can't believe he's actually here, right here in front of us.'

Once the party was seated, the room again became animated. But not as it was before. It was as if everyone was on their best behaviour in the presence of a stern godparent. The previously buzzing conversation was hushed, cups no longer chinked, but heads kept turning to snatch glimpses of this important table with its eminent guests.

Dora soon realised that Verity couldn't stop staring at Hitler and his party. She had ceased eating and drinking altogether, although both the officers were still trying to engage her in conversation.

'Don't gawp like that, Vee. He's nothing special to look at.' Dora thought Hitler looked shabby and insignificant. And she personally considered his moustache ridiculous. Charlie Chaplin wore a moustache with much more panache.

Verity let out an exaggerated sigh. 'Oh, I've died and gone to heaven. I can hardly believe I'm actually here right now, this close to him.'

'We are most fortunate to be here today, in the presence of our Führer,' Friedrich said. 'And I believe that is indeed the famous apple cake, being cut for him at the table this very moment.'

'Then that's what I'm having next time,' Verity said. 'It must be exceptionally good if the most important man in Germany likes it.'

'It is certainly very good here. And look, he takes it with Schlagsahne, just like us.'

Dora glanced towards the table of interest to everyone in the whole restaurant and noticed that two children were being led across to be introduced. There was a girl with long blonde plaits and a fair-haired boy. Both were six or seven years of age. The table's occupants shifted and the children were seated either side of Hitler.

'Oh, look at the little darlings,' Verity said in a breathy voice. 'They can't possibly know how lucky they are, having the chance to actually sit right next to him.'

Hitler put an arm round each child and lowered his head to speak to them one after another. Their mother stood alongside, beaming and encouraging them to speak. But the little boy kept looking up at her and biting his lip as if he was trying not to cry, while the girl's face bore a sulky expression.

They don't want to be there, Dora thought. *They look like I used to feel when I was that age and I was made to politely sit with elderly pipe-smoking uncles and whiskery aunts smelling of lavender and mothballs. The worst part was the kiss goodbye. Ugh, I hope he doesn't try to do that.*

And suddenly, Dora couldn't eat any more of her chocolate and cherry cake. Not because she was too full to finish the rich delicacy, but because the last morsel felt like dry breadcrumbs in her mouth. She laid down her fork and, like Verity, stared at the tableau before her. 'Keep your eyes open,' Father had said, and now she saw clearly. She saw staged camaraderie, a phoney father of the people and the whole restaurant turned into a platform for this performance of fake jovial paternalism.

When the group stood up to leave, the children were returned to their proud, smiling mother and every table rose from their chairs to thrust their arms forward in a salute and shout 'Heil Hitler'. Even the children saluted, eliciting an 'aah, how sweet' from Verity, whose arm also shot into the air.

Dora could not follow suit, although she stood to watch the departure. A man from a nearby table spoke sharply to Heinrich, who glanced at her, nodded and made an excuse, saying, 'Entschuldigen. Sie ist Engländer'. The man shook his head and gave an exasperated sigh before returning to his seat.

But Dora did not apologise. She had no regrets whatsoever. She had seen the truth clearly now and she thought back to that scene she had witnessed earlier in the workshop at Dachau. The workers there may have looked clean and healthy, but she remembered how she had caught a glimpse of their eyes. And she realised that they were dead, without a spark. They were the eyes of ones who lived in fear.

FIVE
ROSA
BERLIN, JULY 1933

Rosa was concentrating so hard on her sewing that she was startled when Josef threw the newspaper onto the table. She frowned at him, then carried on putting the final touches to the silk dress Frau Braun had commissioned from her.

'It's a good thing we were both born in this country,' he said. 'Do you know what they've ruled now? They've decided that Jews who weren't born in Germany can no longer be German citizens! And they're saying the same applies to undesirables, whoever they are! I wouldn't like to be singled out along with so-called undesirables but thank goodness we're both safe from criticism.'

Rosa usually tried to curb her irritation in front of her husband, but her fingers were sore from hours of stitching and her baby daughter Theresia was teething, her cheeks like shiny red apples as she grizzled with the pain, clutching the bars of her playpen. 'Don't be too complacent, Josef. We are fortunate, I agree, but only a few months ago they ruled that Jews can no longer be lawyers. Are they going to weed our kind out of every profession in the end?'

'Oh, that was just to increase the opportunities for Aryan

lawyers. It doesn't mean anything.' Josef stood up and brushed a speck of fluff from his impeccable charcoal-grey suit. He always looked his best as an advertisement for his business, tailoring fine suits for Berlin's more affluent citizens. 'There will always be a need for good tailors and dressmakers, so don't worry yourself about the future of our business. We shall always be in demand.'

Rosa thought Josef had a point. Since they had moved to Berlin from Bad Pyrmont, soon after their marriage three years before, they had never been short of orders. At first, their customers had mostly been businessmen and their wives, but lately they had attracted the attention of high-ranking Nazis, who came for custom-made uniforms as well as suits. And now their fashion-conscious wives were becoming interested in Rosa's dressmaking skills. She was quick to note new trends and studied the magazines for ideas.

She hung the dress out of the reach of inquisitive sticky fingers and turned to pick up her crying daughter from the playpen. 'If we get many more orders for dresses I'll need an assistant. I might employ a nursemaid to help with Theresia, but I can't cope with much more sewing than I already have.'

Josef smiled at her. 'More orders means more profit for us. We shall both need extra hands to meet demand. Don't worry about that, my dear.'

She stretched to kiss him before he left their apartment above the shop and workrooms, but he twisted away from her to stop his daughter's face and hands, wet with tears and mucus, from touching his clothes. 'Not now, my dear. After her bath tonight, when she is clean and dry.'

Rosa wiped the reddened cheeks and found the teething ring that was her child's only comfort. She would rub oil of cloves on her swollen gums to relieve the pain, as Mama had recommended in her latest letter. And perhaps a nursemaid would be needed sooner rather than later, as Rosa suspected that she had felt the first signs of another pregnancy. A brother perhaps for this little one.

Since giving birth to Theresia she'd had two miscarriages and she longed to give Josef all the children they had talked of having when they first married. She prayed that this time she might carry a baby to term. Josef if it was a boy and Esther if it was another girl.

Rosa rocked Theresia until she was calm, then laid her back in her cot to nap. She stroked her daughter's black curls, so like her father's hair. While she was sleeping, she could put the final touches to that dress. Frau Braun would return that afternoon for her last fitting. Hopefully she had not stuffed herself with much more Apfelkuchen mit Schlagsahne since her previous visit and the dress would fit perfectly.

SIX

A GATHERING STORM

SEPTEMBER 1935

Dora kept glancing at the sky as she walked to work that morning. No dark clouds, just wisps of white against the clear blue, but the day felt ominous. And the trees in Bedford Square were already changing colour with tinges of orange and yellow, although it seemed to Dora that summer had barely finished. Leaves were already falling from the beech, plane and lime trees to be kicked and thrown by children toddling with nurse-maids and nannies in the sunshine.

But despite the sun's warmth and the joyful cries, Dora's heart was heavy with apprehension. She had felt on edge ever since her trip to Germany with Verity the year before. It felt as if a storm was brewing. She looked up again, expecting to see darkness approaching, but all around her was the unremarkable everydayness of ordinary life, fully recovered from the trials of the Great War. She wanted to feel as light-hearted as those about her, but could not shake the sense of a doom-laden weight of things to come.

Dora dashed up the steps of Bloomsbury House, the centre for the Quakers' refugee work. She recognised that the storm was not in the skies above London but within herself. Ever since

Hitler had come to power, disturbing news had been flooding out of Germany. The work of the Quaker Friends had begun to feel increasingly urgent. Every day, their office received more and more letters begging for help to escape from the mounting threats in Germany and Austria, pleading for assistance to start new lives far away and free from fear. She took one last lingering look at the blithe figures strolling under the trees in the square, then ran inside the former hotel and up the winding stairs to her office.

Dora hung her light jacket and hat on the back of the office door and refastened the hair slide that clipped back her mousy, straight hair. She was proud to be doing this important job, even if it was sometimes rather depressing reading stories of families suffering persecution and loss of income every day.

When she reached her desk she looked out of the window, somewhat wistfully, thinking that if her fears were soon realised she and Hugh might not be able to marry; they might never be parents and might never have a life together. She twisted the modest diamond engagement ring on her left hand, wondering how long it would be before it could be partnered by a gold wedding ring.

Dora couldn't tear her eyes away from the sight of a nurse lifting a baby wrapped in a long white shawl from a pram. She patted it on the back, then tucked it back into the Silver Cross carriage, adjusted the black hood and rocked it to and fro.

Dora checked the ever-growing pile of unopened letters stacked in her in-tray and sighed. Each and every one had to be answered as quickly as possible and referred to the correct agency if help could be found. And each reply had to be filed correctly with the original query in one of the oak Globe Wernicke cabinets, inherited from a defunct law firm, that furnished her office alongside stacks of noisy grey steel drawers.

. . .

At the end of the day, Dora walked back to the flat as usual, past the stalls packing up in Islington market. She normally found it a cheerful distraction and she might pick up bruised apples or a torn cabbage for a pittance. But today nothing could dispel her dark mood.

As she turned her key in the door, she heard the sound of music. Verity was already home, dancing as she dressed for the evening. Where she was going this time, Dora didn't care, for her cousin seemed to be enjoying a carefree life of pleasure with no thought of what might be happening elsewhere in the world.

The two of them weren't really suited to being close friends, even though they had played together throughout their childhood and attended the same school. But their bond was sealed forever when Verity had caught measles at the age of five. Dora and Verity's younger sister, Honor, had been given strict instructions to stay out of the sickroom. But the giggling girls had crept into the room to cheer up the bored patient, bearing a bag of boiled sweets, with terrible consequences for all of them. Dora fell ill soon after, as did Honor, but, while Dora and Verity both made a full recovery, Honor lost her sight and Dora could never forgive herself for the lasting harm she had caused.

Although both their families moved in similar circles, Verity's titled father was a Member of Parliament and had inherited a huge estate in Yorkshire and additional lands in Scotland. Dora's father, like a number of moneyed Quaker families, was involved in leather goods and had prospered enormously as a result of the Great War, which had created a huge demand for belts, straps and boots for the armed forces.

'Dora, darling,' Verity called as she entered the sitting room, strewn with dresses, glittering evening bags and discarded dance shoes. 'Come and help me decide what to wear tonight. Teddy Rothschild is taking me to a charity ball at the Grosvenor. I can't possibly wear the dress I danced in last week. You've simply got to help me.' Verity's wardrobe had been in

vogue when she came out as a debutante in 1933 and she
fretted about maintaining appearances in fashionable society.

'Which charity is it this time?' Dora couldn't stop herself
picking up a silver shoe and looking for its partner. It had fallen
beneath the sofa along with some discarded bangles.

'Oh heavens, I don't know. More widows and orphans,
probably.' Verity held a long black satin dress against her
slender frame. She was dressed in nothing but peach silk
camiknickers, almost the same shade as her creamy skin, her
perky nipples apparent beneath the thin fabric draped across
her breasts. 'What about this? With my long pearls?' She tossed
her blonde hair over her shoulders and let it fall over one eye.
'Not too vampish, do you think?'

Dora couldn't stop a little smile twitching her lips. 'It's very
elegant, Vee.'

'I'm not sure. If I could borrow Mummy's diamonds it might
just work, but maybe black and pearls is too staid. I really do
want to make an entrance this evening.'

Was she setting her sights on Teddy or was she hoping to
charm another target there tonight? Verity's ambition amused
but also slightly disturbed Dora. She knew that her cousin's
family appeared to be wealthy but were in truth keeping up
appearances. That was why their house in Mayfair had been
sold and Verity was having to lodge with her cousin in Dora's
late Aunt Vera's empty house in Islington, which was not what
Vee's mother, Lady Ponsonby, would have called a 'good
address'. And no wonder she wouldn't lend her daughter her
diamonds; they might disappear in hock to the pawnbroker
round the corner, the morning after they'd made an impression
at the ball.

'Oh, very well, Vee, let's get you sorted out. You've left it
rather late to decide.'

'Don't worry. I'll be ready in good time, darling. I've already
bathed and I only need to brush my hair and powder my nose

again. Look, I've done my face and eyes already.' She batted her heavily mascaraed eyelashes and pouted deep-red lips, making Dora laugh aloud. 'That's much better, darling. You looked a right old miz when you came in. Hugh hasn't been beastly, has he?'

'Of course he hasn't. He's an absolute dear. I'm just worried about the state of the world, I suppose.'

'Darling, I've told you before. It's that dreary job of yours. How you can stand it, I don't know.' Verity twirled in an emerald-green frock with a scooped and draped cowl that revealed the whole length of her back. She did a little filing and typing for an eminent art historian who had a minute gallery and office near the British Museum. The most miserable sights she ever encountered in her working day were images of Christ on the cross and martyred saints pierced with arrows.

'You might be right, Vee. But I do so want to help. People in Austria and Germany are becoming desperate. You should see the bulging postbag that arrives at the office every day. There are tons of them writing to us. We've simply got to help them.'

'Well, why don't they just leave if they don't like it there? That's what I'd be telling all of them.'

Verity threw herself down on the sofa with a jolt, scattering evening purses and beads across the floor. 'Oh, I'm simply exhausted. You choose for me.' She closed her eyes and put a hand to her forehead.

Dora gathered up the scattered gowns and laid them across the back of the sofa. Hints of jasmine from Schiaparelli's Shocking scent wafted from the silky fabrics. Just as well the perfume clung indelibly to all Verity's clothes, Dora thought, as the bottle had long drained dry and until she found herself another rich boyfriend, she wouldn't have the luxury of dabbing more expensive scent on her wrists and throat.

'This one is lovely,' Dora said, holding up a slender gown of pearl-grey satin with chiffon trailing down the back from the shoulders. 'It's understated and elegant and the subtle colour would complement your pearls beautifully.'

The long necklace of perfectly matched and graduated beads was Verity's one good piece of jewellery, inherited from an aunt who had died far too young after experimenting with cocktails and drugs during the Roaring Twenties.

'Darling Aunt Clovis,' Verity murmured. 'She really was such fun. She taught me how to do the Charleston, you know. I was only eight.' She leapt up from the sofa, causing yet more items of clothing to fall on the carpet, saying, 'Come on, I'll show you, then you'll forget all about your miserable penfriends.' She dashed to the gramophone and changed the record, removed the wadding from the trumpet and placed the needle on the disc. Music blared out and she began kicking her legs in time to the tune.

Dora felt nervous as their neighbours upstairs, two staid clerks from the Bank of England, had complained more than once about 'the racket', as they called it. That had resulted in the girls muffling the sound with old dusters stuffed inside the gramophone speaker. But Verity was insistent, grabbing her hands, and soon she too was jigging in time to the irresistible rhythm.

They danced for a few minutes, then, when the tune finished, both collapsed onto the sofa in helpless giggles. 'I've got to meet Hugh in half an hour,' Dora said, sounding breathless.

'Go on then. I'll wear that old grey thing you like so much, if I must. And do you know what, I'm going to knot the pearls and let them trail down my back. That'll cause a stir, don't you think?'

'You'll be the belle of the ball, Vee. But you know you'd impress whatever you decided to wear. You do know that, don't you?'

Verity tossed her hair. 'I don't know what you mean,

darling,' she said, letting the straps of her camiknickers slip from her shoulders till the fabric slid down her lithe body. She stepped out of the pool of silken fabric and threw the shimmering satin gown over her head. It rippled over her bare skin and she looped the pearls round her neck. It was effortless and she looked utterly beautiful.

Dora shook her head. Her cousin was incorrigible. She'd return from the night either engaged to Teddy or glowing with excitement from the thrill of making a new conquest. 'I must tidy myself up and try not to keep Hugh waiting,' she said, kissing Verity's cheek.

But as she went to her room to change her cardigan and make herself look presentable, she thought that, while the raucous music might have finished for the moment, she could not quieten the faint, yet unsettling rhythm of war drums echoing in her heart.

SEVEN
CANDLELIT CONVERSATION
LONDON, SEPTEMBER 1935

Dora tried to convince herself that the dim lighting in their favourite but shabby Italian restaurant in Soho was flattering but she rather thought it was more likely to emphasise her hollow cheeks and the shadows under her eyes. Every table was set with a red and white checked cloth and a candle in a bulbous Chianti bottle, adorned with the waxen rivulets of a hundred previous candles. Dora's fingers always itched to pick at the solid tears dripping down the flask when their conversation took a serious turn.

'You seem very thoughtful this evening, darling,' Hugh said, looking up from the limited menu they both knew off by heart. 'Not your scatty cousin again, is it?' Hugh had shadows under his eyes too, but that just served to make him look kind and caring.

Dora shook her head to rid herself of morose thoughts. She reached for his hand and he wrapped both his hands round hers. His long sensitive fingers and trimmed nails were some of the things she loved about him, along with his dark hair and blue eyes. 'No, I'm not worrying about Vee. Though I've no idea what time she'll be back again tonight. I'm beginning to think that if she doesn't snare herself a rich husband soon she'll wear herself out.'

'You do know that I'm so glad you're not like Vee, don't you, darling? I couldn't afford that kind of life, for a start.'

'Don't worry. This is perfect. Just right,' Dora said, to reassure him that she wasn't longing for jazz bands and cocktails every night. 'I love coming to "our place" and sitting at exactly the same table every single time.'

'Well, that's a relief, I must say. And it's very handy for me dashing to meet you from Guy's.' Hugh's hospital was only a short distance away, so he could whip off his white coat and run off to meet her for dinner at the very last moment when he had finished his rounds.

'Then we must never meet anywhere else, not unless you move to another hospital, that is. Have you decided yet whether you are going to stay?' Hugh had intended going into general practice when he'd completed his training, but money was a problem for his family. Practices meant doctors had to share the upkeep of premises and staff salaries, so it might not be an option for him.

'I'm actually thinking it might be better for me to develop my surgical skills. If we get involved in another war there's probably going to be a greater demand for traumatic injury surgeons than family doctors treating measles and mumps. I'd like to specialise in plastic surgery if the opportunity arises.'

Despite the weak light cast by the guttering candle, Dora could clearly detect his regretful expression from the droop of his mouth. 'Do you really think there's going to be a war?'

'I sincerely hope not, but all the chaps are saying the same thing. Hitler's disrespect for the Treaty of Versailles and his introduction of compulsory military service mean Germany is preparing for conflict. There's going to be a massive demand for medics at some point and we'd better be prepared. I know the general population thinks childhood diseases are dreadful, but the health of our armed forces might well become the priority.'

'Oh Hugh, I hate to say it, but I think you're right. I desperately hope it doesn't happen, but all day I've been feeling that something awful is just around the corner. Every one of those letters I have to open just tells me that life is about to change for us, as well as for all those poor people over there.' She felt tears welling and hoped they couldn't be seen and wouldn't trickle down her hastily powdered cheeks.

'You mustn't worry, darling. We'll be all right, we've got each other. I'll always be here for you.'

'But you might have to go away. You might even have to fight.' She pressed her clenched fist against her lips to stifle her threatened sobs.

'I can never fight, darling. You know that as Quakers we can't. But I can still serve my country by healing. Even if I have to serve as part of an army medical corps, I shan't actually be on the front line.'

Dora took a deep breath. 'Of course, I know that. Ignore me, Hugh. I'm being silly.'

'Look, if I had to register as a conscientious objector, I would. But as a doctor my skills will be needed, so I'll be in a protected occupation. Of course, there are some chaps who are even more principled than I am and in the last war some of them refused even to treat soldiers, saying it meant patching men up only to send them straight back to the front to fight again. But I couldn't do that; I'd always have to help the injured. And I have a feeling that, if the war does come eventually, it will be morally justified.'

'That's what I think too. Oh, I'm so glad we're in tune with each other.' Dora finally managed to smile and squeeze Hugh's hand. 'Shall we order? It isn't going to help anyone if we starve, is it?'

They both asked for the special of the day, vitello tonnato, served with the last of that summer's green beans. And as they were regular customers, Marcello insisted they each had a portion of garlicky potato puree, 'like my mama make me. On the 'ouse for my besta two lovers.' They laughed at his jokes. This was where they had fallen in love, this was where Hugh had proposed and they had celebrated with Marcello's Asti Spumante.

'Gosh, his mama's piled on the garlic tonight,' Hugh said, pulling a face. 'It's delicious, but you might not want a kiss at the end of the evening.'

'Don't be such a chump. I'm eating it too. We'll both reek of garlic. And I'll always want your kisses.'

'That's good to know.' He laid down his knife and fork, then said, 'If you're really certain you'll always want them, I think we should make sure we have plenty of time for kisses before anything happens to change our lives. I think we should get married as soon as possible.'

Dora was in the middle of a mouthful of veal and nearly choked. It took her a minute to chew and swallow, then she took a sip of her red wine before she could answer. 'Really? Are you quite sure?'

'I couldn't be more sure.' He grasped her hand again. 'We don't know what's round the corner right now so why wait? Why don't we grab some happiness while we can?'

'I'd been thinking we'd have to wait. I thought we'd have to have a long engagement until we could see what lay ahead.'

'But don't you see, we don't have to? I know I've still got a long way to go before I can become a consultant or surgeon, if that's what I want, but there's nothing to stop us.'

'I'd love that, Hugh, really I would. But...' She hesitated, hoping this wasn't going to put a dampener on their conversation.

'But what? You do still want to marry me, don't you?'

'Yes, of course I do. More than anything in the whole world.

But...' She rushed her words to get them out before she could hesitate any longer, 'I don't want to start a family. Not straight away, that is. Eventually yes, but I'd like to wait until we can feel more confident that the world will be a safe place for our children.'

'I couldn't agree more, my darling. I couldn't agree more.' He picked up her hand and kissed it. 'Now eat up or we won't have the strength to do anything, let alone keep going until we can have children.'

EIGHT

ROSA

BERLIN, SEPTEMBER 1935

How was this latest ruling going to affect Liese, Rosa wondered. Her German friend had a Jewish husband and now Germans couldn't marry or have relationships with Jews. Isaac was a very successful tax consultant, but would they now be shunned by their neighbours? For years both Jews and Aryans had lived and worked together, but increasingly such close relationships were being discouraged and ordinary Germans were becoming afraid of being seen to fraternise with their Jewish neighbours.

Rosa had to see how her friend was feeling, but when she knocked on her door, Liese was looking angry and was dressed to go out. 'There's another of those despicable posters,' Liese blurted out as she opened the door.

'Where is it this time?' Rosa frowned. 'I'll rip it down right away.'

'Isaac phoned me when he got to the office. He saw it from the bus and I'm glad he didn't hop off and tackle it himself. It's on the noticeboard outside the Jewish cemetery. Have they no respect anymore?'

'They think they can do whatever they like. And they're getting worse.'

'I had to scrape the last one off the board. I expect this one is stuck down firmly as well, but I've got a knife with me.'

The two women walked together as far as the cemetery. Liese pointed out the crude, lurid advertisement for *Der Stürmer*, the anti-Jewish newspaper popular with the brown-shirted Nazis. A headline in large red letters proclaimed *WENN JUDEN LACHEN*, above a collection of cartoon-like, grinning faces, followed by text claiming that all Jews were born criminals.

'Well, that's coming down right now,' Liese said, marching across the road.

Rosa followed and tried to peel the paper off the board with her fingers, but Liese told her to leave. 'It will be worse for you if they catch you doing this. I can deal with those thugs, but if you're involved there'll be real trouble. You know what they're like and you've got to think of Theresia and Josef. Don't risk it. Wait for me over there. I'll get this down in no time.'

Liese waved towards the alleyway across the street and Rosa tucked herself away in the shadows of a doorway and watched her friend slide the knife beneath the gross depiction of members of the Jewish community. Offensive posters like this had been appearing all over the city, but never had one been pasted outside the cemetery before.

Hearing loud footsteps and shouts, Rosa shrank back against the wall, hoping she couldn't be seen. A young man in that familiar brown-shirted uniform clamped a heavy hand on Liese's shoulder.

A gruff voice said, 'Halt. You can't do that.'

Startled, Liese turned to face him. Two of his blond friends stood behind him, their arms folded, waiting to see her reaction.

'This noticeboard is not placed here to be used for such filth,' Liese said, pointing with the knife she had been using to peel the poster away.

'And who says it can't?' He sneered at her, then grabbed her wrist so she dropped the knife.

'You know very well that this is a public noticeboard, not an advertising hoarding. It is extremely offensive and I am removing it.' Liese tugged at the loosened paper and the poster peeled away in her hand. 'There. That's better.'

Rosa admired her friend's boldness, but held her breath, fearing what might happen next.

The Brownshirt gave Liese a hard shove, pushing her back against the board. Rosa heard it crack with the force. 'You're going to have to pay for that.'

'Fine,' Liese said, holding her head high. 'How much do you want?'

'Oh, I don't want money. Do we, boys?' he said, turning to his grinning accomplices. 'We could make a citizen's arrest, but we'd prefer to settle the matter here and now. Make sure you don't try and do this again.'

He swung his arm back and hit Liese on the side of her head, making it jolt back against the board.

Rosa couldn't bear to see her friend being hurt. 'No, leave her alone,' she shouted, and ran out from her hiding place, but one of the gang shoved her with both hands so she fell onto the granite kerbstones of the street.

'It's none of your business,' the Brownshirt shouted. And then she felt a kick aimed at her side and another at her stomach. Searing pain coursed through her body and she lay stunned. She didn't dare protest further in case they turned on her again, but after hearing shouts from the men and screams from Liese, they marched off, laughing about the fun they'd just had.

Liese bent down to Rosa. 'I told you to stay away,' she said, her voice trembling.

Rosa opened her eyes. Liese's nose was bleeding. 'You're hurt. I'm sorry. Did I make things worse?'

Liese tried to smile and helped Rosa to stand up. 'Worse for you than me, I think.'

Rosa's stomach gripped in a painful spasm and she gasped. She bent forward, clutching herself, and felt another intense pain.

'You're really hurt. I'll help you home and then we must call the doctor. Look, you're bleeding.'

Rosa looked at the blood trickling down her legs. 'A doctor won't be able to help. This will be over soon.' She gulped back tears. 'And I'd hoped for a son this time.'

NINE
INTO THE WOODS
SUSSEX, JUNE 1936

Dora lay in Hugh's arms the day after they married in the softest bed she had ever slept in. She was blissfully happy. She had always imagined their wedding would be a small affair, but in true Quaker tradition, the ceremony was held in the Friends Meeting House at Bunhill Fields near Islington and all the members of its congregation were eligible to attend. Despite the crowd, Dora only had eyes for Hugh, brushed and polished in his morning suit. As they stood side by side to say their vows, he had reached for her hand and whispered that she was beautiful. She had smiled to herself beneath the lace veil that her mother had once worn, secured with a band of silken flowers echoing the trim on her long cream satin dress.

And now they were man and wife, lying in a bed in Hugh's aunt's cottage deep in the Sussex woods, far from London. The only sounds were the soft snores of her husband and the twittering of birds in the roses and ivy that climbed the outer walls. Dappled light crept through the deeply recessed windows, hung with flower-sprigged curtains.

Dora slid out of the high bed piled with pillows, her toes

finding the warm sheepskin rug on the wide oak floorboards. Hoping the old cottage would not betray her with creaks as she tiptoed out of the room and down the twisted stairs, she crept into the tiny kitchen and lifted the latch on the back door. Hugh had laughed at finding a crazed porcelain chamber pot under their bed, but Dora preferred to visit the outside privy, despite the chill of early morning. At least it was a flushing toilet, she thought, remembering her sister teasing her that it might be an earth closet in this isolated cottage.

The dim chamber was home to a toad as well as several spiders and, when she emerged into the early morning sun, filtered through the surrounding trees, she startled the garden wildlife. A rabbit dashed into the brambles, blackbirds flew back to their nests and she heard the loud call of a cuckoo. How perfect this simple cottage was; but not every bride would be delighted to find themselves honeymooning in a rural idyll without heating or electric light.

Verity had been astonished to hear that she was looking forward to such peaceful seclusion. 'How drab, Dora. I can't imagine starting married life literally in the middle of nowhere. If that was all my husband could offer I'd be utterly miz, darling. I'd want romance, dancing and champagne. At the very least I'd expect my wedding night to take place at The Dorchester, then I'd want to be whisked off to Paris.'

Dora smiled to herself. She felt country walks and cider were romantic enough. Hugh's aunt had told them there was a good supply of cider from the previous year's apple harvest, so that had made them happy.

She had also heard Verity being flippant about the wedding day itself, saying, 'How very quaint. But it's not exactly a society affair, is it? I'm expecting Westminster and a host of brides-maids when I get married.'

Dora wasn't the least bit offended by Verity's conde-scending remarks. As far as she was concerned, the day had been exactly what she wanted, surrounded by their families and dearest friends. She hadn't expected any different from her cousin. Verity would always be dramatic and demanding and, as befitted her personality, she had worn the most expensive dress of cream draped silk, printed with red roses, topped with a large, extravagant hat decked with an enormous, blowsy, artificial cream flower. Dora thought the outfit was more suited to the Royal Enclosure at Ascot than a modest wedding breakfast in the private function room of the Artillery Arms in Islington. But Verity obviously thought highly of herself, wafting around in a cloud of perfume and scented smoke, brandishing a long black and gold cigarette holder.

The sight of her amused Dora and disconcerted her conservative parents; her mother had said, 'Honestly, that expensive education did nothing to instil any sense in the girl. Thank goodness you're more restrained, dear. That wretched cigarette holder nearly poked Granny's eye out when she bent down to kiss her.'

Dora listened to the chatter of the morning birds for a moment longer, thinking how she'd be happy living this simple life forever. But she soon realised how hungry she felt, so she shook herself and nipped back inside to rekindle the blackened range and boil water for tea.

A local help had been drafted in to rid the cottage of most of its cobwebs, although Dora was sure more had been spun during the night, by fairies at a magical spinning wheel. A strand of spider's silk draped the kitchen window and she could see a web in the ivy tendrils outside, sparkling with dewdrops.

Bread, bacon, cheese and a freshly baked rabbit pie had been stored in a metal meat safe to ward off mice and flies. Milk, butter and eggs had been placed on a stone shelf in the larder, which might once have held rows of preserves but now boasted only a solitary jar of marmalade and a tin of corned beef.

Dora had planned to wake Hugh once the tea was made but

as the kettle whistled, she heard steps overhead and soon he stumbled down the narrow stairs, yawning and rubbing the stubble on his chin.

'Good morning, Mrs Williams,' he said, kissing her on the cheek and hugging her round her waist.

'Tea will be ready in a minute. Do you want to wash and dress first or eat?'

'I'm starving. I hardly ate anything yesterday, there were so many people we had to talk to.' The pub's wedding breakfast had offered a grand selection of cold ham, Scotch eggs and salad, followed by a single tier of wedding cake. But Dora hadn't eaten much either and when they had arrived at the cottage, as the sun was setting, they were both more interested in piling into bed than finding supper.

'The stove is hot and I can make us bacon, eggs and toast. How does that sound?'

'Perfect, darling,' he said, kissing her again. 'And later we can explore the woods. Aunt Hilda reminded me that the blue-bells are long over. She said we should have come in May when there was a sea of blue beneath the trees.'

'That sounds lovely. Maybe we'll come here again next spring to see them. Why don't we walk through the woods and maybe try the pub on the other side of the copse?'

'A perfect day,' he said, hugging her again.

'So perfect we're going to find it hard to leave tomorrow.'

'I know, my love, but this will always be here and Aunt Hilda says we can escape London whenever we like. She's my favourite aunt and understands that we are going to need to find a quiet haven away from our work sometimes.'

'What a dear she is. I'd like that. A little hidey-hole where we can forget the troubles of the world for a short while.'

'As long as I can borrow a car and get petrol, we'll always be able to disappear down here.' The cottage was nowhere near a station and the country buses, though reliable, were infrequent, so a car was the easiest way to travel. 'When I was young I cycled here a couple of times from home, or I'd sometimes take the bus. At the top of Verdley Hill where the road narrows, I always held my breath if the South Downs buses passed each way at the same time – they were only inches away from each other.'

'I'd always be happy to take the bus, darling, but you won't get me to cycle all the way down here from Islington. There are far too many hills.' Dora pushed Hugh away and tied an apron over her nightdress to begin cooking.

He laid the table, poured cups of tea and cut bread for toast. 'Aunt Hilda rarely gets here these days, so I expect we could come whenever we like. She used to spend whole weeks at a time here when she was younger, and I loved joining her for walks through the woods, learning about the wildlife. We were always seeing deer, foxes and badgers. I can show you the badger sett where we once sat on a moonlit night to see the young cubs there.'

'I'd love that, darling. This place is just heavenly.' Dora laid the rashers of bacon in the hot pan and, as they began to sizzle, she fantasised about staying here with her new husband, just the two of them hidden away in the woods, far away from an increasingly troubled world. With a patch of vegetables, some hens and a supply of wild rabbits and pigeons, she could imagine an idyllic life, wanting for nothing.

'Careful, I think the toast is burning,' Hugh said, reaching into the top oven. He rescued the bread just in time. 'Were you daydreaming?'

'I was rather. I was thinking how lovely it would be to stay here forever. But don't worry, darling, I'd soon feel a prick of conscience and want to get back to work. I'd fret about the letters piling up. I couldn't abandon them for long.'

'I know just how you feel. We wouldn't like ourselves if we hid from the task ahead, would we? Just remember that this cottage will always be here to help us heal and be stronger. It will give us the chance to do a better job in the weeks and months ahead.'

'I'll remember that, darling. Now, would you like one egg or two?'

TEN
THE CUPBOARD IS BARE
LONDON, MAY 1937

Dora trudged home from the office thinking about the letters she had dealt with that day. There were now increasing numbers of reports of Jehovah's Witnesses and Quakers being imprisoned as well as Jews. In fact, the Brownshirts wouldn't hesitate to arrest or brutally beat anyone who opposed them.

Surely something like that couldn't happen in Britain. Not with the Englishman's legendary stubbornness and refusal to be told what to think. Or at least the ordinary man couldn't be persuaded, unlike the prejudiced and privileged few such as those in Verity's family, who still thought Oswald Mosley was a fine chap and greatly misunderstood.

Verity had returned with sparkling eyes from some of his British Union of Fascists rallies, often out of breath from a hasty retreat when the events met violent protest. 'It was awfully exciting. He really incites such passion in his followers! I simply can't wait for the next one. I'm going to wear my black coat and dress another time, then I'll feel like I'm really one of them.' BUF members wore black shirts and Mosley himself often wore a black polo-neck sweater.

Dora thought that Verity's conversion to this cause was

partly due to her increased impoverishment, although by many standards she was still relatively well off. She had abandoned the Rothschilds and Aga Khan circle, had a brief flirtation with an Austrian count and was now smitten with one of Mosley's aristocratic followers, Raven Fitzgerald, who had inherited a mouldering family estate in Ireland filled with antiques and silver.

Dora could understand the physical attraction to this tall, handsome Irishman with his deep voice and green eyes, but not to his deeply flawed political views. She had met him once, when the couple had returned from another rally dishevelled and in need of a good wash and hot tea. His Irish lilt was barely noticeable and she immediately felt the power of his spell-binding charm as he bowed his dark head to kiss her hand, saying, 'My dear Dora, how I've longed to meet you after hearing so much about your saintliness.'

Verity was completely under his spell, or perhaps she was more in love with his estate in Ireland. 'It's the most heavenly place on earth, Dora. Virtually a castle, with a magnificent view of the sea. Simply adorable. Raven says it inspires his poetry and wants me to join him there once we've helped Oswald win the fight.'

Since marrying Hugh the previous year, Dora didn't see as much of her cousin as she once had. She and Hugh occupied half of the house while Verity flitted in and out, occupying the top-floor flat that had once housed the dreary bank clerks. However, she made her presence felt throughout the property, with draped scarves on the curved banisters and scattered gloves on the stairs. And – more recently – propaganda leaflets produced by the fascist union littered the walnut and marble console table in the hall.

That evening, Hugh picked up the latest of these missives, saying, 'More of this nonsense again, I see. And I hear Mosley has just come up with a plan to have his own private radio station. On Sark, apparently.'

'That's one of the Channel Islands, isn't it? Why on earth would he want to do that? Hasn't he got enough to do, traipsing around the country, trying to convert the masses?' Dora was preparing dinner, a simple cottage pie. She was too tired after a day of answering desperately sad pleas for help to think of making more of an effort.

'I expect Mosley's being further influenced by the example of the German propaganda machine. He's done a deal with the chap who's inherited Sark. Wants to transmit his views more widely, I suppose, and deliver an alternative message to the BBC.' Hugh twisted the offending leaflet in his hands and offered it to Dora, saying, 'Firelighter?'

She laughed and took it to add to the basket where she kept kindling and paper to light their evening fire. She loved snuggling up with Hugh after they'd both had a long day of work, even though the couch springs were sagging.

Dora finished mashing the potatoes and spread them across the minced beef mixed with diced carrots and onions. She roughly forked the topping to create the crisp browned ridges that she knew Hugh loved and slid it into the gas oven.

At that moment she heard the front door slam and heels clicked across the tiled floor of the hall, followed by thuds as footsteps ran down the stairs to the lower ground floor. Verity popped her head round the kitchen door.

'It smells divine,' she said, then pouted. 'Can you spare a morsel for a poor starving soul?'

'If we must,' Dora said, rolling her eyes. 'Cupboard bare again?' Every couple of weeks, Hugh and Dora felt obliged to share their supper with Verity, who never seemed to think ahead but consumed her supplies until she had stripped her kitchen shelves bare. One evening she told them she had only eaten stale Bath Olivers the night before.

'Finished off all those hard biscuits, have you?' Hugh joked. 'Not even a crust left in your cupboards upstairs?'

'Not a sausage,' Verity said, plonking herself down on one of the serviceable wheelback Windsor chairs that surrounded the scrubbed table and carelessly throwing her coat aside. 'I've not eaten a single crumb since this morning and that was just a wizened old apple. I'm simply famished.'

'You're not as hard done by as the poor people who are writing to us at the refugee centre,' Dora said. 'You have no idea what starving really means.' She began chopping a cabbage with savage strokes.

'Oh, don't try to upset me with your awful stories again,' Verity said. 'I know, poor them, blah blah blah, but don't let them come here and take our workers' jobs.' She picked at the crust of the fresh loaf standing on a bread board on the table, nibbling as she spoke.

Dora held up the hard cabbage stalk. 'In many homes in Germany, this wouldn't be wasted. It would be cooked and eaten. Some people are so desperate they'd even have it raw.' She slammed it on the table.

Verity pushed the stalk away. 'Send it to them, then. Or make it into soup and take it to one of those dreary soup kitchens you're always talking about. I don't care.'

Hugh raised an eyebrow. 'Now, now, girls, we can't have you falling out over a bit of old cabbage. I'm sure you can find a use for it, Dora, then you won't feel so bad.'

Dora threw the stalk into a pot filled with peelings. 'I'll take it to Mrs Harvey for her hens. She chops everything up for them. And in return she gives me fresh eggs from time to time.'

'Maybe we should start keeping hens in the back garden here as well?' Hugh was settled in the rocking chair by the oven, folding back the pages of *The Times*. 'Might be good for us to practise some sensible husbandry, just in case.'

'Ooh, I haven't had a boiled egg in ages,' Verity said. 'Will you let me have one for breakfast, a dippy egg with soldiers, just like Nanny Jenkins used to make for me?'

'You can have one if you boil it yourself,' Dora said. 'I suppose you'll need me to supply bread for the toast as well?'

'Yes please, darling. Oh, you are such a dear. I do love how clever and organised you always are. I seem to be in such a tizz the whole time and never seem to have anything to eat in my flat. Maybe I should take all my meals with you from now on, otherwise I'll fade away and starve in my garret.'

'Oh, come on, the flat's hardly a garret and you'll never starve. Honestly, Verity, you make it all sound so dramatic.' Dora was tiring of her cousin's histrionics and no longer found her as amusing as she once had.

'And anyway, what do you mean, getting hens just in case?' Verity pointed at Hugh with the bread knife, then started to inexpertly hack at the loaf until Dora snatched the knife from her and cut a straight and even slice.

'In case of war, of course.' Hugh shook his head and rattled the pages of the newspaper.

'Oh, that's not going to happen,' Verity said, buttering her bread. 'It's all just a lot of silly talk. Hitler's an utter darling and would never let Germany suffer another war. Look what happened the last time. They don't want that all over again.'

Dora shook her head and thought back to the unsettling news that was reaching her office day after day. Her colleagues were as concerned as she was, although all of them were praying there would be peace.

She just managed to stop herself saying that some of them would shortly be going out to Germany to see for themselves what was happening over there. Even more troubling reports were reaching the office about restrictions on Jewish communities and anyone who dared to criticise the regime. She hadn't yet spoken to Hugh about this possible development and she certainly didn't want her plans debated while her cousin was in the room.

And then, to her surprise, Verity made an announcement. 'Actually, Raven and I are going to visit the country again very soon. We feel we should cement our bond with our German friends. After all, Oswald Mosley and Diana were actually able to get married out there. At the home of Joseph Goebbels as a matter of fact.'

Dora could tell this was a not very subtle hint that Verity was hoping for the same honour as the Mosleys. Really, she seemed to want to emulate everything about them, even down to the possibility of a wedding under the gaze of Germany's chief of propaganda. But Dora couldn't forget the awful scenes Mosley had caused, particularly the dreadful disturbances in the East End of London in October the previous year when his British Union of Fascists had marched in London.

That terrible riot now rejoiced in the epithet the Battle of Cable Street. Verity had returned from that event giddy with excitement and told Dora it had been like fighting in a real war. 'Gosh, you wouldn't believe how thrilling it all was. There were women throwing stones and rotten fruit out of windows all along the street. And emptying out their chamber pots too! It was such a lark!' She'd held out her camel coat for Dora to see. 'But just look at this! I'll never get the stains out!'

Hugh rattled the paper again, calling Dora back to the present moment in the kitchen and the hissing of the stove, where the cabbage was boiling over. Supper was almost ready. Perhaps if she fed Verity well tonight and sent her upstairs with a couple of eggs and some bread for her breakfast, she wouldn't hear any more of her nonsense until the next time the cupboard was bare.

ELEVEN
HANDS UP
LONDON, JULY 1937

Dora wondered if she could find a fresh lettuce and a cucumber. A cold supper would be preferable if the day grew hotter, as promised by the cloudless blue sky. She had taken the bus that morning rather than walking, knowing she'd be hot and glowing if she reached the office on foot, and the bus was already full of shiny-faced travellers, mopping their brows.

At least it wasn't going to rain on St Swithin's Day, she told herself. She didn't really believe the superstition that rain falling on 15 July would result in more rain every day for the next forty days and forty nights, but she didn't really want to tempt fate. The refugee centre was holding a fundraising event in the garden square that weekend and everyone was banking on a fine day. Whatever would they do with all the fairy cakes and crocheted doilies if there was rain?

But first Dora had to put all thoughts of a cool fresh salad out of her mind. Brenda had called a meeting and would be on the warpath if she was late. Brenda Bradshaw, the head of her division, an authority on the refugee situation and a veteran of the school feeding programme the Quakers had established in Germany soon after the Great War, was to announce her plans for a fact-finding mission and Dora dearly hoped she would recruit assistants to accompany her.

As she ran up the stairs to the conference room, Dora could hear Brenda's strident Mancunian voice beginning her address: 'The time has come. Our Quaker friends in Germany are suggesting we must ready ourselves to help desperate families once again. We are already working hard to help those who wish to leave, but I believe many more will soon need our aid.'

Oh dear, had she misread the starting time? She wasn't late, surely? Dora slipped in through the open door, hoping she hadn't been seen as Brenda glanced down at her notes. She sat at the back of the room and focusing on this tall, confident woman who had such a thorough grasp of the increasingly worrying situation. With her sensible, plain clothes and neat, cropped hair, she exuded strength and common sense.

'As many of you must already know,' she said, 'I have been working on behalf of our German friends for a number of years now. I won't bore you with all the details, but I think you can take it that I really do know what I am talking about when I say I fear we are going to be facing a humanitarian crisis of extraordinary dimensions, quite unlike anything any of us have ever seen before. My division is not called the emergency committee for nothing. And it's my belief that the restrictions that are currently being imposed on the lives of Jewish communities are little compared to what is actually happening on the ground and what is likely to happen before long.

'But we need to find out more and assess the situation for ourselves. And for that reason, I am prepared to undertake a journey to Vienna, Berlin and Nuremberg this September and I will require two volunteers to accompany me. Hands up, those who would like to join me.'

An approving murmur filled the room, followed by applause. Brenda stayed standing, looking expectantly at her audience. Dora glanced around her. So far, no one had raised their hand. Were they all reluctant to leave their families? Many of the workers here were female and had children of school age or elderly dependants. Maybe they weren't free to go.

Dora slowly raised her hand, hoping she wouldn't be the only one but also desperately hoping that she would be chosen. She kept her hand in the air as Brenda scanned the room, then noticed another raised arm in the front row. She couldn't see who it was. After a few seconds she realised no one else was volunteering. They were the only ones.

After the meeting, Brenda called the two young women into her office. 'Thank you so much for volunteering,' she said. 'And I believe you have both spent some time in Germany previously and speak the language, which will be very useful.'

'I worked for a family in Munich, who were great supporters of the Nazi Party. I felt increasingly uncomfortable with their views,' said Alice, the girl whose arm had shot up in the front row. 'I was with them for two years, but I decided to leave after attending the Nazi rally in 1933.'

'Interesting,' Brenda said. 'I think that's when we first began to see the light. And what about you?' She turned to Dora. 'Your German is also fluent, I believe?'

'Yes, I've spent quite a bit of time there. Mostly visiting my Quaker friend Angela in Bad Pyrmont, where they hold the annual meeting for German Friends. She has been keeping me up to date with her regular letters reporting on disturbing developments. It's all very worrying. And I attended the Oberammergau Passion Play in the summer of 1934.'

'Aah, yes. That must have been most illuminating. Things were really becoming clearer by then, weren't they?'

'I'm afraid so. There was quite a fervent atmosphere among members of the audience, both during the play and afterwards. And during our visit we also visited Dachau.' Dora lowered her head, remembering her disquiet about both the planned tour and her later realisation.

'You're both very well informed then. I think I couldn't have two better volunteers. So, how do you feel about attending this year's Nazi Party rally in Nuremberg? It's taking place the second week in September. We'll be gathering information elsewhere as well, of course, but I think it will be a good place for us to judge the mood of the populace, going right to the source, as it were.' Brenda smiled at them both. She looked courageous and strong. Dora so wanted to be like her and briefly wondered what Hugh would say if she too cropped her hair that short. But Brenda had never married, perhaps because, like many women of her generation, her chances had been diminished by the loss of so many men in the Great War.

'Won't we need permission to attend the rally?' Alice asked in a timid voice.

'Probably,' Brenda said. 'But many Germans have respect for us Quakers, because we fed their children during hard times soon after the last war. They don't see us as their enemy. At least they don't yet.' She added those last words after a pause, which gave them a finality that emphasised to Dora the seriousness of their mission.

'I think it will be very useful for us to go,' Dora said. 'I want to see it all for myself. We need to fully understand what we might be undertaking.'

'I totally agree,' Brenda said. 'But I must warn you that we will have to be careful. We may be tolerated by the more senior officials in the party, but lower ranks, and particularly the common people who are devoted to their cause, may not wish to hear our opinions of their policies. They do not react kindly to those who criticise the party's actions. We must be circumspect. We must watch and listen, but at this stage we would be wise to keep our views to ourselves.'

Later that day, Dora was in luck. The greengrocer offered her half a cucumber and a slightly wilted Webb's Wonder lettuce. 'It's all I've got left,' he apologised as he slipped them into her string bag. 'It's been nothing but salad all day. But I've got some fresh cooked beetroot left if you're interested.'

She accepted his offer, thinking how she could now make a good supper by hard-boiling a couple of the eggs Mrs Harvey had given her in exchange for kitchen scraps. Verity could find her own eggs if she suddenly turned up begging for her supper again.

TWELVE

ROSA

BERLIN, SEPTEMBER 1936

Dearest Mother,

I had hoped to have good news to give you in this month's letter, but unfortunately, I have miscarried again. It seems that I will not be able to give Theresia a brother or sister until she is much older, maybe never at all.

Ever since I had that unfortunate encounter with some Brownshirts, I have not been able to carry to term and can only last three months at the most. I never told Josef how it happened. He would not be happy to hear that I intervened. He says we Jews have always contributed successfully to the German economy, so if we ignore the changes that are happening around us it will all calm down in good time. But I'm not so sure. Many of our neighbours are leaving Berlin now, saying they are sure the restrictions will become worse. I doubt we shall ever see some of our friends again as they are scattering around the world. Some are going all the way to America, but others are going to live in Amsterdam or Paris. Josef says we would be mad to abandon a successful business and that these unsettled times will all pass and those who leave now will regret abandoning shops and trades they have spent many years establishing.

I hope he is right and that our business will continue. I have employed another seamstress and Josef has had to take on another cutter so we shall keep working hard and I hope that my fears will soon disappear.

Your loving daughter,

Rosa

THIRTEEN
GOOD RIDDANCE
LONDON, JULY 1937

All the way back to the house, Dora fretted about how she was going to tell Hugh that she'd be going to Germany in a few weeks. It wasn't so much the time away that she thought he'd object to; after all, he respected the importance of her work and in fact the value of all that Bloomsbury House was doing for refugees. But she couldn't help thinking that he might not like the idea of her attending the rally in Nuremberg.

She tried to put her worries out of her mind as she planned their supper. She would serve new potatoes, adding a generous sprig of mint from the garden. She had also picked up a thick slice of pork pie just before Sainsbury the grocers closed for the day; the cool green tiles and marble counters had been a welcome haven after the hot dust of the street. She had been coming to this Chapel Street shop since she was a child and the aromas of smoked bacon and cheese always reminded her of shopping with her mother, in the days when the store's floor was strewn with sawdust.

'What are we having tonight, darling?' Hugh was already sitting in the kitchen with a cup of tea. He gave her a kiss on the cheek as he slid his arms round her waist.

'I thought we'd have salad. It's too hot for anything else. I'm just hoping Verity won't suddenly turn up expecting to be fed as well.' Dora quickly put the potatoes and eggs on to cook in boiling water.

'Oh, I don't think you need to worry about her. She's not here.'

'How do you know that? Did you see her go out?'

'No, but she's left you a note. Didn't you see it as you came in?'

Dora wiped her hands on her apron and went up the kitchen stairs to the hall. He was right. There was a note, almost buried underneath that day's post and more of those damned fascist party leaflets. She read it twice, then went back downstairs.

Hugh looked up from his paper. 'Well, what does it say? I hope she's left us in peace for the night.'

'It looks like it. But she hasn't said when she's coming back.'

'Off to another of those ridiculous rallies, is she?' Hugh opened the back door to let in some air to combat the steam of the boiling potatoes and eggs.

'No, she's gone to Germany with Raven. Listen, she says: *It's absolutely beyond exciting, dearest. I am simply thrilled. We are going to stay in Munich where my darling Raven has arranged an apartment for us. He says we shall dine at the Osteria Bavaria, Hitler's favourite restaurant, every night and are sure to be introduced into his intimate circle before long. We are both going to enrol at the language school there to perfect our German so we can converse with the Führer. I'm so excited and happy. It's quite simply a dream come true!*

'Your cousin is completely mad,' Hugh said as he ran a cool glass of water from the kitchen tap and took large gulps.

'I couldn't agree more. Whatever's possessed her to do such a thing? I blame Raven. I wish she'd never met him.' Dora continued staring at her cousin's letter, still hardly able to believe what she had just read.

'Well, she was always bound to end up doing something mad and cause trouble— Watch it!' Hugh shouted. 'The eggs are boiling dry.' He dashed forward to pull the pan from the heat, searing his hand on the red-hot handle. With loud curses, he ran back to the sink and rinsed it under the cold tap.

'Oh darling, is it bad?' Dora turned to help him after she'd rescued the potatoes, which were also nearly out of water.

'It might blister, but luckily I'm not in theatre tomorrow.' Hugh was rapidly gaining an excellent reputation for his surgical skills and was developing a talent for skin grafts for burns, which he said could be vital for mending bodies if war finally came.

Dora drained the remaining water off the potatoes and poured cold over the eggs so they'd peel more easily. 'I wonder if she's told her parents yet. Knowing her, she's skipped off without thinking about them at all. I suppose I'd better phone after we've eaten.'

'Why not do it now? Get it over with, then we can relax after supper. It's such a lovely evening. We can sit outside under the roses.' Hugh gathered a wet cloth to wipe down the garden table and chairs they rarely used.

Dora went out to the phone in the hall and dialled the number. A maid answered at first and, when Lady Ponsonby finally picked up the receiver, Dora said, 'I'm just checking whether Verity has told you she was going away for a bit. I've only just found out.'

'Oh really? That's too bad. I was rather hoping she'd join us here for the weekend. We're expecting a houseful and Verity's always so good at keeping Granny company. Do you think I can telephone her and ask her to change her plans?'

'I shouldn't think so. She's left me a note today saying she's on her way to Munich.'

'Oh, for goodness' sake, that's so inconvenient. Do you know how long she'll be gone?'

'She hasn't said, but it sounds as if she's planning on staying there for quite some time.' Dora thought she'd better not add any details about emulating the Mosleys' wedding or hoping to meet Hitler. This was difficult enough as it was.

'Oh, the wretched girl. How inconsiderate of her. I was banking on her being here to help us entertain in August for the start of the grouse season. Oh, damn it, I'll have to make other arrangements.'

Dora could tell from the bored tone that Verity's mother didn't really care where her daughter was, just about the fact that it was extremely bad timing and interfered with her own plans, particularly for the Glorious Twelfth, when the grouse shooting began on the estate's moors. She returned to the kitchen and Hugh, thinking her own family had always cared far more for her cousin than Verity's parents ever did.

'Well?' Hugh was uncorking a bottle of wine.

'Her mother didn't know and she didn't particularly care. Apart from it being extremely inconvenient.'

'Well, you've done your duty. I've set the table outside. Is everything ready?'

Dora quickly peeled the cold eggs, buttered the potatoes and chopped the crisp lettuce and cucumber. She couldn't find any vinegar for the beetroot and wondered if they'd finished it the last time they'd had fish and chips from the little place down the road.

Out in the cool garden, the scent of the Rambling Rector rose that climbed over the arbour filled the air. Weeds had sprung up here and there amidst the phlox and delphiniums but did little to spoil what had once been a well-kept oasis in the middle of London. They sat down on two creaking Lloyd Loom chairs with motheaten cushions, either side of a rickety bamboo table. Dora thought it was all charming, despite the shabbiness of the furniture.

As they began to eat, Hugh described his plans for restoring the garden. 'We should make space for vegetables, so I think a couple of the flower beds could go. And those neglected fruit trees could be pruned and encouraged to be productive. We might have more apples and plums by next autumn.'

As he waved and pointed with his fork, Dora smiled at his eagerness. This dear man who could mend broken bodies also had the knowledge to repair nature and she loved him all the more for it.

He noticed her amused expression and paused in his description. 'Have I said something funny?'

'No, I'm just enjoying your enthusiasm, darling. What do you think we should plant first? And will there be room for asparagus? You know that's what Vee would be expecting!'

'Certainly not. It takes up far too much space, it takes far too long to establish and it's over in a flash. We'll only have highly productive crops like potatoes, carrots and brassicas. And anyway, she's not here, so she doesn't get a say in the matter.'

He noticed her mock pout and added, 'But maybe we could squeeze in some raspberries. Would that please you and Vee?'

'Oh, I'm not in the least bit worried about what my silly cousin might want. I'm actually rather disappointed in her, running off like that without telling me first.'

'I know she didn't say it would be quite so soon, darling, but she did rather hint the other day that she and Raven would go at some point. So, here's to a peaceful few weeks,' Hugh said, offering Dora a glass of wine. 'It's not very cold, but I did my best, keeping it in the cellar and dousing it in cold water.'

'It's most welcome. Thank you, darling.' She took a sip. 'Maybe we'll have more than a few weeks if we're lucky.'

'Mmm, she wasn't very clear, was she? Do you think she'd like to stay out there?'

'I don't think any of us would like to stay if things get nasty. But I find Verity impossible to predict and she does seem to be turning a blind eye whenever the threat of war is mentioned.'

'Still looking very unsettled, isn't it? How are they taking it at the office?' Hugh frowned as a sliver of beetroot splashed his white shirt.

Dora cut away the pastry on her piece of pork pie. She was never keen on that wrinkled white underside, coated with jelly, rather like puckered flesh that had soaked too long in the bath. 'Everyone's very concerned and the general view is that it's getting worse.'

She scooped a slice of egg onto her fork. Maybe now was the time to tell him. 'Brenda is organising a trip out there, to see exactly how the new laws are affecting people.'

'Very sensible. It's the only way to fully understand what's going on and what you might be facing.'

'She's got tremendous experience and loads of contacts, having spent so much time out there since the twenties. She's going the first week in September.'

'Sounds like she's well informed then. I'll be interested to hear what she has to say about the political climate out there when she comes back, if that's not breaking any confidences. Some very unsettling rumours are leaking out from those who've decided to leave the country.' Hugh dipped his napkin in the white wine and rubbed the stain on his shirt unsuccessfully.

Dora took a deep breath. Now was the time to tell him. 'Actually, what she uncovers won't be confidential and you'll be able to hear it from the horse's mouth, so to speak.' She took great interest in her plate as she spoke, dissecting the deep red beetroot. 'In fact, I'll be able to fill you in myself if you like, because I'll be going with her.'

Hugh's knife and fork clattered a little on his plate. He frowned, then said, 'I'd rather you didn't go, but I know I can't stop you.' He put his hand on hers. 'No, I'm sorry, darling. I shouldn't have said that. It's too important a job for me to care about how I might feel. You're doing valuable work and you've got to get it right. I know you will make a great team.'

'It's not just me. Another colleague is coming with us. Alice Fuller was the only other person who volunteered.'

'Mmm, no one else in the office keen to go?'

'Darling, most of them have families and would find it too difficult to leave them. Alice and I, along with Brenda, have no ties to keep us. Well, apart from me, that is, with my wonderful husband.'

Hugh smiled. 'Go then, with my blessing, and tell me everything you can on your return.'

Dora nodded and returned to her meal. She would tell him everything eventually, she thought, but for now maybe she wouldn't tell him about Nuremberg. And she wouldn't tell him about the rally. She wasn't sure he'd be quite so happy about her being in the midst of a horde of fanatical Brownshirts, spoiling for a fight, ready to turn on anyone who didn't idolise their regime and their hero.

FOURTEEN

EVERYONE'S INVITED
NUREMBERG, SEPTEMBER 1937

'The Nazis always give their rallies a rousing theme,' Brenda said as they pondered their breakfast of white sausage and crisp pretzels, the morning after they had arrived in Nuremberg. 'They're calling this one the Reichsparteitag der Arbeit, which means the Rally of Labour. It's a celebration of the fact that unemployment has reduced since the Nazis came into power. As you can appreciate, for the ordinary German people, who remember the crippling inflation after the Great War, a stable economy and good jobs are vitally important. This is one of the things that has made the Nazi Party so popular – they believe they have the Nazis to thank for this.'

Dora tried cutting into the warm Weisswurst and soon realised that the tough skin wasn't meant to be eaten. She tasted a morsel and recognised the flavourings of parsley and lemon, as well as a spice she couldn't immediately identify.

'Do you think they might be able to make some tea for us?' Alice sniffed suspiciously at the fragrant beer that was being served to every guest in large glass mugs. 'I'm not used to drinking ale this early in the morning.'

'Try it,' said Brenda, taking a great gulp from her tankard.

'It's not at all strong and it's very good for you. It's what the local people always have for breakfast. We've got a long day ahead of us and might not have a chance to get refreshments again for hours.'

Dora peered out of the window at the stream of people already heading towards the parade grounds where the rallies were held. It was early in the morning and the sun was casting a watery light over their surroundings. Like a large number of other foreign attendees, they were being accommodated in railway carriages in sidings on the edge of Nuremberg for two days. The compartments were plain but clean and the food was generous; all the delegates had commented on how clever the enterprising Germans were to think of adapting the train carriages for this purpose.

Dora tasted another portion of sausage meat and finally recognised the elusive flavouring. Of course, it was nutmeg. She happily finished the rest of it, then asked the question that had been concerning her ever since their trip had started: 'I've heard these events attract thousands of people. Are we going to have to queue for tickets along with everyone else?'

Brenda didn't seem at all perturbed by the question. 'We shan't be queuing,' she said. 'We have official invitations and we can go to our seats later than the general crowds. I applied for the authority to attend months ago, anticipating that it would be timely to include this event on our mission. The Nazi Party has extended a welcome to many foreign visitors, so we won't be the only ones there to observe the spectacle.'

'But does that mean they will really welcome our presence and our questions?' Alice seemed nervous. She had been jumpy ever since they'd arrived in Germany.

'I keep telling you,' Brenda said, wiping her lips with her napkin, 'they are more than willing to receive us here. The work our organisation has done in the past, feeding children and helping needy families, means we Quakers are not regarded as opposers of the regime. It puts us in a unique position to observe and record. Remember that at all times and keep your eyes open.'

Alice nodded and finished her meal, having taken only the tiniest sip of the beer. Dora had rather enjoyed the drink but hadn't drunk quite as much as Brenda. She was already thinking of all they had seen since arriving in Nuremberg the day before. Brenda had suggested they should take a short tour of the city before going to their accommodation and in that brief time Dora felt she had gained an unsettling impression of the threats facing certain members of the community.

'Look over there,' Brenda had said even before they had left the station, nodding towards the group of adults and children clad in dark coats although the day was warm. 'That looks like another Jewish family leaving the country. Good luck to them.'

Their pale faces and dark hair meant they stood out against the rosy cheeks and blondness of other passengers. And Dora thought they looked sad to be going, even though it might be safer for them to do so. Their families might well have thrived in this city for years, contributing to its good fortunes as doctors, teachers and tradesmen. But now they were no longer welcome to live alongside Aryan Germans and felt forced to leave.

Before the rally started, Brenda suggested a walk through the city. Dora noticed how clean and well-kept all the streets were. Every cobblestone seemed to be neatly swept, the paint-work was fresh and doorsteps were scrubbed. But as they neared the Jewish quarter, there was a marked change. The streets were narrow and dirty, the houses shabby, and Dora felt that the community was already being confined, squeezed into the least desirable sections of the city.

Later in the day, when it was finally time for them to take their seats at the rally, they walked towards the famous parade ground where Germany showed off its strength and the might of its people. The avenue they walked, like everywhere else in

Nazi-run Germany, was festooned with red banners boasting the party's proud symbol, the swastika. The sun was setting through the trees and fireworks were exploding in the sky. Everyone looked purposeful, cheerful and proud. They took their places in the stadium and Dora became conscious of the vast numbers attending as she surveyed the tiers of seats. How many could there be here? Thousands? No, more – a hundred thousand perhaps.

As the marching of large squads of straight-backed soldiers and servicemen commenced, Dora's head began to throb at the rhythmic sight of rows of men and women performing in unison. Lines of them, drilled to perfection, demonstrating how strong and successful this country now was. Red and black flags were unfurled and waved as the synchronised groups paraded before the main stage. And then there was a thunderous roar as a stream of planes flew overhead in formation, proof of Germany's powerful command of the skies as well as the land.

Finally, a motorcade bearing the leader of all this impressive ceremony bisected the parading troops. The crowds responded to the spectacle and the music with an almighty cheer and cries of 'Heil Hitler!' It was really him at last. Hitler, standing upright in an open car, his arm outstretched as he acknowledged the loyalty of his forces and his people. His entourage proceeded to the main proscenium, where he stepped out onto the stage to an almighty cry of support, then barked out an impassioned speech that electrified his subjects. Dora understood most of the tirade, in which he took credit for the decrease in unemployment and finding jobs for loyal Germans. She glanced at the members of the audience around her. They were all enthralled by his charisma, their faces almost beatific.

As his hysterical speech came to a crescendo at last, the whole performance was enhanced still further by the rich tones of the tremendous organ bellowing the last movement of Bruckner's Fifth Symphony. And all around the stadium, the audience thrust their arms forward in that fervent Nazi salute and shouted their allegiance to him and his policies.

Dora glanced at Brenda, who was holding her arms rigidly by her sides. But beyond her, Alice was being nudged by her neighbour, a large German man, who was frowning at her until her arm began to lift. Dora could also feel the man standing beside her digging her with his elbow, but she refused to look at him.

Once all the marching and shouting had subsided, the man pushed past Dora and her companions, loudly saying, 'Dumme Englischen Frauen.' He must have heard them speaking in their own language before the rally began. His cohorts gave the three women a disgusted look as he switched to English and said, 'You and your sort are a disgrace. Why don't you run back to your country and take all the Jews with you?'

Brenda snapped back at him: 'We'd be glad to take them. You are all mad to drive cultured, talented people away.'

His retort was to spit at her feet. 'Once they've all run off, there'll be more jobs for honest, loyal Germans.' And then he and his friends were gone, buried in the seething mass of people streaming away from the grounds.

'They're losing their professors, their doctors, their scientists,' Brenda said with a sigh. 'Little do they realise what harm they're doing to their country in supporting this madness.'

By now, the light of the day had gone and the whole arena was lit by the brilliant white beams of great vertical searchlights shining all around them, like enormous pillars, creating the semblance of a monumental church. 'They call this effect the Cathedral of Light,' Brenda said in a solemn voice. 'It's known as the Lichtdom.'

Then Dora realised she felt cold, despite the warmth of the evening, and she was trembling. An overwhelming feeling of icy dread enveloped her as she became aware that she had just witnessed the calculated hypnotism of an audience of thousands, an effect extending to the whole city and spreading across the entire country. This was no normal political meeting. This was the rallying of disciples now utterly committed to a terrible cause. Everyone present here, apart from a few independent witnesses like the members of her group, had been seduced by this atmospheric performance of might. Here in Nuremberg and throughout the nation there was no opposition to any laws the Nazis might pass, no objection to any restrictions on freedom. Everyone here believed passionately in supporting the party and its ideology, however flawed, and there could be no question of them ever turning back.

She hugged herself to steady her shaking limbs and chattering teeth. Then slowly, as her breathing calmed, she became aware of the lingering scent of cordite from the firework display overlaying the surrounding smells of tobacco, perspiration and beer. The combination smelt ominous and, after wondering for a moment about its significance, she realised what it meant: this was the smell of encroaching war.

FIFTEEN

AFTER THE PARTY

That night in their comfortable train compartment, Dora was glad of Brenda's reassuring, confident presence. She seemed completely unshaken by the dramatic performance they had witnessed at the rally, although the two younger women felt drained and apprehensive.

'We must keep our voices down. Our views might not find favour with others here,' Brenda said as they shared a flask of hot chocolate. 'But you saw for yourselves how the majority of the population are in thrall to Hitler and his supporters. What we've witnessed today confirms in my mind how dangerous this regime is and how we're going to be facing a situation of the direst urgency before too long.'

'What do you think we might have to do?' Alice lifted her mug to her lips with trembling hands.

'I'd like to think that we could encourage their opponents to speak up,' Brenda said. 'We Quakers have never been shy about voicing our opinions and telling the truth, but we know what will happen if anyone opposes them. They would face the direst consequences. They've already disposed of their main opponents. So, we must continue to offer help to those wishing to leave Germany and Austria. The numbers are likely to increase drastically with the restrictive laws they keep imposing on the Jews. The opportunities for them to live peacefully and successfully are decreasing by the day.'

'Do you mean you think there are going to be even more restrictions?' Dora cast her mind over the laws that had already been passed. 'They've already said Jews can't be lawyers, tax consultants, vets, teachers in public schools, or many other professions. Isn't that enough?'

'I fear this is only the beginning,' Brenda said, dipping a sugared biscuit into her hot chocolate. 'This year has so far been relatively uneventful, but the mayor of Berlin has, as you know, ordered public schools not to admit Jewish children until further notice. And where one city issues such a decree, others are sure to follow.'

'But they're only children,' Alice murmured. 'What harm can children possibly do?'

'It's not because they are children, it's because they are part of a level of society the Germans find it useful to crush, so they can convince the populace they are creating better opportunities for Aryans. Everything they are doing is designed to make this country inhospitable for the Jews. It's clear they do not want people of that faith here any longer, despite their immense contribution to science, culture and trade. It's a despicable attitude and I am sure it's going to become even worse.'

'So, do you think we should be encouraging these people to leave?' Dora was thinking of the hundreds of begging letters she had already opened back in the London office and how many more would await her attention on her return.

'We will help them where we can. Our American Quaker friends are joining us in finding opportunities for a new start for those who are determined to leave. If Germany no longer appreciates their skills, then hopefully other countries will.' Brenda bit into another biscuit, scattering sugary crumbs across her bosom

'I worry that we are going to encounter opposition at home if we have more migrants wanting to come to Britain,' Dora said. 'And there are many who approve of the new German regime.'

'Hmm,' Brenda growled. 'The idiots approve of Hitler and his followers as a shield against what they regard as the menace of international communism. Little do they know that what is to come could well be far worse.'

'But surely lots of Jewish families will still want to leave, won't they?' Alice had acquired a chocolate moustache, which added pathos to her worried expression.

'Aah, but that's just the trouble,' Brenda said. 'Many would like to but can't for various reasons; some can't afford to, many don't want to leave dependent family members, while others think this period of unrest will eventually pass.'

'But many have already left, haven't they?' Dora hoped her efforts in the office had resulted in successful new starts for all those she had met and written to. 'We've helped hundreds of families and individuals find positions in England.'

'Of course. There has been a steady exodus for a number of years now, particularly since the first laws were imposed back in 1933. Those who saw the signs then are hopefully resettled in their new homes and contributing to other countries in the way they have done here in the past. But there are many who think they can still manage to live with these repressive laws, or even that they will change in time. You can understand why someone who has built up a successful business over a number of years would be reluctant to leave it all behind. Not every trade or business is transportable.'

'I know.' Dora sighed. 'I've had skilled men looking for work as tailors and shoemakers who are disappointed when they realise they can't find exactly the same positions as they have been used to.'

'And furthermore, as well as contributing to the success of German society and even fighting in the last war, many Jews have never faced such heightened anti-Semitism until now. Before the Nazi regime gained power, many Germans regarded such views as ignorant and uncultured. Sadly, that is now changing rapidly.' Brenda suddenly looked weary and brushed the biscuit crumbs from her blouse.

'It's hard to understand how the Nazis have gained such a firm hold on the German people,' Dora said.

'I know,' Brenda said with a sigh. 'But when the party won a huge portion of the vote in the 1932 elections its members made sure all dissenting voices were silenced. The brutality they employed to quieten their opponents should have made them unpopular, but they were cunning.'

'And now look what they've done,' muttered Alice in a tired voice, her eyes almost closing.

Dora reflected on all that Brenda had said and felt again the chill of the pomp and spectacle of the parade ground. 'We can't stop it becoming more powerful, can we? It's going to get much worse.'

'No, we can't stop it,' Brenda said, standing up. 'But we're going to be a thorn in their side, asking awkward questions and helping where we can. We don't share their views and I don't mind letting them know that.'

'And we're going to help the children, aren't we?' Alice yawned.

'Failing all else, we shall always help the children,' Brenda said. 'And now we should get a good night's sleep. We shall be investigating the heart of the Nazi organisation tomorrow when we travel to Munich.'

SIXTEEN

ROSA

'I see the party is crowing again about their achievements,' Rosa said as she gave Theresia her breakfast. 'Now they're claiming the credit for getting more work for unskilled Aryans. I think it's more likely because they're kicking Jewish people out of their jobs.'

Josef had been reading that day's paper. He lowered it at the sound of her voice and smiled, shaking his head. 'Now you're not to start worrying again. The government's success depends on helping ordinary people feel they have better lives now, after the Great War. Not everyone is as lucky as us. Many needed work and food for their families. It will soon settle down once more.' He shook the paper and lifted it again, so Rosa couldn't see his expression.

'Huh, you'd think they despised education the way they're telling our kind they can't work at anything that requires half a brain. Don't they realise that some professions depend on knowledge and skill?' Rosa angrily clattered the breakfast dishes as she cleared the table.

Josef continued reading. His silence added to Rosa's annoyance. 'I don't know what they're all going to do if there's another outbreak of something like Spanish flu,' she said. 'Then they'll regret losing all their excellent Jewish doctors.'

Josef folded the newspaper with a great deal of rattling of the pages. 'I'm going down to the workshop, Rosa. We have a business to run and I believe we haven't yet been ordered to stop making good suits and dresses for Germans who can afford them. I'm not listening to any more of this nonsense, we will always be in demand.'

'You say that now,' Rosa threw after him as he went down the stairs. 'Wait till it lands on your doorstep, like it has with many of our neighbours. The teachers, the accountants, the doctors, all of them banned. Then you'll wish you'd listened to me.' She wiped Theresia's hands and face and sent her daughter off to play with her toys until it was time for them to walk to school.

Where will it all end? she asked herself. She had wanted Theresia to attend the public school, but when schools were told not to admit any more Jewish children, she had changed her mind. It had been bad enough, she thought, when the state had banned Jewish teachers so Theresia was attending a Jewish school, with other children from her community only. Perhaps it was for the best, now that ordinary German children seemed to have forgotten their manners, calling names outside the synagogue and chasing Jewish children on their way to classes. Theresia had been scared by their behaviour and Rosa, remembering her disastrous encounter with those young Brownshirts, hadn't dared reprimand them. No, better to turn away, stay quiet and keep working hard than say anything.

SEVENTEEN

THE BROWN HOUSE

As they approached their destination, Dora could not help but admire the magnificent house occupied by the Nazi headquarters in Munich. The Braunes Haus with its impressive stone facade was an imposing testament to power and authority, built by a German aristocrat over a hundred years previously and purchased for the Nazis in 1930. Key officials of the regime occupied offices here and Hitler even had an apartment, as if it was a personal fiefdom.

A young Brownshirt greeted the women politely when Brenda confirmed their appointment with Heinrich Himmler, head of security for the organisation. They were ushered from the entrance lobby into a marbled hall, then to an imposing staircase, and on to an upper office, with a smart young Brownshirt to greet and escort them at each stage of their arrival, until they finally entered Himmler's presence in the Senatorensaal conference room, which was flanked by the red and black flags of the party and guarded by yet more Brownshirts.

Dora felt the overbearing presence of so many stern-faced young men was hardly necessary for a group of three civilised Englishwomen, but clearly the officials considered that no chances could be taken. However, Himmler approached them in a friendly manner, offering his hand to each of them in turn with a slight bow of his head and a waft of cologne. She could tell that his well-pressed black uniform had definitely been made to measure. The shoulders were adorned with oak leaves in silver braid.

'My dear ladies,' he said with a smug smile, 'we are honoured to welcome you to our humble offices. And you are among the privileged few to lay eyes upon our most prized possession.' He waved his hand in a grand gesture at the wall behind him, where a stained red flag was displayed in a prominent position. 'You are in the presence of the Blutfahne, which was splattered with the blood of our brave wounded companions when the Munich police attempted to halt our justified demonstration in 1923. It has rarely been seen by anyone other than senior members of our party.'

Dora thought he spoke with fanatical fervour, similar to the passion she had witnessed at the previous night's rally, as if this flag was a sacred relic and he was a devout pilgrim newly returned from the Holy Land. But Brenda took it all in her stride, giving the faded, tattered flag just the briefest of glances before saying, 'Thank you, Herr Himmler, for agreeing to meet us. We are English Quakers and we are intensely interested in the welfare of Germany. We would like to be enlightened about the aims of the new revolution.'

'Indeed, indeed,' he said, nodding, and indicating the group should take seats around the central conference table. 'We are delighted that our progress is of such interest to your country. And may I say that your organisation has gained great respect in Germany, through your invaluable charitable efforts in previous years of hardship.'

'We have always been ready to help where needed,' Brenda said. 'And we're glad to see families thriving after those difficult times.'

'But now,' Himmler expanded, 'we are continuing to improve life for our population. Ensuring more decent employment for honourable citizens is one of our primary objectives. A million more men have been able to find honest work since the beginning of this year.' His chest seemed to puff with pride as he announced this figure.

'That is indeed a worthy aim,' Brenda said. 'Men need to work to provide for their families.'

'And we are also trying to help the peasants by ensuring they can have their own piece of land. We believe it is important for them to feel they have a stake in our country.' He spoke with such sincerity as he went on, 'We believe we must even up the wage scales as well. Manual workers deserve a decent wage and officials should not be overpaid.'

'Oh, I heartily agree with you there,' Brenda said. 'Everyone should be paid a fair wage. But what about those from the Jewish community? Restrictions introduced in recent years have made it difficult for them to contribute to the country's development as much as they once did. Is it not a great loss for Germany that so much scientific and professional knowledge is no longer available?'

He frowned, indicating that this was an unwelcome question. 'Christians have just as much knowledge and skill as the Jews, but for a long time they have been excluded, crowded out from the professions. And now they too can have a chance to be successful and develop their potential.'

Dora was surprised at the calm manner he displayed in answering this question. It was obvious to her that intelligent individuals were being removed from German businesses, public services and society. Whether they could easily be replaced was another matter.

Brenda remained calm too as she asked her next leading question: 'We in Britain are also very interested in the current methods of suppressing opposition. Recent developments mean there is now no alternative to the Nazi Party. Do you not think that the lack of democracy is less healthy for a nation?'

Dora thought Himmler's smug face, with its little hint of a moustache, was showing signs of deepening in colour. Already florid from rich food and beer, it might turn beetroot if Brenda kept probing.

In a clipped voice that betrayed his annoyance, he said, 'All other political parties have betrayed the Fatherland in one way or another so they can no longer be allowed to endanger our nation's safety. We cannot tolerate alternative views, for the good of the whole country.'

Dora sensed that Brenda was keeping a tight control on her emotions as she said, 'But I believe that pacifists are also being regarded as suspect elements by the current regime. Is it really a betrayal of one's country to work for peace? Our organisation strongly believes in peace and our members here and in Britain consider themselves to be friends of Germany. What do you have to say to that?'

His eyes narrowed as he said, 'Some of your people, along with a number of others, have made insufficient effort to interpret our great national revolution. We will not tolerate disloyalty.' He sat back in his chair with his hands clasped on the table.

And in that moment, Dora saw the crystals of cold ice forming in his eyes behind his spectacles and heard the slice of steel in his voice. She realised his hands were not passively clasped, but were two intertwined fists, ready to mete out punishment at the slightest provocation.

Brenda began to say that the Quakers believe there is God in everyone and that they would nevertheless try to maintain a dialogue with the Nazi movement. But just then they heard the insistent tone of a phone ringing in the conference room and Himmler rose to answer it. The women sat in silence as he spoke, hearing every word he said: 'It's just as we suspected. You must occupy the house and keep guard. Send more men to search thoroughly for evidence. Bring them straight here and we'll deal with them.'

Then he turned back to the group as if their conversation had never been interrupted and his words had not been over-heard. 'Ladies, thank you all for coming. I am glad we have had the opportunity to share our vision and of course we all wish to maintain peace.' He shook their hands one by one and they were escorted from the building in silence by more brown-shirted guards.

Once they were outside, Dora lifted her face to feel the sun and breathe the clean air. She felt as if she had been on the brink of an abyss. 'Did you hear what he said to that caller?'

'I didn't understand it,' Alice said, her pale and frightened face appealing to them. 'What did it all mean?'

'I am afraid, my dear, that someone is going to get very badly hurt.' Brenda looked back over her shoulder at the elegant porticoed building with arched windows on its ground floor. 'I've heard it said that this place is called the Denuntiatur, the place of denunciation, which means this is where people are betrayed and accused of crimes against the government. They bring their opponents here for interrogation, something not everyone survives.'

'Oh no,' Alice said. 'That's awful. Why would they do that?'

'Because they will brook no opposition. Himmler made that perfectly clear. And that is why they are so dangerous.' She took a deep breath as if she too wanted to inhale clean, fresh air, untainted by what they had just been subjected to. 'Come, girls. Let us walk in the park for a while and then we shall visit another Nazi haunt in search of more answers.' Brenda strode ahead, while her two dazed accomplices struggled to absorb all that she had just said.

EIGHTEEN

LADIES WHO LUNCH
MUNICH, SEPTEMBER 1937

Dora stared at the fashionable Munich restaurant in disbelief. 'Is that where we're going next? I thought you said we were here to do research. And I think I've heard the name of this place somewhere before.'

They were standing outside the Osteria Bavaria. Brenda said, 'I thought we'd have lunch here. I've been dragging you girls around from one place to another and you both deserve to have a decent meal before we set off on the next stage of our journey.'

Alice eagerly agreed, but Dora couldn't shake the nagging feeling that there was more to this decision than simply having a good lunch; Brenda didn't undertake anything without a clear reason. As they entered, Dora decided she should remain alert the whole time.

When they were presented with the menu and began to study the list of tempting dishes, the thought suddenly popped into her head that this was where Verity had said she and Raven intended dining regularly once they were settled in Munich. Dora had half wondered whether she should attempt to make contact with her cousin on this trip, but had dismissed the idea because she had wanted to concentrate and use every minute to assist in Brenda's important fact-finding mission. But what if Verity should now walk into the restaurant? What would Brenda think of her association with a Nazi-loving frivolous socialite?

Dora buried her head in the menu, hoping her cousin wouldn't appear. There was no reason to suppose that she ate here every day, after all, even if she had said it would be one of her reasons for living in Munich.

'I think we should make the most of this opportunity to eat well,' Brenda said. 'After this we shall be taking the train to Vienna. That's where the exit visas are being handled at present and I think we should see for ourselves how accommodating the Nazis are being there. I suspect they are making the process as difficult as they possibly can, but I would like to know more.'

All three of them ordered a substantial pork dish with potatoes and dumplings that would satisfy their hunger for the rest of the day. Brenda ordered a light beer with her meal and the girls settled for Himbeersaft, a raspberry cordial.

The restaurant was busy and the tables around them were filling up, but the service was prompt and their food arrived after only a short interval. Dora tucked into her dish with a good appetite, but had taken only a few mouthfuls of the delicious pork flavoured with mustard and marjoram when the chatter and hum of the popular establishment faded away. It was as if an invisible hand had turned the volume knob on the wireless right down to nothing. And Dora felt an eerie chill. It couldn't be repeating itself, could it? This felt like that time three years previously when she had been enjoying chocolate cake one moment and sickened to her core the next.

She glanced at Brenda and saw that she too had noticed the shift in atmosphere. Alice was oblivious, still eating and enjoying her food. Brenda nodded at Dora and turned her gaze slightly to one side. Dora did the same and saw that nearly every

single occupant of the lunch tables was watching the entrance
lobby in total silence.

And then it happened all over again. Flanked by uniformed
guards and officials, parading himself in a humble brown suit as
if he was no more than an ordinary citizen, a bank clerk or an
accountant taking a modest lunch break, it was Him. Hitler.
Dora could not swallow anymore; she nearly choked on the
food in her mouth. And all around them, chairs scraped back on
the wooden parquet floor as all the diners stood to salute him.

The last thing Dora wanted to do was acknowledge his
presence, but Brenda hissed, 'We'd better stand up. But no
salute, mind.' She nudged Alice, who had still barely noticed
what was happening, into standing too. Dora hoped that this
time no one nearby would criticise their behaviour, but luckily
the whole room seemed to ignore them; they only had eyes for
the magnificent presence of their illustrious leader.

And then, as if events couldn't have got any worse for Dora,
they did. For trailing behind the group that had entered was a
slight, fair-haired young woman, accompanied by a tall dark
man. Dora held her breath. She could scarcely believe it, but it
was Verity and Raven who had followed Hitler and his companions into the room and were seated with them at the Führer's
table.

As other diners reseated themselves and resumed eating,
Dora could not face picking up her knife and fork. She stared at
the table. Fortunately, Verity and her lover, or maybe he was
now her husband, had their backs to her. Dora prayed they
would not turn round and catch her eye.

Even from the little she had seen as her cousin entered,
and from what she could see now, Dora could tell that Verity
had changed. Before she had left London she had loved bright
colours, jewels and silk scarves, apart from when she dressed
largely in black to attend Mosley's rallies. Now she was
dressed in a sober, dark grey suit, well-tailored, but stern all

the same. Beneath it was a cream blouse with a neat, buttoned collar and no pearls, as far as Dora could see. Her hair had changed too. She used to visit a hairdresser to have it curled and waved around her beautiful face, but now it was straight and sleek, curving just beyond her collar in a curtain of blonde silk. And she had topped it with a simple black velvet hat that hugged itself around her head without adornment. No net, no flowers or feathers, just this caress of plain black velvet.

Despite herself, Dora had to admit that Verity looked serious and elegant. She had obviously thrown herself into preparing well for her part as a friend and confidante of Hitler. Her mannerisms were more restrained too. Whereas once she had giggled and chattered, danced the Charleston and made silly jokes, Dora could tell from her demeanour that this had changed. Even though she could only see Verity's head and shoulders above the curved back of the dining chair, she could tell that her cousin was quieter, less animated, just occasionally nodding in approval as her hero spoke to the entire transfixed table.

'You're very quiet, dear,' Brenda said. 'Aren't you enjoying your food?'

Dora was jolted into paying attention. 'I'm so sorry. I was slightly distracted for a moment. No, it's all very good indeed.'

But Brenda was not easily fooled. She noticed that Dora could not stop staring at the main focus of interest for the entire restaurant. 'He comes here frequently,' she said. 'It's one of his favourite places. That and the tea rooms.'

'I went there once.' Dora managed to find the words. 'Three years ago, the tea rooms, with my cousin. We saw him then too.'

'And was it like it is now?' Brenda's eyebrows arched as she asked the question.

'You mean the fawning, the sheer adoration?' Dora dabbed her lips with her napkin. She felt sick again. 'It was worse, I think. Children were brought to his table.' She looked up at Brenda. 'Is that why you really wanted to come here?'

Brenda smiled. 'Well, the food is actually rather good. But yes, I wanted to get a closer look for myself. I wondered if the common man would be as easily impressed as those fervent admirers we saw at the rally yesterday. And I have to say, I'm rather afraid they are all in thrall to him.'

Dora looked at her congealing food. It seemed less appetising than when it had arrived a few minutes earlier, but for Brenda's sake she knew she should try to politely eat a little more. Alice was ploughing her way through the whole plateful and didn't seem aware of their quiet conversation.

Dora picked up her knife and fork again, but then hesitated and said, 'There's something else I really need to tell you and I sincerely hope you won't think any the worse of me.'

Brenda looked surprised, but simply said, 'Go on, spit it out.' Then she laughed and added, 'And I don't mean the food.'

Dora managed a weak smile. 'The fact is, my cousin Verity is over there with all of them and Him.'

'Your cousin?' Brenda frowned and glanced across at the table.

'That young woman with her back to us. She came out to Munich determined to meet him one day. I'd no idea she'd managed to ingratiate herself into his inner circle so quickly. She's in love with the man next to her, Raven Fitzgerald. He was one of Mosley's men and she was a sympathiser too, before she left England.'

'Oh dear, oh dear, the poor deluded lass. They'll drop her the minute she puts a foot wrong. And him too, probably. She's only there so Hitler can flaunt his grand British connections. I assume she's from an upper-class family?'

'Yes, they're titled. Verity's an Honourable, in fact, but she rarely mentions it.'

'Hmm,' Brenda murmured. 'How very quaint. The Hon

and the Hun. I expect she thinks it will help, but it's a recipe for disaster. Do you want to warn her?'

'No, I'd rather she didn't realise I was here. She wouldn't be any help to us. She's just an embarrassment. I'm so sorry.'

'Well, try and finish your lunch at least. Who knows when we'll next have a proper meal,' Brenda said, popping a large piece of potato into her mouth with evident relish. 'Don't worry about her, dear. We can't choose our relatives but we can choose our friends.'

Dora tried to finish her meal, but every mouthful lacked flavour and felt like cardboard.

NINETEEN

HEADLINE NEWS

Ever since their return from Munich, Dora had tried not to think too often about Verity. Her cousin was a grown woman and could do what she liked. But Brenda's wise words had emphasised the risk she was taking and, because of her childhood affiliation, Dora couldn't help feeling concerned. Despite her cousin's annoying habits, she had always been fond of Vee and had tolerated her ridiculous ways but now she worried about the company Verity was keeping and how long she'd be safe so close to the heart of this ruthless regime.

Verity's mother phoned from time to time, always expecting that Dora would know when her daughter might be returning. 'The wretched girl never writes to us nowadays and she knows Granny misses her dearly. Can't you persuade her to come home? You've always had such a way with her. She never listens to her father or me.'

'I'm so sorry, Aunt. She wouldn't want to know anyway. She's always had a mind of her own.' But Dora couldn't bring herself to tell Lady Ponsonby that she had caught a glimpse of Verity in Munich and that, whatever her daughter was doing now, she wouldn't be dragged away from her fascination with

Hitler and his cohorts until she was either wholly embraced by her objective or rejected.

The London office was busier than ever and Brenda was increasingly involved in meetings with other charitable agencies, all recognising the growing urgency of their work. She was also lobbying government departments in her attempts to directly involve ministers in making decisions about the number of potential refugees. 'They either seem to think the problem will go away, or are afraid to tackle it because of public opinion,' she seemed to be constantly saying to anyone who asked her about progress.

Dora felt that, despite the clearly ominous signs they had gathered on their mission to Germany, they were failing to solve the issue themselves. Apart from the daily advice dispensed by her office, there was little they could do to hasten or ease the arrival of refugees. Those with assets found it easier to obtain visas and usually already had connections in professions and levels of society in Britain, but the less well off were struggling to gain entry.

In early December, Dora found herself trudging home in the gloomy light cast by the old gaslights that lined the pavements. A soft rain was falling, creating a misty haze around the glowing lamps. It was a dreary end to the day and she tried to comfort herself by thinking of how she and Hugh would have a warm cosy supper, then sit close to the fire and listen to a concert on the wireless. She'd cooked a large stew of beef and carrots the day before and there was enough left to make a pie. If she was quick she could have it in the oven before Hugh returned from the hospital. He always said how he loved to walk in and be greeted by the aromas of a good dinner cooking.

As soon as she was indoors, Dora busied herself lighting the gas stove and making pastry. It had never been her mother's strong point, but their family cook had taught Dora basic techniques, saying, 'Cool fingertips, Miss Dora, that's the trick. Lift them up and get some air into those crumbs.' Thinking of those times, when she'd been wrapped in one of Mrs Lovett's starched white aprons, standing on a stool at the scrubbed kitchen table, brought back happy thoughts. She hummed as she rubbed the lard into the flour and again as she rolled out the pastry on the clean table.

She was just crimping the edges of the pie lid and thinking about making a decoration from the scraps to adorn the top when she heard the front door and Hugh came rushing into the kitchen with a blast of cold air.

He gave her a quick hug round the waist and, as she turned to kiss him, he said, 'I love it when you have flour on your nose,' and he kissed it.

'I don't, do I?' She dusted the tip of her nose with her apron.

'You do now,' he said, laughing and kissing her again. 'What are we having tonight?'

'Steak pie, if I can just get it into the oven.' She beat an egg and brushed the golden wash across the pastry, then cut two holes in the centre of the lid to let the steam escape. 'I was going to show off with some fancy pastry leaves, but I think you'd rather have supper as soon as possible, so this plain pie will have to do.'

'It looks delicious, darling.' He peered in the larder and fetched a bottle of Watneys beer. 'Do you fancy a drop of this?'

'Oh, just a teeny slurp. And maybe I'll throw a drop in the gravy too.' She slid the pie into the oven on a baking tray, then moulded the remaining pastry scraps into a ball and rolled it out. 'I'll just quickly make a couple of jam tarts with this, then I'll put my feet up for a moment.'

In minutes Dora had cut out the tarts with a fluted pastry cutter and popped them in the oven with cubes of bread crust to blind bake. She'd fill them with home-made plum jam later – Hugh loved to have something sweet when he was peckish.

As usual, Hugh was already leaning back in the kitchen armchair, hidden behind a newspaper. Dora sat opposite, feeling more relaxed now he was home and they were together in their warm kitchen. The newspaper rustled as he folded back the page he'd been reading and Dora found herself glancing idly at the columns. But suddenly, one headline jumped out at her: *HUN WEDDING FOR BRITISH HEIRESS.*

Dora leant forward to look more closely. There was a photograph with this article and she found herself reading the words of the headline aloud, followed by, 'What on earth are you reading, Hugh? This isn't *The Times*, is it?'

He moved the paper to one side and peered round at her shocked face. 'No, I left it too late to get one. I found this on the bus. It's the *Express*. Some chap had left it there. Why, what's the matter?'

'Look. Turn it over and look at this page.' Dora jabbed agitatedly at the article until he folded the page back again so they could both read it properly.

Society darling and heiress the Honourable Verity Ponsonby, daughter of Lord and Lady Ponsonby of Featherstonehaugh Hall, wed Mosley acolyte Raven Fitzgerald in Munich at the home of Joseph Goebbels in a ceremony witnessed by Herr Hitler himself. Lord and Lady Ponsonby, the bride's parents, did not attend the wedding and were unavailable for a comment on their daughter's marriage.

'She's only gone ahead and got married,' Dora said in a subdued voice. 'Well, she said she was going to. So, she's got exactly what she wanted, hasn't she?'

'You can't say she didn't warn us,' Hugh said. 'She couldn't have said it more plainly.'

'I know. But somehow I didn't quite believe she could make it happen like this.'

'Do you think she's even told her parents? It looks as if neither of them had any family members present at the wedding, according to this.' Hugh studied the article again.

'Oh crumbs, I'm dreading another phone call from her mother. I hope I'm out next time they try ringing. I'll have to make you answer it.'

'Well, I doubt they'll be reading about it in the *Express*.'

Dora half laughed. Hugh did have a wonderful way of making light of a situation. 'No, I don't think her family have ever read anything other than *The Times* and *Tatler* in their lives. But surely every newspaper in the country is going to leap on this story. It's just so sensational.'

Hugh pulled a face. 'I expect they will. Everyone loves a scandal. Especially a society scandal. There hasn't been anything this exciting since Edward and Mrs Simpson.' The press had crawled all over photographs and reports of that marriage during the summer.

'Oh, Hugh, stop it. I can't bear to think of my cousin, daft as she is, being the subject of such awful gossip. Her parents will be absolutely furious. They were desperate for her to marry into a title and money.'

'But you've got to give it to her. She looks very happy in this picture and Raven is a jolly handsome chap, wouldn't you say?'

Dora studied the photograph more closely. Verity had a sweet smile on her face. She was wearing a headdress resembling a halo that gripped her veil and held a large trailing bouquet in one arm, while the other was linked to her husband's. Raven was dressed formally and his left hand rested on hers, in his arm. He looked protective. On either side of them the uniformed leaders of the Nazi Party, Goebbels and Hitler, appeared to gloat. Look who we have inveigled into our inner circle, they seemed to be saying. Look how our tentacles are now reaching into the upper echelons of British society. They must have been delighted to see the world's press leaping on the news of this marriage at the heart of their regime.

'I just can't bear it,' Dora said. 'She simply doesn't realise what she's doing and what it signifies to them. She can't see what is clearly going on out there.' She jumped up to rescue the potatoes boiling on the stove.

Hugh stood up too and, when she had set down the pan, he put his arms round her. She wept onto his shoulder. 'She'll come running home when it all goes wrong,' he said.

'I hope she gets out while she can,' Dora said through sobs. 'She's blind to the truth and can't see that they are using her. Stupid, stupid girl.'

And then the telephone began ringing and both Dora and Hugh held each other tight and listened until it stopped.

TWENTY

ROSA

BERLIN, APRIL 1938

Rosa was in a hurry. She waited impatiently for the lights to change at the crossroads in the city centre. She'd run out from the workshop to pick up the special mother-of-pearl buttons she'd ordered. If she was quick, she'd have time to sew them on before her client arrived that afternoon.

As the light turned to yellow she began to step off the kerb, but a hand pulled her back, hissing, 'You could get arrested for that. Look at him.' Across the road a man was being dragged away by the police. She turned to thank the passer-by who had saved her. In her haste, she too could have been arrested.

'Will he be fined just for jumping the lights?'

'Oh, they'll probably rough him up back at the police station. They'd have had him if he'd tried to cross diagonally too. Any excuse where they're concerned. An Aryan can get away with a warning, but not the Jews.'

He melted away into the crowds of the city, while Rosa reflected on her lucky escape. If she'd been arrested and held by the police, Josef would have had no idea where she was, Theresia would miss her and her difficult client might refuse to pay. Could such a tiny offence really be worth the trouble? But

as her saviour had said, the police, the Brownshirts and the
Nazis as a whole seemed to look for the tiniest excuse to punish
her race.

Rushing back to the workshop, clutching her package of
buttons, Rosa again felt that ominous pressure of the daily
threats. Josef still refused to take the restrictions seriously. In
fact, he had laughed when he heard of the ruling that Jewish
businesses couldn't change their names.

'Why on earth would we ever want to change our name
anyway when our customers are all queuing up to buy Goldberg suits and dresses? We've always got a waiting list and we've
had to employ our new cutter and a seamstress, to cope with the
demand.'

Rosa tried her best to be as optimistic as Josef. We are fortunate, she told herself, having a business that is still able to be
profitable. But many of our former neighbours are not doing so
well.

She thought of those whose former professions were now
closed to them, the lawyers, accountants, teachers and many
others, who were struggling to make a living and had had to
move out of their homes and find less expensive accommodation. She and Josef might still be doing well for the time being,
but would it continue or would new laws affect them too? How
much more could the authorities take from people?

The latest ruling, pompously entitled the Order for Disclo-
sure of Jewish Assets, required all Jews to report property in
excess of 5,000 Reichsmarks. Rosa shuddered at what this could
mean. It seemed to her that the government was weighing up
the value of the Jewish community in comparison to ordinary
Germans. And that there would come a time when they would
announce that the Jews were far too rich and that those assets
really should be shared by the state. What could she and Josef
say they owned? They'd paid for a long lease on the shop and
apartment, and they owned the machinery and the tools of their

trade and couldn't run their business without them. It scared her.

As she approached their shop in the fashionable quarter of the city, she felt proud to see the window display advertising their skilled services. A dark, well-cut suit made by her husband stood alongside a draped silk dress that was one of her most popular designs. But then her heart sank as she recognised a man in a threadbare, soiled suit sweeping the street. He had once been a professor at the university. Head lowered, he didn't turn towards her, so their eyes never met.

Rosa swallowed her fear. She knew that every unemployed Jew could be forced to do menial work. Perhaps this wasn't his choice. More likely he had been ordered to do it to humiliate him still further. She couldn't bear to look at him. She ran up the stairs to their apartment and began to cry.

TWENTY-ONE

A NIGHT TO REMEMBER

The atmosphere in Bloomsbury House was grim. Dora braced herself every time she went to the office, wondering how many more pitiful letters were awaiting her attention. Since the beginning of the year it seemed that every restriction the Nazi regime could invent was being applied specifically to the Jews and she felt pain for them every time she heard of yet another new discriminatory law.

In April all Jews had been required to register their assets. 'How dare they,' Brenda had exploded at one of their team meetings. 'Greedy monsters like Goebbels and Göring are totting up what valuables they can lay their hands on. They just want to know exactly how much these industrious people have built up through years of hard work. There is no justification for it whatsoever.'

Then in July it was announced that Jewish doctors would not be able to treat Aryans. Never mind that many of them were the best doctors that their German patients had ever had and that many Germans would have preferred to stay with a doctor they had known and trusted for many years. 'It's madness,' Hugh said when he heard of the decree. 'All honourable doctors subscribe to the Hippocratic oath. It doesn't matter what your faith or background is, you are there to heal everyone. They are shooting themselves in the foot and will find they have no one competent left to treat the sick and injured. Idiots!'

Dora agreed with Hugh, but inside she felt that growing sense of dread as each new sanction was announced. August of that year brought a law that she found particularly ominous, by which any Jew whose name didn't make their ethnicity clear was required to add the name Israel or Sara to their passport and identity documents. She found herself saying to Alice, who was equally shocked, 'It's so there'll be no way of hiding from them. What other hideous schemes can they possibly dream up?'

She hadn't imagined that the next development would come from another quarter altogether: a neighbouring country. Early in October, they heard that Switzerland was insisting that all passports belonging to German Jews should bear the initial 'J'. The Swiss Alien Police were demanding that Germany should provide a symbol to identify Jews at their country's borders. What it actually meant was that old passports had to be surrendered and then only passports with a 'J' were valid.

Dora heard the news with a sinking feeling. 'It's so they can't slip away easily,' she said to Brenda, who had a thunderous face.

'We knew it was going to get bad,' Brenda said. 'We saw the signs early on. But how could we know exactly what form it would take?'

Just over a month later, they all realised that events were really taking a serious turn for the worse. Brenda had asked Dora to accompany her to Berlin for another meeting with their German counterparts and Jewish representatives. 'We must make them see the need for urgency,' Brenda said of their journey. 'I have a terrible sense of foreboding. They won't stop now.'

Dora thought so too, when she told Hugh of her decision to

make another trip to Germany: 'I have to go with her. She is so strong, but even a forceful woman like Brenda needs company, someone to raise the alarm if there's a problem.'

'I don't like the thought of you going at all,' Hugh said, holding her tight. 'I hate thinking of how you have to face those thuggish Nazi brutes but I know you will both be sensible and take care. You can go with my blessing.'

'And if I see Verity,' Dora said with an impish smile, 'shall I tell her we miss her terribly and want her to come back home?'

'Heavens, no. I don't miss that silly little flibbertigibbet one bit. She can stay over there as long as she likes. She hasn't started producing sprogs as well now, has she?'

'Darling, you know that I haven't the faintest idea what she's been up to. And she hasn't been keeping her family informed either. That's rather selfish of her, I think. I know they haven't always been the most affectionate parents, but she ought to write to them now and again. They must wonder what she's involved in and who she's meeting.'

'With their sympathies I don't suppose they'd mind hearing her news...' Hugh laughed and attempted to imitate Verity's gushing tone of voice. '"Dearest Mummy, today we had tea with darling Hitler. He does so love his apple cake"... and so on in similar vein.'

'Yes, all very funny, darling. But not so amusing when you think she might be persuading others in her former circle to think the same way.'

Dora remembered this exchange when she and Brenda were returning to their hotel after dinner at the British embassy on their second evening in Berlin. The November night was turning cold, hinting at a bitter winter to come. They walked through Kurfürstendamm Strasse, one of the main shopping areas in Berlin, equivalent to Bond Street and Regent Street in

London's West End. As they passed the displays of expensive clothes and furnishings, Dora's eye was caught by a striking red dress in a shop window. 'Gosh, what a lovely frock,' she said to Brenda, who cared little for fashion and tended to always dress in shades of navy or brown. 'I don't normally hanker for clothes, but that is just gorgeous.'

'It would certainly suit you,' Brenda said, admiring the stylish garment on the mannequin. 'We can come this way tomorrow if you want a closer look when the shops open again.'

'Maybe better not.' Dora laughed. 'I might be tempted to buy it.' She looked longingly at the draped fabric, wishing she could feel its silky texture in her fingertips. 'It would be lovely for Christmas though.'

'Then we'll definitely come this way again in the morning,' Brenda said with a tolerant laugh.

As they continued their walk back to the hotel, they began to notice groups of men gathering in side streets with an underlying growl of menace. 'I don't know what's happening,' Brenda said, 'but I think we should quicken our pace and get back as quickly as possible.'

When they entered the hotel, Brenda went straight to the front desk and spoke to the concierge. 'Has something just happened? We couldn't help noticing crowds gathering outside.'

'Nothing of any consequence to concern you, madam. A little local difficulty, that is all.'

As Brenda led the way upstairs, she turned to Dora and said, 'We'll see, shall we? Local difficulty, my foot! Keep your door locked tonight, my dear. We'll know one way or another by the morning.'

Dora locked her door as instructed and prepared for bed but as she rinsed her face at the bathroom sink she thought she heard shouts far below, outside the hotel. She peered through the curtains and couldn't make out anything, but went to bed feeling uneasy.

Later that night she woke suddenly. She could hear the thump of footsteps running along the corridor and angry voices. She wondered whether to open her door, but then thought it safer to stay inside. She went to the window and gazed out upon the night-time city. A wave of shouting, screaming and the clanging of sirens reached her ears.

Dora was trying to make sense of it when she heard a knock on her bedroom door. 'It's only me,' she heard Brenda say in an urgent voice.

She unlocked the door and Brenda entered, patting Dora on the shoulder. 'Don't be alarmed. We are quite safe here, but I'm afraid our Jewish friends are in terrible trouble.' She strode across to the open curtains and looked out upon the city.

'It's started,' she said, shaking her head. 'Look out there. See the fires?'

Dora stood by her side and realised that she wasn't just seeing the lights of the city. Here and there, across the panorama of Berlin visible from her hotel window, was the bright flickering of flames and smoke billowing into the night sky. 'What on earth is going on?'

'It's the deliberate, wanton destruction of Jewish property,' Brenda said. 'They're targeting synagogues, businesses and homes. All in retaliation for something innocent people didn't warrant or commit. And all sanctioned by this corrupt government, which is egging them on to further frenzy.'

Dora felt sick, even though she knew she was safe in the hotel with Brenda. But what about their friends, their colleagues, the concerned people they had met with recently – were they safe? Or were they too being subjected to the will of the mob?

TWENTY-TWO
LET THE FIRES BURN
BERLIN, NOVEMBER 1938

Towards mid-morning, Brenda judged that it was quiet enough for them to venture out of the hotel. As they walked through the reception to the entrance, the concierge urged them to stay inside: 'We cannot be responsible for your safety, madam. There is still some unrest on the streets.'

But Brenda was bold enough to resist his cautious tone. 'Thank you for your advice, but we are official representatives of English Quakers and the British government. We are here as witnesses to this folly and it is our responsibility to report with our own eyes on this destruction and persecution.' She strode to the revolving doors, wielding her rolled umbrella as if it were a weapon. Dora followed, similarly armed, hoping they would not encounter any trouble.

In the immediate vicinity of the hotel there was no evidence of rioting, but a smell of smoke drifted on the air, hinting at fires still smouldering throughout the city. As they proceeded towards the main areas of business, the damage became obvious. The streets were littered with broken glass from shattered shop windows. Every premises identifiable as Jewish had been vandalised. Granite kerbstones, prised up from the city's roads, littered the pavements and many had been used as ammunition to smash the glass.

'How could the authorities have let this happen?' Dora stopped to look upon the devastated shops in horror. 'Just think of the poor people whose businesses have been ruined, whose homes have been destroyed. This is criminal damage.'

'Oh, they didn't just let it happen, they positively encouraged it,' Brenda said, pursing her lips in disgust. 'I spoke to our contact at the embassy. He said Goebbels gave orders to every section of the Nazi Party, ordering brutal reprisals against the Jews in every city, town and village throughout the land. It's not just Berlin that's firefighting and sweeping up broken glass this morning, it's like this across the whole country and probably hasn't stopped yet in some places.'

'But why? What is the point of them wrecking their own towns and cities?' Dora shook her head in disbelief as she took in the sheer destruction all around them.

'The party despots have been waiting for an excuse to do something like this and a damn fool handed them one. Last night a member of the German embassy in Paris was assassinated. The government has blamed the attack on a young Jew and claims all the Jews are responsible for this official's murder.'

'But that simply doesn't make sense. What, one man commits a rash act of madness and this is the result?' Dora spun round, surveying the sheer extent of the damage.

As they continued to walk through the city, heading towards an area where smoke was still spiralling into the sky, Brenda said, 'The Jewish communities have not experienced aggression like this since the Middle Ages. I'm afraid we shall see that there will be worse yet to come.'

Dora was deeply saddened by all she was seeing and hearing. How could people approve of the destruction of their own city? Walking carefully, treading around the shards of glass that littered every pathway, they reached one of the burning buildings, still smouldering with glimpses of red embers.

'What was this place?' Dora could not tell from the collapsed brickwork and timbers what the property had been previously.

'This was the Fasanenstrasse Synagogue,' Brenda said. 'The rioters destroyed hundreds of synagogues last night and there have been a number of deaths. I've been told they even targeted a hospital for sick Jewish children and drove them out in their nightclothes, in bare feet, over broken glass. They attacked the doctors and nurses there too.'

'Whatever happened to normal human decency?' Dora clamped her hand over her mouth as she looked in horror at the smoking rubble.

Behind them they heard a low male voice: 'We were forbidden to use any water on the fires. We were forced to watch until the whole place had burned down.'

They turned round to see a weary, uniformed fireman gazing in despair at the charred mess. 'I heard the alarm go off in the early hours. I cycled to the fire station immediately, but I wasn't allowed to take the fire engines out.'

'You mean you were actually prevented from doing your civic duty?' Brenda looked incredulous. 'You, a man who is a trained, responsible professional, was barred from helping?'

He shook his head. 'I wasn't even allowed to open the doors to the fire station. One of my friends, who lives near here, warned me. He said he was beaten up when he came down here and wanted to put out the fire. I can't see the sense in it.'

'There's no sense in it,' Brenda said, looking over at some men in brown uniforms standing nearby with arms folded, admiring the smouldering pyre. 'I think you should be careful talking to us, but I want to know more. Do you know who did this?'

'Them,' he said, his eyes flicking towards the groups of

Brownshirts. 'And they beat up anyone who tried to put it out. They rounded up the local Jews too and made them watch. They only let us firemen use water when one of the Party members was afraid that his own property nearby was going to catch fire as well but even then we had to stand and watch as this house of prayer was reduced to ashes.'

'What a sorry state of affairs,' Brenda said, shaking her head. 'And what good will it do the fools?'

Dora thought she could see a glimmer of tears in the fireman's eyes. He heaved a sigh and said, 'As I was watching it all burn, I couldn't help but think, whose turn will it be next? Will the same thing happen to our churches? Have they no respect for anything anymore?'

He turned away as if he couldn't bear to look at the destruction any longer. His shuffling steps were a sign of the misery Dora felt all around her. She felt herself coming close to tears. 'Poor man,' she said. 'They're preventing people from obeying their instincts. Even a good man like that couldn't be allowed to behave with simple decency. It's so dreadful.'

Brenda looked back at him walking off with his head bent. She shook her head with despair. 'It comes to something when an honest citizen isn't allowed to carry out his duty, but I'm afraid this is how it's going to be from now on. When good men can't take steps to halt the evil around them.'

'It's so sad,' Dora said. 'I used to love this country, but now...' She could feel her bottom lip trembling and took a deep breath to stop the tears.

'Come,' Brenda said, holding Dora's arm and turning her away from the sad pile of ash and charred timber, 'we mustn't become disheartened, we must stay strong. Maybe we have been fortunate to be present at this time to bear witness. We are lucky to have seen it for ourselves and now we can tell others, so we can be prepared.'

'Of course,' Dora said, biting her lip. 'I realise that. We're here to gather information and make a full report on our return to London.'

Dora found it comforting to hold Brenda's arm as they made their way back towards the hotel, weaving around the debris. Men were starting to clear the streets, but some had clearly been injured. Dora couldn't stop herself from pausing to ask one man with a bandaged head how he had been hurt. He looked over his shoulder, maybe wondering who might witness this interaction. 'They forced us to watch the fires last night,' he said. 'And now they are making us clean up their mess. And,' he added with another wary glance, 'they say we have to pay for the damage ourselves.' He turned back to his sweeping.

'But that's not fair,' Dora said, as Brenda pulled her on towards the hotel.

'I'm not a bit surprised. Typical of them to make it all the responsibility of the Jews. They'll be vicious and punitive at every turn. I've been told the authorities have cancelled all insurance payouts to Jewish businesses and homes, so the poor victims will be held responsible for all the repair costs. They're bleeding them dry.'

Brenda's grim tone kept hammering home the severity of the situation. And as they walked past the last row of damaged shops Dora realised that, apart from the shards of glass and bricks that now littered the shop windows, many of them were also now empty. She slowed down, then stopped to look more carefully. She was certain that most of the goods displayed the day before had gone. 'Do you think the shop owners might have managed to salvage their stock in time?'

'I doubt it very much,' Brenda said in her matter-of-fact way. 'More likely that the mob have pinched it all for themselves. The owners wouldn't have dared confront them. Those that did would have been set upon. They're arresting Jewish men all over the country now and sending them off to concentration camps.'

Dora remembered her one visit to Dachau with its false show of industry and order. She knew that it was no longer pretending to be like that; reports had filtered through of horrific punishments meted out in all the camps.

They took a few more steps along the street until Dora realised that they were in the area where she had admired the red dress the day before. She looked around, trying to identify that particular shop, until her eyes rested on a broken window. The sign above the door read Goldberg, so it too was a Jewish business. There were no dresses or suits in the window now, just two broken white plaster torsos that had once modelled the clothes.

Dora stared at the shattered dummies, which looked like fragments of skeletons. Only yesterday they had been draped in silken fabric and pinstriped worsted. Now they were stripped. Who was wearing that red dress now, she wondered? And what kind of person would want to destroy a Jewish dress shop, but would have no objection to feeling the caress of stitches made by the hand of a Jewish dressmaker next to their skin?

Oh well, she told herself, with a deep sigh. *I didn't really need it. I was never really going to buy it. And I already have a dress for Christmas.* But still the tears came.

TWENTY-THREE

ROSA

NOVEMBER 1938, BERLIN

That night had begun with a low rumble of threatening shouts that seemed to crawl from the back streets and alleyways until it reached the city centre. Rosa heard it as she read to Theresia and settled her for the night.

Josef came in for supper that evening looking anxious and harried. 'We should be safe up here,' he said, striding to the window and looking down on the street below. 'I've locked all the doors on the ground floor and barricaded the stairs.'

'Whatever is happening? Why are you so worried?'

'A member of the German embassy in Paris has been assassinated and now all Jews are going to have to pay for it.'

'Paris? I don't understand, why should that affect us?'

'They're looking for any excuse, any excuse at all to blame us, to destroy our people and our businesses.'

Rosa was stunned. This was Josef, the man who had maintained that they would survive, that they would always continue to do well. She had been the one with doubts and now he too, was fearful. 'We must try not to alarm Theresia. She is already asleep.'

'Bring her into our room. Keep her with us tonight.'

Just as Rosa was carrying her sleepy daughter into her own feather bed, she heard the first sounds of breaking glass. Theresia barely stirred, so Rosa tucked her up and lay beside her, holding her tight, praying the mob would stay on the streets and not break into her home. Waves of shouting, crashing and splintering reached her as she covered her daughter's ears, then gradually the sounds washed away as the hordes raged through other areas of the city.

In the grey hours of early morning, she crept from the bed and found Josef slumped in an armchair by the window. One of the panes had been smashed and shards of glass lay on the carpet. 'They didn't get past the shop,' he said, looking at her with red-rimmed eyes. 'But our business is in ruins.'

'Have you been down yet to look?'

'No, I didn't dare. I've watched them all night. The city is burning, Rosa. They've all gone mad. No one can stop them. We must stay hidden until we are sure it is over.'

But it won't be over, she thought. *This is just the beginning. They will have a taste for it now.*

Two days after that terrifying night, Josef had insisted on leaving their apartment. 'They damaged our buildings and businesses,' he said. 'It's not right that we should have to pay for restoration. A group of us are going to demand compensation and the right to claim insurance.'

He had pulled his expensive overcoat over his smart suit, donned his hat and set off. That was the last she had seen of him. Theresia kept asking for Papa, they had no bread or fresh milk and she had no news.

'Stay here and don't move,' she told Theresia. 'I'm just going down to our shop for a minute.'

She crept down the stairs and unlocked the door that separated work from home. It was not as bad as she had feared. The main windows were smashed and the finished clothes that had been on display were gone, but the workshop was undamaged. They'd been lucky. The shop had not been set alight and they still had their sewing machines, threads and fabrics. Perhaps they could start again.

She went to the main door and looked through the broken glass panel onto the street, where she saw Liese, treading her way carefully through the debris. 'Is there any news?' she asked her.

'They've all been arrested. Isaac went with them. I told him not to, but he said they'd need someone good at figures.' Liese shook her head. 'The fool. They were never going to listen to them.'

'What, all of them, arrested?'

'Them and half the Jewish men in Berlin, I think.' Liese's mouth trembled and she began to cry. 'It's hopeless. I've been trying to plead with the police, but no one will listen.'

'But they only went to ask for what's right. They weren't doing any harm.' Rosa felt empty and sick at the same time. 'Where are they now?'

'A labour camp. Sachsenhausen, so everyone is saying.' Liese dabbed her eyes with a sodden handkerchief. 'I'm so afraid I will never see him again.'

Rosa put her arms round her friend and they held each other, both trying to draw strength from their friendship. 'Sachsenhausen is only a few miles from Berlin. They're only trying to scare them. They could all be sent back very soon.'

'And there's more news.' Liese sniffed, drawing back from Rosa and looking her in the eye. 'Another of those damn laws. As if we don't have enough of them already.'

'What is it this time?'

'All Jewish businesses are closed down.'

Rosa gave a bitter laugh. 'What? They destroy our premises and then they won't let us rebuild? So now we're not even allowed to earn money to feed our families? What are we meant to do?'

'It's a vendetta. A legal one, but cruel all the same. When our men come back there will be nothing for them. Soon they'll all be sweeping the roads. They don't want your sort here anymore, Rosa. Remember what Goebbels said in his speech to the police here months ago.'

Rosa remembered all too well. Josef had made light of it, but she had been chilled when she heard reports that Goebbels had said the Jews must get out of Berlin. No, they weren't wanted. Maybe as labourers, but not as intelligent, skilled people.

She stood for a moment, taking in the devastation all around them. The ruined shops and homes, the hopeless people picking at the debris. 'Come inside. We'll manage. And we'll keep hoping our husbands come back soon.' Rosa put her arm round her friend. They had to stay strong for each other and for their children. As they climbed the stairs, Rosa felt sick again. It couldn't be, could it? Not the sickness of fear and anxiety, but the nausea of new life?

TWENTY-FOUR
SAVE THE CHILDREN
LONDON, NOVEMBER 1938

The day after their return to the London office, Brenda stormed up the stairs to find Dora. 'Right, that's it. They've really done it now. We've got to start planning in all seriousness. They've set their sights on the children.'

Dora was startled by Brenda's appearance. She was red-faced and furious. 'All Jewish children are to be expelled from public schools,' she said, marching around the office. 'I told you this was going to happen, when it started in Berlin a year ago.'

'But they can still go to other schools, can't they? Jewish schools?'

'Probably, until they attack those too and close them down. But don't you see? This is yet another level of poisonous discrimination. Children who have always played together and been taught together soon won't feel safe being seen together. Aryan children will be encouraged to turn on those they once regarded as their playmates and friends. It's so insidious, Dora. Infecting even the children with their ridiculous prejudice, for goodness' sake!'

Other members of the office, including Alice, heard Brenda shouting and came to see what was happening. Anxious faces peered round the doorway, then Brenda pushed her way out through the little gathering impatiently, saying, 'There's no time to waste. I have to go right away. I must organise an important meeting. If we can't get more adults out of danger, we'll have to concentrate on the children. The government's got to listen to us.'

Dora could guess what that meant. Brenda was going to contact high-level officials in all the refugee organisations, including World Jewish Relief, and coordinate a delegation to batter the government into taking more refugees at speed.

'I'll have to put the pressure on the Intergovernmental Committee on Refugees,' Brenda said. 'Neville Chamberlain might not like the idea, but I think Baldwin and Samuel Hoare, the Home Secretary, are on our side. And I reckon I can pull some strings with prominent Quaker families, like the Cadburys and Rowntrees.'

Dora closed her eyes and prayed that Brenda would be successful.

Six days later, Brenda returned to Bloomsbury House triumphant, waving a sheaf of paper. 'We've done it,' she cried. 'Parliament has agreed. It took some doing, but they've agreed to let us bring in an unlimited number of child refugees. It was Samuel Hoare who swung it in the end. Good old Sam! They've said we can give the children temporary refuge in Britain as long as there is no recourse to public funds.'

The office filled with excited workers, cheering and clapping at this news. Then Brenda held up her hand and said, 'To work, everyone. Time is of the essence. We need donations, sponsors and lists.'

Dora felt quite breathless when Brenda finally left the room to galvanise more help. She knew that the pace of their work was going to become even more frenetic now but she couldn't wait to tell Hugh the news.

That evening, when he asked why she looked so pleased and she told him, he said, 'The papers are full of it. And they've printed big extracts from Hoare's speech.' He folded back the pages of his newspaper. 'Listen to this: *There is an underlying current of suspicion and anxiety, rightly or wrongly, about alien immigration on any big scale...*'

'That's why they've resisted for so long,' Dora said. 'And now each child will need a sponsor so they don't cost the state a penny.'

'Gosh, that's going to take some doing. You're not going to have to do all of it, are you?'

'No, there's a coordinating committee representing all of us but it might mean going back to Germany to help tie things together.'

'You mean you might have to go again?'

'I'm rather afraid so. It's frightfully complicated. The Home Office only has offices for issuing visas in Berlin and Vienna, and there are people all over Germany and Austria who are desperate. They have to contact their nearest British consul, but I just know that's going to be terribly difficult for some of them.'

'Does that mean you'll have to go back to Berlin?'

'I don't know yet. We think the trains might be allowed to leave from there and, if this is just for the children, we'll need to think about escorts. We can't ask the Jewish organisations to do it because their members will be at risk themselves, so I rather think it is going to come down largely to the Society of Friends, which means people like me and Alice.'

'It's clear from what the papers are reporting that Quakers are playing a major role in this crisis.' Hugh turned back to his newspaper. 'They're saying Hoare had met a Quaker representative, who told him they'd asked Jewish organisations about the attitude of the parents to such a scheme. And listen to this, he actually said in his speech, *Jewish parents were almost unanimously in favour of facing this parting with their children and taking the risks of their children going to a foreign country, rather than keeping them with them to face the unknown dangers with which they are faced in Germany.*'

'That must have been Brenda. She stormed off to tell them the facts. She's so forceful and well informed. How could anyone, even someone as important as him at the top of government, resist her arguments?' Dora couldn't resist a wry smile, thinking of her determined colleague.

'I'll have to meet this Brenda of yours one day,' Hugh said with a laugh. 'She sounds quite formidable. But then so do the parents who've said they'd rather send their children away. That takes some courage too.'

Dora thought of the people she and Brenda had met on their last trip. Their quiet stoicism, their belief that their faith could survive even this had impressed her. But the thought that they could bear to part with their children caused tears to prick her eyes.

'What's the matter, darling? I thought you'd be pleased now you've got what you and your colleagues needed to get going?'

She shook her head. 'I am, but it's just that I can't help thinking how it must feel to even think of having to part with a child. It's going to be so hard for families. And if I am going to help escort groups out of Germany, I wonder how distressing it will be for the parents, the little children and me. There are bound to be some emotional scenes on the platforms as the trains prepare to leave. Am I strong enough to do it?'

'You'll do it with great compassion,' Hugh said, drawing her into his arms. 'Suffer the little children to come unto me.'

'Yes, it is rather like that, isn't it?' Dora smiled and enjoyed being held safe in his arms for now.

. . .

The next few days were a frantic melee of letters, phone calls, agreements, confirmation of funding and checking transport. 'I can't believe this,' Dora nearly shouted at Alice. 'The Germans are now saying the children can't leave through any German port.' They had been hoping that groups wouldn't have to travel great distances before boarding a ship and could depart from Cuxhaven, the port nearest to Hamburg, which was not far from Berlin.

'Why ever not?' Alice paused in her envelope-stuffing; they were mailing requests for sponsorship to interested parties.

'Because they're saying they don't want their ports sullied by Jewish children. The disgusting cheek of it. They're going to make them travel far further than necessary, all the way to Holland. That's going to make the journey so much longer and harder.'

'They're not going to make this easy, are they?' Alice sighed. She too had agreed to act as an escort for the transports, but had made it clear she wasn't looking forward to it.

'I think this is just the start of them making our job as difficult as possible. Damn German officials, they don't want the Jews in their country but they don't want to help them leave either. We're going to have to be prepared for every obstacle to be thrown in our way but I'm not going to let them stop us saving the children.'

Dora could feel her heart racing and her temperature rising. She was becoming as furious and passionate as Brenda and knew she would need to channel every ounce of determination to beat the Nazis and deliver her charges into safety.

TWENTY-FIVE
BE MORE BRENDA
VIENNA, NOVEMBER 1938

Dora hammered on the locked cell door. 'You're making a terrible mistake,' she shouted. 'We're here with the authority of the British government.' She wished she'd been given an official document to prove the legitimacy of her mission, but she had nothing to show the police.

After a moment, she heard a reply, but it was just the cry, 'Den Mund halten!' in an aggressive tone. *'Shut up!'*

How could this have happened? Surely Brenda wouldn't have found herself in such a spot?

Dora and Alice had been trying to meet their contacts in Leopoldstadt, the Jewish quarter of the city, but, to their surprise, every entrance to this area was roped off. Many of the buildings, were drab and neglected with flaking paint, missing tiles and broken windows.

'What's happening here?' Alice said. 'Does this mean we can't go in?'

'I'm not sure if it's to keep the residents in or us out,' Dora had said, and had then called across the street to a woman carrying a basket within the barred section of the quarter. 'Good day to you. We've come here to meet representatives in your

Jewish Community Office. I have been told to ask for Herr Friedmann. We're here to help you. Can you tell us where to go?'

The woman looked nervous, but edged a little closer to them and said, 'Herr Friedmann? The diamond merchant? How can that help us? We aren't allowed to leave the quarter or even cross the road. And you should see what they did to our homes that terrible night. Kristallnacht, they're calling it now. Many of our houses are in ruins.' Tears appeared to be welling in her eyes, but then her expression changed to one of terror and she scuttled away down a narrow passageway and out of sight.

As the woman fled, Dora felt a heavy hand on her shoulder. She turned round to find herself facing two stern police officers. 'You're under arrest,' one said.

'But we're here on official business. We've done nothing wrong.' Dora tried to sound commanding, but she felt like a child caught stealing sweets.

'We're arresting you for a public order offence and we're taking you to the police station to be formally charged.'

'But we have every right to be here,' Dora said, trying to be bold despite her racing heart. 'We are English Quakers here to arrange the transport of Jewish children with the knowledge of your government. We have done nothing wrong.'

Alice grew quiet and pale and shrank against Dora's side.

Despite her protests, Dora soon realised that she and Alice had no choice but to accompany the two armed men. Perhaps she could make them see reason, perhaps once they fully understood the purpose of her assignment they could even help her. But she couldn't help thinking that this would never have happened to Brenda.

And now both girls were locked in a dingy cell reeking of urine and the door was slammed shut. Alice burst into tears as the heavy metal clanged. 'I don't like this! I want to go home.'

The cell was bare apart from a filthy bucket and a rough wooden bench, where Alice perched, her face in her hands.

'There's no point in crying, that's not going to help us.' Dora felt irritated by her friend's tears, although she almost wanted to do the same herself. But what would Brenda do? She'd fight, she'd argue with them, she wouldn't stand for this nonsense.

'Are they going to unlock the door now?' Alice asked tearfully.

'They told me to shut my mouth, but I'm not finished yet.' Dora thought some more, then shouted, 'We are British nationals here on official business. I shall be informing all the newspapers how you treat Aryans who come to undertake legitimate charitable work in Vienna. You had better listen to me, because the British embassy will soon be asking why we haven't yet returned. This will become a diplomatic incident if you don't release us immediately.'

She listened at the door, but could only hear mumbling voices and shuffling footsteps. Alice buried her head in her hands, weeping, while Dora strained to listen for any signs that her words had been understood and were gaining a response.

Eventually the door was unlocked by a contrite senior policeman, who took them both to his office. 'My sincere apologies, ladies. My men thought you were residents of Leopoldstadt causing a public nuisance. There have been some disturbances in that quarter recently and we are alert to any further unrest.'

Dora thought it was far more likely that the only unrest had been caused by the Nazis themselves, but she nodded and brushed down her coat as if she was wiping away all traces of that disgusting cell. 'Your men should have listened to us properly in the first place. We only wanted to make contact with the community centre in the Jewish quarter. We are here with the full knowledge of both our governments, to arrange the transport of children to England. If you are not going to help us visit the centre in Leopoldstadt, then we must appeal to the highest authority for explicit permission to avoid further misunderstanding.'

Frowning and looking worried, the officer said, 'We are deeply sorry for this error. Tell me what we can do to make amends.' He seemed genuinely concerned – or he was afraid what his superiors might have to say about the fuss Dora was clearly capable of creating?

Dora hesitated for a moment. Who should she say she needed to see? She knew she had to deal with the Jewish organisations, but if there was going to be resistance whenever she and Alice tried to enter their section, she was going to waste precious time. Who could give her the authority to arrange such meetings? It had to be a high-ranking official, but she could hardly insist on seeing the Führer – or could she?

And then she remembered Brenda telling her who would make the final decision on whether children could leave the country. 'I want you to arrange an appointment for me with Eichmann,' she said in a clear, firm voice conveying determination and concealing her underlying trepidation. 'I understand that he has the ultimate power to assist us. You can contact me at the Hotel Bristol with details. If you can do that for us, I shall refrain from contacting the newspapers for now.'

'Of course. I promise I will see what can be arranged.' The officer bowed and waved them out through the station.

They walked past him and out into the street. Dora breathed a sigh of relief. She had no idea whether he could accomplish her audacious request, but she told herself that Brenda wouldn't have settled for anything less than a face-to-face meeting with the man who had the ultimate power to say yes.

Later, as they entered the grand hall of the imposing Hotel Bristol in the centre of Vienna, lit with glittering chandeliers, a smartly dressed man approached them across the black and white chequered floor. He clicked his heels as he came to a halt, bowed, then said, 'Good afternoon, ladies. We are collecting funds for the Winter Aid Appeal. Would you both like to make a donation?'

Dora sized him up with her new-found confidence. 'And what are you going to use the money for?'

'It's for children,' he said with a smile, holding out a labelled tin. 'All the donations collected will be used to help the children of needy families.'

'That's excellent. We're both English Quakers. I'm sure you're aware of how much we've helped German families in the past. We're supporting Jewish children now.'

The man's pleasant expression changed immediately at these words. 'Oh, no. This money isn't going to be spent on any Jewish children.'

Alice had already pulled out her purse, but Dora stopped her extracting any coins. 'Then I'm afraid we cannot possibly make a donation, you'll have to try someone else.' She turned away from him, thinking Brenda would be proud of her.

TWENTY-SIX

THE YES MAN

Adolf Eichmann stared at Dora from the height of the dais on which he was sitting, relaxed, with crossed legs, in a gilded chair. A large black dog sat by his side, gazing devotedly at his master, who was stroking the hound's pointed ears. After staring at her dismissively for a moment, he said, 'I don't deal with women in these matters.'

Dora was shocked by his rudeness. This Monday-morning appointment had been confirmed by an official message delivered to her hotel. He had known very well that he would be meeting a woman and she had arrived promptly. She was very glad that she had been told to attend alone and that Alice was waiting for her back at the hotel. Her anxious colleague would have been trembling with fear in this awkward situation.

She knew that Eichmann was trying to intimidate her and make her nervous but she was determined not to let her fear show, although she could feel her heart beating faster. Now he was SS-Obersturmführer, he was charged with the administration of the Central Agency for Jewish Emigration in Vienna, housed in the palatial former home of Albert Rothschild in Prinz-Eugen Strasse. She had no choice but to negotiate with him if she was to obtain formal clearance to organise the trains and evacuate the children.

Dora had approached him expecting to shake hands, but this was his unwelcoming response. Although she was thrown by his impolite arrogance, she was determined not to show it. He was just trying to unnerve her. So, she threw back her shoulders and held her head high. 'My mission is authorised by the British government. They have given permission for thousands of Jewish children to be brought to the United Kingdom. We have arranged sponsorship to care for them and would like your authority to proceed with transporting them by train out of your country.'

In answer to this statement, Eichmann delivered a scoffing laugh and turned to the officials standing either side of him. 'Did you hear that? What a crazy English woman,' he said, patting the dog, which licked his hand. 'And just how do you think you're going to manage that? Do you have a letter of authority from your government?'

When Dora regretfully said she didn't, but that her official position could easily be verified by contacting the British embassy, Eichmann told her to sit down. She sat and waited for his response.

He stared at her and his lip curled as he said, 'Show me your hands.'

She laid her hands demurely on her lap, wondering why he'd made such a strange request. Perhaps it was so he could see whether she was wearing a wedding ring.

But what he said next shocked her even more. 'Pull your skirt up a bit.'

Dora seethed at his utterly insulting behaviour and didn't follow this second instruction. Who on earth did he think he was talking to? She wasn't a woman of the street – and indeed any woman from any walk of life would have rightly felt offended at this request. She could feel every fibre in her being telling her to get away from this dangerously rude man, but she knew she couldn't leave until she had the result she needed.

She stared back at this extremely arrogant high-ranking Nazi official in his pressed and embellished black uniform, challenging him with her steady, calm gaze. He was not that old, probably only in his early thirties. For a second she thought how Verity would have been impressed by him, with her fondness for high-ranking uniforms. Maybe she could have charmed him. He was really quite good-looking; some might say he had matinee idol good looks. But his ice-cold eyes conveyed no humour, no charisma, only an innate sense of superiority.

Dora told herself he was simply trying to humiliate and unsettle her, and was determined he would not succeed. She ignored his ridiculous instruction and took a deep breath before she spoke. 'I would like to discuss with you how the departure of Jewish children could be arranged,' she said, mustering as much assurance as she could. 'I believe you are the right person to ask and I am sure you would not object to Jewish children leaving your country. You no longer have any interest in their education or their welfare.'

'They are of absolutely no consequence to us,' he said with a careless shrug and pressed a bell. This instantly summoned another man to their meeting. He was older, bearded and dressed in a black coat and hat, which suggested to Dora that he might be a member of the Jewish community. She wondered if this could be the representative she had been meant to meet in Leopoldstadt, the Jewish quarter of the city.

'Herr Friedmann, come and join us,' Eichmann said, beckoning him closer. 'Have you met this mad Englishwoman before?'

The newcomer shook his head and Eichmann said, 'This young woman doesn't have any form of documentation from the British government to support her claim that she will be allowed to bring children into their country. So, what do you say that we take her at her word? Let's put her on the spot and see if she can organise a transport of children and see how she's going to pull it off.' He pointed at both Dora and Friedmann and said, 'You've got till Saturday morning. After that I may not be quite so considerate. Kindertransport indeed! Let's see if you can do it.'

Friedmann looked at Dora with some concern as Eichmann continued: 'We'll let her work out how she's going to get them over the border and into her country. A mad Englishwoman and a Jew. This should be interesting.' He laughed and dismissed them both with a wave of his hand.

Once they were outside in the street, Dora turned to Herr Friedmann and shook his hand. 'I'm so pleased you're here. I was meant to meet you sooner, but we were arrested trying to enter Leopoldstadt. I'm a representative of British Quakers and I'm here because my government has given permission for the transport of thousands of Jewish children to Britain. Our London office has been working hard to collect donations to make sure this can happen.'

'Now the new laws forbid me from running my former business,' he said, 'I'm in charge of the affairs of the Jewish Community Office. You will have to work through me and the Palestine Office to coordinate the collection of the children. We are going to have to work very fast.'

'Then I must go back to the hotel immediately and make a call to London,' Dora said. 'There's so much to coordinate and someone will have to go to Holland to speak to the Dutch authorities as well. We're going to need their cooperation if we're not allowed to depart from a German seaport.'

Dora crossed the road with her companion, but just as they reached the other side they heard the screech of tyres. Friedmann stepped behind her, seeming to shrink against the wall. 'We should get away from here this minute,' he said. 'We don't want to get caught up in this.'

'Why, whatever is happening?' Dora couldn't resist looking back at the building they had just left. A queue of Jewish men was being forced to line up against the wall by several Brown-shirt thugs wielding cudgels.

'Come away, don't look,' Friedmann said, his hand cupping her elbow, trying to pull her from the scene.

'No, just let me watch for a moment. I have to know what's going on. It's important for me to know about all developments here,' Dora said, even though she could feel herself shaking with fear. She knew Brenda would have insisted on being an eyewitness, so she felt she had to do the same. 'Those men were queuing in an orderly fashion for visas, weren't they?'

Herr Friedmann gave an expressive shrug. 'Who knows? But then who knows the real purpose of the so-called Central Agency for Jewish Emigration? Are they facilitating departure to a destination of the applicant's choosing, or is it chosen for them?'

And in that horrible moment of clarity, Dora realised that the office they had just left was a sham. It was not like others she had visited, legitimately dispensing passports and visas. Like the other fakes and facades she had seen in this corrupt regime, it was masquerading under a grand title, a civilised persona, to mask its true intent, to remove the country's Jewish population by any means possible.

But still, she felt she had to ask Friedmann the obvious question: 'Do you think those men were going to the Emigration Office to apply for permission to leave the country?'

'It is very possible, but I fear others may have decided they should have a speedier departure now. Look...' Friedmann pointed to the shining black cars, which had reversed up the street and turned, and were now roaring back towards the queue.

'Oh, they can't possibly—' Dora clamped a hand over her mouth. Thank goodness Alice wasn't here to see this. The cars rammed the queuing men, who had no chance of escape. Those who weren't killed on impact were beaten with cudgels by the brown-shirted guards. Thuggish shouts interspersed the screams of the dying and the droning of the engines, and a haze of blue exhaust filled the street.

Dora felt sick and couldn't stop her body from trembling, but she forced herself to turn away from the terrible carnage. 'It's so shocking, I feel so helpless,' she blurted, steadying herself with a hand on the wall. 'I wish we could have helped, but we must leave right away. I have to report immediately to London and there isn't a minute to waste.'

She and Friedmann hurried back to the Hotel Bristol with an increased sense of urgency to start work. It was 10.30 a.m. on a Monday. They had less than a week to organise the transport.

TWENTY-SEVEN

THE FIRST TRAIN

BERLIN, DECEMBER 1938

Dora wanted to reach out to all the children arriving at the station, scoop them up in her arms, calm them and tell them they would soon be safe. But there were so many of them and there was so much to do. She had to keep a clear head and deal with them quickly and efficiently.

The days since her disturbing meeting with Eichmann had been a whirlwind of activity. Since the British government had sanctioned the immigration of Jewish children on 21 November, hundreds of families had begun registering their children, hoping to reserve a place for them on the trains.

But this first group was not accompanied by anxious parents. No mothers and fathers stood on the station platform, waiting to wave goodbye to their young ones. There were no tearful farewells for these refugees for they were Waisenkinder; they were already orphans.

'Is there really no one here to see them off?' Dora asked Herr Friedmann, who had collected this straggling queue of orphaned children. They were not well prepared for their journey, in ill-fitting coats and sweaters. They were wearing shoes, but most had holes and few of them fitted well. The orphans were an assortment of ragbag vagrants, their names printed in large letters on tags tied to their lapels, like badly wrapped parcels.

'Their orphanage was burned down in the state-sanctioned riots early in November,' he said.

One of the boys heard him saying this and added, 'The soldiers woke us up. We were in our pyjamas, we didn't have our shoes on.'

Herr Friedmann shook his head in despair. 'Driven out in the night they were, along with the home's directors, wearing nothing but their nightclothes. We've had to help them manage as best we could ever since but at least now they might stand a chance.'

'They haven't even got any luggage,' Alice said. 'Not even a change of underwear.' She looked anxious and Dora knew that the strain of the last few days was telling on her. She'd had to stay behind in Berlin processing applications, while Dora had travelled to Amsterdam to obtain clearance to cross the border.

'They'll be well looked after when they finally arrive,' Dora said, trying to sound confident. It had all been such a rush, liaising with the hostels back in England that would house the orphans temporarily. She hoped they were well prepared to greet these children with nothing but the clothes they stood up in. They had already been warned to have hot baths and nit combs ready as the children would be travelling with unwelcome guests as well as themselves.

'Welcome,' Dora said, stopping to help a little boy board the train. 'You can sit anywhere you like.'

His eyes widened. 'Are you coming with us?'

'Yes, Harry,' she said, reading the name on his label. 'And do you have a friend you want to sit with?'

He shook his head. 'My best friend isn't allowed to talk to me now. After we had to leave the school, he couldn't play with me anymore.'

Dora blinked back the threat of tears and noticed Alice doing the same. 'But now you are going to make new friends and all will be well.'

He climbed aboard and passed down the corridor as Dora and Alice turned to the children next in line.

'They've brought very little to eat with them,' Alice said. 'A crust of bread and an apple isn't going to be much help if the train is delayed.' The journey was expected to take at least fifteen hours and that was if it was allowed to go straight through non-stop.

Dora turned to Herr Friedmann. 'Is there any chance we can arrange some more food for the journey? Some of these children look undernourished as it is.'

He shook his head. 'Sadly, that is true of many of our people in this city these days. But I will see what I can do. I am sure some of our community will want to spare a little something if they know it is for the children.' He disappeared through the mob of guards keeping watch over the train and Dora hoped he would be in luck.

She and Alice were continuing to check the children onto the train when two guards pushed past them and entered the carriages. 'What do you think you're doing?' Dora called, but they rudely ignored her. She ran after them as they marched down the corridor, peering into the compartments filling up with children, who shrank back into their seats in terrified silence at the sight of these menacing intruders.

'What do you want?' Dora demanded of them when she had caught up with the two men. One of them had just grabbed a paper bag from a little girl and tipped the contents out onto the floor of the carriage. It contained nothing but a wizened apple and a hard crust of bread.

'We have orders,' he growled. 'Jews aren't allowed to take money and valuables out of the country.'

'They don't have any money,' Dora said. 'They're all

orphans. You burned down their orphanage. The only home they knew was destroyed by you and your kind.'

He shrugged and made another child stand up, then felt his pockets and the hem of his shabby jacket. 'They all do it,' he said. 'Sneaky Jews. Can't trust them.'

'Are you going to terrify every child on this train? I insist that you leave right now. They have nothing but the clothes they're wearing, surely you can see that?'

He shoved the boy back onto the seat and pushed his face so close to Dora's that she could smell the stink of the onions from the wurst he must have eaten earlier. 'Just got to be sure, haven't we?' Then he and his companion barged out of that compartment and into the one next door.

Dora hugged the little girl whose food had been snatched away and picked up the scraps she had brought with her. 'Don't cry,' she said. 'We'll soon be leaving his sort behind us. They won't harm you while I'm here.' But would they, she wondered? The Nazis seemed to have no respect for anyone and she fervently hoped she could escort these children to safety without further incident.

When all the children allocated to that particular train, a total of 196 orphans in all, had been seated and Dora and Alice had calmed the fearful, dried the tears and reassured the older ones that they would be leaving soon, Herr Friedmann came rushing across the platform with a cloth bundle and bulging pockets. 'It's not much,' he said, showing them dried fruit, cooked potatoes and yet more crusts of dry bread, 'but it's all that can be spared. Many of our community will go hungry today because they have been generous to these children.'

Dora looked at the paltry offering and wondered how the Jews of Berlin would last the winter if they were already so short of supplies. 'Thank you,' she said. 'And you must thank your friends too. We shall see that the children are fed properly once our journey is over.'

'And now I must leave you,' he said. 'I would have gladly come with you as another escort, but I think I am needed here to continue processing the applications. Word is reaching many more families and we shall soon be helping hundreds more.'

Dora pressed his hand. 'Thank you for helping us. This is only the start of our work here, I know. We are going to be busy for quite some time.'

'I pray we shall have enough time,' he said. 'We shall keep working as long as the border is open to us, but after that, who knows?' He shrugged, holding out his hands in an expression of despair.

'We shall pray too, shan't we, Alice?' Dora and Alice stepped onto the train. Leaning out of the window, they felt the engine start to shudder in preparation for its journey.

Friedmann shook both their hands, then reached deep into his pocket. Dora thought perhaps another crust or apple had slipped down into the lining, but it wasn't fruit or bread, it was a small tin, sealed with layers of sticky tape.

He pressed the package into Dora's hand, saying, 'For luck. You have maybe heard that in Jewish cemeteries, my people lay stones instead of flowers. Here in this tin is a stone from my homeland. You should carry it with you always and it will bring you good luck.' He stepped back and waved at the train as it began to creep out of the station, and waved at every window as it passed, as the children peered out at what might be their last glimpse of Germany.

Dora stared at the wrapped tin and at the dark-bearded man scurrying away in his black hat and coat. What a strange gift. But she valued the sentiment. She put the package in her hand-bag, hoping that the luck it conveyed would take her and her charges away from Berlin, decked with the scarlet flags of Nazi power, and safely into Holland.

TWENTY-EIGHT

ROSA

We couldn't leave now even if we wanted to, Rosa thought bitterly. *Not that I want to leave unless I know for certain that Josef isn't coming back.*

Several of the Jewish families she had known well had left Germany in the last few years, but since the destruction of Kristallnacht in November, a new ruling made it impossible for any Jew to leave of their own accord. We missed our chance to escape, she told herself. But where would we have gone? It was all very well for those with relatives in other countries that welcomed talented workers, but she and Josef were German-born and bred and their family members were all in northern Germany, not Holland, France or Britain.

She rubbed her cold hands together and pulled her mittens over her thin wrists for warmth. Light snow had fallen yesterday, although, unlike most Berlin winters, this year had so far seen more days of fog and rain than of snow. But it was still cold in the apartment they had once been able to heat with coal.

While Theresia was occupied at school, Rosa had started chopping up their furniture for firewood. Fuel was impossible to find, let alone carry back to the apartment. She hoped if Josef returned, he would not object to her destroying his favourite chair to keep their child warm and boil water for washing and cooking.

Liese had offered to help Rosa fetch kindling, but she was suffering too. Her son and daughter still attended the public school, but lately they had been coming home greatly upset after boys had chased them and thrown stones: 'The other children are calling them Mischling and saying they aren't good Germans.'

'What on earth does that mean?' Rosa hadn't heard the word before.

'Oh, it's some darn stupid classification the party came up with a while back. Because their father is Jewish, they are only half German, so according to our beloved government that means they don't fully belong to the German race.'

'How ridiculous. They speak German and they look German, don't they? So you mean other children are picking on them?'

'It seems so.' Liese's eyes filled with tears and she shook her head in despair. 'Children can be so cruel.'

But it seemed to Rosa that they were cruel because they were encouraged to be so. And that made her even sadder. If Liese's children could be reviled by their schoolmates when they were only half Jewish, what did that mean for Theresia, whose parents were both Jewish? Did she even have a future here?

She picked up the next chair and hit the legs with savage strokes of her axe. Splinters flew across the carpet. No one would hurt or upset her child who would return today to a blazing fire and nourishing chicken soup. Rosa put a hand to her stomach. At least the sickness seemed to affect her only in the mornings. She too could manage a bowl of soup later.

TWENTY-NINE
IT'S ONLY GLASS
BERLIN, JANUARY 1939

Dora glared at the two guards striding up and down the corridor of the train. She knew by now that this show of intimidation might well cease during the journey out of Germany and into Holland. On her very first trip, once the guards had checked every compartment, terrified every single child and inspected every paltry food parcel, they had retreated to the baggage hold and spent most of the time smoking and dozing. Hopefully these two would do the same, once the train had left the station and their superiors couldn't check how diligent they were being.

But within minutes Dora heard crying and had to rush to comfort a little girl who had just been frightened by these men. She put her arms round the child, saying, 'They're going now, they won't come back.'

The child sobbed into Dora's thick tweed coat. 'I'm scared. Bad soldiers hurt my father, they burned down our house.'

Dora gave her another hug and led her back to her seat in the carriage. 'Please don't worry. The soldiers can't hurt anyone here while you're with us. And you will stay with some very kind people when we get to England.'

The child looked up with the saddest expression. 'The

soldiers broke my bed. They ripped my mattress and pulled out all the feathers. And I can't find my best doll anymore.'

Dora bit her lip, trying to stifle the emotions that surged through her every time she heard such tales. It was not an uncommon story. The callous destruction of those nights in November, when towns and cities turned on their Jewish communities, was still being repeated. Casual cruelty and violence were almost part of everyday life for many poor families, including this little girl's.

She left the compartment and looked down the corridor. The guards were taking their time; since these children weren't homeless orphans, there was more for them to inspect. Many came from middle-class homes and had been well prepared for their journey by their parents, aunts and uncles and grandparents. Well dressed and well shod, they all had clean, shining hair and scrubbed faces. They had luggage too and that was what was delaying the guards, who were insisting on opening every case and rifling through the clean clothes that had been pressed and folded and neatly packed.

Suddenly another bundle of white underwear was thrown out of a compartment into the corridor, followed by an embroidered nightdress. Dora sighed. That would mean more tears for sure.

Hurrying towards the pile of dishevelled garments, she heard swearing – and a cracking noise – as the guard's boots stamped on the linen. He bent down to see what he'd trodden on, then threw it back on the floor in disgust and proceeded to the next carriage.

Dora picked up the garments and shook them free of grit. Luckily the guard's boots hadn't been thick with mud and the items weren't torn. Glittering shards fell from the nightdress. Looking closely, Dora could see there was silky thread between the fragments. Sometimes parents hid jewels in hems and the heels of shoes. But this was just a glass necklace or bracelet, a treasured keepsake that had been wrapped into the folds of the garment. He must have thought he'd found diamonds. No wonder he was so annoyed.

A young girl knelt down beside Dora and reached for the tiny pieces of glass. 'My grandmother gave me this necklace for my birthday,' she sobbed. 'Now it's all broken.'

'Let's pick it all up carefully,' Dora said, checking the name tied to the girl's coat. 'Look, Ilse, some of the beads are all right. They're not broken. There might be enough to rethread or add some new beads. Here, take my hankie and we'll wrap it all up in that for safety.'

The girl sniffed and picked up every tiny bit. Dora tied a knot in the handkerchief so it formed a little bundle and pushed it into the child's coat pocket. 'There you are, you won't lose any of it now.'

'They thought I had diamonds,' Ilse said. 'They said they could tell by the quality of my clothes and my luggage that I must have money or jewels. They ripped open my lining and then searched my case.' She opened her coat to show Dora the slashed silk and ripped hem, then burst into fresh tears. 'But I haven't got anything hidden away. My mother just wanted me to look respectable.'

'I know, dear,' Dora said, putting her arm round the child. 'They are suspicious of everyone. Let me help you pack everything away again.' She folded the nightdress and underclothes and rescued other garments that had been thrown onto the carriage floor. Other occupants in the compartment were sitting in stunned, frightened silence, some sucking thumbs, others huddled into their winter coats as if they could make themselves invisible.

'Thank you,' Ilse said, taking her case from Dora. 'You're the first Aryan who's been nice to me in a long time. Will there be more people like you in England?'

Dora could barely speak; she continued to be shocked at the

cruel prejudice these innocent children had experienced. As far as she was concerned, her behaviour was nothing out of the ordinary, she was just being normal and decent. 'Lots of English people will welcome you,' she managed to say. 'Now go back to your seat and rest. They won't come back and bother you again.'

Dora could hear more shouting and crying along the corridor. These two guards were being particularly officious. As far as they were concerned, the children looking clean and well-dressed meant there was a greater chance that they could find something of value.

So far, she and Alice had not been subjected to such treatment – their clothes had not been torn, their luggage not emptied out onto the floor – but what if that should change? Dora felt for the tin Herr Friedmann had pressed into her hands, containing its good-luck stone. It was hidden deep in her coat pocket. If she had known at the time that he was a former diamond merchant, would she have questioned his gift or even refused to take it?

Soon after her return to London from their first Kindertransport, she had received a brief letter from Amsterdam, addressed to her at the London office.

Please send the diamonds given to you for safe keeping by our uncle Herr Friedmann.

She remembered staring at the sealed tin, which bore no identifying marks of any kind. It had lain at the bottom of her handbag ever since he had given it to her. That night, she had told Hugh about the letter she'd received. 'I'm not going to open the tin, but if it really does contain diamonds I'd feel very concerned about sending them by post. I couldn't be sure they would reach their destination. I think I should deliver them in person. It wouldn't be out of the question.'

'Can you do that? Will there be time to stop off in Amsterdam?'

'Or maybe I should ask them to meet me at the port to save further travel?'

'If that little tin really does contain diamonds, you have a huge responsibility,' Hugh said. 'This consignment might mean the chance for another person to start their life afresh. Jews can no longer take money or valuables out of the country, so smuggling them out with you was the only way.'

'Oh Hugh, am I really a smuggler? I had no idea what he'd given me.'

'Of course you didn't know, and if you had known, what would you have done then?'

'I'd have been terrified that I might be caught with them.'

'Exactly. This Friedmann was doing you a favour by not telling you. Your guilty face might have given the game away. But now you have to decide how to get them to their rightful owners. It sounds to me like they're all in the diamond business.'

Dora thought hard. 'I think I should take them to the address on this letter. That's the only way I can be sure it will end up in the right hands.'

'And to think, darling, that I told you that lucky-stone business was nonsense! Good thing you didn't take my advice and throw the tin away.'

And Dora smiled to herself, remembering Hugh's teasing remarks. A smuggler she was indeed, and at the end of this journey she'd be leaving Alice and another escort they'd recruited to help the children board the ship, while she took a detour to Amsterdam.

THIRTY
THE CITY OF DIAMONDS
AMSTERDAM, JANUARY 1939

Dora shivered and wished she had a thick fur stole round her shoulders, like many of the smartly dressed women she passed, as she tried to find the address the Friedmanns had sent her. The air was bitterly cold, despite the glints of winter sun on the frosted barges and the glittering waters of the canals. How appropriate, she thought, that on her first visit to Amsterdam, the City of Diamonds, everything should sparkle like the famous gems, which had been cut, polished and traded here for hundreds of years.

She checked her bearings on her map and looked across the canal to the row of tall five-storeyed houses with arched gable roofs. And she couldn't help wishing that Hugh could have been here with her to appreciate the elegant architecture. She knew he would have loved exploring Amsterdam. She glanced down at her modest engagement ring, set with three small stones, nestled above her wedding band. Verity had barely contained her disdain for its insignificance, but these tiny diamonds were all Hugh could afford at the time and they were beyond price for her.

Dora crossed the little arched bridge spanning the canal,

heading for the house she was seeking, in the middle of the terrace. She looked again at the address on the letter that had been sent to London, to be sure. She had written back before departing once more for Berlin, but in these uncertain times who knew if every letter arrived and every recipient waited patiently for the promised visitors? She looked over her shoulder before she approached the house, to reassure herself that no one was interested in this modestly dressed English woman and no one could possibly know she was carrying a valuable consignment of gems. Once again, the old Verity entered her thoughts. How she would have loved this smuggling adventure. But Dora doubted dear Vee could have curbed her excitement and carried off the mission without drawing attention to herself.

She knocked hesitantly on the narrow door, willing it to open soon. It felt like an age until she heard steps inside, maybe descending stairs, then the clicking of soles across the hard surface of a tiled hallway. When the door opened, she was greeted by a bearded man, dressed in a formal black suit.

'Herr Friedmann?' Dora said, 'I am Mrs Williams from London. I believe you are expecting me. I wrote to inform you of my intention to come and see you in Amsterdam.'

'May I see your papers first?'

Dora had been expecting this. After all, it isn't every day that one is invited into the very heart of the diamond business. 'I can show you my passport and travel documents,' she said, holding out the relevant papers.

He took his time to check them all, so while he was studying them she asked, 'May I also enquire who you are, before I enter the building?' She had thought about this too. Herr Friedmann in Berlin had entrusted the package to her, knowing that he intended it to be passed on, and she had to be certain that she was delivering the diamonds into the right hands.

'Of course. You are very wise.' He pulled identity papers

and a business card from his pocket, confirming that he was Josef Friedmann of Friedmann diamond merchants, Amsterdam. 'And now, if you are willing to proceed, I shall take you to meet Herr Friedmann senior, the head of our family company.' He stepped aside and waved her through into the hallway, which was paved with a geometric pattern of black and white tiles.

Although the house was narrow, it also extended a fair way back and Dora soon realised it was much larger than she had at first thought from her view of the modest exterior. No wonder it had taken a while for the front door to be answered. Josef led the way down the long hallway, on and on, to a staircase at the back of the building. Beyond, she could see a workroom where men with eyeglasses were bent over desks equipped with scales, lit by bright lights. She assumed this must be the heart of the operation, where stones were weighed and assessed.

After climbing two flights of narrow stairs and a walk down another long corridor, Dora was ushered into a panelled room with a polished desk and leather chairs. A tall stove decorated with blue and white Delft tiles radiated a welcome heat. 'Please wait here for a moment,' Josef said, waving to a chair before the desk.

He left the room and, instead of sitting, Dora took a step towards the large windows that gave a clear view of both the street below and the canal. As she was enjoying the sunlight on the sparkling water and the passing barges, just like a Dutch painting, she heard soft steps behind her and turned to see an elderly bearded man, again dressed all in black.

'Mrs Williams, thank you so much for coming here in person,' he said, inviting her with a gesture to take a seat. 'I hope your journey has not been distressing or tiring for you. Some refreshments will be with us shortly.'

'I was very concerned to make sure this little parcel ended up in the right hands,' Dora said. 'When that letter arrived in

London, I have to tell you I was really shocked. I'd no idea I was in possession of anything of value. When Herr Friedmann handed me the package in Berlin, he told me it was simply stones, for good luck.'

The Dutch Herr Friedmann spread his hands in an apologetic gesture. 'What can I say? My cousin thought it better for you to be unaware of the great responsibility he bestowed upon you, so you could be an innocent courier. How might you have betrayed yourself on your travels through Germany if you had known the truth?'

'Exactly. The guards on the train are always checking our passengers. My husband said I was a smuggler.' Dora couldn't help smiling. 'But a courier sounds far less sinister.'

A woman wearing a smart tailored suit arrived, bearing a silver tray of fragrant hot chocolate, served in glasses set in silver cup holders. She set one before Dora, along with a tiny glass of transparent liquid and a saucer of sugary Jodenkoeken, the sweet biscuits served throughout Holland.

'Your good health,' Friedmann said, holding out his liqueur glass to chink against Dora's. He then drank the contents in one gulp, smacking his lips.

Dora sipped it cautiously. She thought it might be straight gin, which she had only ever drunk occasionally and with the addition of Indian tonic water. But it warmed her insides on this bitterly cold day.

'You have the package with you?' He held out his hand.

Dora opened her handbag and took out the wrapped tin. She placed it in his hand and noticed how he seemed to test its weight in his palm. He then moved to the desk, opened a drawer and took out a knife, a jeweller's eyeglass and a pair of miniature scales. He spread a black material across the desktop and sliced open the layers of packaging round the tin, then tipped the contents out onto the cloth. The stones looked nothing like the diamonds Dora had seen set in rings. They could have been little more than worthless sandy pebbles. If Hugh had encouraged her to dispose of the tin, or had suggested opening it, neither of them would have realised that the contents were of value.

Friedmann ran his fingers over the gems as if he was counting them, then weighed each one and recorded its weight in a notebook he had pulled from his pocket. When he'd finished, he folded the cloth over the stones and smiled at Dora. 'You have no idea how much this means to us,' he said. 'This little consignment is worth the lives of several families. It could mean life or death to them. We are immensely grateful to you.'

'I'm glad to have been of service. I've begun to realise how desperate people are. I hope this may help. Will the rest of your family be able to get out of Germany now you have these?'

'I have every hope that they will find a way,' he said. 'We will have to work fast, but this will definitely increase their chances. And we are also supporting those who have already left and made the journey to Amsterdam. Many of our people were stripped of their valuables before they were even allowed to leave.' His eyes beneath bushy white eyebrows creased with amusement as he added, 'But we have ways and means to foil them and are becoming ever more inventive with our possessions. Hollow walking sticks and umbrella canes have turned out to be very useful.'

Dora smiled. 'I'm very glad to hear that you can keep some of your valuables from their greedy grasp, but I'm sorry to say that I too have seen the guards in action, even with the children, checking their clothes for hidden money and gemstones. So, I really hope that the families you are able to help can rebuild their lives and will be safe once they are in Holland.'

'But who knows how long for?' He gave that expressive shrug Dora had seen before in his cousin. 'The Netherlands are safe at present, but we fear that Germany will set its sights on our borders as well before too long. Many of our people have already departed for America and Britain and more are likely to do so soon.'

'But this country was neutral in the last war. Surely the Germans aren't a threat to Holland?'

'Aah, but the German regime is both greedy and vicious. Nowhere is safe.' He stood and beckoned to her. 'Come with me, I want to show you something.' He led the way into the next room, where there was a huge display of graphic black and white photographs.

Dora stared at the pictures, trying to make sense of what she was seeing. All the photos were of posters and placards, in shop windows and on noticeboards. They were all in German and every single one was violently anti-Semitic. One announced *No Jews welcome here. Jews forbidden*. One after another, harsh cruel messages, banning Jewish people from businesses and activities. 'Where have these come from?' she asked, baffled by the sheer number of them, spread across an entire wall.

'Dear friends of ours, non-Jews, have been making trips into Germany for several years. The Wieners began taking cycling holidays across the border back in 1935 and were utterly shocked at the number of posters scattered across the country-side, so near to the Netherlands. They were so horrified they thought they should begin making a record of them, as an indication of the growing mood of the German people. There were only a few when they first started and now there are more than they can count.'

'It's appalling that there should be so many. I hope your friends didn't land themselves in trouble. I know of people who have been attacked for suggesting that such posters should be removed.'

Friedmann actually managed a little laugh, 'But who would think to challenge two healthy Aryan Dutch citizens taking photographs on a cycling holiday? It is ironic, don't you think, that instead of charming pictures of German farms and countryside they have been returning with such convincing souvenirs of the increasingly menacing German attitude.'

'It's simply dreadful, I can see why you are so concerned about what might happen here in the Netherlands as well.' Dora continued trying to memorise the awful signs. She had seen quite a few in her time in Germany, but displayed like this it was so clear that anti-Semitism was rife and that Jewish communities were at great risk. 'I wish we could do more to help.'

'My dear, you have already helped more than most and I understand that you have a great deal of important work to do. Children are the future, so they must be saved.'

Dora sighed inwardly at this reminder of the tremendous task ahead of her and her colleagues. 'Yes, I must go straight back to London and then I will have to return to Berlin to escort the next consignment.'

Friedmann nodded and shook her hand, clasping it with both of his. 'Go back and tell your friends what you have learnt today. Tell them we have seen it coming. They should be afraid for any country bordering the greedy Germans. The Dutch may have done much to halt the waters of the sea, but I doubt they can stem such a tide of hatred.'

Dora thanked him for his hospitality and left the house deep in thought. Germany bordered so many countries. Not Britain, of course, but were France, Poland, Belgium, Denmark and the others all at risk? The Germans had already moved into the Rhineland and Sudetenland, and Austria was being treated as an extension of their country. She suddenly felt over-whelmed by the enormity of the work ahead in whatever time they had left. She, Alice and Brenda were struggling to work as quickly as they could. They could save some of the children, but what about all the others who would be left behind?

THIRTY-ONE

A CRY FOR HELP

Dora couldn't be sure if it really was her. But in amongst the dark-haired, anxious parents thronging the busy station platform, that jaunty black hat, that blonde hair marked her out. What on earth was Verity doing here? There had been no news for months. Not even her parents had heard from her, and ever since that shocking wedding photo had been splashed across the front pages of the national press, Lady Ponsonby had ceased phoning Dora to ask whether she'd had a letter from her errant daughter.

Calling to Alice to continue checking arrivals onto the train, Dora dashed through the crowd of mothers and fathers waiting to see the train depart, to catch a last glimpse of their children. Despite the clamour of the station, Dora called out, 'Verity, is that you?' Her voice melted away into the melee of engines, announcements and general hubbub of greetings and farewells.

The slight figure was beginning to turn away. Soon she would be lost from sight. Dora hesitated, knowing her main responsibility was to the children filing onto the train. But there was still time and she wanted to seize this opportunity to grab Verity, ask what she was doing here, ask if her marriage was happy, ask her if she would ever come home. She surged through the clustered groups of frowning parents, some dabbing their eyes, some grimly silent.

'Verity,' she shouted again and somehow her voice carried through the fraught atmosphere and reached the ears of her cousin.

Verity turned. 'Dora? Is that really you?' She held out her hand.

'What are you doing here? Are you and Raven living in Berlin now?' Dora was surprised by the change in her cousin's appearance as she took in Verity's sunken cheeks, her hollow eyes. She was still elegant in her fitted charcoal-grey coat and her black hat, but she was a shrunken version of her former self. And everything about her was a little less polished than it had once been. Her clothes needed brushing, her shoes were scuffed and her lips bore only a trace of faded lipstick.

'Oh, thank goodness,' Verity said, almost tearfully. 'I was so hoping I'd find you. I'd heard that English Quakers were helping to take Jewish children to England and I guessed you'd be involved, but I couldn't be sure you'd actually be here this time.' She clutched Dora's hand in a fierce grip. 'Oh, Dora, dearest, thank goodness I've found you.'

'I've been coming backwards and forwards for quite some time. This is my fifth trip. I don't do every single one, but I'll keep doing them for as long as it's needed. We really don't know how much time we'll have in the end and there are so many families applying for help. Have you and Raven left Munich? Are you both living in Berlin?'

'No, we're not – that is, I mean... he's not.' Her face crumpled and she took a deep breath. She was trying her hardest to remain composed.

'Where is he, Vee? Please don't tell me he's left you?' Dora had a sudden inkling that the handsome, wayward Irishman had not fulfilled his promises.

Verity lifted her chin and looked directly at Dora. 'He certainly hasn't. Not voluntarily, that is.' She bit her lip. 'He's somewhere… somewhere awful. Dachau, I think.'

'But why on earth…?' Dora glanced back at the train. Children were still entering with their packages and little suitcases. Alice was still smiling encouragement. She thought she'd have a little time to find out what was behind her cousin's arrival.

'They think he was one of the plotters.' Verity seemed to spit out the words. 'They don't trust anyone now.' She turned slightly to look behind her, then peered over Dora's shoulder before continuing. 'But he'd never betray his friends. He simply wouldn't.'

'I don't understand. Do you mean Raven's been arrested? What plotters? And have you heard from Raven?'

'No, they say he's helping them. They came in the night, Dora! In the middle of the night. He was dragged from our bed. His last words to me were, *pray for me, my love…*' She sniffed and found an inadequate lace-edged handkerchief in her coat pocket. 'Ironic, isn't it, how we once visited Dachau as tourists? Do you remember? Little did we know!'

Of course Dora remembered and she felt Verity's dread at the thought of what her husband might be suffering there. If Hugh had been in a similar position, she would have been beside herself.

'Are you quite sure there is no justification for his arrest?'

'Absolutely certain. We thought they were all our friends. But you know what happens if they suspect someone isn't on their side. You've simply got to help me.' She gripped Dora's arm, her fingers digging through the thick cloth of her cousin's winter coat. 'You've got friends here and all over Germany, you've got to help me get him out of that dreadful prison.'

Verity's pleas were pitiful and Dora felt her pain and distress acutely. 'Dearest Vee, I'm not sure what I can do to help. Have you talked to the ambassador yet? Tried anyone at the embassy here?'

'Oh, them, they're not the slightest bit interested. I tried asking for help and they said we were no longer of any concern to them. Not deserving of their protection. Can you believe that? We're both still citizens of the United Kingdom, after all.'

But Dora could believe it. Verity and Raven had made their allegiances all too clear when they decamped to Munich and cosied up to Hitler and his cohorts. The British government couldn't trust them, so why should they help them? 'Then you'll just have to try there again. And maybe appeal to your parents as well. Your father still has some influence, surely? He knows the ambassador, doesn't he?' She hugged Verity tight. 'Oh, I wish I could stay and help you, but I can't. You must call your parents and beg them to help.'

'Oh, they don't want to talk to me either. They've made it perfectly clear that I've brought shame on the family name, by marrying an Irishman, for a start.' Verity gave a slight, scoffing laugh. 'I think that has infuriated them even more than any connections I may have made over here.'

'I'm sure they'd help you if it really came down to it. They're your parents, after all. But what exactly has Raven done, or not done? What is he accused of?'

Verity looked around her again, as if she was afraid of being overheard. 'Hitler and his men are absolutely paranoid about another assassination plot. Raven's done absolutely nothing, but they've rounded up a whole group of perfectly innocent men, all associates of ours. They've no hard evidence, none whatsoever.'

'Then surely their case will fall apart and then they'll have to release him.' Dora glanced over her shoulder. The train was making more urgent sounds. She couldn't stand here much longer.

'You don't know what they're like. Or what they're prepared

to do to find evidence.' Verity began to cry again, dabbing at her eyes. 'He might not survive their interrogations.'

Dora reached out to comfort her cousin. 'Vee, dear, I'll see what I can do. But I can't stay a minute longer now. There's nearly three hundred children on this train and I simply have to go with them. Write to me in London, let me know where I can find you.' She hugged her cousin, then turned away and began to walk quickly towards her charges. 'I'm really sorry I can't stay, but I'll come back again very soon.' She waved at Verity, who stood still for a moment, her mouth twisting with emotion, before rushing off through the milling crowd without saying any more. And was it Dora's imagination, or was that blonde head followed through that mass of dark coats?

Dora ran the last few yards to the train and climbed aboard just as the guard blew his whistle to signal immediate departure. She caught her breath and looked back through the open carriage window. Verity had gone, but her distress stayed with Dora. She tried telling herself her cousin had made her bed and would have to lie in it, as their school matron used to say to them when they were children, but that couldn't quell her unease. Verity may have been annoyingly dizzy and easily influenced, but this was still Vee, the girl she had known since childhood, the girl with whom she had crept down in the middle of the night, when they were children, to steal dried fruit and biscuits from the kitchen for their midnight feasts. They had argued and made up, teased each other and laughed, and now, despite her cousin having turned her back on her country, Dora wished she could help her.

THIRTY-TWO

ROSA

BERLIN, MARCH 1939

It was time to leave, Rosa decided. Ever since that terrible night she and Theresia had continued to live in the apartment above the business she and her husband had proudly owned, hoping Josef would soon return. But she no longer felt safe in this devastated area. With the name above the shop defiled, but still obvious to anyone who cared, they were marked out as Jewish. Not only had their livelihood been destroyed on Kristallnacht, but Jewish businesses were no longer allowed to operate. It could only be a matter of time before they were forced to leave. All around them shops and homes were being taken by greedy Germans who didn't care about the fate of their former occupants. It would be best if they left while they could still keep some of their possessions.

Rosa had packed most of their wardrobe and as she emptied the bottom drawer of her armoire, she looked sadly at the baby clothes she had saved from when Theresia was tiny. Her pregnancy had progressed well so far. Maybe she could dare to think that this time she would carry her baby to term. Since that dreadful day of the attack, when she'd tried to defend Liese, she had suffered three more miscarriages. But now more than five months had passed, perhaps all would be well. She added the tiny garments to her case, hoping they would be used eventually.

'Come, Theresia,' she called to her daughter. 'Have you finished packing your doll and her dresses?' Scraps of fabric from the business she once loved had been used to make fine clothes for her child's favourite toy.

'Mama, why do we have to leave? Can't we wait for Papa to come back?' Theresia hugged her doll to her chest and appealed to her mother with her deep-brown eyes.

Rosa bent down to her little daughter, now nearly seven years old. How could she protect her from all that was happening around them? She had been terrified that terrible night of violent carnage. 'Papa will know where to find us. Liese will tell him for us and I have written to him as well. We are going where we shall be welcome.'

Rosa added these last words trying to feel certain that it was true, but she could not be sure. It might seem safer, being surrounded by more members of the Jewish community, but how welcome would they really be? That part of Berlin was known as Scheunenviertel, or barn quarter, in reference to the poor housing built by refugees and it was becoming crowded with immigrants from the east. Once, she had never imagined that she too would be forced to live in such a deprived quarter of the city, but now it was the only option for anyone without a dependable livelihood.

Rosa wondered if she would find any work there at all. After restitching the hiding places in her hems and seams, she had packed her sewing box, filled with reels of thread, pins and needles, but perhaps she would have to search the city for jobs that would pay. Women would still require new clothes if they could afford the fabric, or alterations if they had to make do.

She took a last look at the apartment where she and Josef had once been so happy. Many of the finer decorations, the mirrors, the pictures, the rugs had gone, sold to buy food now that work was so scarce. Most of her furniture she'd burnt during the winter months. Liese had promised to help her with a cart to carry the bed and a couple of chairs to her new home, but she too was struggling since her husband had been arrested.

Rosa sighed and helped her daughter tie her bundle. The proud dressmaker now looked like a refugee herself, going to join the other lost souls in an area of the city she had once shunned, but which now might be the only place she could go.

THIRTY-THREE

SHE MADE HER BED

On her first evening back in London, Dora opened her heart to her husband. 'I felt so desperately sorry for Verity but there was nothing I could do in the time. She'd turned up just minutes before the train was about to leave and my first responsibility was to the children. Alice couldn't have managed the whole journey without me.'

'Of course you had no choice but to leave her there,' Hugh said, beating eggs for a quick omelette for her supper. 'I've no sympathy for her at all, quite honestly. She turned her back on you and her family. Not to mention her country. No wonder she didn't have any luck at the embassy.'

'But, darling, if only you could have seen her. She was a shadow of her former self. I'm afraid that she's going to make herself ill. How she's managing, I can't begin to think. I'd be sick with worry if I was in her shoes.'

'It's all very distressing, I know, darling, but you've got to admit she's brought this on herself. It's her own fault.'

Dora couldn't help thinking that Hugh could try showing a smidgen of sympathy. Verity may often have been annoying, but he had always been amused by her antics. 'Well, yes, but she didn't ask for her husband to go to prison, did she? And the worst kind of prison, as we now know.'

Hugh sighed. 'Yes, that's most unfortunate. More and more rumours are coming out of Germany every day. It's not looking so rosy now, is it?'

Dora shook her head in exasperation. 'I was never in any doubt about what they were really up to in Dachau. I knew it all those years ago. I could just tell from the way those prisoners looked. Their eyes told me they were deeply afraid. And do you know, a report has reached the office that, since that time, that wretched place has continued to put on a good show. Sometimes they even dress the guards up as prisoners to pretend everyone is hale and hearty. Such deceit!'

Hugh put his arm round her. 'Chin up, darling. You need to stay calm. If you're going to continue undertaking these harrowing train journeys, you've got to look after yourself. You'll be no good to all these children if you wear yourself out fretting about your errant cousin.'

'I suppose you're right, though I did wish I could have helped.' She thought back for a second, recalling her last glimpse of Verity. 'And I can't be certain about this, because the station was crawling with people all dressed in dark coats, coming and going, but I rather think she was followed when she left.'

'You haven't heard from her yet, I suppose? It might even have all blown over by now.' Hugh hugged Dora tight, but even his strong arms and warmth couldn't dispel her fears.

It was nearly a week since Dora had encountered Verity in Berlin. She had only been home a day after escorting the children to their various destinations. Some were met at Liverpool Street station by pre-arrangement with relatives, some were placed with foster-families or accommodated in hostels. All needed reassurance and comforting hugs after their tiring travels.

Every transport was upsetting to one degree or another. Sometimes the guards were brutish, emptying every case in every compartment, so the children had to scrabble to reclaim their clothes and toys. They had so little, but the few possessions they had brought with them were a precious reminder of loving homes and families they might not see again for a very long time. Everyone associated with the Kindertransport told the children that this would not be for long, that they might only be living in Britain for a matter of months. But Dora felt a deep gnawing inside that told her they might never return to their homeland and see their families again.

She was due to make another trip to Berlin less than a week after returning home. Alice wouldn't be going with her as her mother was in ill health and wanted her daughter close by. The London office couldn't spare another worker to go with her, so Brenda said she would join the next transport herself: 'I'd like to see first-hand how it's all operating and it will be useful to report back to our sponsors on that end of the operation.'

Dora was secretly glad she would have Brenda's company rather than Alice's. Her younger colleague was hard-working, but she was also timid and each encounter with a harsh official, a rough guard, a deeply distressed child, bruised her and Dora wasn't sure how long she could stand the pressure of this work.

Then, just days before they were due to leave, Dora received a letter from Berlin. It wasn't from Verity, but from a friend of hers, and said:

Your cousin has asked me to write to you to tell you that she is under arrest. Her husband has still not been released and she has been taken in for questioning. She is now in Plötzensee Prison and hopes you may be allowed to visit her there on your next trip to Berlin.

Dora felt faint at the word 'prison'. She rushed to show the letter to Brenda and said, 'I have to do something. I hope there will be enough time for me to see her. I know everyone is saying she has brought this on herself, but it's awful to think this is happening to a member of my own family. She looked so frail when I last saw her, I feel I have to try and help her.' She breathed deeply, trying to calm herself.

'Of course you must try to visit her. If their prisons are as awful as we've heard, she will need your support. You should pack some spare clothes and medication; she may well need it. And I think you should go on ahead of me to give you enough time to arrange a visit. They may not allow you to see her immediately.'

Dora rushed home that night to pack her case and tell Hugh she would be leaving sooner than expected. She didn't have time to prepare a last supper, so they ate fish and chips out of newspaper in the kitchen. 'I'm sorry I've got to go again so soon, but I never expected to hear that Verity would be arrested as well.'

'I imagine they suspect she has some useful information, if they are trying to round up known associates,' Hugh said, dousing his chips with vinegar and salt.

'I'm hoping she's being well-treated, but it makes me cringe to think of her being held with common criminals. It might be truly awful in there.'

'Try not to worry about it too much. Knowing your charismatic cousin, she's probably charmed one of the guards into bringing her hot water and a sprinkling of cologne.'

But Dora couldn't help thinking of the sad figure she'd met in Berlin, clutching her arm and begging for help. Verity's fabled charm was not much in evidence then and she doubted that she would be able to conjure up a winning smile while she was so worried about Raven.

. . .

When Dora arrived in Berlin, she knew she would have to act quickly. The next consignment of children had to be her priority, so anything she could do for Verity had to be achieved within the first two days. But when she approached the prison, she was told she wasn't allowed to see her.

'No visitors,' the guards at the entrance said.

'But she's my cousin and she's British,' Dora pleaded.

'It makes no difference. She's a political prisoner.'

Dora decided she would have to try another route. She went to the British embassy on Wilhelmstrasse and asked to see the British ambassador, Sir Neville Henderson. She had every confidence that he would agree to see her; after all, he had sometimes dined with her father and occasionally stayed at Verity's family home, and she and her cousin had both known him since they were young. He had a reputation for diplomacy and firmly believed that Britain could achieve peaceful relations with Germany. She was sure he would agree to see her even though he and the embassy had not been willing to listen when Verity had applied to them previously.

But it was not to be. Dora's request was passed down the ranks within the embassy and the only person she was permitted to meet was a very young and lowly assistant attaché by the name of Rufus Carrington. 'I'm afraid that Sir Neville is not available,' he said, seating her on a hard chair next to his bare desk in one of the embassy's smallest offices, far from the grandeur of the opulent rooms where the ambassador entertained and held important meetings. 'His diary is extremely full and this is rather short notice.'

'I'm terribly sorry about that. I've only just arrived in Berlin for another mission, escorting a train filled with Jewish children back to Britain. I've very little time available as they have to be my first concern but can you at least help me get permission to visit my cousin? The prison told me visitors aren't allowed.'

Carrington frowned and scribbled something on his

notepad. 'Aah yes, you're part of the Kindertransport, as the Germans are calling it, aren't you? I can ask the authorities about your cousin, but I'm not very hopeful. If, as you say, she is being held as a political prisoner, they're very unlikely to let anyone in to see her.'

'She may have made some rash decisions, but she's the least political person I know,' Dora said. 'She was just highly impressionable and easily influenced. Just a silly girl who had no idea of the consequences of her associations.'

'I remember seeing the photograph of her wedding in all the papers,' Carrington said with an apologetic smile. 'I thought at the time it wouldn't go down very well.'

'It certainly didn't. Not with her parents nor any of the establishment,' Dora said ruefully. 'But I don't suppose she thought about that at the time. She was far too starstruck with Raven and all the Nazi hierarchy.'

'Hmm, that's the trouble. They're all very good at posing in glamorous uniforms and making connections in high society.'

These wise words hinted at Carrington's good judgement, despite his fresh-scrubbed cheeks. Dora remembered Verity's unwise flirtations with young Nazi officers all those years ago in Oberammergau. She had never been one to see the truth beyond the gloss.

'But I'm begging you to see if you can help. She's very delicate. I thought she looked so frail when I saw her a couple of weeks ago. I really don't think she should be in a prison – and after all, whatever stupid things she may or may not have done, she is still a British citizen.'

'Of course. I'll take that line with them. I certainly agree that we should get her out if we can. They tend to send political prisoners on to Sachsenhausen and I should think that's the last place you'd want her to go. It's getting quite a nasty reputation.'

Dora felt a sick chill grip her stomach. Whatever Verity had done, she could not let her suffer in one of the regime's cruel prisons. 'And what about her husband? Do you think there is anything you can do to help him?'

'From what you've said about his supposed involvement in an assassination plot, I very much doubt we'd be able to pull any strings there. I'll make enquiries to see if I can gather any information about his situation, but I have to warn you there may not be good news. If his case has already been heard and a sentence has been passed, we may not be able to change the outcome.'

Dora sighed. 'Poor Verity, she was so desperate to help him when I saw her.'

'I'm rather afraid he won't be released and, to be honest, anyone who has a link to any kind of plot doesn't last long. They always receive the death sentence.' Carrington looked as serious as his boyish face would allow. 'I really am awfully sorry. Perhaps you had better prepare your cousin for the worst.'

Dora was shocked. She hadn't thought it would come to this and she couldn't imagine telling Verity that she'd never see Raven alive again. She'd been hoping she could get help to free her cousin, but if Raven was executed, what would Verity do then? She'd be a widow, alone in a country on the brink of war, far from her family and friends, with only the memory of her brief marriage to comfort her.

THIRTY-FOUR

VISITING HOURS

It was two days later and Rufus Carrington looked very pleased with himself. His almost-smooth cheeks were pink, nipped by the cold outside the hotel and his race to find Dora. 'You're going to be allowed to see your cousin. It seems the ambassador still has some pulling power after all, despite his busy schedule.'

'You mean I can visit her in the prison?' Dora had hardly dared to believe she would be able to see Verity this time after being refused entry when she had tried in person. As the hours had slipped by, she had begun to think a lowly clerk from the embassy would be unable to achieve a result.

'No, you can't see her at the prison. She's going to be brought to a police station in the centre of the city tomorrow morning at nine o'clock. You'll only be allowed to see her for fifteen minutes.'

'Oh dear, that's not very long and I'm meant to be checking children onto the train at that time. We're due to leave at ten tomorrow.'

'I'm sorry, but that's the best I could do. There's no room for negotiation. This is all they're prepared to offer and they won't compromise. I can't ask Sir Neville to beg them for a more convenient time. I think you're lucky they're letting you see her at all.'

'I'm so sorry, I didn't mean to sound ungrateful. Thank you – and please thank Sir Neville too. I'll write to him as soon as I can, to thank him myself.' Dora shook Carrington's hand warmly and continued, 'I'll make arrangements somehow for tomorrow with my colleagues.'

'I wish I could have made it easier for you, but I think we have to accept whatever they're prepared to offer.' He waved goodbye and Dora prepared to break the news to Brenda, who had arrived the night before.

'Don't fret about it, dear,' Brenda said in her sensible manner. 'We'll just have to manage. We've got those nice people from the Jewish Community Office helping as well, so we shouldn't have any trouble checking the children aboard while you're visiting your cousin. It all seems to be running quite smoothly these days.'

'I suppose it's better than having to run all the way across the city to the prison itself,' Dora said, trying to make the best of this awkward situation. 'That would have taken up much more time and this way I won't be far away from the railway station. But it would have been much more helpful if I could have seen her today when we're free.'

'I expect they have their reasons, my dear. Perhaps they want to get her ready for the meeting.' Brenda raised an eyebrow.

'Oh, what are you thinking? Is there something wrong with this arrangement?'

'I expect they don't want you to see how prison has affected her and they may want to present her in a good light.'

Dora suddenly pictured Verity in a dank, chilly cell, furnished with nothing but a pallet of straw and a bucket. She remembered how frail her cousin had seemed the last time she'd seen her; she hadn't fully considered the impact of prison life on her. She might be suffering from the restricted diet, the cold and the cramped conditions. She might now be unwell or, too terrible to even begin to think it, she might have been ill-treated.

'Oh, I think I see what you're implying. I do hope she hasn't suffered and isn't unwell. She didn't seem at all strong when I last saw her.'

'Then seeing you, and knowing you are doing all you can to help, will be a great morale booster for her. And you brought supplies with you, I hope?'

'Yes, I've made up a parcel for her, which I hope they'll let her have. I expect it will get checked, but it's only clean underwear, stockings, soap and aspirin.'

'All very sensible, dear. How can they possibly object to that?'

'Maybe I should add chocolate as well?'

'If she doesn't get a chance to eat it, I'm sure someone else will.' Brenda smiled and patted Dora on the back.

The following morning Dora rose early, ate a minimal breakfast and set out for the police station so she would arrive well before the appointed time. She had slipped slices of bread and cheese from the hotel buffet into her pocket in case she had the chance to pass those on to Verity as well.

As she walked briskly in the frosty morning air, her breath dampened the inside of the scarf covering her nose and mouth.

She reached her destination in only ten minutes. She looked at her watch and realised she was nearly twenty minutes early. But perhaps Verity was already here and she'd be allowed to see her straight away, or even have this extra time with her? Dora entered the station and approached the officer on duty.

His stern face told her she wouldn't be granted any favours, but he marched off to check. On his return he told Dora that the prisoner hadn't yet been transferred, but she could wait on a chair in the corridor until she arrived.

'Will I be able to give her this parcel while she's here? It's nothing much, just clothes, medicine, soap and chocolate.'

'Nein. We must inspect all goods sent to prisoners.' He held out his hand for the package and took it away.

Dora sat down on the hard wooden chair, her hands tightly clasped, her back straight and alert. Now, more than ever, she sensed how precarious Verity's situation was in this unforgiving atmosphere. From somewhere else in the building she could hear the clang of heavy doors, muffled cries and harsh shouts.

She couldn't stop herself glancing frequently at her watch, feeling that with every tick of the second hand her chances of helping were fading fast. If Verity didn't arrive soon, Dora would have hardly any time with her. But all of a sudden, the corridor seemed to fill with guards and a tiny figure was being bustled along with them, shielded by the uniformed figures. Despite the broad-shouldered men either side of, in front of and behind her, as if she was a ruthless criminal likely to escape, Dora caught a glimpse of a hollow-cheeked face as they marched to the far end of the police station.

When the hands on her watch finally reached nine o'clock, a police officer fetched Dora and escorted her to a bare room, where Verity was seated behind a desk. A guard stood beside her and another stood in front of the closed door.

Dora was allowed to sit opposite and reached out to clasp her cousin's cold hands, bound with handcuffs. The white wrists projecting from the sleeves of her black coat were almost skeletal. She was bareheaded and her normally gleaming hair had become a dirty blonde, though it had at least been combed.

'Darling Vee, I'm so glad I could manage to see you. I got here early but they wouldn't let me in at first. Tell me what you need and how I can help. Do you want me to contact your family?'

Verity spoke in a faint voice through dry, cracked lips that hadn't seen the balm of lipstick for a while. 'They won't believe I wasn't part of it. I'm so tired, I need to sleep.'

Dark circles framed her bloodshot eyes, not the mascara she had once employed. 'And I can't help them if Raven isn't with me. I know nothing about his friends.'

'Keep telling them that. They'll have to believe you eventually and let you go. I've tried to get help at the embassy. That's how I was able to come and see you. And I've brought some things you might need, underwear and so on. Is there anything else I can get for you?'

Verity shrugged and shook her head wearily. 'I just want to know that Raven is safe and they haven't hurt him. He's innocent, I know he is.'

Dora remembered Carrington's words of warning but how could she tell this exhausted, despondent girl that she might never see her husband again and that he might have already been sentenced to death? She rubbed Verity's dry, chilled hands to warm them: 'Keep hoping, dearest.' That was all she could say.

But before either of them was able to say very much more, the guard behind Verity pulled back her chair, grabbed her arm and made her stand up. Dora could see clearly how her clothes hung from her thin frame, even though she was wearing a coat. He marched her to the door, saying, 'The time is up.'

Dora was shocked at how abruptly their brief meeting had ended, and now Verity was being marched away with a body of armed guards as if she was a dangerous prisoner. But she caught the words her cousin shouted out as she disappeared down the corridor, 'Save Raven for me, Dora. Save him.' And as Dora watched her go, she realised Verity was being almost dragged by the burly guards, her feet barely touching the ground, leaving behind her a scent trail of unwashed clothes and dirty hair.

THIRTY-FIVE
MAKE UP YOUR MIND
BERLIN, MARCH 1939

Brenda was waiting for Dora on the platform when she rushed back there in plenty of time before their departure. 'Were you able to see your cousin, dear?'

'Only briefly. It wasn't even the full fifteen minutes they'd promised. And I realised after the guards had taken her away that they hadn't given her the parcel I'd taken to the police station. I had to hand it in for inspection before I even met her so I've no idea if she'll ever get it.'

'They were bound to do that but hopefully your gifts will reach her eventually.'

'Oh, I do hope so. She looked so pathetic and I could tell she's not being well-treated. Much more of this and she'll be getting seriously ill, I'm sure of it.' Dora glanced at the list of names Brenda was ticking off on her clipboard. 'How are you getting on?'

'We're well over halfway through. It's lucky for us you were able to get back here so soon. I'll carry on here checking them off while you hop on the train and see how they're all settling in.'

Dora walked through the carriages, smiling at the nervous children already seated. Dark-eyed faces stared at each other, most of them clutching vital parcels of food for the journey. Some chattered excitedly, others leant out of the window, waving to their families outside, but many had sunk into a fearful silence. The compartments captured the smell of scrubbed faces, damp wool and the coal-fire fumes of the smoking engine.

Above the chatter of those making friends, sounds filtered through from the station concourse. The huge black steam engine was already throbbing, like a tense athlete crouched to spring from the starting block, and the platform was filled with anxious parents holding little hands, while those who had already deposited their children on the train wrung sodden handkerchiefs. Shouts from porters and the fractured shrieks of the tannoy jarred with harsh orders from soldiers, while mothers and fathers called out final messages to their young ones: *'Write soon. Tell Onkel Fritz we shan't be far behind you. Give our love to Tante Hilde.'*

Dora walked along the corridors looking into each compartment, reassuring the occupants that she would be with them for the whole of the journey. They were all doing their best to be brave and not show their fear to parents outside still watching and waiting.

Halfway down the carriage, she was suddenly aware of a strange woman entering the train and darting into the compartment nearest the exit. Parents weren't allowed on the train; they had to say their farewells on the platform.

Then the woman emerged with a little suitcase, clutching the hand of a reluctant girl of about seven dressed in a dark blue coat with a red woollen bonnet and matching mittens. They left the train hurriedly and, through the window, Dora could see the woman bending down to talk to her child on the platform.

Perhaps she has a last message for her daughter, Dora

thought, watching the pair for a moment. The girl must have had a place on the list of passengers and maybe the mother had forgotten some vital instruction.

As Dora continued to watch them, the mother and daughter re-entered the train and went back to the same compartment. Dora imagined the conversation they might be having, the instructions a caring parent might give a child going to stay with relatives or strangers. Now she'll settle her child down and tell her to be a good girl on the journey and when she arrives at the other end.

A few more minutes passed while Dora checked the children further down the corridor. As she was doing so, she noticed the same mother, who had been watching from the platform looking agitated but waving to her daughter, suddenly dart forward and board the train yet again.

Surely she'd already given her daughter enough of a lecture, Dora thought, stepping out of the compartment into the corridor. But to her surprise, she saw the woman dragging the child out again with her little case. They both left the train and returned to the crowded platform, where the mother once more bent down to speak with her daughter.

Perhaps I should speak to that mother, reassure her that her child will be safe and well cared for, Dora told herself. But at that moment an argument broke out between two boys in the carriage and her attention was diverted. When she looked again, the mother and daughter were no longer on the platform.

Dora glanced at her watch. The train should be leaving very soon. She walked down the corridor so she could lean out of the carriage door and check the time by the huge station clock hanging over the concourse. And maybe she should double-check with Brenda that they had their full consignment of children.

As she neared the end of the passageway, she saw the anxious mother again. She was pulling her crying daughter out of the compartment once more. Dora was shocked. This was the third time the woman had removed her child. It was not only upsetting for the girl but also for the other children in the carriage.

Dora dashed forward and called after her, 'Please don't go. Your child will be safe with us.' She ran to the doorway, but the mother was already dragging the tearful girl through the massed crowd. She raced after them, but the bodies surging towards the throbbing train made it impossible to follow.

She heard the piercing shriek of the guard's whistle above the hubbub and ran back to the carriage. Peering out of the open window, she could see the back of the woman weaving her way through the tight knots of worried parents and grandparents towards the station exit. She was carrying her child in her arms so the little girl was looking back towards the train over her mother's shoulder. That bobbing red dot of a bonnet, framing her black curls, stood out among the sea of grey, black and dark blue coats and hats. And as Dora watched and felt the train start to gird its loins to move, the girl waved. Was she saying goodbye to the new friends she had made?

Dora was dumbfounded. What was the child thinking? She must be so confused by her mother's actions and she'd seemed upset to be leaving the train. She must have been told why she was going to make the journey, but then suddenly she was torn away from all that had been promised.

And the mother? Three times she'd placed her child on the train and three times she'd removed her. She had bought her daughter a precious ticket to a land of safety, packed her case, dressed her in her best winter coat for the journey, sat her on the train and then, at the last minute, taken her away. In the end she couldn't bring herself to send her darling child off into the unknown with strangers. Torn between what she knew and what might be, she had chosen to keep her daughter with her, to keep her here in Berlin, where Jews had already lost their jobs, their businesses and their homes. How could living in squalid conditions and queuing for scraps of food be better than sending her child to a country where she would be fed and able to go to school in safety?

How many other parents had made the same heartrending decision? Dora was reminded once more what an immensely painful choice all of them faced, hoping the threats would come to nothing, praying that life would return to what it had once been. All the children on the trains, apart from those who were orphans, had families who loved them and were reluctant to part with them. But their parents and grandparents had deemed it better to send them away, rather than risk further danger here in Germany.

What would I do in similar circumstances? Dora wondered as the train began to steam out of the station. Keep my child close and try to shield her from the deprivation closing in around us? Is that a better choice? Or take a leap of faith and send her far away, out of danger? I wonder how soon that mother will come to regret her decision.

She closed the carriage window and turned back to find the compartment she'd been allocated. On her way, she passed Brenda, who, said, 'You look very tired, dear. Why don't you try to rest? Close your eyes for a little while. The children won't need our attention for a bit.'

'Did you see that woman take her child off the train? I could hardly believe it. She just couldn't make up her mind. She took her on and off three times.'

Brenda frowned and gave a tut of disapproval. 'Oh, what a shame. The poor dear. And that means there's a spare seat on the train. We could have taken one more.' She shook her head, then rested it against the cushioned back of the seat and shut her eyes.

She was right: they could have saved one more. But had that woman just saved her child or condemned her? Dora stumbled to her seat, slumped back and closed her eyes. As the darkness of sleep came to her, she could see the little red hat bobbing through the black crowds, bordered by the rippling of those wretched red Nazi banners, proclaiming their superiority over the miserable hordes trying to escape.

THIRTY-SIX

ROSA

Rumours were rife in Scheunenviertel; some of them Rosa didn't want to hear. But the subject that interested her enormously was the story that British charities were taking Jewish children to safety in Britain.

'Several trains have already left,' Liese said. 'They started in December. Maybe you should think about sending Theresia. It wouldn't be forever, just until things get better.'

Rosa hardly dared to think about the idea. It seemed to her that parents could only bear to be parted from their children if they had no hope for the future. And what would Josef think if he returned and found their daughter had gone?

After asking around about how this was being arranged, she queued at the Jewish Community Office to speak to the man in charge, Herr Albert Friedmann, a former diamond merchant. He had a kindly face. She hoped that everyone taking children away from their families was as kind.

'And have you heard from your husband since he was arrested?' His hand hovered over the list of names on his desk.

'Not directly,' Rosa said, clutching her daughter's hand. She had never told Theresia what she feared the most. 'But I received a message from a man who was released from Sachsenhausen last month. He said Josef sent us his love and told us to keep the faith.'

Friedmann nodded. 'Of course. And do you think your husband would be in favour of you applying for a place for your daughter?'

Rosa paused. Josef would want to see his child one last time before she disappeared, possibly forever. She knew her thoughts were written on her face. 'How many more transports do you think there will be? Do I have to decide now?'

'If you really want her to go, it would be best to put her name on the list right away. We don't know how long they can continue and there is huge demand for places.' Friedmann laid down his pen. 'And once you have registered your child, you can't change your mind and let the place be wasted.'

Surely she had done the right thing, applying for a visa and a place for her daughter? Life was sure to get harder. Rosa ran her hand over her swelling stomach. Was it her imagination or was she larger than she had been with Theresia?

The day before the train was due to depart, Rosa prepared her daughter for the journey. 'I've decided that you deserve a special holiday in a country where there is plenty of food. You are going to have a lovely ride on a train with lots of other children and all of you will be happy together and go to school in England. Won't that be fun?'

'Can you come too, Mutti?'

Rosa shook her head. 'It's a special train, just for children. But you can take Elsa with you. Look, I have made a bag for all her clothes.' She showed Theresia the carpet bag she had stitched from a scrap of velvet, embellished with cord handles. 'Would you like to pack everything for her?'

Theresia smiled, then began folding her doll's dresses. 'Can she have a red hat like mine, so we look the same?'

Rosa bit back her tears and nodded. 'Of course, she must have a hat. You must both look very smart when you arrive in England.' She reached for a piece of red felt and threaded her needle. By concentrating on her stitches, she could hide her distress.

The next day, she packed a suitcase, gave her daughter provisions for the journey, told her she was going to have a wonderful adventure, dressed her warmly and let her take her favourite doll with its own bag of hand-stitched dresses. She watched Theresia take her seat on the train, heard the rumble of the engine, smelt the steam billowing from the chimney, waved as her daughter peered through the carriage window, then felt the awful, searing pain of separation. If this baby growing inside her didn't survive, if Theresia never came back, she'd have lost her only child...

And then she couldn't do it – or could she? The first time she took Theresia off the train, she told herself she was just checking that her daughter understood why she had to leave her homeland for another country. The second time she gave her instructions about how she was to behave with the kind people who would care for her. But the third time she couldn't explain; she just had to run away with her before she broke completely.

'I'm sorry, Liebchen,' she sobbed as she ran, holding her crying child in her arms.

'Why can't I go on the train, Mama? Why can't I go?'

'I can't bear to lose you and Papa wants to see you when he comes back. He wouldn't like it if I sent you away.'

But when she reached their squalid new home, she wept again. Was it the right decision? Could she have been stronger? And how was she going to cope if this pregnancy produced more than one child?

Theresia curled up on the bed, opened the bag of little

clothes and began to dress her doll. She sang to herself. And as she watched her, Rosa hoped her daughter would forget about the train.

THIRTY-SEVEN
NO TIME TO REST
LONDON, MARCH 1939

'You look quite done in, darling,' Hugh kissed Dora and hugged her as she slipped out of her coat. 'I hope you're going to stay at home for a while and rest before you do another trip.'

'Alice and Brenda are doing the next one, so I won't have to travel again for a couple of weeks. I can stay home tomorrow, but then I must return to the office to deal with the paperwork.'

Hugh frowned. 'You look to me like you could do with more than a day to recover, but I know you won't listen to the advice of a mere doctor. Still, I can make dinner tonight and bring back fish and chips tomorrow, so you won't have to cook.' He took her apron off the hook on the kitchen door and tied it round his waist.

Dora had to laugh. 'It suits you. What are you making?'

He flourished a frying pan and bowed. 'Egg and chips with brown sauce, madam. I picked up the best chips in Islington on my way home and the hens have been laying well, despite the cold, while you've been away. Would madam like one egg or two?'

'That sounds perfect. I'll have two. Are you sure there are enough?'

'Plenty. Mrs Harvey's chickadees have been doing their duty on a diet of scraps and cold chips. And in the absence of your scrounger of a cousin, the eggs are all ours.' He glanced at Dora. 'How was she, by the way?'

Dora couldn't help herself; tears sprang to her eyes as she began to tell him. 'Oh, Hugh, it was awful. It was so difficult arranging to see her and then we only had a few minutes together, with guards standing over us the whole time. Verity didn't look at all well and I don't even know if the parcel I took for her ever ended up in her hands. Those wretched men probably kept it for themselves.'

Hugh laid down his pan and put his arms round her so she could bury her face in his solid, comforting shoulder. 'You did your best, darling. Don't upset yourself.'

'But I can't help thinking how I'd feel if you were arrested. Verity's so lost without him – and the awful thing is that I was warned by the man at the embassy who helped me that Raven is very likely to be given a death sentence, even if they can't prove he was part of a conspiracy plot. And I simply couldn't bring myself to tell her that. Whatever is she going to do if that happens?' Dora's tears began to flow freely and Hugh held her tight until she was quiet.

'Your cousin and her husband both knowingly entered into a dangerous situation, darling, with dangerous associates. You can't do any more than you already have.' He gently sat her down and looked serious. 'You mustn't feel responsible for her or for him. Your duty is to your task. Save your strength for the children.'

Dora blew her nose and sniffed. 'I'm just tired, that's all. I won't find it so hard once I've slept properly. Trying to rest on a train with upset children doesn't make for a good night's sleep. I'm pretty exhausted.'

'Then as soon as you've eaten your supper, it's bedtime. I'll clear up down here and you mustn't do a thing. I'll put a hot-water bottle in for you right now, so you can just crawl in and fall asleep straight away.'

'That would be lovely.' Dora yawned. 'Now, how long is it going to take to fry those eggs?'

The next morning, Hugh left early for the hospital, but brought Dora tea and toast in bed before he did. 'Now remember what Doctor Hugh has prescribed,' he said, bending down to kiss her. 'Bed rest all morning, then nothing more than light duties around the house. Or better still, curl up with a book by the fire.'

'I'll be good,' she said, reaching for the toast, thickly spread with butter and marmalade. But after she'd eaten it and drunk her tea, she began to wonder what might greet her in the office if she didn't go in for another day. The begging letters had been piling up before she left and she knew how many more arrived with each delivery. She swung her legs out of bed and made a plan. After a relaxing bath she'd go in for just a couple of hours. Then she could easily be back for the afternoon and Hugh would never even know she'd disobeyed his instructions.

An hour later she caught a bus to Bloomsbury House to begin work. As she'd expected, trays of post awaited her, even though Alice had been processing requests every day in her absence. She began opening envelopes and had barely read more than a couple when Brenda came into the office. Clearly, she hadn't felt the need to take time off either after their long journey back from Berlin the day before.

'Aah good, there you are. I'd just tried telephoning you at home. I thought you were going to take the day off.'

'I was, but I couldn't really relax. I slept like a log but this morning I thought I couldn't sit at home doing nothing, knowing all this was piling up here. It just didn't feel right.'

'Good for you. But leave that for the moment. You've had a

call from the embassy in Berlin. Someone called Rufus Carrington. Wants you to call him back as soon as you can.'

'Oh, that's the lovely chap who helped me get permission to see Verity. He must have some news. I'll try ringing him right away.' Dora knew that it sometimes took a while to book an international call, so in the meantime she began imagining all the developments Carrington might be able to report. She hoped fervently that it would be good news and that he was phoning to tell her Verity had been released and Raven had been found innocent of any plot.

Nearly an hour later, she was put through to the embassy and listened to the frustrating clicks and hisses on the line until Carrington answered the call. 'Hello,' she said. 'What's happened? I hope it's good news.'

'Some of it is,' he said. He sounded very sombre. 'Your cousin has been released.'

'Thank goodness for that. How is she? Do you know?'

'She's in hospital. And I don't know how long for.'

'I knew that prison wasn't good for her. I could see she wasn't in great health when we met that day.'

'No, it isn't just that. Well, I mean, the prison conditions weren't conducive to good health. But no...' He hesitated again as if he was reluctant to say more. 'When are you coming back? You are going to come back soon, aren't you?'

'I'm not meant to be coming for another two weeks. My colleagues here are taking the next Kindertransport. Why? Do you think I should come sooner?'

'I do rather. You see, she's been injured. That's why I don't know how long she'll be in hospital.'

'What, you mean because they ill-treated her in the prison? Are you saying they beat her?'

'No, nothing of the kind.' She could hear him take a breath, trying to pick his words carefully. 'I'm very sorry to have to tell you this, but she tried to shoot herself.'

Dora's heart lurched, imagining Verity, silly old Vee, dramatically shooting herself by accident and spurting blood. 'She did what?'

'She managed to shoot herself in the head. She only grazed herself, actually, but it was quite nasty and, more to the point, there's concern about her mental state.'

'What? Why on earth would she want to do such a thing?' Dora could feel her heart thumping at quite an alarming rate.

Carrington gave a slight cough, then spoke. 'I imagine it was her reaction to the news about her husband. I'm dreadfully sorry to have to inform you that he was executed, only hours before she tried to take her own life.'

'Oh, my goodness. Poor Verity, she must be beside herself. That's simply dreadful. I know you told me it might happen, but nevertheless it's a terrible shock.' Dora could feel herself slumping on the chair next to the desk, as if she no longer had the power to sit upright.

'And I'm afraid, to make matters even worse, his death and the deaths of the others were pretty awful.'

'You mean there was a firing squad? Or were they hanged?' Dora was starting to feel faint. If the news was affecting her like this, how on earth could Verity stand it, hearing that her darling husband had been killed?

'Regrettably neither. They're rather fond of using a guillotine for anyone they consider to be a traitor. I'm so sorry to be the bearer of such awful news.' Carrington sounded genuinely sorry, but perhaps that was because Raven had a British passport, despite his birthplace. This kind of diplomatic complication would hardly help the ambassador in his delicate peace negotiations.

Dora could feel the bile rising in her throat. She struggled and took a deep breath before saying, 'Oh my goodness. I must go to Verity.'

'I'm so sorry I've had to tell you this. I realise it must be the most dreadful shock.'

'It's not your fault. You've been extremely helpful.' Dora couldn't think of anything else to say. That handsome rascal Raven with his silly jokes, his love of whisky and his love of Verity, dead, his body mutilated; it was all too horrible to contemplate.

'Perhaps you can let me know when you are coming back to Berlin,' Carrington said. 'And if there's anything else I can do to help, please don't hesitate to contact me.'

Dora let him go. The man had probably never expected to have to deliver such devastating news when he first applied to join the diplomatic service. She continued sitting, her whole body trembling, until Brenda looked through the doorway.

'My dear girl, whatever's the matter? You're white as a sheet. Not bad news, I hope?'

Dora took a deep breath. 'I'm afraid it is rather. My cousin's husband has been executed.' She held back the flood of tears threatening to come and added, 'He was beheaded.'

Brenda sat beside her. 'Utter brutes. They're totally ruthless.' She gave Dora's hands a comforting squeeze. 'What do you want to do? If you think you should go to your cousin immediately, you must. You can go as soon as you wish and stay out there until it's time for the next Kindertransport. Alice can stay here and I'll join you in Berlin as soon as I can.'

'Thank you. May I try calling my cousin's family immediately from here? They may wish to go to her.'

But Dora had no luck. The butler answered and she couldn't bring herself to leave such a grim message with him, so she left her desk to send two telegrams at the nearest telegraph office on her way back to Islington. The first message, to Lord and Lady Ponsonby, Verity's parents, said:

VERITY IN BERLIN HOSPITAL STOP GOING TO HER TODAY STOP

The second was to Rufus Carrington:

LEAVE   FOR   BERLIN   TONIGHT   STOP   TELL VERITY STOP

As soon as she had done that, she raced home to pack and write a brief note for Hugh.

> *Darling, the most dreadful news from Berlin. Verity in hospital, Raven executed. I have to go immediately. I'll be back with the next Kindertransport. All my love, Dora. xx*

She knew he would be disappointed when he arrived back that night with a double portion of fish and chips to find her gone. But she couldn't stay. Her misguided cousin needed her help and she had to get to her side as soon as she possibly could.

THIRTY-EIGHT

THE WORST NEWS

Dora was directed by a nurse to the far corner of the hushed ward lined with two rows of iron-framed beds, shrouded in white sheets and tightly tucked grey blankets. Apart from the low murmur of subdued voices, there wasn't a sound until Dora began walking across the wooden floor in her sturdy brogues. Her loud, echoing steps made her feel she was intruding in this place of quiet healing.

Shrunken in a nest of white pillows and sheets, her head bandaged, Verity reminded Dora of the Egyptian mummy she had seen as a child in the British Museum. Her closed eyes were circled with shadows and her face was pale.

'Vee, darling,' Dora whispered, 'It's me. I've come specially to see how you are doing. The man at the embassy telephoned me.' She lightly touched Verity's hands, clasped together over the folded top of the crisp sheet.

Verity's eyes sprang open with a gasp as if she was startled. 'I'm sorry to wake you,' Dora said. 'I wasn't sure if you were asleep.'

'I wasn't,' her faint voice said. 'I can't sleep.' She turned her head a little to look at Dora. 'Did you know he's dead? They've killed my darling Raven.'

'I know, dearest. I'm so sorry. I left London as soon as I was told what had happened.' Dora leant forward to kiss her cousin's cold cheek. 'Do you want me to help you leave here and go home?'

'Home? Our home here?' Her eyes seemed vacant and Dora couldn't help wondering how much damage a bullet might have done to Verity's brain, despite them having told her it was a minor injury, little more than a surface wound.

'No, not here, Vee. I was thinking you might like to come back to England. You're very welcome to come back to your old flat in London. Or, if you'd rather, you could go to your parents, as they'd be there all the time to care for you. We all want to look after you.'

Dora made the last statement confidently, but she had had a phone call from Verity's mother shortly before she'd left the house with her suitcase. Lady Ponsonby's verdict included the words *that girl always was one to make a scene... we'll never live it down... I don't know what her father will have to say about this shocking business.*

Dora knew that her own parents would never reject one of their own in need, no matter what the problem was, but the Ponsonbys were somehow a quite different, unsentimental breed. 'If the doctors think you're well enough to leave, I could take you to my hotel for the time being, until you can decide. Would you like me to ask them if you can leave today?'

'Ask who? What do you want to ask?' Verity's voice was vague and shaky, underlining her confusion.

'Your doctor, dear. I'm going to ask whether they're happy to discharge you into my care. And if they think you're fit enough to travel, I can take you back to England with me. In a few days' time, I'll be escorting another group of children. I'm sure we can find a seat for you on the train.'

Verity grabbed Dora's wrist with a surprisingly strong grip. 'But Raven... he can't come with me...'

'I know what's happened, dear. It's just awful and I'm so sorry about that. But this means that you're free to leave Germany now. That might be the best thing, don't you think?'

Verity's sunken eyes filled with shimmering tears. 'He has to go back to Ireland. His family is buried there. I can't leave him here all alone. He needs me.'

Dora realised she hadn't even thought about Raven's body. Could she arrange for him to be returned to Ireland? Or had his corpse already been disposed of in Dachau? She wasn't sure how to handle this without upsetting Verity any further.

'I'll ask the embassy for help,' she said. 'I'm sure they will know how to organise that. But it might take some time, with official red tape and so on. Maybe it would be best for us to travel back home together and wait to hear when that can be arranged. It would give you time to regain your strength and then we could all help you make plans for a proper funeral.'

Verity's tears flowed and she sobbed. 'I'd like that. I don't want to stay here anymore without Raven. I want to go home now.'

Dora remembered Lady Ponsonby's cold response to the news of her daughter's distress and wondered if the lofty standards of Featherstonehaugh Hall would help or hinder Verity's recovery. Maybe it would be better for her to recuperate in the London flat, even though Dora and Hugh weren't at home during the working day. Or better still, perhaps she should stay with Dora's family, in the calmer surroundings of the more modest country house in Hampshire, where she would be treated with gentle sympathy and escorted walks to see the carpets of primroses. 'Let me find a nurse and make enquiries,' she said.

Two hours later, they were safely back in their hotel room. Verity was freshly bathed with washed and combed hair, lying on the cushioned bed, sipping beef tea and nibbling toast. The bandage round her head had been removed before they left the hospital and now bruising and a strip of plaster were all that remained of her self-inflicted injury. She whispered answers to Dora's gentle questions and said, 'How long can we stay here?'

'The train leaves in three days and it takes at least fifteen hours to reach the coast of Holland. So, with good weather for the crossing and if there's no trouble from the guards they insist on sending with us, it takes two whole days to get to Britain. Then we all pile onto a train to Liverpool Street. Would you rather stay here until you feel stronger? I must say I'd rather not leave you behind though.'

Verity gave a weary shake of her head. 'No, I don't want to be here alone. If I'm on my own I won't stop thinking about what they did to Raven. I hate them. All of them. They were our friends and they betrayed us.'

Dora reflected that her cousin had always been a girl for extremes and wasn't surprised to hear the once-passionate Nazi lover had become a fervent Nazi hater after what had happened. 'Then you really do have to leave Berlin with me. You can stay and rest here until the last minute. I'll take care of you on the journey, but I'll probably be looking after about a hundred children as well and my colleague Brenda will be dealing with the others.'

'Children.' Verity's face crumpled again. 'He wanted children so much. We both did.'

Dora sat on the bed and put her arm round this sad, shrunken figure. 'It's all so sad, Vee. I'm so terribly sorry. I hope the long journey won't be too hard for you.'

'It won't be as hard as prison. And I was held in one of the better ones. It was filthy, cold and cruel.'

'They didn't hurt you there, did they? Please tell me they didn't.'

'No, not me. But other prisoners were beaten and whipped.

It was ghastly. And Dachau would have been even worse...' She began to weep again. 'My poor, darling Raven.'

'Try to rest now, dear. Get some sleep.' Dora kissed Verity on the top of her head, removed the drained cup of bouillon and pulled the quilt over her. She needed to make a plan and decided to call Rufus Carrington at the embassy.

'Have you seen Mrs Fitzgerald yet?' he asked when she got through.

'She's here with me right now. She's been discharged and I brought her back to the hotel. I'm hoping she'll be well enough to travel in three days' time. I'm planning to take her back to England with me on our next trainload. I can say she's one of our chaperones. But, I've just thought, will she have any trouble returning to Britain, given her associations?'

She could hear Carrington clear his throat before he answered: 'I'll have to double-check, of course, but I should think we could turn a blind eye.'

Dora sighed with relief. 'Then I've got just one more question. And this might be a bit tricky: it's about her husband.'

'Go ahead. What do you need to know?'

'Will the authorities allow his body to be brought back for burial in Ireland? That's where the family estate is and Verity is desperate for him to return home.'

There was a strange silence before Carrington answered. 'I'll have to make enquiries, of course, but I rather fear that there may not be an actual body to be returned.'

'But there must be. He was executed in the prison, in Dachau, wasn't he?'

Carrington cleared his throat. 'That's what we've been told, but I'm afraid his body and those of his fellow conspirators were incinerated immediately. The ashes will probably have already been disposed of. There's no longer anything to claim. I'm so sorry.'

Dora's heart sank. How could she tell Verity this when she

was pinning her hopes on taking her husband back to the land of his birth? She would decline still further and maybe make another attempt on her life. This awful news had to be kept from her.

She took a deep breath. 'Can you make enquiries all the same? She's in a desperate state. I simply can't tell her there's no hope.'

THIRTY-NINE

WHERE'S MY LIPSTICK?

BERLIN, MARCH 1939

Dora kept doing her best to distract Verity from asking questions about taking Raven's body back to the UK. 'The embassy is making enquiries for you. These things apparently take a little while as there's all sorts of paperwork.'

'But I have to travel with Raven. I want to bring him home with me.'

'All in good time, dear. It just isn't possible to do so immediately. Besides, it will be better for you to go home and recuperate for a while, then come back if you have to.'

But would she ever be able to? Dora asked herself. Would the authorities allow an alien under suspicion to re-enter Germany and what if war was imminent by then? She might never be allowed to return to the country that had once so enamoured her and Raven.

Verity looked a little brighter after a couple of good nights' sleep and Dora was reassured that her appetite seemed to be slowly returning, so she could concentrate on her other reason for being in Berlin. 'I have to meet Brenda this morning with the Jewish Council to check through our passengers for the transport. Will you be happy staying here? I expect I'll be gone for most of the day, but it would be good for you to rest and take lunch in the hotel.'

'I won't be going anywhere. I might even have lunch sent up. Off you go and don't worry about me.' Verity picked up a book and yawned.

Dora didn't like to leave her cousin alone for so long, but was acutely aware of how much detailed work was needed to ensure all the children had the correct papers and could complete their journey. Brenda couldn't easily do it all without her help. 'Very well then, I'll see you later. Don't exert yourself.'

At the end of a long, tiring day checking documents with Brenda, Dora returned to the hotel, looking forward to a hot bath and then a quiet dinner. She entered the bedroom and was surprised not to see her cousin still lying on the bed where she'd left her that morning. She hadn't noticed her as she walked through the hotel lobby to the lift, but thought perhaps she had taken herself downstairs to the lounge for a change of scene, maybe to enjoy tea and Sachertorte. Or maybe she had decided to return to the flat where she'd been staying to collect her possessions. She had come to the hotel with nothing but the clothes she stood up in.

Dora was weary and decided to run her bath straight away. She was sure that, when she emerged from the bathroom wrapped in a fluffy towel, she'd find Verity lounging on the bed again, having read hardly any of the book she'd started that morning.

The hot water, perfumed with a few drops of cologne, was soothing after dealing with worried parents and fretful children under the watchful eyes of interfering Nazi officials. Dora leant her head back on the edge of the bath, cushioned by a folded towel, and closed her eyes for a moment.

She could feel her mind starting to drift towards dreaming

and shook her head to stop herself falling asleep. She sat up, splashing her face, and hauled herself out of the delicious bath. She had just wound a large white towel round her torso when the bathroom door burst open and Verity screamed at her.

'How could you not have told me? You lied to me. He's never going to be able to come home with me, is he?' Verity's eyes were surrounded by black rivulets of mascara diluted with tears. Red spots of anger stood out on her pale cheeks and her lips were slashed with scarlet. 'Why didn't you tell me they'd already destroyed my darling husband's body?'

'Oh, Vee, darling, I'm so, so sorry. The embassy said they'd check for me. They didn't know for certain. I just didn't want to worry you further until we knew more. Please don't upset yourself. I thought I was doing the right thing.'

'You had no right to do that. I hate you.' Verity swung her handbag, but Dora ducked in time and the bag hit the bathroom mirror.

'Come and sit down,' Dora said, her heart thumping as she guided her cousin out of the bathroom, away from the shattered glass. 'Where have you been?'

'To the embassy, of course. I had to know the truth. I can't believe you didn't tell me.' Verity threw herself down on the bed, her body trembling with great sobs.

Dora sat down beside her. She hadn't expected this development. 'Who did you see there? Who told you?'

At first Verity's voice was muffled in the depths of the quilted bedspread, then she turned her tear-streaked face to look at Dora. 'A little weed called Carrington deigned to see me after I'd made a scene. He took me into an office, offered to calm me down with a brandy and then told me everything. He said there's a slight chance he can get the ashes for me, but he didn't sound very hopeful.'

'Dearest Vee, I'm so sorry. I should have told you myself but I wasn't sure of the facts at that time. I wanted to be certain before I said anything. Carrington has been very helpful throughout. It was him who arranged for me to see you in prison and then he told me you were in hospital. I'm sure he was only trying to be kind.'

'Oh, he was that, all right,' Verity gasped between sobs. 'He was making sure I didn't embarrass his precious embassy and wanted to keep me well out of the way of the senior officials and his wretched ambassador. He didn't want them seeing and hearing a hysterical Englishwoman screaming the place down.'

'Oh dear. I'm sure he felt dreadful having to break the news to you.'

'Not half as dreadful as I feel. How would you react if you'd just been told your darling Hugh had not only been executed but they'd destroyed his body as well and there was nothing left for you to bury? They had no right to do that to my darling, darling husband.'

Dora rubbed her cousin's shaking shoulders. 'I really had hoped there would be better news. I'm so terribly sorry. But don't you see, there's nothing to keep you here now. You can come home with me, the day after tomorrow. I really don't want to leave you feeling like this.'

Verity pulled the coverlet over her head. 'I just want to die and never have to think about this ever again,' she said in a muffled, strangulated voice.

'I know, darling. But we all love you and want to keep you safe. I'm not going to let you out of my sight.'

Dora stood up and finished rubbing herself dry. 'I'm going to get dressed again now. If you feel up to it, we'll go down for dinner but I'm quite happy to have it sent up to our room.'

She let Verity lie there for half an hour or more, her sobs quietening, her shoulders gradually becoming still, while she dressed. As she sat at the dressing table, applying powder and lipstick, she caught sight of her in the mirror. Her cousin was sitting up, running her fingers through her hair.

'How are you feeling?' Dora said. 'I'm quite hungry. Do you fancy joining me downstairs in the dining room?'

'I've lost my lipstick,' Verity said. 'Raven loved me having red lips. He wouldn't want me to hide away as if I was ashamed. He'd tell me to show them what I'm made of.'

'Here,' Dora said, 'feel free to use mine but wash your face first. Your eyes are all black. I've mascara here too, if you can't find yours.'

Verity eased herself off the bed and went to the bathroom to splash her face. She dried herself, leaving dark stains on the white towel, removing a reminder of the filth in the prison where her husband had been slaughtered. Then she grabbed the lipstick from Dora's outheld hand and drew a fierce slash across her lips. 'Let's go,' she said. 'I'm starving.' She combed her hair and settled her black hat at a stylish angle over her blonde waves.

Dora watched the transformation with amazement. Verity had always been highly dramatic, able to act the part, and now she was playing the role of the wounded widow with conviction. But she was acting with determination and aplomb to show her enemies they couldn't break her. Dora was immensely proud of her and knew that Raven would have applauded his wife's convincing performance too.

FORTY

FRIENDS AND ENEMIES

'It's hard to believe she's a grieving widow,' Brenda said, glancing at Verity, who was sitting on a bench playing pat-a-cake with a little girl on the station platform. Dora's cousin was smartly dressed, although all in black, and had made an effort with her hair and make-up.

'She's trying very hard,' Dora said. 'She's putting on a brave face, playing a part, but I think once she's safely home she'll probably break down again. I'm just glad she's agreed to come with us.' She glanced around the station concourse, wondering how many of the men in dark coats were passengers or parents and how many were there to ensure her cousin left Germany, probably never to return.

'Do you think she's being watched?' Brenda also looked over her shoulder, surveying the gathering crowd. 'Have you noticed anyone?'

'I'm sure we were followed from the hospital when I first collected her the other day and again this morning when we left the hotel. And I've no idea who might have seen her going out and making a scene at the embassy the other day. They'll be glad to see the back of her, I should think.'

'Did you ever find out how she'd got hold of a gun? I hope she hasn't still got it in her handbag.'

'Oh crikey, I hadn't thought about that. It's the one thing I hadn't thought to ask her.' Dora ran her mind over the chaotic contents of Featherstonehaugh Hall and wondered if it was an heirloom Verity had collected there, or perhaps an unusual gift from her eccentric grandmother. It would be just like her to think a dainty pearl-handled pistol was a suitable going-away present. 'There was no sign of one when we collected her belongings yesterday.'

'Well, she seems to be keeping occupied for now, at least,' Brenda said, glancing across, then ticked off another pair of young passengers on her clipboard. 'Why don't you take these two onto the train and find a seat for your cousin in one of the compartments?'

Dora was glad to see Verity onto the train; she had feared that she might change her mind at any moment and suddenly decide she had to storm the embassy again or, worse, the Reichstag in her anger at the injustice of her husband's end.

'Verity, dear,' Dora said, ushering the children forward, 'I have two more passengers who need your company. Meet Jack Hedman and his sister Hilde.' She put a guiding arm round the two children. The little boy was clutching a teddy bear to his chest, the little girl a doll. 'And now let's find you all seats on the train.'

Leading the way down the corridor, Dora said, 'I'm going to put you in the second compartment along and I'll be in the first one, nearest the entrance, then you'll always know where to find me.' She or Brenda always chose to sit there so if additional guards entered the train at any stops they were able to speak to them immediately. The guards' presence was always disconcerting for the most nervous of their passengers, but could sometimes be smoothed over with a polite word from either of them.

'Hold my hand,' Verity said to the little girl she had already befriended. 'We can sit together for the whole journey if you like.'

Dora was glad she had persuaded her cousin to join this transport. Not only was she relieved to be taking her away from the country of her husband's death and her imprisonment, but the presence of innocent children in need of comfort seemed to be helping her too. She couldn't remember Verity ever taking an interest in the family's younger nephews and nieces before, but perhaps the vulnerability of these unfortunate girls and boys, separating from their parents, was appealing to her better nature.

Once the group was settled in their seats, Dora returned to the platform to help with further arrivals and calm anxious relatives. Most children were accompanied by one or more parents, some with just a grandparent, some with an aunt. An associate of Herr Friedmann brought a group of orphans, thrown out of their orphanage by an angry group of brutish Brownshirts.

'Where is Herr Friedmann?' Dora asked, hoping to see him again and check that her consignment to Amsterdam had produced the desired result.

'He has not been seen for some time,' the man said. 'We fear he has been arrested, following the latest edict.' He saw her look of incomprehension and added, 'As of now, all of us have to hand in any precious metals and stones we possess.'

Dora's heart sank. She knew that was not good news and that her good friend might well have had more valuables in his possession and might not be seen again. 'I'm so sorry to hear that. And his family?'

'We fear for them too, for the same reason.' He shrugged and went on, 'Who knows whether he did anything wrong, but who could blame him if he smuggled some valuables out of the country before it was too late.'

If only we could rescue all of these persecuted people, Dora found herself thinking. Life is becoming so hard for them, stran-

gling them little by little. But they have the courage to send
away the things most precious of all to them, more than gems or
gold can ever be. We're scooping up their children, which is
distressing in itself, and leaving their families to face whatever
the regime may devise next in its programme of destroying these
communities. She shook her head to rid herself of these deeply
depressing thoughts and forced a confident smile for the children next in the queue to enter the train. 'Just go along the
corridor to the first compartment with spare seats,' she said,
waving them aboard.

She was just about to turn round to check in some more
passengers when two men in long black coats, with black hats
pulled down low over their brows, barged past her and entered
the train. Dora started to say something, but Brenda rushed over
to her. 'They're Gestapo. You'd better go after them. I think it
might be to do with your cousin.'

Dora jumped back onto the train and went to the second
compartment. One man was hauling Verity to her feet, despite
her urgent protests, while the other stood guard in the corridor.
The young passengers in the compartment were frozen in their
seats, all cowering, some whimpering in terror.

'What is happening here?' Dora felt her heart fluttering
with fear as she tried to sound authoritative. 'My cousin has a
valid ticket and has an important job helping to look after the
children on this officially authorised Kindertransport.'

'We have further questions for Frau Fitzgerald,' the man
said, dragging Verity out of the compartment towards the exit.
The second man followed, holding up a badge. 'We have unfin-
ished business with this lady.'

Dora could tell that Verity was clenching her jaw to stifle
her urge to scream. Her painted red lips were set in a thin, hard
line but her eyes were wide with fear.

'Verity, darling, I'll contact the embassy right away. They'll
soon sort this out,' Dora called after them as the men began

marching that delicate figure across the platform towards the street. Dora could see a black car waiting by the exit.

'Don't worry, darling,' Verity called out, adopting the imperious tone her mother, Lady Ponsonby, always used to intimidate anyone who crossed her. 'They know I have nothing for them, they're just trying to cause a scene. I'll be back before you know it. Don't you worry.'

Brenda joined Dora and they watched the threesome reach the car, which then drove off at speed. 'She's right,' Brenda said, 'they're only doing it because they can. Those two are thugs. I'm sure they'll release her again very soon.'

'I'm still worried though,' Dora said. 'What if they put her in prison again? She's not fully recovered and she's in a fragile state, mentally and physically. I really wanted her to leave with us today, so I could keep an eye on her. Oh, I hope they don't hurt her. I'm going to call Carrington anyway. She was cleared of all charges, so they shouldn't come storming in and terrifying the children like this.'

'I agree with you,' Brenda said, pushing Dora towards the phones. 'Go and make your call. I can cope for a while. It's all going smoothly apart from this.'

Dora raced to find a public telephone and was soon being put through to Carrington. 'Now what's happened to her? Typical,' he said, once Dora had explained. 'They just want to put the wind up us and she was a perfect excuse. Leave it with me and I'll see what I can do. What time is your train leaving?'

'It's scheduled for twelve and you know what the Germans are like about punctuality. That's the one thing they and the Italians have got right so far.'

'So, we've got two hours, maybe a little more.'

'But what will you do if she isn't released in time for the train?' Dora was desperate to get Verity away.

'Don't worry, I'll make sure I know where she is and what's happening. If she doesn't make this train, I'll try to get her onto the next one out of the country. I promise I won't let you down. She may have been a fool in the past, but she's one of ours and we have to look out for her.'

'Thank you so much. I know I can trust you and I'll leave it in your hands. I sincerely hope she returns soon. She was settling down so well with the children too.'

'If I can get her released, I'll bring her to the station myself. I'll do my best.'

Dora breathed a small sigh of relief. He was a good man; junior, but good nevertheless. She hurried back to join Brenda again. 'Carrington's going to do what he can, but he can't promise he'll get her released before the train is due to leave.'

'Poor dear man had enough trouble with her at the embassy the other day,' Brenda said, raising her eyebrows. 'He's not the only one who will be glad to see her leave.'

'Oh, I'm so sorry to give you all this worry on top of everything,' Dora said, her voice starting to break. 'It's quite enough having to deal with all our passengers, let alone this.'

'Get away with you. Get yourself back on that train,' Brenda said, pushing Dora away with a brusque smile. 'Some of those children will have been quite shaken by what just happened. Go and tell them we aren't expecting any more Gestapo to come forcing their way on board today and they're all quite safe now.'

But are they? Dora thought as she went back to her charges, wondering how she could explain Verity's sudden exit. *Can any of us feel safe until we are across the sea and back home?*

FORTY-ONE

FOR WANT OF A SHOE

'When is the nice lady coming back?' The little girl Verity had played with whispered her question hesitantly and put her fingers in her mouth, as if she didn't dare ask any more.

'Very soon, I hope,' Dora said, hoping none of the children understood what had really happened or noticed how disturbed she felt. She thought quickly for a valid excuse. 'She'd forgotten to pay a bill before leaving. That's all. She'll be back as soon as she's sorted it all out.'

'She left her shoe behind,' a boy said, pointing down to the floor of the compartment. Verity's black court shoe lay on its side.

Dora picked it up and laid it on her cousin's seat, next to her abandoned handbag. She felt tears pricking her eyes. She hadn't realised the men had been quite so rough in manhandling Verity off the train and she hadn't noticed her limping. They were so tall and strong, they must have virtually carried her, feet dangling, across to the waiting car.

'Oh dear,' Dora said. 'They were all in such a hurry, she didn't realise she'd lost it. Still, it's here for when she gets back.'

Soon, I hope, but will it be soon?

Having calmed the children, she returned to Brenda and they continued the task of checking the papers and tickets of the arrivals. Most of the parents put a brave face on bidding farewell to their children. One mother grasped Dora by the arm, saying, 'I thank you with all my heart for taking my daughter. You are good people and will receive your reward in heaven.'

And a grandfather with a long white beard and the ringlets of an Orthodox Jew held her hand and bowed over it, muttering a prayer she couldn't understand. Dora was deeply moved by how all these people agonised about sending their young ones away. How dreadful for them to even have to think that they should part from them; but it was clear they firmly believed that what might come next would be worse than had happened before and so had finally reached this momentous decision. No parent should have to make this choice, she kept thinking, but this is right for these times. Of course it is right.

She herself smiled bravely, along with Brenda and their various Jewish helpers; they all kept up a cheerful appearance despite the waves of sadness crowding around them. And Dora kept checking her watch and glancing at the station clock, wondering if Verity would be released soon or not at all.

'If she doesn't make it, are you sure your chap at the embassy will look after her once we've left?' Brenda leant across to Dora as they checked off the last child and the hands of the clock jerked towards midday.

'I think I can rely on Carrington to do his best,' Dora said, comparing the time on her watch yet again. They had barely five minutes left. 'I have to trust him. There's nothing else I can do. If she misses this train, he will make sure she catches another.'

'Well done,' Brenda said, giving Dora's shoulder a reassuring pat. 'I wish I could help too, but the children have to come first, I'm afraid. They're our priority. We've given these parents our word.'

'Don't worry about me. I know that. I'm worried, of course, but I won't let you down.'

'Good girl. I knew you wouldn't, but I'm very sorry you've had to deal with all this extra trouble.'

Dora really appreciated Brenda's steady presence, but she still hung in the doorway of the train as they readied themselves to leave Berlin. She scanned the platform and station entrance, slowly pulling the door towards her, but she kept the window open as the clock ticked towards the last few seconds.

The tannoy announced the train's departure and the first blast of the guard's whistle pierced the air. Dora felt she had failed, even though she had helped over two hundred children to board the train. But there, all of a sudden, she saw two figures darting at speed through the crowd, one of them waving a black shoe in her direction.

It was Verity and Carrington. Dora flung open the carriage door, just as the train started to edge slowly forward. 'Quick, get on now,' she shouted above the rumbling noises of the engine. 'I'll grab you.'

She thrust her hand forward, grabbing Verity's arm and pulled her aboard just in time. 'Thank you so much,' she called to Carrington, who stood panting and dishevelled on the platform, waving, as they left the station.

'Oh, my goodness,' Dora said, hugging her cousin. 'You were cutting it fine. I was beginning to think you'd never get here.'

'Me too,' Verity said. 'I knew it was touch and go. Rufus found me some shoes so I could run.' She looked down at the dark brown brogues she was wearing. 'He pinched these from one of the embassy secretaries. They're not quite me, are they?'

Dora could have cried with relief. Verity sounded almost like her old self, already on first-name terms with her saviour and commenting on the inappropriate style of the shoes. 'Oh, darling Vee, who cares about some silly old shoes? They got you here in time, didn't they?'

Verity held out her court shoe. 'I don't know what happened to the other one, but when they dragged me away, my feet were barely touching the ground.'

'I wanted to stop them, but there was nothing I could do.' Dora couldn't help a few tears of relief escaping.

'Don't cry, darling,' Verity said, hugging her. 'I'm here now.'

'Was it beastly? They didn't hurt you, did they?'

'Oh, they were a bit rough, but nothing terrible. I wouldn't be surprised to find a bruise or two on my arms from their great ham fists, but compared to what they're capable of doing, I got off very lightly. They plonked me down on a chair at the police station and started going over all the questions they'd asked before about who'd been involved with Raven and so on. I couldn't add anything to what they already knew. They just wanted to make a damned nuisance of themselves, that's all. Good call of yours getting hold of that Rufus chap. He's not such a weed after all.'

'He's an all right sort, isn't he? I don't know what I'd have done if I hadn't known who to call immediately.'

Verity looked down at her borrowed shoes again. 'These really are awful, but he saved the day finding me these. I hope the poor girl doesn't have to go home in stockinged feet. I didn't catch her name, but when we get back I'll wrap them up and send them off to Rufus so he can return them.'

'He'll do that for you. He's utterly reliable.' And then Dora remembered. 'Anyway, your other shoe is still here. It dropped off near your seat.'

'Thank goodness for that. Then I can get rid of these monstrosities and wear my own shoes again.' Verity broke into a great smile. 'And at some point I must get a hat. Mine fell off somewhere along the way. I can't be seen in widow's weeds without a decent hat.'

Dora laughed and hugged her. Dear Vee. Her cousin was slowly coming back to life – maybe not for long, as she was sure there would be moments of gloom and grief – but she was still the same old Verity inside.

FORTY-TWO
ROSA
BERLIN, MARCH 1939

Rosa shrank back into the bread queue, hoping she wouldn't be noticed and that the police wouldn't pick on her next. An old man was their first victim, slammed against the wall by three burly men.

One of the policemen ripped open the lining of the man's coat and triumphantly held out a ring and a gold chain. 'This belongs to the state, you greedy Jew,' he shouted, slapping the old man around the head. His brutal accomplices jeered and kicked their target, then sauntered off to find another suspect.

Since when, Rosa thought, clenching her teeth. Since when has the state had the right to take everything of value from us? We are not the only ones to have put our trust more in gold than in cash after the crippling inflation of previous years. Somehow she had missed the ruling published in February, requiring Jews to turn over all precious gems and metals to the state without compensation. But even if she had been aware of it, she wouldn't have wanted to hand in everything she had saved, not when she was desperate for money.

'I don't like to ask,' Liese had said when she visited one day with more fresh bread than Rosa was ever able to buy, 'but do you want me to keep anything for you? You do know that if you're ever found to have kept your jewellery, you could be punished.'

Rosa knew she could trust her best friend. Perhaps it would be a good idea to let her have one or two pieces for safe keeping. 'But you could be in trouble as well if they find out you are helping me.' Liese was already an enormous support, finding extra food for her friend and Theresia. 'I'll give you this gold chain, but you must sell it to cover the cost of the food you keep bringing us. I can't have you always paying for that yourself.'

Liese weighed the chain in her hand. 'I'll keep it safe for you. There may well come a time when you'll need it.'

'Why are they doing this to us? If they take away our livelihoods, our means of earning to feed our children, what are we meant to do? Give them everything until nothing is left?' Rosa shook her head in despair.

'I'm glad I can help you,' Liese said, hugging her friend. 'You need to eat well in your condition.' She glanced at Rosa's swelling waist. 'Does Theresia know yet?'

'No, but I must tell her at some point. This pregnancy feels different somehow. I'm relieved it's gone well so far, but I'm surprised at how quickly I've got bigger. And that's not just because of the food you've been bringing us either.' Rosa managed to force a small smile and cradled her stomach, feeling the frequent movements inside.

Liese hid the chain in her jacket pocket. 'I'll come again very soon. Look after yourself and keep your valuables well hidden.' She laughed and kissed Rosa, then left.

Rosa wondered if she had hidden her valued possessions well enough. She knew that few in her increasingly poor community obeyed the ruling if they could help it. Why would they? Why should they give up what might save their lives, bribe a policeman if they were caught crossing the road and buy food for their children? But every time a family was forced to move out of the home they had lived in for years, thugs tore open mattresses, pillows, suitcases, and searched every crevice, in the belief that all Jews had hidden gold and gems. Well, maybe they all did. They had to do whatever they could to hold on to what they had earned with hard work.

Rosa's skill as a dressmaker was not greatly in demand these days, although her ability to create garments from old curtains and bedspreads was appreciated by many. But her greatest skill was in concealment. Everyone was growing clever at finding ways to hide their few remaining valuables, but she excelled. Where most filled pockets and hems with stones and gold, she was more inventive. Who would think to feel beneath the horn buttons of her winter coat? Who would question the weight of Theresia's doll, which she had restored with invisible stitches while her child slept?

Rosa smiled to herself at her deception. She would not be left with nothing. She had lost her husband, her home and her business but she still had her child and the one to come. She was determined that they would all survive.

FORTY-THREE

WHERE'S AUNTIE?

At Liverpool Street station, Dora hugged Verity before waving her off into a taxi. 'You must go straight back to the flat. Hugh might be there with supper. Tell him I'll join you both later when we've sent all the children off to the right places.'

Arriving in London at last, after a final train from the port of Harwich, was theoretically the end of their tiring journey, but in fact it was also the next arduous stage. Every child was due to be met by a relative or representative of the host family or hostel. Each had to be united with the correct person or destination and with their chaperones. The children were all exhausted by the long trek from Berlin and patient form-filling had to be endured before they could be released.

This recent journey had not been as stressful as some, Dora reflected. Once the drama of Verity's arrest on the train was behind them, she had proved to be a most helpful assistant. She had played with the children, sung to them and encouraged them to sleep when they became too tired. She had gained their confidence and was a most comforting companion, so much so that Ruth, the little girl who had first warmed to her, was sad to see her go and pleaded with her to stay. 'I must leave now,'

Verity had told her. 'And Ruth, your great-aunt, will soon be here to collect you.'

But as the crowd of children dwindled, as each claimed child waved goodbye to their travel companions, Dora began to worry. Ruth's great-aunt was apparently based in London, so she would have expected her to be one of the first to sweep her niece up into her arms. She kept looking around for anyone who seemed to be searching the group and looking lost, hoping that at any moment a woman would come rushing through the station entrance to take her great-niece back to a warm, welcoming home.

By the time they had seen nearly all the children handed over to their hosts, more than an hour after the train had arrived, Brenda was looking worried too. 'I've never known this to ever happen before,' she said. 'But I've often thought that we might have no way of hearing if a relative was suddenly ill or not available for some reason.'

Dora glanced at Ruth, still sitting on the station bench, legs dangling. She was hugging her doll, but her eyes were drooping. The child was tired out and Dora longed to scoop her up and take her somewhere warm and safe. 'What's the protocol if the relative doesn't turn up? Do we have one?'

Brenda shook her head. 'We haven't had to deal with it previously. We could send her off to one of the hostels, I suppose, but they're better suited to the older children.'

Dora glanced across at Ruth again. The child was only six. She had expected to be met by her great-aunt, her grandmother's sister. She'd never met her, but she did at least know of her. Ruth was very shy and timid and although she had warmed to Verity, she had been withdrawn when anyone else spoke to her.

'I'm not sure a hostel is the right solution for her,' Dora said. 'Let's wait till the last minute and see if the aunt turns up. I can't bear the thought of her going some place where she won't be loved.'

'We'll hold on,' Brenda said. 'There may have been a hitch we don't know about.' She too kept looking around the station, hoping the anxious aunt would come scurrying up at any second, but the place was full of busy travellers going about their business, taking no interest in the little figure nearly asleep on the bench.

Another half-hour later, all the other children had been claimed. Papers had been signed, addresses and identities supplied, to ensure that everyone was sent to the right destination. Only one lonely child remained.

'Well, we've got to make a decision,' Brenda said. 'We can't stay here all night. The aunt knows she can find us at the office, so I suggest I take her home tonight, then we'll have to see if we can find out what has happened in the morning.'

Brenda bent down to the little girl and gently touched her shoulder to wake her. 'I'm afraid your auntie hasn't turned up to collect you, so we think you should come home with me for the night.'

Ruth's eyes widened and her chin trembled. 'Why isn't she here? Mama promised Tante Hilde would be here.'

'We don't know why she hasn't come, dear. Maybe she isn't well. But we'll find out soon enough.' Brenda held out her hand, inviting Ruth to walk with her.

But Ruth pulled away. 'No, I want the nice lady. I want Vee.' She'd heard Dora using her cousin's nickname and had taken to it. 'I want to go home with Vee.' Her tears came thick and fast in great sobs.

Brenda rolled her eyes, then looked at Dora. 'Can you take her home? She might be prepared to go with you if she knows your cousin is there.'

'Verity's only staying with us for a day or so. She might go to her parents or mine eventually, but she's there at the moment.' Dora knelt down to be close to Ruth. 'Vee is staying at my house. If you want to see her, you can come home with me. Would you like to do that?'

Ruth nodded through her tears and slid off the bench, putting her hand into Dora's. 'Vee's nice,' she said, gulping back hiccups.

'Good girl,' Brenda said. 'Now off you go with Dora and get a good night's sleep. We'll sort all this out in the morning.' She waved them off towards the taxis and marched herself to the Underground.

By the time they arrived at the Islington house it was dark and the gaslights around the square glowed with their haloes. 'This is where I live with my husband and Vee,' Dora said as she fumbled with her key. But before she could unlock the door, it was flung open by Hugh and he threw his arms round her.

'You're here at last,' he said, pulling her into the hallway and kissing her. 'I was worried you'd got lost.'

'It always takes ages, sorting everyone out,' Dora said. 'And we've got a visitor.' She looked down at Ruth, trying to hide in the folds of her coat.

Hugh bent down to shake Ruth's hand, but she pulled away from him and covered her face with Dora's skirts. 'Never mind,' he said. 'I'm very shy too.' He stood up, smiling, 'Have you eaten?'

'Not for ages. Is Verity here? I sent her off as soon as we arrived at Liverpool Street.'

'She's upstairs in the flat but I gave her supper before she went up. I'll warm yours up again in the oven. What about this little one? Will she eat with you?'

'I think she'd better, then I'll take her upstairs to see Vee. She's very fond of her, so she might settle better with her tonight.' She looked down at Ruth and said, 'We'll see Vee in a minute, but first we'll have supper in the kitchen.'

Leaving their cases and coats in the hall, Dora took Ruth through to where Hugh was warming plates of fish and chips and heating milk. The food was soggy, but it was welcome and although Ruth ate very little, she managed a few chips and drank the milk.

'Now let's see if we can find Vee,' Dora said and Ruth willingly followed her up the stairs, clinging to her hand.

Dora knocked on the door to the upper flat and then opened it a little. The lights were off and she guessed her cousin had already gone to bed. 'Verity,' she called out. 'Sorry to wake you, but we've got a visitor for you.'

Entering the flat, Dora switched on the light and began making up the bed in the spare room. 'You can sleep here tonight,' she said, 'but first I'll take you to the bathroom and you can have a quick bath after that long journey.'

'No,' Ruth said, folding her arms in protest. 'I want Vee.'

At that moment, a yawning Verity, wrapped in a dressing gown and pyjamas, stumbled through the door of the room. 'Sorry, I couldn't wait up. I was so tired.'

'I'm sorry I had to wake you. Ruth has been asking for you. Her aunt didn't turn up, but we don't know why, so I thought she could stay here with you.'

'Of course you can, darling,' Verity said, bending down and opening her arms wide. She hugged Ruth. 'Poor poppet, we'll look after you.'

'I thought she should have a bath first,' Dora said, 'but she doesn't want to.'

'Of course she doesn't,' Verity said, walking away with Ruth. 'She's too tired. That can wait till the morning. She can sleep with me tonight, can't you, dear?'

Dora saw Ruth nodding and listening to Vee's every word. It wasn't what they normally did after a long journey with children from all kinds of backgrounds, but what harm could it do?

The worst that could happen with a grubby child was a flea bite or two. And her own bed and Hugh were beckoning.

FORTY-FOUR

BATHTIME

Dora had agreed with Brenda that she wouldn't rush into the office the next day but she was keen to find out what had happened to Ruth's great-aunt, so soon after Hugh had left for the hospital, she urged herself to get out of bed.

She was still in her nightclothes and dressing gown, making tea and toast in the kitchen, when Verity came downstairs to find her. 'How did you and Ruth sleep?' Dora yawned. 'Sorry, I've only just got up.'

'Never mind, I need you to come upstairs.' Verity's face was drawn and Dora thought she could glimpse hovering tears.

'What's the matter? Ruth's not ill, is she?'

'No, but you've got to come and see for yourself.' Verity led the way upstairs, talking and looking over her shoulder at Dora as she went. 'She refused to get undressed last night. Wouldn't do it herself or let me help her. She went to sleep fully dressed. But I thought, well, what does it matter just this once? The poor little dear is tired out, so why not let her sleep? Then this morning I ran my bath and when she was awake, I suggested she should have one too. It took some persuading, I can tell you.

She wouldn't let me touch her. Insisted on undressing in the bathroom and getting into the bath on her own.'

'She's not scalded, is she? Was the water too hot?' Dora knew how the geyser could suddenly gush great spurts of extra-hot steamy water into the bath.

'No, nothing like that. I was very careful and she wouldn't be able to reach the heater, anyhow.' They were at the top of the stairs now and Verity was wringing her hands as they approached the bathroom. 'I didn't mean to pry, but I thought I should make sure the door wasn't shut properly, just in case. And once I was dressed, I peeped through a crack in the door, just to check... and well, look. See for yourself.'

Dora put her eye to the thin gap between the door hinges and the doorframe. She had a clear but limited view of the bathroom and the bath, and the back of the child facing her. She couldn't help but gasp, and put her hand to her mouth.

'In heaven's name whatever is that?'

'You can see it quite clearly, can't you? There's no mistaking it, is there? Who could have done that to her?' Verity's face was white with horror.

Dora forced herself to look again. 'Poor girl. It must still be terribly painful.'

'That's what I thought. Now, I'm going to be really gentle, but I think we should ask her how it happened.' Verity draped a very soft white towel over her arm.

Dora looked once more. The little girl was thin, but not unbearably so. Her bony shoulder blades looked like angel wings, as she washed herself. But across her back there was a livid scar, red, raised and raw. The poor child bore the mark of a swastika: she had been branded.

Dora felt sick with horror and knew Verity felt the same way. But this was no time to worry about how they were both feeling. It was hardly surprising the girl hadn't wanted anyone to touch her or undress her and had shied away from Hugh. 'You go in first,' she said. 'We don't want to frighten her.'

Verity nodded and slowly opened the door a little, releasing a waft of damp air scented with talcum, air-dried linen and paraffin from the hissing stove heating the room. 'Ruth, dear,' she said in German, 'I'm coming in with a towel for you.' She entered the room and knelt down by the bath. 'Will you let me help you out?'

The little girl looked up, still holding the bath sponge under her chin, hesitant but not afraid. Then she put out her arms to Verity, who wrapped her in the towel and lifted her out. Sitting on the bathroom chair, she spread a second towel over her knees and pulled Ruth onto her lap. 'There now,' she said in a soft voice. 'Isn't it nice to be clean and warm again?' Ruth leant her head against Verity's chest and sucked her thumb.

'Do you mind if I come in too?' Dora poked her head round the door. 'I'm not even dressed yet either. Aren't we lazy girls today?' Ruth gave a shy smile as Verity gently patted her skin dry.

Dora came into the steamy room and sat on the side of the bath, pulling the bath plug out as she did so. 'How did you hurt your back, dear?' The water began emptying with a glug and a swirl.

Ruth pressed her face into Verity's chest again and didn't answer. 'You don't have to tell us,' Dora said, 'but we'd like to make sure it gets better. Is it still very sore?'

Ruth nodded, then turned her face slightly to peer at Dora. 'Mama said it will take time to heal. She put butter on me and then special cream.'

'You have a very clever mother. May I take a closer look?' Ruth flinched slightly, so Dora added, 'I won't touch you, I promise.'

Hugging her so Ruth felt safe, Verity let the towel drop to waist height. The shocking injury was clearly healing, but it was still livid and weeping. The brutally cruel mark taunted and shocked them both and Verity quickly draped Ruth's shoulders again.

Dora calmed herself with steady breaths to control her horrified reaction. 'It's not infected, so your mother did the right thing. But how did it happen, dear? Can you tell us?'

'Boys, nasty boys,' Ruth murmured. 'After school one day. They said they'd make me more German. They laughed.'

'How could this have been allowed to happen?' Verity whispered fiercely, switching to English, her eyes sad but blazing. 'A child, hurt by other children.'

'They've been schooled to hate,' Dora said. 'Taught to single out those who are different.'

'They made a fire,' Ruth said. 'They held me. It hurt me a lot.' She began to cry and Verity held her tight and kissed the top of her head.

'There, there, dear, it is healing. You are quite safe now. Nothing like that can ever happen here in this country.' Dora looked into Verity's eyes, then switched to English. 'It looks as if it will fade in time, but I'd like Hugh to take a look if she'll let him.'

'Not yet,' Verity said. 'It's far too soon. There's no harm in waiting a while, is there? Let her get used to all of us first.'

Dora stood up. 'You're right. I think that would be best. But once I'm dressed, I have to go into the office to see if we can find out anything about her aunt not showing up yesterday. That's where she's meant to be, after all. There's eggs, bread and cheese in the kitchen larder. Help yourselves when you and Ruth are ready.'

Dora went back downstairs, her mind reeling from the sight that had just confronted her. She could eat barely a mouthful of toast. As she dressed, she realised she would have to report this terrible discovery to the office and she couldn't help wondering what other unspeakable unseen nightmares might have travelled with any of the Kindertransports from Germany. Many of the children had already seen or suffered cruelty that they should never have experienced in their young lives. But while she and her colleagues had all worried about them having the correct papers, finding hosts and bathing the children to dispel alien bugs, she had never imagined that she would be faced with such dreadful horror.

FORTY-FIVE
NOT WELCOME
LONDON, MARCH 1939

Dora still felt weary, despite having slept well overnight. But she was fired up with disgust at what she and Verity had discovered and couldn't wait to write a report on this appalling treatment of a child she and her colleagues had saved from further harm. As she thought about how she would describe Ruth's abuse, she had to remind herself to control her anger and pick her words carefully.

Making notes while her mind was still freshly imprinted with the dreadful image, she wondered whether the injury would be better described and recorded with a photograph. That would record the wound more graphically and clearly, along with her notes, in case they ever had to justify their actions. But perhaps taking a picture could wait a while, until Ruth felt safer and trusted them completely. That scar was not going to disappear soon and in fact, Dora feared it would never fade entirely. The poor girl had been cruelly marked, quite possibly for life, and it was no wonder her mother had been convinced she would be better sending her daughter out of the country.

When Dora went to see Brenda in her office, her first question was about Ruth's great-aunt: 'Do we have any further news of the family?'

'We've checked back on the files and everything seemed to be in place. There's no telephone, so I've sent a telegram asking her to contact us as soon as possible. But I've no idea how old she is or whether there is anyone else living at the property.'

'Well, there's no problem with Ruth staying with us for now. She was very happy to see Verity again. And I think her dependence may be doing my cousin some good, helping her to forget about her own problems.'

Dora looked down at the report she had just written. She could hardly bear to tell Brenda what she and Verity had discovered that morning. 'But I think you ought to read this first. It's about Ruth. She is going to need very careful handling.'

Brenda took the brief account, read it, looked up at Dora and then read it again. Her lips tightened as she frowned and said, 'I'd heard that such dreadful deeds were happening, but I never thought it would be perpetrated on a child and such a young one at that. German children are being taught to be monsters. What kind of a nation are they breeding, now that boys can even think of such an act?'

'I'm as horrified as you are. The poor child was reluctant to undress, let alone take a bath. Her aunt is going to be horrified when she meets her and finds out, if her mother hasn't already written to tell her about the injury.'

'And you think her back is healing? You don't think she needs immediate medical attention?'

'I'm pretty sure it's getting better. Not that it's ever likely to disappear completely, I'm sorry to say. But I thought I'd get Hugh to take a look once she's got used to him. It's too soon to make her expose herself to anyone other than me and Verity. She's very wary, but she trusts us both. But I'll tell him, of course, and he did have a lot of experience with children before he switched to plastic surgery.'

'That sounds very sensible. You don't need to frighten the child any further. Gently does it, I'd say. She's lucky to be with the two of you.'

Dora pictured how trusting Ruth was of Verity, how comfortable she had looked on her cousin's lap, wrapped in a soft white towel. 'We're very happy to look after her. She's no trouble and we so want her to feel safe and happy. Let me know as soon as you hear anything about her aunt.'

Much later that afternoon, Brenda looked into Dora's office. 'There's still no answer from Ruth's relatives. I'm beginning to think that something might have happened to them. I wonder if we ought to go to the address and check for ourselves. After all, we still have a responsibility to Ruth's mother to deliver her to the right destination if we can.'

'It's Hampstead, isn't it? I could run up there and then go straight on home afterwards.'

'If you don't mind, that would be a good idea. Try to phone me once you know what's going on.'

Dora was happy to pull on her coat and leave the stuffy office, despite the late-afternoon chill outside. After taking a bus up to the heights of Hampstead, once she had been deposited near the heath she felt was out in the countryside. She breathed the cleaner air, far from the grimy streets and the choking smog of fires and fumes, looking down onto the haze of the metropolis. The sun was beginning to sink, casting a glow over the city, and as street lights sparked into life she heard the final sharp evening call of a blackbird.

The address she had been given wasn't far away and as she approached, she could see lights in a ground-floor room, which she took to be a sign that someone was home. She knocked on the front door and soon heard shuffling steps in the hallway. The door was opened by an elderly man wearing a droopy brown cardigan and baggy corduroy trousers. His spectacles were perched on the top of his balding head, which was streaked with greasy strands of grey hair.

'Mr Leibowitz?' Dora smiled at him. 'I'm here on behalf of your niece, Ruth. She was meant to be collected on arrival at Liverpool Street station yesterday. We were expecting her great-aunt to be there to meet her.'

'Aah yes, of course, come in, come in.' He shuffled down the tiled corridor to a room lined with books, where a gas fire popped and puffed into the airless atmosphere that smelt of pipe smoke and old manuscripts. He waved Dora to a sunken sofa, half piled with books and papers, then sat down in a sagging armchair and picked up a meerschaum pipe, which he tried to relight.

'My apologies for my study. So much work always.' He shook his head, then tapped the contents of the pipe out into an ashtray. 'My wife, Ruth's great-aunt, is not well. She had a fall and is recovering in a nursing home. I'm afraid I forgot that she had promised Hannah that she would give the girl a home here. As you can see, it is not at all suitable for a young child, but what could I do? Hannah had got it into her head that Ruth had to leave Germany and come here. I told my wife it wasn't necessary. These things have happened in the past and will again. But neither of them would listen to me.'

Dora was not quite sure if he fully understood the current situation in Germany. By now, surely everyone was aware that anyone of Jewish descent was in extreme danger?

'Was your wife in favour of Ruth coming here?'

'For Hannah she will always agree to anything. I had no part in the matter. Let her come if you wish, I said. But I will not be involved. We are old and should not be troubled at our time of life with children.'

Dora tried to judge his mood and considered what was best to say next. 'When do you think your wife will be able to come home? And do you think she will be fit enough to look after Ruth?'

He shrugged and spread his hands expressively. 'Who knows? A broken hip at her age... I don't think she should be running around after a child. We may have the room here in this house, but a young girl needs to be looked after, fed and taken to school.'

Dora glanced around her. The sitting room was cluttered, but warm and comfortable. Presumably the rest of the house was in reasonably good order. But did she want to see Ruth brought to a home where she was not going to be welcomed? Was this somewhere she would feel safe and loved? Mr Leibowitz seemed more concerned with his troublesome pipe than with his great-niece, as he continued to fiddle with a pipe cleaner and then pack the bowl with fresh tobacco.

She decided to make it clear that she thought Ruth's mother had very good reasons for wishing to send her daughter abroad. 'Did Hannah tell you and your wife much about what has been happening in Germany?'

'Oh, we all know that country is going through much change,' he said. 'But move to the Netherlands or France if you don't like it. I have seen such disruption before and will do so again. It will all pass over before too long.'

Dora was shocked that he seemed so unconcerned and couldn't resist delivering an impassioned account of her work. 'I have just returned to Britain with a trainload of two hundred children whose parents all believe they must leave the country as a matter of urgency. They have made the heartbreaking decision to send their children away, believing they will be safer here, with us. It is not the first such transport I have undertaken and I hope it won't be the last. And Ruth is just one of those children. If you believe that there is no real danger in Germany and Austria, then why are their parents prepared to send them so far away, knowing there is a chance they may never see them again?'

He shrugged again, expressing more lack of interest than lack of knowledge. 'Who knows? Time will tell.'

Dora stared at him, unable to believe he could be so blinkered. 'Mr Leibowitz, I have to tell you that these children will be far safer here in Britain than in their own country. And I have also been to Amsterdam recently and I believe that the Netherlands will also come under threat in the near future.'

She could feel her anger building. He might be an old man, but he was a stupid old man. 'And in case Ruth's mother has not already written to your wife to tell her how dangerous life is now becoming, I have to tell you that your great-niece, little Ruth, who is only six years old, was subjected to the vilest abuse before she was sent away. That poor little girl has been branded on her back. Some young Nazis have branded her with a hot iron in the shape of a swastika. Now, what do you think of that?'

His face crumpled and paled. He hung his head and shook it from side to side. 'I don't know when my wife will be able to return. We cannot manage to have Ruth here, you must make other plans.'

Dora stood up. 'Don't worry, I will. I shall arrange for Ruth to be cared for by people who will love her.' She opened her handbag and left a card on his desk. 'But if you or your wife change your minds, this is where to contact me. And in the meantime, I shall write to Ruth's mother and tell her what has happened and that we have had to make alternative arrangements. I shall be assuring her that Ruth will be safe and well in our hands.'

She left him crouched in the armchair, his head in his hands as if he was ashamed or just didn't want to hear any more from her. She couldn't bear to look at him any longer.

'Don't worry, I'll let myself out.'

Dora slammed the front door shut with a mighty bang, glad

to be away from that man's insensitivity and blindness. She breathed the clean air of the Heath, detecting the inviting scent of woodsmoke from fires lit in welcoming, loving homes. A dog walker passed by, giving her a nod, then went in to a house where lights blazed. And Dora thought she'd like nothing better than to run home and show Ruth how to cook crumpets and muffins on a toasting fork by the fire, to prove to her that not all fires were menacing.

FORTY-SIX

ROSA

Theresia knelt beside Rosa on the bed. She patted her mother's rounded stomach, clearly visible through her patched skirt. Rosa had unstitched some of the pleats but still couldn't fasten the button to the side. 'Mama, how many babies are inside you?'

'Why do you ask, darling?'

'Because Frau Goldmann says you look like you are going to have twins. What's twins?'

'Two babies,' Rosa whispered. Could it be? Was that why she seemed so large, despite her restricted diet? She favoured Theresia when food was available, giving herself just enough to take the edge off her hunger.

'I want twins. One baby for you and one for me.' Theresia laughed and rocked her doll as if it was a real baby.

Rosa stroked her daughter's dark hair and thought of the few baby clothes she had managed to bring with her. Two babies, if they both survived, would need more vests, nappies and shawls. Perhaps she could ask her neighbours for anything that would help clothe them; even wool or cloth to make garments would be welcome. But everyone was facing hardship these days and people had little to share. The laws on property and valuables meant everyone was poor or had hidden what treasures they still had.

She hoped the human spirit was still generous when it came to young ones, but she often had to shield Theresia's eyes from the shocking sight of starving children on the street, slumped and unable to move. She was sure the boy they had seen asleep yesterday when they queued for bread was already dead. But still she didn't regret taking her child from the train and keeping her with her.

'We shall have to ask Frau Goldmann if she or her neighbours can lend us some baby clothes if we have two, won't we?' Her neighbours were struggling just as much as she was, but Frau Goldmann organised a soup kitchen, collecting peelings and bones, so there was the chance of a hot meal every day.

There was still little news of the men who had been arrested in November. Rumours circulated about the harsh regimes in all the prison camps, but she tried to keep hoping that Josef was still alive and would return one day. He would not be as optimistic as he once was, but they could rebuild their life together. Or could they? The mounting restrictions on Jewish livelihoods made her feel as if they were being slowly strangled. Josef had once laughed at the futility of being forbidden to change the name of their business, but what would he make of the ruling that Jews could no longer even have a business? He too would surely despair.

Rosa smiled at her daughter, but inside she felt dread. Living conditions were not at all what she had been used to. A single toilet for the whole block and a tap for washing and laundry made it difficult to stay clean and healthy. Despite her best efforts, she and Theresia were constantly bitten by the lice that crawled over them and the whole community. However would she be able to keep two tiny babies safe now? She instinctively felt the waistband of her skirt and the hem of her jacket. Her few remaining valuables might soon be needed to feed herself and her growing family.

FORTY-SEVEN
THE TICKING CLOCK
BERLIN, APRIL 1939

Dora had been tempted to stay in London instead of embarking on yet another train journey so soon, but as Alice seemed to be increasingly nervous on these trips, she decided it would be better if she accompanied Brenda once more. Besides, Ruth was settling well in Verity's company, so she didn't feel the need to be there all the time.

As she noted each child's name and ensured their identity and contact details were firmly pinned to their coat, Dora couldn't help wondering what history each of them might be carrying along with their little cases and bundles of food. So many had already suffered abuse from former schoolfriends and neighbours. She hoped that none were bearing painful scars like Ruth, but who could tell what was hidden away beneath the layers of winter coats and warm sweaters? She watched to see if there were any who shied from an adult's touch or flinched if anyone came close, as Ruth had done at first.

It was becoming more evident, too, that life was getting harder for these children and their families. They were thinner and greyer than the first groups she had encountered in December. Their clothes were no longer as clean nor in such good condition as those she had met earlier on. It was clear to Dora that despite the efforts of their families, who were trying to provide their children with the best they could manage, obviously their means were diminishing and they were struggling to maintain a decent standard of living.

Is it any wonder, Dora thought to herself as she helped another little boy and his sister onto the train, their threadbare elbows a reminder of poverty, when every means the Jewish communities had of providing for their families was being eroded? On top of the restrictions already in force and the businesses that had been destroyed the previous year, there were so few opportunities now for Jews to earn enough to live on.

That was quickly followed by Hitler's decision to authorise the forced emigration of Jews from the Greater Germanic Reich and the establishment of a Central Office for Jewish Emigration in Berlin. But where would they be told to go, Dora wondered? It seemed unlikely that they would be allowed to choose for themselves and she had the awful feeling that their final destination had already been chosen for them.

Everything would be taken from these people: their livelihoods, their property and their money. Every time she thought about how rapidly new restrictions were being imposed, she felt a sickening fear that, however hard she and her colleagues worked, they would never be able to do enough in time.

In addition to the Jewish children she and Brenda had been used to taking on the transports, there were also some from Aryan families who were being subjected to persecution, with family members even being imprisoned. And today, she had dealt with the mother of a boy whose leg was strapped into calipers and another whose daughter had a serious speech impediment. 'We are afraid he will be taken from us,' the boy's mother had whispered, helping him climb awkwardly into the train carriage. 'They're sending children with problems to special schools.' She paused, hesitating to reveal more. 'But they don't come back, you know. They never come home again.'

Dora wasn't sure she had understood immediately, despite the stories, but the mother had added, 'He's very bright. It's only his leg, but they only want perfect children now.' Dora had heard the rumours of hospitals and schools that seemed to have a higher degree of mortality than normal. Would there be no end to this cruelty?

She glanced at the huge station clock hanging over the concourse of Berlin's Friedrichstrasse station. She couldn't hear it ticking above the clamour of the loudspeaker announcements and the rumbling of trains arriving and departing, but she was aware of it eating up the time they had left. Today, the hands were gradually ticking their way round the enamelled clock face to the appointed time for the train's departure, but she also felt acutely conscious that the number of hours available for the saving of lives was shrinking. How many weeks and days did she and Brenda have left to continue their vital work? How would they ever find enough time? There was no deadline for the final train from Berlin; they could only keep working at this steady pace, reassuring worried parents, calming frightened children, telling themselves that, despite the urgency of their task, this all had to be accomplished calmly and correctly.

As Dora helped the last child onto the train, noticing with a pang her darned socks and scuffed shoes, she caught sight of a man running into the station entrance from the street. His hat flew off and as he bent to pick it up, she realised who it was. He was encumbered by a large cardboard box under one arm.

'Mr Carrington,' Dora called, stepping forward to help him. 'What a surprise. We're due to leave in just a few minutes.'

He was trying to catch his breath so he could speak. 'I knew you were here,' he gasped, 'I was hoping I'd find you in time.'

'Has something happened? Your secretary received the shoes, I hope?' Dora had remembered to return the shoes that

Verity had borrowed during her frantic departure from Berlin a few weeks earlier.

'Shoes? Aah, yes, she was very glad to have been of assistance.'

'So, what urgent mission brings you here today?' Dora looked over her shoulder at the clock as she heard the first blast of the guard's whistle. Brenda was standing in the doorway of the carriage, beckoning.

Carrington thrust the box into her hands. 'It's his ashes. Mr Fitzgerald's ashes. At least I hope so. I managed to get them for her.'

'Thank you so much, but I must go,' Dora said as the whistle blew again. Brenda was still holding the door open and Dora began to run towards it. 'Thank you for all you've done.' She reached the carriage and stepped aboard at the final blast of the whistle.

'I hope it helps her,' Carrington shouted above the noise of the chugging engine, trotting alongside the rolling carriage. 'Please give her my regards. Say I hope it will bring her some comfort.' He waved his hat as the train left the station and his final words faded away in the steam and the grinding of the great engine's wheels.

Dora stared at his disappearing figure as the train gathered speed. She clutched the box to her chest. It was heavy and she peered inside. She could make out the top of a blue and white pottery jar with a golden finial, rather like an ornate biscuit barrel. How Carrington had managed to obtain these ashes for Verity she couldn't imagine. Had he pulled strings in diplomatic circles, or been to the prison himself? There hadn't been time to ask questions, though she would have dearly liked to. She realised she'd barely had time to thank him properly either and resolved to write on the journey and post the letter once they crossed the border into Holland.

Brenda had moved along the carriage corridor and was

remonstrating with the two guards who had been assigned to accompany this transport. They had clearly been upsetting the children as usual, inspecting luggage and turning out pockets. It happened with every single journey and nothing untoward had ever been found. The Kindertransport organisers from the Jewish Council emphasised to parents the terrible consequences involved in hiding valuables in the children's cases and in their clothing. It simply wasn't worth it, whatever the value.

As Brenda finished her reprimanding and entered her own compartment with a haughty toss of her head, one of the guards caught sight of Dora closing the flaps on the top of the cardboard box. 'Was hast du da?' he shouted, striding towards her.

Dora, still unsettled by the sudden appearance of Carrington and his last-minute presentation of the box, didn't answer immediately. Her voice was not as forceful as it would normally have been when she finally said, 'I'm taking it back to England. It's my' – and then she didn't know what she should say – 'it's my cousin's ashes – no, not my cousin's, my cousin's husband's ashes.'

She could feel herself flushing, growing hot. She knew her explanation sounded ridiculous and that she looked extremely suspicious. 'Gib es mir,' the guard said, holding out his hands. His colleague followed him and stood right behind him in the narrow corridor.

Dora had no choice. She didn't want to pass the box to him, but the guards were both armed. She had to let him take it from her.

He ripped open the top of the box and stared at the contents. His partner leant over and removed the jar's top, holding it by its delicate little finial handle. 'Ein gutes Versteck für Diamanten,' he said. And then he stirred the contents with his index finger.

Dora was horrified and tried to protest. 'Those are human ashes,' she said. 'You mustn't touch them.' At least she hoped that it was only ashes and that Carrington hadn't been persuaded by some unfortunate person to conceal valuables that should have been surrendered to the state. What would happen to her and the whole transport if they found anything suspicious? Would the train have to return to Berlin?

The first soldier gave a careless shrug, then knelt down. He pulled the jar out of the box, then tipped everything out onto the floor of the carriage. At first glance it looked like fireside ash, but when she looked more closely Dora could see that the pile of grey ashes was coarser, sandier, flecked with brown and white.

The second guard also knelt down for a closer look and ran his fingers through the sandy pile, spreading it across the dirty corridor floor. 'Nichts,' he said. 'Es ist nur Asche.' Then they both stood up, pushed past Dora and stomped away over the ashy debris, leaving the jar and its lid rolling on the floor as the train thundered along the track.

Dora stared at the mess, feeling helpless. How callous they had been. But she wasn't surprised they hadn't believed her; so many Jews were trying to send valuables out of Germany in secret, hoping to save a fragment of their lives and provide for an uncertain future. It was lucky that it was only ashes and not diamonds like the time she had unwittingly carried the gems for Herr Friedmann. If there had been contraband hidden inside the jar, she would have been arrested immediately and taken off the train at the first stop.

She was still staring at the empty jar lying on its side, the crushed box and the scattered remains, feeling shaken by the whole incident, when Brenda emerged from her own compartment and called out to her, 'Have you had a spot of bother? Can I help at all?'

And Dora couldn't stop herself. All the tension of the last few days, the worry about how little time was left, the insensitivity of the guards, built up inside her and she began to cry. 'It was for Verity,' she said through sobs. 'And now look at it.' She pointed to the clumsy boot print in the middle of the ashes.

'Her husband, I assume,' Brenda said, joining her and looking down at the dusty, sandy remains strewn across the floor. 'We'd better clear it up and save what we can.' She marched back to her compartment and returned with a hair-brush and a stiff piece of folded card. 'It's not the best brush and dustpan I've ever used, but it'll have to do,' she said, easing herself down to her knees.

Together, Dora using her own hairbrush, Brenda sweeping with hers, they collected every tiny speck and fragment that had been tipped out and returned them all to the jar. And as they swept, Dora knew the ashes would now be an amalgamation of soot, dust and fibres from the train's corridor floor. But when she remembered Carrington's words, she wondered whether he had ever been convinced that these were indeed the final remains of Raven Fitzgerald and only his. Perhaps from the beginning this had only ever been a placebo, a sop to soothe Verity and make her feel she still had a part of her husband. Dora decided she could never tell her what had happened, nor what she suspected.

When Brenda finally heaved herself to her feet, she said, 'Your man Carrington is a good sort. That jar looks like it once held crystallised ginger. Perhaps he was given it as a present at Christmas.'

And Dora realised the jar was similar to the ones her mother gave elderly relatives in happier times. She couldn't help smiling at last. Dear Raven, preserved for posterity in a ginger jar. She was sure he'd have been amused by that. But what was Verity, who had wanted to bring him home in her arms, going to think when Dora brought him back?

FORTY-EIGHT
DUST TO DUST
LONDON, APRIL 1939

Dora didn't see Verity until the morning after her return. The train from Harwich had been late and it had taken them until well into the night to finish dispatching the children to their various destinations. By the time Dora reached Islington, Hugh was the only one waiting up for her.

'Ruth has started school now,' he said, 'and Verity will be up early with her tomorrow morning. You'll see her when she gets back, after you've had breakfast.'

Dora yawned over the late supper of scrambled eggs he'd prepared. 'It's probably better that I can talk to her while Ruth isn't here. That box I lugged all the way back here contains Raven's ashes. Or at least I hope so.' She described the unpleasant incident on the train and Carrington's unconvincing words about the provenance of the jar's contents.

'I'd imagine all the products of incineration in a place like Dachau would be piled up together,' Hugh said. 'They're hardly likely to identify each separate body.'

'So, it could literally be anyone in there,' Dora said, staring at the box.

'Or the remains of several unfortunate individuals,' Hugh said. 'You're not going to tell her that, are you?'

'Oh, my goodness, absolutely not. I've been worrying enough about having to bring it back myself when she had wanted to do that for him. I couldn't possibly let her think it isn't even him.' She paused and yawned again. 'I just hope she doesn't inspect the contents too closely. I can't promise there aren't bits of fluff and fibre mixed up in there as well, from when we swept it up off the floor on the train.'

'Raven would have found it hilarious, I'm sure,' Hugh said. 'From what I remember of him, he had no time for protocol and ceremony. Don't worry about it. I'm sure Verity will just be glad to have him back, in whatever shape or form.'

After a late breakfast of toast and marmalade the next morning, Dora waited for Verity to return from taking Ruth to school. When she heard the key in the front door, she ran up the steps from the kitchen to greet her cousin in the tiled hall.

'Vee, dear, how is Ruth settling in?' She kissed Verity's cold cheek.

Her cousin was flushed from her morning walk and looked bright and cheerful. 'She's loving it and already picking up new phrases in English every day. It's so good to see her making friends. After her dreadful experience and the way the Nazis are making children turn on each other, it's wonderful for her to be with normal children who want to play with her.'

'I'm so glad. It's the best thing for her. And I think even if the great-aunt does suddenly recover and want to have her after all, we might suggest she stays with us.'

'Oh, I do hope so. Ruth will thrive if we can keep her. Let's hope the old biddy decides she could never cope.' Verity laughed. 'That sounds awfully unkind, doesn't it? But you know what I mean.'

Dora laughed with her. 'I know exactly what you mean.

And I totally agree. Now, come and join me in the kitchen and tell me everything that's happened while I've been gone.'

Over more tea and toast, Verity regaled Dora with stories of Ruth's progress and her growing appetite. 'We had Chelsea buns for tea the other day and she loved them. So, I think on Saturday morning we will walk to the baker's and I'll let her choose whatever she wants. It sounds as if her diet had become extremely limited and she's revelling in the variety of cakes, buns and biscuits we have here. She said her mother was only allowed to shop for food at the end of the afternoon, when the stores had hardly anything left.'

'I'll have to come along with you,' Dora said. 'I'd love to see her face when she chooses. And I'll have to have an Eccles cake, my favourite.'

'Of course, you must come,' Verity said. 'You must see lots of Ruth while you're here. I assume you'll have to go away again very soon?'

'I'm afraid I will. So many families have registered their children for a place. We simply can't deal with them fast enough. I'll have to keep going back until the authorities put a stop to it.'

'Or unless things take a turn for the worse and you can't carry on,' Verity said, with a long, drawn-out sigh. 'It's going to happen eventually, isn't it?'

Dora gave a weary nod. 'It's looking that way. We just don't know how long we might have. So, we've got to keep on working hard, collecting the children, for as long as we can.' She drained her cup of tea, then thought she should get to the point.

'By the way, I bumped into Rufus Carrington again on this last trip. He turned up at the station shortly before we left. In fact, he popped up at the very last minute, just as the train was nearly ready to go.'

'Oh, really? What did he want? Those awful shoes got back to the right girl, didn't they?'

'Yes, they did. That wasn't the problem. No, he'd brought something he specially wanted me to bring back for you.'

Verity looked puzzled. 'For me?'

'Yes, darling, for you.' Dora stood up and fetched the crumpled cardboard box she'd left on the top of the dresser. 'He'd been able to collect Raven's ashes for you.'

Verity nearly dropped the box in surprise as Dora put it into her hands, but pulled it firmly onto her lap, holding it tight with both arms. 'This is Raven? *My* Raven?'

'That's right, darling. He's come home to you.' Dora hoped she sounded confident and that Verity wouldn't inspect the ashes too closely. 'I know you really would have liked to bring him back yourself, but I could hardly refuse when Carrington had made a point of rushing to the station specially. I think he'd gone to a lot of trouble.'

Verity took the blue and white jar out of the box and lifted the lid. Peering in, she said, 'It's not very much, is it? A whole person, reduced to dust.'

'Ashes to ashes, dust to dust,' Dora murmured.

Verity dipped her forefinger and thumb into the sandy contents, took a pinch, rubbed it between her fingers, then let it fall back into the jar.

Dora held her breath, hoping she wouldn't detect any alien debris in the ashes.

'Raven's in here,' Verity said, replacing the lid and standing the jar on the kitchen table. 'He's home at last. I'm glad you brought him back to me.'

'When you've had time to think about it, you might want to make plans to travel to Ireland, to his family estate. That's what you'd wanted to do, wasn't it? To take him home?' Dora was watching her cousin closely. She couldn't detect any tears or trembling of her lips; she seemed totally calm.

Verity stroked the jar. 'He's here now, that's all that matters.

I think I'd like to keep him here.' She looked at Dora. 'He said he'd always wanted children. He'd have loved Ruth and she's dark-haired like he was. If I keep Raven here, he'll see how well she's doing.'

FORTY-NINE

ROSA

Exhausted and drenched with sweat, Rosa lay back on the hard pillow made from a bundle of old clothes. 'Can I see them?' She held out her arms to take the two tiny babies, wrapped in clean rags.

'A boy and a girl,' the midwife said. 'Both healthy, although smaller than usual.'

Rosa gazed at the cross, red faces. 'Fetch Theresia, so she can meet them.'

Frau Goldmann, who had cleared the room to give Rosa some privacy during her labour, bustled off to fetch the child. Despite being a gossip and rather bossy, she had been a great help, fetching the midwife when Rosa's waters broke.

A few minutes later, Theresia rushed into the room they normally shared with another family, followed by Liese. 'Let me see,' the little girl demanded. 'Can I hold one?'

'Sit on the bed beside me and hold out your arms.'

Theresia sat obediently as she was told and took one of the bundles onto her lap. 'What are their names?'

'I thought we'd call the girl Esther and the boy should be Josef, of course, after your father.' *I'll call them whatever I like,* she told herself. *They aren't going to be Sara and Israel, no matter how the law now tells us all Jews should be named.* 'Do you like those names?'

Theresia nodded, then said, 'Who's the boy and who's the girl? They look the same.'

Rosa looked over to Liese and said, 'Perhaps we should have different coloured bonnets or ribbons for them.'

Liese nodded. 'That would be a good idea. I'll sort that out right away, then we'll always know which is which.'

Rosa smiled in thanks. Her loyal friend visited frequently and her blonde hair meant she could visit shops with less trouble than the Jewish residents whose lives were severely restricted.

'And in eight days' time, you should have the mohel come to perform b'rit milah,' Frau Goldmann said. 'Your husband would expect that to be done according to our tradition.'

Rosa nodded her assent. She was too tired to argue with this forceful but helpful woman and it was true that if Josef were here, he would expect her baby boy to be circumcised. But looking down at her babies' faces, she felt anxious about doing anything at all that would cause them pain. All she wanted was to keep them safe from harm. And how was she going to do that with the constant introduction of new laws making normal life impossible?

'Look, Mutti,' Theresia said, tugging her mother's sleeve. 'Esther is sucking my finger. She's hungry.'

Rosa reached for the little bundle. She was tired and longed to sleep, but she knew her body would respond to her babies' needs. If she encouraged them to suckle, her milk would soon flow and she could give them both the best nourishment of all, despite the lack of food for adults and older children.

'Hold your brother while I feed Esther,' she said, exchanging the babies. 'Once she's had enough, I'll let him have a turn.'

Rosa stroked her newborn girl's soft downy head, still damp from her arrival. She could feel her breasts responding as if they already remembered feeding Theresia when she was a baby. In the midst of all this chaos, cruelty and hunger, this felt like a blessing. And for a moment, the sheer miracle of a mother's body, able to give birth and then provide sustenance, flooded her with wonder.

FIFTY
BABY DOLLS
GERMANY, MAY 1939

How could a woman bear to give her tiny babies away? Dora was still shocked by what had just happened. She cradled the basket on her lap and gazed at the peaceful faces of the twins. They were so vulnerable and she was now responsible. She looked again at the two photos tucked in the envelope in the basket. Not casual Brownie camera snaps, but posed studio portraits taken by a professional photographer. It was clear that these babies had been born to a middle-class, bourgeois couple with aspirations, people who could never have imagined they would be reduced to desperate, despised undesirables.

As the train rumbled away from Berlin and through the countryside, Dora realised she had to make a plan. It was all very well telling her charges that the twins were a secret and hoping the guards on board wouldn't make a further appearance, but this journey might not proceed as smoothly as some previous trips had. Unlike the other children, the babies were not authorised to join the transport. They didn't have visas or tickets. She had to think of a way to ensure they wouldn't be discovered.

Dora turned to the boy beside her and looked at his name tag: 'Gabriel, I need you to do something for me.'

He looked up, eager to help. He was one of the older children, about twelve, and had already shown himself to be responsible, helping the others load luggage into the overhead racks and calming some of the younger ones when the guards had yanked open cases.

'I want you to go and find Miss Bradshaw, the other lady who was helping me at the station. Her compartment is further down the corridor, near the entrance. Please go and tell her it's very important that I speak to her right away, but I can't leave my seat. Can you do that for me?'

He nodded with a smile, jumped up, opened the door to the corridor and dashed off. In minutes he was back, closely followed by a flustered Brenda.

'Whatever is the matter, dear? Are you feeling unwell?' Brenda leant over Dora, looking closely at her, as if she expected to see her developing a fever. 'And what on earth do you have there on your lap? Have we been honoured with the delivery of a luxury hamper?'

'Nothing like that. See for yourself.' Dora opened the lid and, as she did so, both babies flexed their tiny pink fists and made little mewing cries.

'Oh, my word, however did this happen?' Brenda lowered the blinds to the windows facing the corridor. She eased herself into the empty seat next to Dora and Gabriel closed the compartment door and stood with his back to it.

Dora explained how the basket had been thrust into her hands with no explanation and that the only documentation enclosed with the babies was the letter. 'The train was just about to pull out. I didn't have a chance to ask questions. If we get checked again, that piece of paper won't be enough. I'm terrified that we won't be able to protect them. Whatever are we going to do?'

Brenda put a steadying hand on her shoulder. 'We are going to do our job. We are going to make sure no harm comes to these little ones – or any other child on this train, for that matter. But I tell you what I think might help.' She stood up and let Gabriel return to his seat. 'Firstly, I am going to move into the compartment nearest to the goods van. Then, if our friends decide they are going to come round on another inspection, I will do my best to delay them. And Gabriel here will come with me and will run to warn you.'

Gabriel's face lit up with pride and he sat up very straight. Dora couldn't help giving him an approving smile, despite the seriousness of the situation. 'And secondly,' Brenda added, 'we must be prepared in case other guards enter the train at a checkpoint, as they often do. They usually enter from the goods van end. We must think of something that will stop them wanting to even think of entering this compartment.'

'I know,' Gabriel said brightly, holding up his hand as if he was answering a question in the school classroom. 'We must pretend we are all very ill.'

'Clever boy,' Brenda said. 'That's it. This compartment will be in quarantine. We shall say we have an outbreak of, let's say measles, and we have confined all the children showing symptoms to this area.' She looked around at the seated children, all listening intently, and explained in German that they would have to act convincingly if it became necessary.

'But what if one of the guards insists on inspecting this basket? It wasn't here when the men who are already on board went through the train earlier. They could well realise they didn't see it before.' Dora couldn't help thinking how like a food hamper it looked and how tempted the guards might be.

Brenda studied the children in the carriage. 'How many of you have brought dolls with you?' Five hands shot up, from girls who were still young enough to play with dolls. 'And you and you' – she pointed to two more young girls– 'would you each like a doll to play with?'

Both of them nodded shyly. 'Right then,' Brenda said. 'If Gabriel warns us that the guards are on their way, all of you are going to be cradling your dolls, just like they were real babies. Only you two' – she pointed again to the two little girls who hadn't brought dolls – 'will be holding the babies from the basket. I want you both to sit near the window and turn towards it, so your pretend dolls can't be seen properly. The guards will just think all you sick children are comforting yourselves with your toys.'

She looked at Dora, who was hardly daring to think they could get away with it. 'But what if the guards come inside? They'll be able to tell right away that the babies are real. I daren't think what they would do if they found out that there are no valid tickets for them.'

'We're not even going to think about it,' Brenda said. 'We're all going to act our parts if we have to. And that basket won't be so obvious if you shove it up onto the luggage rack behind the other cases.' She opened the compartment door. 'Let's step outside for a moment.'

Dora placed the basket with the sleeping babies on her seat and followed Brenda into the corridor. She was feeling increasingly nervous about the situation they were all facing. 'If we're found out, there could be consequences for the whole transport. It could mean the whole trainload of children is turned back to Berlin and we're never allowed to take any more of them in future.'

Brenda looked back into the compartment once the door was closed. The children could no longer hear their conversation in English. 'You and I both know what these cruel men are capable of doing. What chance do you think those babies would have if they were discovered on this train without the correct authority? I dread to think what would happen to them. We have to do everything within our power to keep them hidden and keep those guards away from them.'

Dora nodded in agreement. She hated to think of rough hands hauling the basket away, ignoring the babies' needs, neglecting them or, worse still, ending their lives once they discovered the children weren't Aryan.

'They'd know soon enough that they were both Jewish. I've put the mother's letter in my handbag, but the little boy would have been circumcised soon after he was born. That's the custom and to the Germans, that's as clear a sign of his identity as any official papers.'

'Exactly. I doubt they'd even make it back to Berlin if they were discovered.'

FIFTY-ONE
LIPSTICK ON COLLARS
GERMANY, MAY 1939

Dora didn't dare close her eyes. She was tired, but felt she had to stay alert throughout the journey in case there was a sudden signal from Brenda, who had moved to the compartment nearest to the goods van with Gabriel.

The children were tired too, worn out from hours of queuing that morning as well as hours of packing and preparation the day before, but she needed to ensure that they knew exactly what to do if the guards made another tour. 'Let's all pretend we're feeling ill,' she said. 'How ill can you all make yourselves look?'

There was some giggling as the boys pretended to be sick, making retching noises, and the girls recoiled in disgust. 'I think it's more likely that if you had measles you'd all feel very tired,' Dora said. 'And maybe some of you would just cough a little bit.'

They rehearsed weak coughs and weary sighs until Dora was satisfied they could all put on a fair show. Then one boy put up his hand and said, 'I had spots when I had measles. Spots would show them we're ill.'

'What a very good idea,' Dora said. 'Now how can we give you all spots?'

After a burst of laughter, several hands went up and there were shouts of *paint, red ink, crayons!* But no such materials had been included in anyone's luggage. Looking at the disappointed faces, longing to be made up for their acting debut, Dora thought of the red lipstick in her handbag. It was a recent purchase from the cosmetics counter in Jones Brothers on the Holloway Road and she'd hardly used it. Her brand-new vivid Elizabeth Arden Victoire would be enough to dot a couple of faces and redden a few cheeks to create the impression of a feverish high temperature.

She found the gold tube in her bag and opened it. It seemed a shame to waste it, and she wished she was more like the old Verity, who had always been a great advocate of lipstick and rouge and usually carried both in her handbag.

Dora held up the glowing lipstick so the children could see what it was. 'Now I'm not going to use it on all of you, because some of you don't have the measles yet, you're just sickening for it. But I need a couple of volunteers. Who wants to look spotty?'

The boys, of course, all wanted to look ill and Dora gave two of them convincing measly spots. Then she gave two girls flushed faces, rubbing the colour across their cheeks so they really did look as though they could have a temperature.

'We'll see what happens and maybe I'll do some more measles for the rest of you later,' she said. 'But next I want the girls with dolls to show me how they'll wrap them up and cradle them like real babies.' They all obliged with scarves and shawls as if they had been used to doing so all their lives.

'And now we'll have a practice with the real babies, as they've woken up and want some milk.' Dora helped the two little girls who had been selected to move to their seats facing the window, away from the corridor. She settled a baby on each lap, showed them how to crook their arm to support each tiny head and then helped them both offer the babies the milk that had been packed in the basket.

At first they wouldn't suckle and one pulled away from the teat, but once they'd had a taste of the tepid milk, they began to drink. With full stomachs the babies soon became drowsy again and slept in their young carers' arms. Dora decided not to change them at this point, partly because she wasn't sure what she would do with dirty nappies, which would be an obvious giveaway.

'Well done, girls,' she said. 'You've done that beautifully. The babies will do very well with you.' She returned the sleeping infants to their basket and said, 'There's just one other thing I think we can do to discourage any guards from coming in here. What else might you find in a sick bay or quarantine ward?'

'A notice!' shouted one of the boys. 'A keep out notice!'

'Right then, who's got paper or card to make a sign?'

'Me!' yelled another child, pulling down their case and taking out a sketch pad of thick paper.

'Perfect,' Dora said, flattening the paper on the floor. She thought for a moment, then, taking out her lipstick again, she searched for the words for sick bay and measles and wrote: 'Krankenstation. Masern'. *That might do the trick*, she thought, as she taped it with sticking plaster to the window facing the corridor and then pulled down the blinds. *If they ask why the compartment is dark, I can say it's because measles affects the eyes as I know all too well. And now we're as ready as we can be.*

Despite her determination not to sleep, Dora must have dozed off for all of a sudden she felt an urgent hand tugging her sleeve. 'They're coming,' Gabriel said and Dora realised that the train was no longer moving. They must have stopped at a checkpoint or station.

She glanced around the compartment. Several children were also asleep, flushed either with sleep or with a supposed fever. The two little girls by the window were awake and alert, ready to take their charges. Dora placed the babies in their arms and turned them away from the corridor to face the outside window, also shaded by a blind. The other girls had either fallen asleep holding their dolls or had quickly resumed their position with them nestled in the crook of an arm like real babies.

'Gabriel, are they our old guards or new ones?'

'These ones just got on the train. There's three of them and they were angry with the other guards for sleeping in the goods van. Miss Bradshaw is talking to all of them now.'

Good old Brenda. Dora told herself she'd buy them time, delaying the soldiers a while. Hopefully she could placate them too, so the arrivals didn't reach Dora's carriage in an even worse mood. She quickly tucked the basket behind some cases at the far end of the luggage rack.

'Good boy,' she said. 'Now go and squeeze yourself into the next compartment. We can't have you catching measles too now, can we?'

'It's all right,' Gabriel said. 'I've had it already. But I know what you mean. We've all got to pretend this is real.' He slipped out of the door and disappeared.

Dora took a handkerchief from her handbag and dampened it with water from her flask. Bending over one of the boys dotted with lipstick, she said, 'We're going to make it look as if I'm trying to reduce your temperature if they come along here. All you have to do is lie back with your eyes closed and look as if you have a very bad headache.'

He did as he was told and Dora crouched close to him, her wet hankie ready to soothe his feverish brow. When she finally heard heavy steps approaching, she cupped the back of his head with one hand and dabbed his forehead with the damp cloth.

She looked up when the steps halted outside the compartment. She could just see the group through the clear gap at the edge of the blind. There in the corridor were three uniformed soldiers and Brenda. The men were pointing and laughing. Dora heard them joking and heard one of them say, '*Mit etwas Glück warden sie geblendet.*' They laughed some more, then moved on. Brenda gave Dora a thumbs-up behind their backs.

Listening to their retreating steps, Dora tried to continue acting her part. How could those heartless men say with any luck the children would be blinded by their illness? She knew to her cost only too well how deadly measles could be. Not only could the disease kill, but the eyesight could be severely affected, often leading to a lifetime of blindness. She swallowed her fear, along with a momentary flashback of Verity's sister, Honor, racked with fever as a child and now nobly negotiating the extensive family house with her white stick.

She carried on tending to her pretend patient. Usually, these inspections began at one end of the train and finished at the other, but she wasn't going to take any chances; she said in a low voice, but loud enough for everyone to hear, 'Well done, children. Just carry on until we know they've finally gone for good.'

The compartment was quiet and still, as if everyone was holding their breath, and in that hush, Dora thought she suddenly heard the tiniest of cries. She looked across at the two little girls. Both of them were gently rocking their charges and both turned to look at her with slightly worried expressions. The babies must be hungry again or need changing. The cries were not yet loud enough to be heard outside the compartment, but Dora had heard a hungry baby's desperate cries when she had visited her sister. If they weren't quickly quietened, they might be heard further down the train.

But somehow, maybe because they had seen it done before or maybe because it was maternal instinct, even in ones so young, the two girls each gave their baby a knuckle to suck.

They fed their bent fingers into the babies' mouths and soon all was quiet again.

Dora breathed a sigh of relief. She knew it couldn't last long and hoped that soon she would see Gabriel or Brenda giving her an all-clear sign. And better still, that the train's wheels would begin to turn again and they would be even closer to a land of safety.

FIFTY-TWO

ROSA

Rosa paused in writing her letter to her mother. She had not heard from her in several months and wondered whether this letter would even reach her, but she had to unburden her thoughts after her rash act that morning.

She glanced at her daughter. The child was still silent, curled on the bed, clutching her doll tight to her chest as if she feared that it might be given away as well. As they ran back from the station, Theresia had held her mother's hand tight. Did she remember the time she had sat on the train in readiness for a long journey, or did she fear that she too might be abandoned? Rosa had tried to explain that there wouldn't be enough food for a growing baby brother and sister, and that this was the best way to help them grow up strong and healthy. But Theresia had hung her head and sucked her thumb.

Taking a deep breath to quell her tears, Rosa read again the words she was using to justify the painful choice she'd felt forced to make:

My dearest Mother,

I cannot yet tell whether I have made the best decision of my life or the worst. Today I gave my babies to a stranger in the hope that they would be taken away to a safer place.

I am writing this with tears on my cheeks and milk leaking through my blouse, praying that I have done the right thing. How I wish you were here, so I could have talked to you first and listened to your wise advice.

Ever since the twins were born two weeks ago, I have been so afraid for all of us. Food is so scarce and milk for little ones is unobtainable. I worried that my milk would not last long with two hungry ones and little food to sustain my supply and then what would I do? If they weakened and were ill, there would be no medicine for any of us. Every day, in this filthy house where we are all crammed together, children and the old are growing weaker and new babies are dying. And I fear there is little hope of Josef returning, so I had to decide what was best for my children.

I fed the twins before I ran to the station with Theresia at my side. I settled them in a wicker hamper with a supply of napkins and two bottles filled with my own milk. Then I ran to the train and threw the basket at a woman who was just about to close the door to the carriage, without explanation. All I could say was, please take them. Then I ran, crying as I ran, clutching my one remaining child's hand, hoping that the train filled with children reached England safely.

What should I say to Theresia? How do I explain to her that I couldn't send her away but this might be better for her baby brother and sister? And in any case, how can I be sure I am right?

When we came back, she sat on a far corner of the bed, knees drawn up to her chest. She won't speak, she just sucks her thumb and sits there rocking backwards and forwards. Her doll is tightly gripped in her arms as if it was a baby. She is

*sleeping now, thank goodness, and I hope that soon I too can
sleep and wake knowing that I will not regret this.*

Rosa signed the letter as she always did, hoping it would
reach her mother. But maybe it never would. She had thought
that writing these words might lighten her heart a little, but now
she felt that the burden of guilt would never leave her and that
she had wounded not only herself but Theresia.

With her daughter sleeping, Rosa slipped out of the house
to post her letter. She caught sight of the clock on the church
outside the Jewish quarter. It was ten hours since the train had
been due to leave. The babies should be nearing the Dutch
border by now. They might have already been fed from the
bottles she had filled and be in need of more milk. And
suddenly, with just that thought, as if she had instructed her
breasts to respond, Rosa felt them swell and ache, ready to
perform their duty. She could feel the warm milk seeping
through her clothes, trickling down her shrinking stomach. But
there were no babies here to drink it.

FIFTY-THREE

SAFE AT LAST

HOLLAND, MAY 1939

Dora woke with a start from a dreamless sleep. Her neck was stiff from sleeping upright in her seat and the train had stopped. She peered through the window and, with relief, realised they had crossed the border and were now in Holland. Once they were safe in a neutral country, the guards who had accompanied the train could no longer exercise their authority and luckily there hadn't been any more unscheduled stops and inspections.

The compartment door slid open with a jerk to reveal a beaming Brenda. 'Well done, all of you,' she said, clapping her hands to wake the sleeping children. 'Dutch volunteers are waiting outside with hot chocolate and good things to eat. They always look after us well when we get here.'

She turned to Dora. 'And I've told them we need warm water and clean napkins for our youngest refugees. They'll be here in a minute.'

Dora stood up and stretched, yawning as she did so. 'Thank goodness we're here at last. That was such a tense journey.' She looked at the children opposite and couldn't help but laugh. The boys' faces were blotchy where their lipsticked measles rash had smudged. 'And we might want to clean everyone else up too – we can't arrive in England with lipstick all over their cheeks.'

Brenda laughed too. 'They performed wonderfully. It certainly did the trick.'

Behind her in the corridor, Dora could see a woman bearing a jug and bowl of hot water, followed by a younger woman holding a child of about eight months. 'We have an offer of breast milk for the babies,' Brenda said. 'This young mother has plenty to spare and is willing to feed them both.'

Dora was a little shocked. Wet-nursing was a practice she'd heard of, but she didn't think it was practised in England these days. But it was a perfect solution as the bottles that had been supplied were now empty and the infants were awake and crying lustily. Both were swept up by the two women, who expertly changed and cleaned them. Then they were clasped in plump arms as they latched on to the creamy breasts laced with blue veins, a babe on each side, while the woman's own child sucked her thumb as she sat beside her mother in Dora's seat.

The rest of the children were also wiped clean with fresh warm water and taken outside to eat squares of chocolate, soft white bread and sweet cakes. Dora always found the Dutch so welcoming and generous after the harsh treatment they generally received while the trainload was still on German soil. It made her feel like crying tears of relief to see how the children were transformed by such kindness. Apart from the love they had received from their own families, in Germany they had mostly known only indifference and abuse.

Brenda tapped Dora's shoulder, interrupting her reverie of the suckling babies. 'Now we're in safe hands, we need to have a word about what will happen when we reach the end of our journey.'

They stepped into the corridor and out of the carriage into the fresh air. Dora could see the harbour opening out to the sea, with boats, bridges and beaches. Further inland she imagined fields coloured with ribbons of bright reds and pinks, where tulips were in full flower. It was the peak of springtime and she was relieved to have left the oppression of Germany and be in a free-speaking, tolerant country.

'We need to talk about those little ones,' Brenda said. 'We've got through the worst bit, but now we've got to decide what to do next.'

'I've been thinking about it,' Dora said. 'I don't know whether you'll agree, but I want to take them back home with me. I can't bear the thought of them being handed over to some faceless institution.'

She waved a hand to forbid any interruption. 'I know there are wonderful children's hospitals and marvellous foster-parents, but I feel that young mother chose to give *me* her precious children. I'm not saying she might not just as easily have given them to you, if she'd seen you, but she literally pushed them into my hands. And that makes me feel immensely responsible. She had no idea whether I was an official representative or a casual helper, but she saw me and she trusted me.'

Brenda nodded sagely. 'I can understand how you feel. We have no prior arrangement for these babies. We know nothing of any family connections they might have in our country. But are you absolutely sure you want to do this?'

'I'm thinking of Verity and Ruth too. I think between us we can make it work. And besides, Hugh was a paediatrician before he started specialising in surgery. I really do feel that I owe it to that mother to honour her trust in me. All she said to me was *please take them*. Nothing else, just that. No explana-tion, no arguing, just *take them for me*. She must have been so desperate, so afraid. I don't want to let her down.'

'Very well, my dear,' Brenda said, putting an arm round Dora's shoulders. 'We'll give it a try. If you find it all too much, then we shall have to think again but I can see why you feel this way. And perhaps you should take a break for a little while before taking on another transport.'

Dora gazed out to sea at the green of the water, the blue of the sky, and longed for the end of their trip. The crossing always took around eight hours, but the ocean looked calm today, so perhaps it would be an easy voyage without the seasickness they often experienced.

Back on the platform, they helped the children collect all their belongings from the train and trekked off to the ferry terminal. Brenda carried Dora's case as well as her own, so Dora could cradle the basket with the contentedly full, sleeping babies. The Dutch women had provided more clean napkins and had washed and refilled the bottles with milk for their journey. Most of the children were cheerful after their delicious refreshments and looking forward to crossing the ocean, as few of them had ever seen it before.

Hours later, they all arrived at Liverpool Street station and Brenda and Dora completed the transfer of all the children to relatives, foster-parents and hostels. The babies were fretful, needing a change and more milk. It was difficult attending to their needs in the midst of the noisy station. 'I'd better come back with you,' Brenda said. 'You can't manage your luggage as well as the basket.' They had also acquired an emergency supply of newborn baby clothes from one of the charities that had turned up to collect some children.

Once they were settled in the relative peace of a taxicab, the women each cradled a baby and a bottle. The infants soon settled down, even though Dora suspected they would need changing again once she reached home.

'You do realise you're not going to get much rest tonight, don't you?' Brenda laid the baby against her shoulder, patting its back.

'I think Verity might be eager to take over,' Dora said. 'I

hope we don't come to regret this but I've been thinking that she might be glad to have another couple of needy creatures to take her mind off her troubles. This will certainly be a distraction.'

'They'll be that all right, but I can see joy ahead too.' Brenda's voice softened, her Mancunian vowels becoming less acute than usual. 'I never expected to have children, nor did I ever want them, but I can see the attraction with helpless little ones like these.'

'Hugh and I hope to have a family of our own one day, but we've promised ourselves we'll wait until we're sure we're in a safer place. If there's a war coming, I couldn't feel comfortable bringing children into the world.'

'Understandable, my dear. We don't need you making more trouble for yourself.'

'And it feels as if I'll have enough family to worry about for the time being,' Dora said, wiping away a dribble of regurgitated milk from her shoulder, where the baby's head had rested. Oh dear, she was going to smell of milky sick rather than cologne when Hugh gave her a welcome home kiss.

FIFTY-FOUR

SURPRISE VISITORS

The moon was rising over the communal gardens in the square by the time their cab reached the house. Hugh must have heard it stop with its motor still running, or picked up their voices, as he'd opened the door before they'd even had time to knock.

'What's all this?' he said with a smile on seeing the two of them laden with cases and the basket. 'A delegation?'

'No, darling, this is Brenda Bradshaw. I needed help as I'm rather loaded down.'

'Good evening, Mr Williams,' Brenda said. 'Don't worry, I shan't be staying, but Dora couldn't have managed this all on her own.' She passed over a case, plus the bag of baby clothes and napkins.

'Because we have unexpected visitors,' Dora said, stepping inside the hallway and lifting the lid of the basket in her arms.

'Oh, my word.' Hugh stared at the sleeping babies. 'You do like collecting waifs and strays, don't you?' He peeled back the blanket to look more closely. 'You'd better come into the kitchen – it's the warmest place.'

'I hope you both manage to get some sleep tonight,' Brenda

said, giving them a wave and turning back to the cab, which was still waiting outside.

Once she had gone, Hugh took the basket and they went through to the kitchen. He placed it on the table and removed the nearly empty bottles. 'I'm sterilising these right away. I don't suppose they've been washed properly on your journey, have they?'

Dora sank into the armchair near the stove. 'We had nothing prepared for them, Hugh. This was totally unexpected.' She launched into the story of the twins' arrival on the train and the steps that had had to be taken to conceal their presence. And although she was tired out, she found herself laughing when she told him how she had given the boys measles. 'It was very effective and kept the guards away from us, but I was rather sorry to waste my precious lipstick,' she said, just as they heard steps on the stairs.

'And what was a waste of your lipstick?' Verity's voice called from the hallway as she rushed to join them. Wearing her dressing gown and slippers, she had clearly been preparing for bed.

'It was put to good use actually,' Dora said, and repeated her tale of deception. 'We had to do everything we could to protect the twins. It was the most terrifying and nerve-wracking journey I've ever undertaken.'

'Clever you, darling,' Verity said, peering at the babies, now stirring in their woven crib. 'Gosh, Ruth is going to adore these little sweeties. They're simply gorgeous. Are we keeping them?'

Dora glanced at Hugh, who was filling the baby bottles with boiling water. He raised his eyebrows in a questioning look. She hadn't got this far in her account. 'I told Brenda I thought we could cope. I feel a huge sense of obligation to the young mother who gave the babies to me. She practically threw them into my hands, so she must have thought she could trust me. So yes, I would like us to keep them. What do you both think?'

Hugh cleared his throat in what might have been intended as a non-committal comment. Verity immediately swung round to look at him, standing there with the bottles in his hands. 'You can't possibly be doubting that is the right decision! Of course we have to keep them.'

Dora sighed. 'I'm far too tired to have a long debate about it now. We'll talk about it properly tomorrow.'

Verity glanced again at Hugh and the bottles. 'Have you enough milk for those? Should I put a note out for the milkman?'

He frowned. 'Might be a good idea. We usually manage with one pint a day. But better still, we should get proper baby milk powder. Can you get some after you've dropped Ruth off at school?'

Verity nodded. 'And I think it would be best if she doesn't see these two adorable little ones until she comes home from school. I'll never get her to go in if she knows we've got them. She'd want to stay here all day to help.'

Dora couldn't help smiling despite her tiredness. She was looking forward to seeing Ruth again and it would be a joy to see her delight in the tiny babies. It would make her feel she was part of a real family.

'Should I get any other supplies?' Verity asked. 'How are you doing for nappies, creams or whatever else tiny babies might need? I've absolutely no idea, but I'm perfectly willing to learn.'

Dora looked at Hugh. 'I've not much idea either. We're all new to this, apart from you.'

'Being a paediatrician isn't quite the same as being a wet nurse,' he said, rolling his eyes. 'I can check them over, but I'm not that familiar with small baby problems.'

Verity gave a squeal of delight. 'You know what we should do? Get Nanny Jenkins down here. She's got absolutely nothing to do these days. Daddy's tucked her away in the lodge house and she's simply bored stiff. I haven't been up to see her for ages, obviously, but the last time I was there she said chasing me around with a hairbrush when I was naughty was the happiest time of her life.'

Dora couldn't help laughing, in spite of her weariness. Verity had been a wilful child and the family's nanny, who had potty-trained and chastened two generations, was a firm but kind force for good. 'That might not be a bad idea for a while. Do you really think she'd come all the way here?'

'I'm sure she'd absolutely adore it. Two tiny babies and a little schoolgirl? What could be better for the old dear? I'll get hold of her first thing tomorrow morning. Mummy won't approve, of course, but I'll phone the house and ask one of the maids to take Nanny a message.'

Dora could imagine how news would travel in that rambling house. But if the telephone was answered by staff, there was a good chance Lord and Lady Ponsonby wouldn't get to hear about this for a while. 'What do you think, darling?' She glanced at Hugh.

He looked somewhat bemused by this suggestion. 'Look, if you both think she could be useful and you both like her, then I've no objection. I'll leave it to you two to decide where she'll sleep and which room will be the nursery.' The tall, three-storey Islington house had rooms that were unused, filled with old furniture. 'As long as I can have some peace and quiet down here, I won't mind.'

'I'll sort everything out and make arrangements, don't you worry,' Verity said. 'Oh, how exciting! She's such a dear. You're going to simply love her!'

FIFTY-FIVE

NO NONSENSE

Nanny Jenkins was a tiny but forceful figure. As soon as she arrived early in the evening, having travelled down on the express train from York to King's Cross station, she took charge.

'Now then, Miss Verity,' she said, 'You're to leave everything to me. I may be ancient, but I won't have any trouble managing these two bairns. And as for you, Miss Dora, I believe you have important work to be getting on with, so you'd better be seeing to it.'

Dora and her cousin couldn't help but pull faces at each other. Not only was Nanny refusing to treat them as responsible adults, she was also refusing to refer to them by their married names. 'Let me show you to your room and the nursery, Nanny,' Verity said. 'And if there's anything you need or want changed, just say.'

'This young miss can come with me and help, for now,' Nanny said, taking Ruth by the hand, and they followed Verity up the stairs together.

Dora watched them go. Ruth had been so excited when she'd come home from school to see the babies. And when they'd explained that Verity's old nanny would soon be arriving to help look after them, she'd said, 'Like my oma when I was little.' She was speaking English every day now, although it was often interspersed with German names and terms. This was the first time Ruth had referred to another member of her family and Dora wondered if the grandmother had been against her leaving Berlin or had encouraged her parents to organise her departure to a place of greater safety.

Verity came running down the stairs a few minutes later. 'Nanny's approved the rooms, thank goodness, but she thinks Ruth should have her own room now, up on the top floor. She's happy about that, but can you come and help me? And we need to take tea upstairs right away. Nanny's parched after her journey – and she'll be taking supper with us tonight.' Verity shot the last few words over her shoulder as she dashed away to prepare Ruth's new room.

Following her instructions, Dora took a tray upstairs, adding Bath buns she'd bought from the bakery that morning. She found Nanny bustling around in the bathroom, running hot water and saying, 'Ruth can have her bath first, then I'll use some of the water for the little ones. As you don't have a baby bath here, it would help if you can find me a large bowl, preferably enamel.'

Dora ran back down the stairs to search for a bowl. She was sure she'd seen one somewhere in the house at some point. She began by looking in the scullery, then the cellar. Having found one large enough and rinsed it out to meet Nanny's approval, she ran upstairs again. She was beginning to think she might be sent on many errands now this tiny termagant was here. The thought of escaping to the office, despite her desire to see how the children fared, was starting to appeal to her.

After delivering the bowl, she went up the final flight of stairs to the top floor to find Verity attempting to turn a mattress on a single bed in an upper room. Ruth had been trying to assist, but it was too heavy for her.

'Let me help you,' Dora said, taking one side so they could settle it onto the bedstead. 'This is one of my favourite bedrooms,' she went on. 'It's got a lovely view of the garden square and you can see all the way to St Paul's Cathedral.'

'I like it up here too,' Ruth said. 'I used to have my own bedroom at home, but when they made us leave our house, we all had to share the same room for everything.'

And Dora was reminded yet again of what this little girl had already seen and suffered in her life. 'Well, now you can have this room all to yourself and you won't hear the babies if they cry in the night.'

'I think I might move up here too,' Verity said. 'It would be nice to be away from the noise and be next to Ruth if she needs me. Nanny will be more than happy to have the whole floor below to herself. You remember how she always loved being totally in charge.'

'I like her,' Ruth said. 'And can I choose a cover for my bed?'

Dora had opened a blanket box filled with bedspreads and pulled out a paisley eiderdown and a patchwork quilt with squares and diamonds of blues and yellows. 'Go ahead,' she said, 'you can have whatever takes your fancy.'

At that point they heard Nanny call up the stairs: 'Miss Ruth, time for your bath.'

Ruth pointed to the quilt, then ran off, leaving the cousins to finish making the beds and plumping pillows. 'Have you told her about Ruth's injury?' Dora asked as she struggled to fold the top sheet into a neat hospital corner over the mattress.

'I explained it all over the phone and then again in more detail when I collected her from the station. She hasn't seen the scar yet, of course, but she'll take it in her stride. I know she's fierce, but she's a complete and utter darling. I think Ruth is going to love her. I know I did, despite the spankings with the hairbrush!'

'Well, I don't think Ruth is ever going to need any of those. What did you say when you told her about the twins?'

'I told her how they had been given to you and she said the sweetest thing.' Verity's mouth twisted in a strange way and her eyes seemed to shimmer with tears. 'She said all the mummies and daddies are being very brave. And she's glad the twins' mummy was brave and decided to send us her babies.'

Dora felt a lump in her throat too. This little girl who'd suffered so much was showing such intelligence and understanding. She felt that with sympathetic support Ruth would survive the time ahead, even if it turned out to be as tragic as she feared. If only the boys who had hurt her had half her sensibility, but she feared their sort would not grow to be men of empathy and tolerance.

Verity sniffed loudly and pulled a hankie from her sleeve. 'Oh, do stop it, Nanny won't approve of us going all miz. Come on, help me make up my bed too. Then we can go and see the babies having fun in their bath.'

Dora managed to laugh, even though she too needed a hankie to wipe her eyes. 'What a pair of softies we are. You wouldn't catch Nanny blubbing like this and getting all sentimental.'

'Good thing too,' Verity said, flicking her with a starched pillowcase. 'Last one to the bathroom's a ninny.'

FIFTY-SIX

ROSA

Dearest Mother,

You cannot believe the relief I felt today on receiving a letter from London. I am astonished that it reached me, since we have been moved from house to house as more refugees have been thrown into our community. Families no longer have a room to themselves any more. We all have to share, no matter what we were used to in our former lives.

The letter confirmed that the Kindertransport reached London safely with all of its passengers, including my babies. I have been given an address for them and have been told that they are in good health. I was informed that they will not be placed in an orphanage but will be cared for by the woman who took the basket and her family, which includes a little girl who had travelled on a previous train.

I am so happy that they are safe and well. I showed Theresia the letter, which was written in German, so she knows that her siblings are thriving. She is still very quiet, but she is not rocking to comfort herself all the time now. I think she is slowly beginning to understand why I had to send the twins away, when I say that we would not have had enough food for them as well as ourselves. Today we were lucky to get the last heel of bread from the baker. So many have nothing but peelings to boil for soup.

I hope that you, dearest Mother, and all our family are also well. I miss your letters, but maybe they too will find me one day.

Your loving daughter,

Rosa

FIFTY-SEVEN

NO MORE BABIES

LONDON, AUGUST 1939

Dora wanted to spend her last evening at home reading a story to Ruth and rocking the twins to sleep, but she was finding it difficult to break away from Hugh.

'I really don't like the idea of you going back to Berlin tomorrow,' he said, throwing his folded newspaper down on the kitchen table. 'Just look at what's happening. It's getting more and more unsettled by the day.' He jabbed his finger at the page in question. 'You could find yourself stuck out there when the bubble finally bursts.'

She glanced at the news report. *The result of Sir Neville Henderson's visit to Hitler is not yet revealed, but he will be arriving in London tomorrow morning.*

'It's all arranged,' she said. 'Brenda and I are flying out there to save time. I have to go with her, because this could very well be the last chance we have to save more children.'

'Look, darling, I appreciate all that you and your colleagues have done, but I care about you very much. I don't want you landing yourself in a dangerous situation just as the Germans decide to pull a fast one. I'd never forgive myself if you couldn't get back before war breaks out.'

'That's not going to happen and you know it. I'll be home before you've even had time to miss me.'

'It's too risky, Dora. With the Germans sending Ribbentrop to Moscow, to sign some non-aggression treaty or other with Russia, it's making me very nervous. I wish you'd change your mind.'

'I can't and I won't. I'm sorry, darling, but I have to give it one last chance. There are hundreds of children still waiting to be brought out of that dangerous country. They're dealing with far greater dangers, day after day, than anything I'd ever face. Bit by bit they're clamping down on anyone the regime thinks can't contribute to the state. The latest edict is appalling – ordering the reporting of little children with disabilities. They make me sick.'

Everyone in Dora's office had been shocked by the ruling from the Reich Ministry of the Interior that all physicians, nurses and midwives had to report on any child under the age of three with any severe mental or physical impairment. Brenda, pronouncing on this order, had said, 'Mark my words, it's not going to stop there. It's the thin end of the wedge. Soon they'll be disposing of anyone, old or young, Jewish or Aryan, who can't contribute to the economy and isn't perfect in mind and body.'

Dora left the table and walked as far as the door to the hall. 'I'm popping upstairs to say good night to the little ones. And I can tell you now that if this transport succeeds and we're allowed to continue, then I will be going back again and again for as long as there are children in need of our help.'

She turned on her heel before Hugh could utter another word and dashed up the stairs. She knew that she and Brenda might face a difficult time, but it couldn't be any worse than anything they'd already encountered on their many trips to Germany. Threats, rudeness, obstructions, delays, even brief imprisonment were nothing, in her mind, to the danger those children faced if they weren't brought out of Germany, a country that didn't value them or protect them. She was determined to keep rescuing these vulnerable young people.

She stopped on the first floor of the house, where Nanny Jenkins was rocking two cradles, bought from a second-hand shop in Islington, one with each hand. 'Let me take over for a bit,' Dora said in the quietest voice she could manage. 'You nip down to the kitchen and make yourself a cup of tea.'

Nanny left on tiptoe and Dora took over the rocking duty. The twins had grown so much since they had first landed in her arms. Where once they could be tucked head to toe side by side in that basket, now they needed beds of their own. Their cheeks were plump and their chubby arms and legs with their rings of flesh resembled fat sausages. As it was such a warm night, Nanny had laid each of them down on the mattresses in just a vest and a nappy, so Dora could see their rounded tummies too.

It was soothing after her confrontation with Hugh to gently rock them while their eyes closed. Gazing at their rosy faces in turn, Dora wondered how much more they would have developed by the time she returned. Already they looked with knowing eyes when they were held and kicked vigorously when they were bathed. And if she, who wasn't even their birth mother, could feel regret at missing them for the next week, whatever did the woman who had given birth to them and suckled them for their first two weeks of life feel?

Dora knew nothing of their mother's current circumstances. She had written to the address on the letter as soon as she was safely back in London and had written with news of their development every week since, but had heard nothing back. Perhaps her letters hadn't reached her; or perhaps their mother had tried to write in return but her letters were held back for some reason. Or, unbearable to think, perhaps she was no longer at that address, had been forcibly removed, or even sent away to a prison to join her husband. Thinking of the likely outcomes made Dora all the more determined to do her job, to go back to Berlin and rescue more children.

Her thoughts were disturbed by Nanny beckoning from the doorway. 'You can go back to your husband,' she whispered. 'I've brought my supper up with me and I'll eat in my room in case they wake again.'

'I'll run up to Ruth quickly. I must see her tonight as I'm leaving so early tomorrow.'

'They'll all be here well and thriving when you get back, Miss Dora,' Nanny said with a sympathetic smile and a nod of her head.

Up on the top floor, Ruth was listening to Verity read *Hansel and Gretel*. They had begun reading her traditional German fairy stories, omitting the more macabre ones, to help with her English. She recognised the familiar tales and loved hearing the translated versions and learning the equivalent words for witch and so on.

'Shall I take over for a minute?' Dora let Verity slip away after she'd kissed Ruth on the head.

'I like that story but I don't want another one tonight,' Ruth said. 'I want to know how many children will come on the train with you.'

Ruth loved hearing that Dora and Brenda were saving even more children and finding places for them to stay. 'There should be about two hundred this time,' Dora said. 'But I know there are many more hoping to travel on still more trains in future, if we have time to organise them.'

'You're going to save all of them, aren't you?' Ruth's eyes were wide and appealing as she held Dora's hand.

'We hope to, dear. And other countries are trying to help too. Holland has said children can stay there as well and there are people helping in nearby countries where there are other Jewish children.'

'If the Germans come here, will I have to go somewhere else?'

Dora was shocked to be asked this question and wondered what news was filtering through to Ruth, now she was at school with children who might repeat overheard conversations. She and Verity were careful never to talk about the likelihood of war and the possibility of invasion. There was only one way she could answer her: 'You're going to stay with us for as long as you and your parents want you to. England is safe, you must remember that.'

She covered Ruth with just a loose sheet as that night the top-floor rooms were even hotter than those below. 'Go to sleep now and don't worry about anything. I have to leave early tomorrow, but you're so busy at school, making new friends and helping with the babies, you'll hardly notice I'm gone.'

'I have a new friend,' Ruth said. 'Her name is Mary and she is teaching me lots of things.' She yawned, so Dora kissed her cheek and turned to go.

'Don't bring any more babies back,' Ruth said, sleepily.

Dora smiled to herself, thinking she had never intended collecting the two she had brought home. But each time she undertook one of these trips, she never knew what surprises were in store, nor what risks she might encounter.

FIFTY-EIGHT

THINGS HOT UP

BERLIN, AUGUST 1939

The sweltering heat of Berlin was just as oppressive as it had been in London, yet still the children arrived in their winter coats. Dora could understand their parents' desire to equip them as best they could for the colder months ahead, but she encouraged them to slip out of their heavy coats as soon as they had claimed their places on the train. She was wearing a light cotton summer dress and felt sorry for the overdressed children with their perspiring, red faces.

Brenda was fanning herself with her clipboard as they welcomed the last few passengers for this consignment. 'Once the train gets going, it won't seem so bad,' she said. 'We can open the carriage windows for a bit of a breeze.'

'I'm hoping we've enough water for the journey,' Dora said. 'They're all arriving thirsty enough as it is.' Few of the children carried flasks or bottles, though most had the usual packages of food prepared by loving mothers and doting aunts and grandmothers.

'I'll do a last check,' Brenda said. 'It won't do to run out if we get delayed or stuck in a siding when we're checked over. The last couple of times the soldiers have been very difficult and unpleasant.'

Both the guards assigned to travel with them on the train and those who came aboard if they were stopped were becoming increasingly jumpy. They too were aware of increasing tension between Germany and Britain, they too were wondering if this was the day the trigger would be pulled and they would receive new orders directing them to stand by for war, to leave these easy duties behind and head for the front.

Dora was thankful that the station concourse was shaded by a vast arching roof that gave the train and its waiting passengers some protection. They would all have been even hotter if their platform was out in the open, under the blazing sun. All around the station the scarlet Nazi banners hung limply, as if they too were drained by the heat.

She glanced towards the entrance, where the last few children were arriving, escorted by parents or other relatives. And then she recognised the familiar figure of Rufus Carrington coming towards them at a rapid pace.

She smiled and waved to him and, as he came closer, said, 'Mr Carrington, to what do we owe the pleasure this time?'

'I'm afraid it's not good news,' he said, catching his breath after his rush to the station. 'I knew you were all here and would be leaving this morning and I thought I should come myself and find you the minute I heard.'

Now Dora was alarmed. Surely war hadn't been declared already? 'Whatever is wrong? We're due to leave very shortly.'

'I know, that's why I thought I should come right away. We've just this minute heard – there's been a directive from the Home Office. They're stopping the Kindertransports.'

'Stopping them? But when?' Dora felt her heart thudding with shock.

'That's the problem. As of now.'

'But why? We've just checked through a whole trainload of

over two hundred children, all expecting to travel today. Their parents have already agreed to them going.' Dora looked over her shoulder at the anxious young faces pressed to the windows of the carriages and the clusters of families waiting to see the train depart.

'I don't know why it's just happened, exactly. I think they must believe we're reaching a critical point in negotiations with Germany. I must say it's very tense at the embassy. Everyone there is on tenterhooks.'

'I'm sure they are,' Dora snapped impatiently. 'We all know that things are reaching a crucial stage but these children have been told they're leaving today. They've all said goodbye to their families. It's a very sensitive and emotional time for them.' She looked around at the groups of relatives still standing nearby, watching and waiting, holding each other's hands, trying not to break down in tears. 'We can't let them all down.'

Carrington shook his head. 'I'm dreadfully sorry, I don't know what to say. I realise it's awful timing.'

'What's going on here?' Brenda approached them. 'Is there a problem, young man?'

He looked flustered confronted by Brenda's solid no-nonsense attitude. 'I've just been explaining—' he began.

'They're stopping the transports,' Dora blurted out. 'They can't really do that, can they?'

Brenda calmly asked for a full explanation and Carrington repeated exactly what he had just told Dora, finishing by saying, 'I'm so sorry to be the bearer of bad news. I've no idea exactly how this is going to be implemented and what it means for you right now, I just felt you had to know immediately.'

'Quite right, Mr Carrington,' Brenda said. 'It was very good of you to come in person and find us. However, as I have received no official communication on this matter what-soever, at this stage I consider that this transport has already been authorised and should proceed as scheduled. If the decision had been taken on high to halt this particular journey, then I am sure we would have been given prior notice. Don't worry, I shall take full responsibility for carrying on as planned.'

She shook Carrington's hand and thanked him again. 'Come along, Dora, we have our full quota for this trip and must prepare to leave in a couple of minutes. I'm sure we shall learn more in due course.'

The two women began to walk towards the waiting train, but Carrington darted after them and caught Dora by the arm. 'Forgive me,' he said, 'but could you pass my regards on to Verity— I mean Mrs Fitzgerald? I do hope she is in good health and a better frame of mind now.'

Dora looked into his eyes and saw genuine concern there. 'I'll do that. And thank you for thinking of her.'

'Please tell her I'd like to call on her when I return to London, if I may.' His face flushed and he stood forlornly on the platform as they boarded the train, which pulled out of the station only seconds later.

Dora looked back at him. He had taken off his hat and waved it as they rumbled out of Berlin. Had she misunderstood or had this self-effacing man just revealed his feelings for Verity? What a surprising match that would make, the modest diplomat and the dramatic widow.

She caught up with Brenda in the train corridor. 'What do you think is going to happen now?'

Brenda looked furious, with beetled brows and pursed lips. 'They can't stop our work just like that without prior warning. And it's not just this consignment we should be worried about, there's another three hundred travel documents already processed for the next transport. Just think of the distress this would cause all those desperate parents.'

'I know, those poor people. I can't bear to think how they'll feel. Those families have all agonised over making such an enormous decision and to think they might then have the chance taken away from them. It's just awful.'

'Stay calm, my dear. We'll do everything in our power to make sure it all goes through,' Brenda said. 'And not a word in front of the children, mind.'

The two women spent the next couple of hours checking that all the children were settled, before allowing themselves to rest in their own seats. Dora couldn't help turning the matter over and over in her mind. It must be true that the Home Office had decided to cancel the transports if the news had reached the embassy. But why hadn't it reached her and Brenda? Were they not to be consulted about such an important decision?

As the journey rumbled on, Dora must have eventually fallen into a deep sleep, for she woke with a start when the train stopped with a screech of brakes. She opened her eyes, thinking they must have been delayed at a checkpoint, and braced herself for officious soldiers disturbing the children. She stepped out into the corridor to see Brenda also peering out of the window. 'It's not a check, it's the border,' she called back. 'But something is happening. There are officials walking down the platform and none of the usual welcome committee.'

Dora looked out too. They had become used to the friendly farmers' wives greeting each trainload with much-appreciated supplies, but today none of that was waiting for them.

'I'm going outside to see what's happening,' Brenda said, donning her straw hat and taking her handbag. 'Tell the children to stay in their seats.'

Dora watched her alight from the train and walk to meet the uniformed men coming forward to meet her. There was much nodding of heads, waving of arms and pointing of fingers before Brenda returned to the train.

'It's worse than I feared,' she said. 'The children aren't going to be allowed to travel through Holland. The Dutch govern-ment has been told that this transport won't be admitted to

Britain.' She leant back against the walls of the carriage and closed her eyes, breathing fast.

'So what are we going to do now?' Dora was almost shaking with shock at this news. 'They can't do this to us, can they?'

'I'm afraid they can and they have, my dear. Diplomats! What kind of diplomacy behaves like this with desperate people? I despair of them, I really do.'

Dora caught Brenda's wrath in her words and began to feel angry herself. 'But what are we meant to do now?'

Brenda took a deep breath and pulled back her shoulders. 'We are going to have to take this train back to Germany. We have no choice. We'll tell the children there is a problem with the paperwork. They're used to people always asking questions about the right papers, so they won't get too worried. And I've told the Dutch that if they won't let the children into their country, the least they can do is bring us supplies for the return journey. They've promised that will be here shortly, after the train has picked up more fuel.'

Dora was trying to calm herself. Food would be welcome, but she couldn't help thinking that she and Brenda had failed in their mission. This transport was meant to offer two hundred children salvation and a future, not deliver them straight into the jaws of the monster that was growing stronger and more audacious by the hour.

FIFTY-NINE

EVERYBODY OFF

The trainload of confused children returned to Berlin in a dejected mood, despite the offerings of soft bread, chocolate and milk the Dutch had delivered before their departure from the border. Some of the older passengers, those in their early to mid-teenage years, had noticed that the train was retracing its original journey and approached Dora and Brenda. The two women found themselves compelled to answer their awkward questions more fully than they would have liked.

'We're hoping that this is simply a misunderstanding that can be sorted out once we get back to Berlin,' Brenda said. 'We're so sorry and we know it's very worrying for you. If you can, try and keep it to yourselves. We don't want to frighten the younger children.'

But Dora and Brenda couldn't help feeling unsettled themselves and when they finally arrived back in the city, they found the station was busier than ever. All around them people were piling onto trains with bursting luggage and there were impatient queues at the ticket office. There was a general sense of frenetic energy, anxiety and fear. Dora had to prevent desperate passengers trying to push their way onto the train still filled with children.

'It looks like everyone's in a panic and trying to get out of the city as soon as they can,' Brenda said.

Members of the Jewish Council were waiting for them with worried expressions, as were a number of parents. And alongside these expectant faces, Dora could see Rufus Carrington. She jumped off the train and ran to speak to him. 'We can't take the children off the train until we know exactly what is happening,' she said.

He sighed. 'All I'm officially allowed to say is that relations between His Majesty's government and Germany are strained.'

'And what's that supposed to mean? We've all known things have been tense for ages.' Dora was feeling impatient and wanted a straight answer.

'Young man, you tell us the truth, right this minute.' Brenda had noticed him there too and had marched across for an explanation. 'We need to know exactly what is going on. Now don't try pulling the wool over our eyes.'

He looked over his shoulder before speaking in a low, confidential voice, as if he didn't want to be overheard. 'The official line,' he said, 'is that relations are strained, but what it really means is that we're aware of German movements on the Polish border and we're rather expecting that Poland may be invaded imminently. And if, or rather when, that happens, the British government will issue an ultimatum and the next stage will be a declaration of war.'

'It's a tinderbox,' Brenda muttered. 'It's all about to blow up in our faces.'

'I'm rather afraid it's looking that way,' Carrington said. 'I'm so terribly sorry you couldn't get the children across the border and through Holland. As soon as I heard about it, I knew you'd all have to come back. And I was sure you'd stay with them rather than carrying on back to England without them. I knew you wouldn't leave the children on their own.'

'Of course we couldn't have left them. We were meant to be taking them to a safer place. They were meant to be escaping this terrible country.' Dora was nearer to tears than she had been throughout their whole journey. 'It's our duty to make sure we look after these children from start to finish but it seems we're just going to be handing them back to their families again, to face whatever terrible challenges the Nazis decide to throw at them next. We haven't achieved anything at all.'

'But you've done so much already,' he said, trying to reassure her. 'Your organisation has sent thousands of children to safety. That's an enormous achievement.'

'That's all very well,' Brenda said. 'But this is no time to start patting ourselves on the backs. We need to deal with the children we've got here right now. I'm going to talk to the local committee members and parents. They need an explanation and an apology.'

'I wish I could do something to help,' Carrington said. 'I know this isn't the result you wanted.'

'It certainly isn't what we wanted,' Dora said. 'And what about those who were expecting to come with us in the near future? There's another three hundred candidates with certified travel documents already waiting to travel. What are they meant to do now?'

'I'm afraid those papers will be invalidated,' he said. 'They're not going to be allowed to go with you. They'll all be staying here.'

'But they won't be able to stay, will they? Not for long at any rate. You know very well what's happening here. It's already started, hasn't it? People are being forced to move away to other countries, supposedly to free up jobs and homes here for Aryan Germans. They're even taking children away from their families if they aren't fit and healthy. There's no hope for them whatsoever if they stay here.' Dora couldn't help breaking into tears at the end of her outburst.

Carrington looked embarrassed by her emotions. He looked over towards Brenda and caught her eye. She nodded and came across as soon as she had finished talking to the other officials.

'Pull yourself together,' she said briskly. 'No point in upsetting the children now, is there?' She handed Dora a clean hankie. 'Dry your eyes and we'll go onto the train and tell the children that they are being collected out here on the platform. It's all arranged.'

'But what will happen to them?' Dora sniffed and gave her nose a good blow.

'Nothing for the moment. They'll go back to their homes and orphanages and carry on as normal. And we'll just have to wait to hear if the situation changes. Now get a move on and deal with the children. And after that we've got to see if we can get a train out of here ourselves.'

'I can help with that,' Carrington said. 'It's the least I can do. I'll join the queue at the box office over there and see if I can get tickets for you.'

'And if we can't get away today, can you and the embassy find us somewhere to stay in the meantime?' Brenda was back to being calm and efficient, dealing with the immediate problem.

'I'll see about the tickets first, then check the hotels,' Carrington said, then ran to join the ever-increasing queue of shuffling hopefuls laden with cases.

Dora sniffed again, told herself not to be so stupid, then boarded the train. 'Right, everyone,' she said as she went from one compartment to another. 'I'm terribly sorry, but there's been a mix-up and you're all going to have to go back home for now. Collect all your things and follow me.' She smiled brightly, even though she could feel her heavy heart weighing her down.

The children were obedient, filing off the train with their cases and coats. 'I don't want to put my coat back on,' one little girl said. 'It's too hot and that soldier tore the lining when we got on the train.'

'You don't have to wear it if you don't want to,' Dora said, thinking how shocked the child's mother or other guardian would be to see the rips in the satin lining of the once good coat. Unfortunately, it always happened to some of their passengers while the guards were searching for smuggled valuables, which they never succeeded in finding. And now that parent would not only be disappointed that their daughter hadn't been whisked to safety, but would also realise that even the train journey itself was not risk-free. If the Kindertransports were reinstated, would she be willing to send her daughter off again into the unknown, or would she be more inclined to keep her close by her side?

Finally, all the children had left the train and been assigned to their destination. Brenda looked as exhausted as Dora felt. 'I must say, I'd rather like a night in an hotel before taking another train journey,' she said. 'Let's hope we can catch our breath before we have to start all over again.'

Carrington came running towards them, waving two tickets. 'You can leave tomorrow. After that I wouldn't be too sure. And I've managed to find you a room for the night at the Hotel Kaiserhof. They could only offer one room, I'm afraid, so I hope you don't mind sharing.'

Dora frowned, 'Isn't that the hotel favoured by the Nazis? Hitler himself is rather fond of it too, I've heard.'

He flushed, as he was wont to do. 'I'm afraid it is, but there isn't much choice tonight. Just about everywhere is full. It seems a lot of people are staying over while they wait for transport out of the city. It's all a bit chaotic, I'm afraid.'

'Never mind, Dora. It will do. I'm sure we can put up with it for one night.' Brenda shook Carrington's hand. 'Thank you. It's very kind of you to find a room for us. Now, I'm sure you're needed back at the embassy. This must be a very busy time for you all.'

'It is rather. But I got permission to leave my desk to see that you had accommodation and the means to travel tomorrow. We're all aware that this unexpected situation has been rather hard on you.'

'Well, that's an understatement if ever I heard one,' Brenda said with a sardonic smile. 'But none of it is your fault and we're very grateful to you for all you've done for us.'

Carrington turned to Dora. 'Please don't forget my earlier request. About Mrs Fitzgerald.'

'I hadn't forgotten. I'll be sure to tell her and to say that you have been most kind. Thank you.' Dora shook his hand and dipped to pick up her case, but he was there before her and took Brenda's case too.

'The least I can do is help you into a cab. The hotel's a bit of a walk from here.' He strode ahead, balancing the two suitcases, but when he reached the entrance his face fell; there was a huge queue waiting for taxis.

'Never mind, Mr Carrington,' Brenda said. 'We know the way and we're far from helpless. You get back to your desk and carry on with your work. That's much more important.'

'No, no, I'll walk with you. It's on my way.' He picked up the cases again and strode out into the street.

Dora started to rather hope he would soon leave as he kept asking questions, hovering by her side. 'How is Mrs Fitzgerald getting along now? Do you think receiving the ashes helped her to come to terms with her husband's death?'

What could Dora say in truth? Verity had gratefully received the urn – or preserved ginger jar – but hadn't done any more with it or mentioned any plans to take the ashes to Ireland. 'To be honest, Mr Carrington, I think she is still getting over the shock. But what seems to be bringing her the greatest comfort are the children we have staying with us now.' She told him the story of Ruth and the twins, and noted his surprise.

'But that's wonderful. It sounds as if she has a natural talent with them.'

'To tell the truth, Mr Carrington, it has been a complete surprise to me. I've known Verity since we were children and I'd never known her to have such sympathies before. It has been a revelation.'

As they reached Wilhelmstrasse, where the embassy was located, he handed over their cases, saying, 'I'm afraid I must leave you now, but please don't hesitate to contact me if I can be of further service.'

They thanked him again and walked the last ten minutes to the hotel side by side. 'What a nice, decent man,' Brenda said. 'I do hope he and the embassy staff are all well-treated when they finally bring down the curtain.'

SIXTY

ROSA

BERLIN, AUGUST 1939

Rumours were rife in Scheunenviertel, but perhaps the whole of Berlin was asking what would happen next, Rosa thought. Those with access to newspapers and radios said Germany would soon be at war, while others only wanted to concentrate on finding their next crust of bread.

'If there is another war,' Liese said, her eyes bright with hope, 'that might be good news for our husbands. Jews fought bravely in the last war and men will be needed to fight again.' That day she had brought Rosa cooked potatoes and boiled eggs – they wouldn't be hungry for once.

'True, but will they be fit enough to fight when they are released? You know what is being said about those camps. If anyone is lucky enough to come out alive, they are no longer the men they once were.'

'But we must keep hoping, Rosa. We cannot give up hope. Just like you hope for the children you sent away. Have you heard any more?'

Rosa hadn't told Liese exactly how she had delivered her twins to the train. She was too ashamed and worried. She had let her think she had been able to gain a place for them legitimately. 'I haven't had any more news, but I tell myself that my twins are thriving and must be learning to speak English by now. I make Theresia laugh by telling her that she now has an English brother and sister and that when we all meet again, we shall have to ask them to teach us and not the other way round.'

'Of course, that will be their first language. They will be English children. And if there is a war anything like the last one it will be quite some time before they can come back here.'

If at all, Rosa thought. If ever. And if they do return one day, will we still be here? Will Theresia ever meet her brother and sister again?

'If there is a war, will you stay here in Berlin?' Rosa knew that Liese had relatives in the countryside. 'German cities are bound to be targets for bombs.'

'I think I'd have to take the children away. And if Isaac came back and couldn't find me, he'd guess I'd gone to stay with my family. What about you?'

Rosa shook her head. 'Sadly, we don't have choices like you do. I suppose I could try to get to my family in Bad Pyrmont, but escaping to another Jewish community wouldn't guarantee our safety. It could be like jumping from the frying pan into the fire. Anyway, I haven't heard from my mother for some time, so I really don't know if they are still there. As you know, we keep hearing how Jews are being forced to resettle in the east – they may all be in Poland by now.'

Liese hugged her friend. 'I'm so sorry I can't be more help to you. If I go, I won't stop wondering how you are both coping.'

Rosa hugged her back. 'You've been a wonderful comfort to us throughout, keeping us well and hopeful. But you must leave if you think it will be safer for you and your children. Besides, if I stay in Berlin, Josef will be more likely to find me when he returns.' She'd noted that Liese had said 'if' her husband returned. But she still had hope. She laughed. 'He'll be surprised when I tell him he's got to learn to speak English too.'

Rosa tried to shrug off her fears about a possible war, her doubts about the future. Today was all that mattered. Today she had to queue for bread, today she had to ensure Theresia still went to her Jewish school in their poor district, today she had to boil water to wash her remaining child. Today was all that mattered. Tomorrow would come and she would face its challenges when she woke.

SIXTY-ONE

COCKTAILS AND COLOGNE
BERLIN, AUGUST 1939

The imposing Hotel Kaiserhof in Wilhelmplatz was right next to the Reich Chancellery and was considered to be the grandest and most up-to-date hotel in Berlin. It was where Hitler had returned to meet his cohorts to announce he had been elected chancellor, six years previously.

'I must say, it's a bit of a treat being put up in a place like this, despite the clientele,' Brenda said as they stepped through the colonnaded entrance into a vast, brightly lit, high-ceilinged hall filled with a swarm of field-grey military uniforms and stylishly dressed women. 'Don't catch their eye,' she added as they headed towards the reception desk through a cloud of cigarette smoke and cologne.

'You'd think they'd have better things to be doing at a time like this, rather than swanning around a posh hotel,' Dora said as they waited to catch the attention of the receptionist. 'Maybe they don't believe war is imminent.'

'It doesn't surprise me they'd rather be having cocktails,' Brenda said. 'But then they've always liked the good things in life, for all their so-called social principles.'

At that moment, a heavily cologne-scented officer in a black and silver uniform came up behind them. 'Good evening, ladies. I couldn't help overhearing your conversation. You are English, I believe. Won't you join my fellow officers and myself for a while this evening? We should be most grateful for the pleasure of your charming company.'

'I'm terribly sorry, but we must decline your very kind invitation,' Brenda said. 'We have a long journey ahead of us tomorrow. We intend taking supper in our room and are looking forward to an early night.'

'But I'm afraid I must insist,' he said, taking hold of the cases they had set down on the floor of the reception area while they were standing at the desk. 'We are most interested in hearing about your journey and your time in Berlin.'

'But we're very tired,' Dora couldn't help blurting out. 'We have been travelling for the last two days. We must rest.'

Brenda gave her a withering look, then spoke to the officer. 'Please convey our apologies to your colleagues, but we cannot possibly accept.'

'It will only take a moment of your time.' The officer was joined by a second, equally smart uniformed man, all gleaming buttons and slicked-back hair. 'We must insist. You may join us here at our table in the hotel or we may have to suggest taking our conversation elsewhere, which might not be quite so convenient, nor so salubrious.'

In that instant, they both realised the atmosphere had chilled and they had no choice but to comply with these determined officers. After collecting their key, they followed the men to a corner of the salon, where they were forced to sit on a velvet banquette seat, hemmed in by the men who sat either side of them, facing two more equally smart and scented officers across the circular table.

'I am sure you will enjoy taking a glass of *Sekt* with us,' the second officer said. 'In case you are not familiar with it, this is the sparkling wine of Germany. The French can boast all they like of their champagne, but this wine is superior, produced from our country's famous Riesling.'

They could not refuse him and sipped the glasses set before them. It was most refreshing after their long day, but Dora couldn't enjoy it as the persistent questions began and continued.

'You must tell us what two such charming ladies are doing here, visiting Berlin at this particular time.'

Despite the extremely polite manner in which they phrased their enquiries, Dora felt a shiver run down her neck, but she detected a suppressed laugh in Brenda's reply.

'I am sure you gentlemen must have better things to do, considering your country's present state of affairs, than idly passing the time drinking *Sekt*.'

'Dear ladies,' said the first officer with a wolfish smile, 'I can assure you we are most interested in your reasons for being here and we are willing to make this encounter a pleasant one. I'm sure you will agree that this is a much more conducive ambience for civil conversation than a police station.'

'I really can't think why you would need us to talk to you there.' Brenda's voice was level and calm, with not a hint of nervousness. 'We are merely British charity workers representing Quakers in England.'

'Indeed? And what brings you to Berlin?'

'I am quite sure you already know all about our reasons for being here. You and your people take a very close interest in all the comings and goings of foreigners in your country. And why you should be so interested now, when you should be looking to your border with Poland, I cannot think.'

He laughed, a brittle laugh. 'Ha, so clever. News travels fast, does it not?' He looked around at his colleagues. 'I think we need to probe a little deeper, don't you?'

Dora was clutching the stem of her glass so tightly she

feared it might break. She hoped Brenda could continue deflecting their questions.

'And what about your young companion? Perhaps we should ask her what you've been up to?' He turned his steely gaze on Dora.

His blue eyes were cold and his thin lips weren't smiling. She dreaded having to answer him and hoped her quivering lips didn't reveal how frightened she really was.

'Just tell us exactly what kind of work you two have been doing,' he said. 'And then we can let you retire to your room for a comfortable night. I'm sure you would prefer that to some of the other establishments we are able to offer.'

Dora glanced at Brenda, who nodded as if she was giving her assent. 'We have been to Berlin several times over the past year, actually. With your government's permission, we have been arranging for children to leave Germany and come to live in Britain temporarily.'

'Delightful,' he said. 'What kind of children, may I ask? Is your country that much in need of young blood to strengthen its workforce?'

Dora's mouth felt dry and she quickly took a sip of the *Sekt*; it tingled as she swallowed. 'Jewish children. We've been taking Jewish children to Britain.'

'Oh really? Are you sure you're not taking our healthy Aryan boys and girls away?'

'No, I think they've only been Jewish children so far.' Dora knew this wasn't strictly correct as some journeys had also included a few disabled children, whose families knew their future was bleak if they stayed in Germany.

'Well, we don't care if you take the dregs of society, do we?' He slammed the table with the flat of his hand and laughed along with his fellow officers. 'If you don't get rid of them for us, we'll have to do it ourselves eventually. You've been saving us the trouble.'

'But we couldn't enter the Netherlands with our latest consignment. That's why we've been travelling for the last two days and why we had to come back to Berlin.'

He took a cigarette from a gold case and took his time lighting it. 'And now even your own government doesn't want these Jewish children. They've sent them back to us so we can deal with them.'

Dora hated everything about him: his tone, his words, his laughter, his languid flicking of ash. She had to bite her tongue to stop herself answering back.

'But are you sure that's all you've been taking? We can't trust the Jews, not even their children. They're not above stealing valuables that rightly belong to the Reich and smuggling them out of the country.'

With a flip of her heart, Dora remembered the little tin Herr Friedmann had pressed into her hand all those months ago. Thank goodness she hadn't accepted anything like that since.

'My friends,' he said, addressing his colleagues, 'I'm sure the ladies will understand if we take a quick look at their luggage while they are here.'

One of the other officers smirked and slammed Dora's case onto the table, clicked open the catches and tipped out the contents. Her underthings and stockings, both clean and not-clean, fell out in a pile.

Dora was mortified by the public exposure of her personal belongings. Despite the chattering crowd around them in the salon, all drinking and laughing, she could only see and hear what was in front of her. He picked up a pair of her knickers, stretched them with both hands, holding them up so anyone could see. And then his companion handed him a penknife and he slashed the lining of her case and groped underneath the material.

'Nichts,' he said and reached for Brenda's suitcase. He

opened it and placed it so the lid was upright, shielding the contents. He rummaged through her effects and suddenly, with a triumphant smile, held up a glittering brooch.

'That's not mine,' Brenda said with a scoff. 'I've never seen it before in my life.'

Dora hadn't ever seen Brenda wear any kind of jewellery, not even a ring. She wasn't that kind of woman. But could she perhaps have been persuaded to hide some valuables for a desperate Jewish parent? Her mouth was dry with nerves as she realised they could both be imprisoned for this. On the brink of war, these officers had no regard for the niceties of diplomacy and were enjoying toying with her and Brenda for their own amusement. She set down her glass and clenched her trembling hands in her lap, hoping that her fear was not apparent to these arrogant men.

'Perhaps you have forgotten you were taking it to sell for one of your Jewish friends?' the smoking officer said with a sly smile. He held out his hand and examined the brooch. 'This looks very like real diamonds to me, of considerable value. What do you think?' He passed it to the officer next to him.

'Smuggled diamonds. They always think they can get away with it,' he said, weighing it in his hand.

'Perhaps we should have it verified first before we start accusing these dear ladies of smuggling.' The first officer turned to the women and said, 'You won't be going anywhere tonight. We shall make sure of that. We will let you know in the morning if you are free to catch your train.'

Dora's heart was thudding so fast she thought she might faint; she felt so dizzy. The officers must have planted that brooch. But could they arrest them and detain them? What if they missed their train and were imprisoned on the eve of war? She desperately wished she could call Carrington at the embassy.

'You all know jolly well that we have nothing whatsoever to

do with that jewel, whether it's real or paste,' Brenda said. 'Now, if you've finished your little game, my colleague and I would like to go to our room.' She stood, gathered the contents of the cases together in handfuls and started to repack their luggage.

Dora stood up too, though her whole being was trembling, and the man beside her slid across the banquette seat so they could both leave the table. 'Allow me to escort you to your room,' he said. 'And for your safety I will post a guard outside your door tonight.'

'That really won't be necessary,' Brenda said, holding her head high. 'I shall inform the British embassy of this meeting tonight.'

He followed them all the same as Brenda led the way to the lifts. All three passengers stood stiffly, shoulder to shoulder, as the bell boy took them to the third floor.

When they reached the room allocated to them, Brenda unlocked the door and ushered Dora inside, then turned to deliver one final retort to their unwelcome companion. 'We are now going to order room service. We shall expect no further trouble from you. Good night to you.'

Inside the room, Dora slumped onto the bed. 'That was horrible. They can't really accuse us of smuggling, can they?'

'Of course not,' Brenda said. 'The whole thing was a charade, designed to intimidate us. They were enjoying themselves. Now, why don't we order some delicious food? You must be hungry. I know I am. And it might be a good idea if you phone your young man at the embassy and tell him what's been going on. After all the trouble he went to, getting us tickets for the morning, he certainly wouldn't want us to miss our train.'

SIXTY-TWO

GIVE MY REGARDS

BERLIN, AUGUST 1939

Dora barely slept that night. She couldn't stop herself thinking about their chilling encounter with the German officers. The thought that a guard had been placed outside their hotel room door also unnerved her. They could never sneak past him. And what if a new accusation was made against them in the morning? If they were marched to a police station for questioning their departure would be delayed and who knew when they might be able to book more tickets with so many trying to escape Berlin now that the drums of war were beating?

Brenda's soft snores rose and fell in the twin bed next to hers. She'd had no trouble falling asleep after their supper and a refreshing bath.

Once they had ordered food through room service, Dora had called Carrington. She couldn't speak to him immediately as the switchboard operator said he was in a meeting, but he rang the hotel about twenty minutes later.

'Is everything all right there? You've got the room I booked for you?'

'Yes, it's fine. We're having supper brought up but we had a rather bruising encounter with some German officers, downstairs, just after we arrived. Oh, sorry, not literally bruising, I meant annoying and awkward.'

'In what way?'

'They insisted we joined them at their table and then, after a few questions, they went through our cases and found a brooch. They tried to suggest that we were trying to smuggle diamonds out of the country.'

'There's no way it could have been slipped into your luggage by someone else?'

'Only by them. We're convinced they were trying to plant it on us. They've left a guard outside our door and we were told they would check whether the diamonds were real, then let us know if we could leave tomorrow.'

She heard him take a deep breath on the other end of the line. She also thought she heard some unusual clicking, as well as other, distant voices. 'Don't worry,' he said. 'I'll make sure you'll be able to leave tomorrow. It's getting rather frantic here, but there's no point in them hanging on to you.'

'What's happening now? We're completely in the dark here.'

'I can't say much but I will say this to you and to anyone else who is listening in on this conversation: you will both be allowed to leave the hotel tomorrow and will be able to get on the train home. I will meet you in the foyer in the morning and take you to the station myself. There will be no more of these ridiculous games.'

Dora was reassured by the confidence in his words, but however much she repeated them to herself in the middle of the night she still couldn't sleep. She felt that the Nazis were becoming more and more daring and that any protection previously afforded to her and Brenda by their charitable status and nationality no longer counted for anything.

. . .

In the morning the two women both washed and dressed, then Brenda cautiously unlocked the door and looked up and down the corridor. 'Well, that's a surprise. There's no one here,' she said with a shrug. 'Maybe your man's words did the trick last night.'

After a hasty breakfast they met Carrington in the vast lobby, which was buzzing with uniforms and bustling staff. 'I've got a cab waiting outside,' he said, taking their cases and leading the way through the glass doors.

He was red-eyed and looked exhausted. In the taxi, he said, 'It's been pretty busy all night. I couldn't really tell you anything on the phone in case it was tapped but the ambassador has been called into a meeting with Hitler himself. And the Germans have stopped all telecommunications beyond their borders. It's really coming to a head now, so it's a good thing you're getting out today.'

'What do you think is going to happen next?' Brenda asked the question; Dora couldn't speak as she was so nervous and holding her breath.

'It looks as if they are going to find a pretext for invading Poland any minute now. Then our country will have to issue an ultimatum, giving them time to withdraw, which they will almost certainly refuse to do. After that' – he drew a deep breath – 'if they don't meet the deadline, Britain will issue a declaration of war.'

He put his head in his hands and, as he lifted it again, Dora thought she could see the sheen of tears in his reddened eyes. He swallowed hard and said, 'When that happens, we will stop the clock in the embassy and close everything down.'

Dora felt sympathy for this kind, thoughtful man, facing such a critical time. 'And what will happen to you, the ambassador and all the staff?'

He tried to smile. 'Oh, we'll all be all right. We expect that, shortly after that, the Germans will cut our phone lines and

send troops in to detain everyone. After a few days, we'll probably be exchanged for the staff at the German embassy in
London and then we'll all be able to come home. It will all be
quite civil.'

'But nevertheless distressing for you,' Brenda said. 'We shall
be thinking of you as events unfold.'

Dora stared out of the window, deep in thought. People
were scurrying through the streets, many of them with suitcases
and bags. If ordinary Germans were supporting this corrupt
regime, why did so many appear to be leaving a sinking ship?
The regime was strong, the Nazis were confident and arrogant,
but perhaps normal people were sensing what might be about to
happen and weren't in favour of this aggressive stance.

When they reached the station, which was just as busy as
the day before, Carrington carried their cases to the waiting
train. They had a few minutes before departure and Brenda
said, 'I want to thank you most sincerely, young man. Your help
has been much appreciated. I hope you bear up with fortitude
as the next few days unfold.'

He shook her hand and then turned to Dora. 'I'll think of
you when you are back in London,' he said. 'I hope you will find
that the children you rescued are thriving.'

'I'm sure they will be,' she said. 'And you don't need to
remind me again about your special message for my cousin.
Please come and see all of us when you finally return. We'd be
delighted to see you again and hear how you've managed
through this crisis.'

She thought her last words seemed to please him; his smile
was stronger as he shook her hand and doffed his hat.

Once they had found their seats on the crowded train and
stowed their cases in the overloaded luggage rack, Dora leant
back with a sigh of relief. Surely nothing could stop them
leaving Berlin now? She closed her eyes for a second, just to
enjoy the moment, and when she opened them again and

scanned the platform she saw that Carrington was still standing there. Perhaps he felt he couldn't leave until the train was actually on its way, bearing them back to the Netherlands and on to Britain.

Brenda saw her watching and said, 'He's a very decent young man. His sort have been trying to control this explosive situation, but it sounds as if the balloon is going to go up at any moment.' She sighed, folded her hands in her lap and closed her eyes. 'Now let's rest while we can.'

At that moment the whistle blew, the train began to roll and Dora could finally close her eyes and sleep.

SIXTY-THREE
HOME SWEET HOME
LONDON, AUGUST 1939

'I can't tell you how relieved I am to have you home at last, darling. I've been dreading the news every day,' Hugh said, almost lifting Dora off the floor with his bear hug.

'And I can't tell you how glad I am to be back,' she said, burying her face in his shirt-sleeves. His familiar smell, of Imperial Leather shaving soap with a top note of hospital disinfectant was deeply comforting. 'That last night in the hotel in Berlin, I barely slept, even though I was worn out. I began to think they were prepared to conjure up any kind of false pretext to keep us there. I was so afraid we wouldn't get away.'

'But you're here now and you won't be going back.'

'I don't see how we can, unless the ban on the transports is lifted. But we're devastated to think of the children we nearly saved. We've had to leave hundreds of them to their fate. And it's not just those who were on that particular train either. So many other families had struggled to obtain visas for their children and thought they were going to be able to send them away soon too.'

'You've done so much, darling. You knew it would come to an end one day.'

'I know, but we had to keep going while we could. And now I doubt that anyone who is Jewish, or who objects to the regime, will ever be able to leave. It's so depressing.'

'It has to reach a head soon, it has to. It's just a matter of time.'

'Do you know, I sort of feel as I've been waiting for that moment forever. We've seen it all coming for ages, haven't we?'

Hugh kissed her again and led her into the kitchen. It was late at night and the house was quiet. He prepared scrambled eggs and made her sit down with a cup of tea. It was a warm balmy evening and the back door was open, so the scent of roses wafted inside. A moth made a desperate dive for the overhead light, bruising its wings on the hot lightbulb.

'Have you all been well here, while I've been gone?' Dora sipped her tea and felt herself finally beginning to relax after the last few stressful days.

'The babies are thriving, Ruth has made more friends at school and Nanny Jenkins is ruling the roost. I must say she's done Verity a power of good. Keeps her busy doing chores and shopping for the little ones. She hasn't mentioned Raven once.'

'So no more talk of taking his ashes to Ireland?'

'None that I've heard. I think that jar is still sitting on that table on the landing upstairs. And at this rate it may well sit there until we know whether there's going to be another war or not.' He slid the steaming plate towards her.

She glanced at the creamy, golden eggs. There was buttered toast on the side of the plate. 'Are you sure we can spare this much?'

Hugh winked. 'We've got plenty, and plenty for the foresee-able future as well. While you were away, I got us some hens. Ruth is loving them. We finished the hen house and run over the weekend, settled them in and the very first morning she wanted to go out and see if they'd laid.'

'And had they? That soon?'

'They certainly had. Ruth was thrilled. And, you'd have loved it, darling, she wore a little apron Nanny Jenkins had made for her and carried a basket to collect the eggs. She looked adorable.'

Hugh had such a broad smile as he recalled the scene and Dora suddenly felt two conflicting emotions. The first was regret that she had not been there to see the little girl's delight, while the second was a wave of love for Hugh at seeing his fondness for this child and her progress after her trauma. Here was the father he could be, if they were one day able to have children of their own.

'You're looking sad, darling,' he said. 'Are the eggs not to your taste or are you worn out?'

She ate another forkful for him to show that the supper was perfect. 'I'm just tired. And so happy to be back with you and our family.' And as she said that, she momentarily thought that this might be it, this might be their family. For if the war happened and dragged on, they might be content with this little family, the twins and Ruth, here in the house where she and Verity had once been single young women.

A shuffle of slippers in the hallway caught her ear and Verity tiptoed in, wearing cool silk pyjamas. 'I didn't want to disturb you,' she said, hugging Dora, 'but I thought I could hear you. So glad you're safely back. I've been so worried.'

'Well, I'm here now and I won't be going anywhere for a bit. I won't be able to.' Dora quickly related the story of the halt to the transports and how upsetting it had been having to return their young passengers to Berlin.

'Gosh, darling, how dreadful for all of you. Those poor little mites. I can't bear to think how it must have affected them. When I think of dear Ruth and all she's suffered, I could never contemplate sending her back to that.' Despite her concern, Verity looked up at Hugh and said, 'You couldn't manage to conjure up another cup of tea, could you, darling?'

Hugh wearily shook his head with a smile, put the kettle back on the stove, rinsed the teapot and added three fresh scoops of tea.

'Please don't say anything to Ruth. About the children going back to Berlin, I mean,' Dora said. 'She wanted me to go back there and help, but I think she'd find this setback too upsetting. She just didn't want me to come back with any more babies.' Dora just about managed a smile at her final words.

'Gosh no, two is quite enough. Though Ruth simply adores them. They're getting quite smiley and she rushes off to see them every single day after school. I think they're really good for her.'

And then Dora remembered the message she had promised to deliver. 'Oh, and I almost completely forgot. You remember Rufus Carrington, the chap from the embassy?'

'How could I possibly forget? He's the dear man who saved me when those brutes dragged me off the train. I certainly owe him, even though he's got terrible taste in shoes.' Verity was laughing as she recalled the incident, dreadful though it had been at the time.

'He was the hero of the hour again on this trip too. He saved Brenda and me from an awful lot of trouble. I don't know how we'd have managed if he hadn't been there to help. And I don't just mean carrying our cases and taking us by cab to the station on the last day. But what I also wanted to say is that he was very sweet and concerned about you. Wanted to know how you were getting on and passed on his regards. He was quite insistent in fact, and mentioned it more than once.'

'He is rather sweet. A bit drab, but sweet all the same.'

'Vee, I think he rather likes you. I hope you don't mind, but I found myself saying that when he gets back to England he'd be very welcome to call on us.' Dora was studying Verity's face. Was this inappropriate for a widow of less than a year?

But a little smile flitted across her cousin's face with a slight flutter of eyelashes as she said, 'Well, why on earth not? He's been a good friend, hasn't he?'

Dora caught Hugh's eye as he poured fresh tea and passed a cup to Verity. He raised an eyebrow and she understood his meaning. The old Verity might be re-emerging. Not quite the same as she once was, but alive nevertheless.

SIXTY-FOUR

LONDON CALLING

At any other time it would have been the perfect Sunday morning. Dora and Hugh had woken early and taken their breakfast of boiled eggs and toast in the kitchen. They'd let the hens out of their run but left the collecting of eggs to Ruth, who now regarded it as her personal responsibility and took great delight in proudly bringing them indoors every day.

After they'd eaten and scraped their crusts and eggshells into the food box for the hens, Dora and Hugh held hands as they walked to the Meeting House for Sunday Meeting, which was even more subdued than usual. Rows of Friends sat with their heads bent, silent as they hoped and prayed. Everyone was still within their own thoughts, praying for peace and knowing that the day was going to bring dramatic news one way or another.

When they returned to the house, Verity had already peeled potatoes and seared the beef ready for the oven. She looked up as they came in and said, 'I thought we were going to need a good lunch, whatever happens.' She didn't often assume control in the kitchen, but the apron suited her.

Nanny Jenkins carried the twins out into the garden and

laid them in the Silver Cross pram that had been brought down on the train from Yorkshire. Despite lulling three generations of Ponsonbys to sleep on long strolls, it was still sturdy. Ruth was told she could rock the pram and walk it around the garden, but she was not to come indoors until she was called.

All four adults gathered round the kitchen table and Hugh ceremoniously switched on the radio. According to the clock it was five minutes before the quarter-hour, but Hugh checked his watch all the same. They heard the final stirring strains of 'Finlandia', the rousing hymn composed by Sibelius earlier in the century to support Finland's opposition to Russian oppression. Earlier that morning they had heard an announcement on the radio telling them to stand by for an announcement from the prime minister at 11.15 a.m. precisely.

As they sat waiting for the music to finish, Dora gazed out into the garden. It was a sunny day, the roses were still in flower, the hens were scratching in their run, Ruth was singing to the twins as next door's cat rubbed its head against her legs, asking to be stroked. But the adults sat in silence, hands clasped in laps or clenched on the tabletop, waiting.

As the music that had punctuated broadcasts all morning finished, they heard the level tones of the announcer say, *This is London. You will now hear a statement from the prime minister.* Verity's hand crept towards Dora's and gripped it tight while they listened to Neville Chamberlain's weary voice.

> *I am speaking to you from the cabinet room at 10 Downing Street. This morning the British ambassador in Berlin handed the German government a final note stating that unless we heard from them by 11 o'clock that they were prepared to withdraw their troops at once from Poland a state of war would exist between us. I have to tell you now that no such undertaking has been received, and that consequently this country is at war with Germany.*

Dora closed her eyes as he continued to speak. She heard Nanny Jenkins' gasp and Hugh's intake of breath and felt Verity's hand tighten on hers. When Chamberlain had finished speaking, various announcements were made regarding the precautions the population should take and warnings about gas masks and shelters, but Dora couldn't listen any longer. It seemed that a great silence had fallen upon them all as they sat there with their own thoughts and fears. She opened her eyes and glanced at the kitchen clock. It should have stopped at this momentous time, she thought, just like the clock in the embassy in Berlin was now being stopped, just like all of normal life had just stopped.

Then Hugh broke the silence: 'I think what we now need is something to stiffen our resolve.' He opened the glass door of the dresser, took out four glasses and poured each of them a large dry sherry.

'That's just the kind of medicine I'd have recommended,' Nanny Jenkins said. 'Though my single malt is all the way upstairs in my room.'

'Here's to a short conflict,' Hugh said. 'May it be over by Christmas.'

'They're saying children should be evacuated from London,' Verity said. 'Do you really think that's necessary? Ruth is so settled in her school, I'd hate to move her.'

'What do you think, Hugh?' Dora rather agreed with her cousin. Everyone in London had been carrying a gas mask for over a year now and children had been rehearsing with them in their schools. 'We've got the cellar after all, that should protect us, shouldn't it?'

'I'm not sure,' he said, studying his cuffs. 'We don't know exactly what kind of weapons might be deployed. I think we'd sleep easier if the children were somewhere safe.'

'I could take them all back to Yorkshire,' Nanny Jenkins

said. 'We'd be far away from any big towns and cities. They'd be perfectly safe there.'

'But how would you manage? And I'd miss them all terribly, especially Ruth.' Verity looked almost tearful.

'You wouldn't have to miss a thing. You'll be coming with me, Miss Verity. An extra pair of hands would be most welcome. We'd get a girl in from the village to help with the washing too. And I'd need you with me to keep your mother and grandmother out of our hair – we wouldn't want them poking their noses in too often.'

'But we won't all be able to fit into your lodge house, would we?'

'Of course not. That's why we'll be staying in the big house. If your parents object, you'll have to talk them round. And little Ruth can go to the village school. She'd thrive there.'

Dora loved hearing Nanny's common-sense attitude to this shocking announcement. And it helped her to make up her mind about how she would face this uncertain future. 'And I'll stay here to continue our work at Bloomsbury House. We won't be able to go abroad to escort any more children, but there'll be plenty of work for us to do with the refugees who've already come here and any others who may manage to get out. There might be an exodus from the Netherlands soon.'

Hugh clasped Dora's hands. 'I know my skills will be needed, unfortunately. I'll either be here in London or go wherever I'm needed.' For a few seconds they all sat there, each of them resolved to do their best at coping with what might lie ahead.

And seconds later, they all jumped with alarm as they heard the blast of a siren, followed by the sound of shouting in the street. 'Surely not so soon,' Dora said as she heard Ruth scream with fright outside in the garden.

Nanny Jenkins ran to fetch the children with Verity, Dora rushed to switch on the cellar lights and Hugh dashed out to the street, then helped them all down the rickety stairs. They stayed there in the musty basement for about fifteen minutes, until Hugh said, 'I'm going up to check what's happening. I can't hear anything outside now.'

He came back ten minutes later and, as he opened the door, they could all hear the single continuous note of the all-clear signal. 'It was a false alarm. Apparently, a plane was seen flying up the Thames.' He laughed, 'It was a French plane too. Trust the French to put the wind up us all. Oh well, it's given everyone a taste of what's to come and a chance to improve our shelters.'

'We'll find some cushions and blankets,' Dora said. 'We might as well be comfortable.' She thought she should sweep away the dust and cobwebs as well if they were to stay hidden underneath the house for any length of time.

Nanny Jenkins went back out to the garden with Ruth and the twins. Dora could see her laying the babies down on a blanket on the lawn to kick their legs and gurgle. *We should all enjoy the last days of the summer*, she thought, *before we're in danger from the bombs and poison gases that people are saying might engulf London.*

Hugh offered everyone a second sherry and when they all declined, decided he'd have another anyway. 'We'd better stock up; we'll need plenty of stuff like this for our nerves from now on.'

'And I'd better get on with lunch,' Verity said, quickly blowing her nose on a hankie plucked from her apron pocket. 'We need to eat well while we can.'

'I'll help you,' Dora said.

She drained the parboiled potatoes and handed Verity the bean slicer. Her cousin was not a practised cook, but was quite capable of stringing the home-grown runner beans they had succeeded in growing through the summer.

'At least we'll have lots of lovely fresh vegetables if we go up to Yorkshire,' Verity said. 'And we should have a good supply of eggs and milk from the farm.'

'I'll miss you all, of course, but I think it's a very sensible idea.' Dora dotted the potatoes with lard, then slid them into the oven alongside the beef.

'Maybe I'll have to learn to milk cows and drive a tractor up there, if all the male farmhands have to go off and fight.'

Dora laughed. The thought of her elegant socialite cousin working outside had once seemed impossible, but now maybe it wasn't. She glanced at her. Verity's hair was simply curled under, tied with a plain black ribbon. She wore a pale blue cotton dress, topped by that sprigged apron, and her usually bright red lips were bare. But she was still beautiful, plain and unadorned as she was.

'Oh, Vee, how I'd love to see you getting your hands dirty on the farm. That would be so funny. What on earth would your mother say?'

'Oh, knowing her she'd think of some fashionable, charitable cause desperate for her support and insist that I help her.' Verity frowned. 'Though I'm thinking that Daddy will have to change his mind about Mosley. That might not go down too well now. He'd be better off demonstrating he's changed his sympathies by offering to house wounded officers or some such worthy thing.'

Dora turned her attention to podding the last of the summer's peas. They'd had a plentiful crop, owing to the good weather and Verity and Ruth's help in watering the vegetable patch. The peas were picked regularly and were smooth and green, not wrinkled and hard. 'I think I'll make us a crumble,' she said. 'What do you fancy? Apple or gooseberry?'

'Let's go mad,' Verity said. 'Why can't we have both? I want this to be the most perfect Sunday lunch we've ever had. All of us here together for maybe one last Sunday.'

SIXTY-FIVE

LOST LUGGAGE

Dora decided to walk home after work that day. She had felt stifled in the office, surrounded by pitiful letters from parents who now knew they would never be able to send their children away from danger. She had written again to the mother of the twins and also to Ruth's mother, in the vain hope that she would ever receive a reply from either of them. Yet she knew she was obliged to tell them of their children's progress and the imminent move to Yorkshire. It had been decided to give Verity's parents and staff time to prepare a suite of rooms for their young guests, hence the delay in leaving London. There had been no further response from Ruth's aunt in Hampstead either, but she had to write to that address too. Sometimes it felt as if she and her household were the only ones loving these children and taking pride in their well-being and development.

Just as she turned the corner of the garden square opposite the house in the early-evening sunshine, she saw a familiar figure mounting the steps to press the doorbell. 'Mr Carrington,' she called, 'Is that really you?'

He turned towards her with a smile. She thought he looked older and thinner. As he did so, the door opened and there was

Verity, her hair covered with a scarf, her figure with a full-length floral pinny. She looked like a charlady, but Carrington's cheeks flushed pink at the sight of her and he held out his hand in greeting.

Inside the house, Verity shooed them through to the kitchen and filled the kettle for tea. 'I don't know what you must think of me,' she said, whipping the scarf off her head and running her fingers through her hair. 'We've been packing all day long and it's simply chaotic upstairs. Nanny Jenkins is so very particular and I have to do everything exactly as she says.'

Carrington sat meekly, waiting for the offered cup of tea. 'I must apologise if I've called at an inconvenient time but I wanted to come as soon as I could.'

'That's perfectly all right,' Dora said. 'When did you get back?'

'We only arrived in London yesterday. It might have been sooner, but the Germans insisted on recalling all their embassy staff from every country first before any of us could leave.'

'And were they simply awful to you? After the declaration that we're at war, I mean?' Verity poured tea at the table.

He accepted the cup and a digestive biscuit, smiling and shaking his head. 'They were actually very polite and treated us all very well. It looked a bit alarming to begin with, when the soldiers arrived at the embassy, late that very first afternoon. They were armed and accompanied by Gestapo. They cut the phone lines, then they took us all to a very decent establishment, the Hotel Adlon.'

'Oh, very nice indeed,' Dora said, knowing the luxurious hotel's reputation for grandeur. 'Did they let you stay there in comfort, until it was time to come home?'

'No, after a couple of days we were moved to Bad Nauheim, a few hours away from Berlin, under armed arrest. It was pretty cushy though, as it's a resort, so we were quite comfortable. Arrangements were eventually made through Swiss diplomats to exchange us for the German embassy staff here in Britain. All very civilised.'

'Gosh, but it must have been tense, all the same.' Verity leant forward, her hands embracing her cup, her eyes totally fixed on Carrington. 'You must have all been terribly worried about when they'd let you leave, even so.'

'Well, I can't say it's something we want to repeat but I think we have to thank our ambassador for it being so bearable. From start to finish, he's been the supreme diplomat, despite what some are saying. He couldn't persuade them to let us take all our effects out of the country though. Our stuff is all still in limbo in Switzerland.'

'Oh, you poor thing. Have you come home with absolutely nothing?'

He stopped being serious and almost chuckled at Verity's overdramatic show of concern. 'They must have thought we might be smuggling valuables or top-secret documents out of the country. I don't know if we'll ever get it all back.'

'But thank goodness you're all safe and well,' Dora said. 'It could have been much worse for you. And what will happen now?'

He sighed and said, 'I'm not entirely sure. The ambassador wants another posting, but we all know he's in ill health, so that's unlikely. As for me, well, I suppose I'll have to join up. Or my fluent German may possibly take me somewhere else.'

Dora guessed what he could be implying. Linguists were valuable, particularly nondescript ones. He might not have a front-line role, but could be deployed in some shady branch of an unnamed service tucked away out of sight. 'We'll all have to do our bit, I suppose, wherever we're needed.'

'And I imagine you'll still have your work cut out here, despite the unfortunate halt to your Kindertransports?'

'Indeed.' Dora sighed. 'The office is inundated with cries for help. Most of the time all we can do is advise. But we act as a central point for families to stay in touch too, as much as they can in the circumstances.'

'And we're off to Yorkshire,' Verity said. 'I'm rather looking forward to it. We think it would be the safest place for the children. Oh, do you know about the children here?'

'I'd heard,' he said with a nod towards Dora. 'It's wonderful that you've been able to give a home to a few unfortunates at least. But you must have your work cut out.'

'Oh, we called on my old nanny to help. She couldn't wait to take charge down here and escape from her tedious retirement.' Verity giggled, 'I can honestly say it's been the most fun since she's been with us. I knew nothing about babies and little children before, but it's been utterly joyful.'

'Apart from when Ruth ate too many strawberries that time,' Dora added.

Verity grimaced. 'Oh, yuk, yes, that was disgusting! She's wary of them now. But I think it was all that cream more than the fruit.'

'And how long do you think you might stay up in Yorkshire?'

'Who knows? Everyone's saying that children should leave London as soon as possible, if they can. Many have already left, whole families and entire schools, I believe.'

'The station was full of them when we came back yesterday,' Carrington said. 'It reminded me of you with your train-loads out of Berlin. Lines of them, all tagged with labels and little suitcases. Very young, some of them. But lots smiling and looking as if they thought they were off on a jolly holiday.' He looked thoughtful.

'And then there's you with no luggage whatsoever.' Verity laughed. 'Whatever have things come to?'

They all went quiet for a moment and in that stillness they heard cries from upstairs and then the patter of feet on the main staircase and down the steps into the kitchen. Ruth peered round the door. 'Vee, Nanny wants to know what's keeping you?'

'Gosh, I'd better go.' Verity leapt up. 'She's an absolute tyrant.' She held out her hand. 'Mr Carrington, it's been delightful to see you again. Do keep in touch.'

'Rufus, please,' he said in a hesitant voice. 'I'd like you both to call me Rufus.'

'Very well, Rufus, and you must call me Verity.' She fluttered her fingers at him from the doorway, then they heard her scampering up the stairs.

Dora smiled to herself at this exchange as Carrington, now Rufus, glowed with happiness. Verity had also seemed to twinkle as she basked in his admiration of her.

Ruth hung back, shyly staring at their visitor. And Dora realised that she hadn't introduced her. 'Rufus, this is Ruth, who I told you about. She has been living with us since the spring, because her aunt in London was no longer able to take care of her.'

They shook hands and Rufus said, 'Do you like living here and learning to speak English?'

'Yes. I have lots of friends and we all speak English.' Then she frowned and said, 'But I'm forgetting how to speak German. I'm worried my mutti won't understand me when I see her again.'

Dora realised, to her shame, that she had spent so much time encouraging Ruth to speak her new language that she had quite forgotten about the voice of her homeland. How could she have done that? Of course the child mustn't forget everything about her birthplace and her family. Despite the dangers she'd faced, she hoped to return to her mother one day.

But Rufus patted the chair beside him and said, 'Wir können jetzt Deutsche sprechen, wenn Sie möchten.'

Ruth nodded and sat beside him. A beaming smile spread across her face as she spoke to him in rapid swoops of excited

German. Words tumbled from her as she talked of her school-friends, how she helped care for the twins and how she loved to visit the baker and choose cakes for tea.

Dora stared at them both for a second, then had to excuse herself and stand outside in the garden. She breathed deeply for a moment, hearing the rhythmic conversation continue behind her, the words and laughter indoors blending with the soft soothing clucks of the hens in their run.

The lump in her throat melted away and her tears didn't spill over. But her heart warmed as she thought how beautiful life could be when, only days after war had been declared between the two countries, an Englishman could converse in German with a Jewish German in the spirit of peace and friendship. One day, it would no longer be remarkable and all faiths would be able to live together in harmony.

SIXTY-SIX

ROSA

As a skilled dressmaker, more used to working with silks and finely woven wool, Rosa found the coarse fabric offensive to both her eye and her touch. She detested the crude design, printed on rough yellow cotton. Yellow, the colour for plague and pestilence since the Middle Ages, was also traditionally the colour that singled out the Jews. Thick black lines printed on the crude material formed the shape of a six-pointed star, the star of David. The single word *Jude* was stamped in the centre, as if it was an insult. And to make matters even worse, she'd had to buy these ugly emblems with her own money.

From that month, every Jew in Berlin and every child over the age of six was meant to buy four stars so every one of their outer garments would carry one. As if there was a need for so many stars when hardly anyone owned more than one coat or jacket now, Rosa thought as she stabbed her needle into the offensive material.

Produced by the well-established factory Geite Fahnenfabrik, the stars were being distributed to Jewish communities across the country. The company was more used to manufacturing flags and banners than insults, but they had willingly

accepted the lucrative order for a million stars. And the Association of German National Jews had been forced to agree to
distribute the hateful badges. They bought them in at three
pfennig and sold them on for ten pfennig each.

Why must they profit from us? Rosa asked as she pinned the
first star to her daughter's coat. But she assumed the organisation would use the money for essential medicines and food for
the community. And she also knew she was luckier than some.
She'd been able to sell a bracelet she'd kept hidden in the lining
of her coat to buy the stars, but some people couldn't spare coins
for badges when they were desperately in need of bread.

Threading her needle with matching silk, Rosa made her
first stitches, turning the edges of the fabric for a tidy finish. If
they were being forced to wear these crude emblems, then she
and Theresia would have the best and the neatest in their whole
community. She was not going to spoil their clothes, shabby
though they now were, with badly sewn stars. No, theirs would
be the smartest – and also the most secure. Theirs would never
fall off their clothes by accident. They couldn't risk being seen
without a star. The ruling stated that there would be severe
punishment for anyone who failed to wear it. And rumours
confirmed that the penalty usually meant being shot dead on
the spot.

'Mutti, why do we have to have stars on our coats?' Theresia
held up one of the unsewn emblems and held it against her
dress. Now nine, she was nearly old enough to understand, but
Rosa continued to spin a fable to shield her from the awful
truth.

'Because we are very special, Liebchen. We are better than
the ordinary Germans. We aren't like them.'

'Better than Liese?'

'No, Liese is special too, but in a different way. She is kind
and loyal.'

Rosa hoped her friend would stay safe, far from Berlin and

the war, with her family in the countryside. Liese had written a couple of times, but Rosa couldn't be sure if her own replies were ever received. She hoped they would see each other again when the war was over, but who knew who would survive these turbulent times?

Rosa had given Liese the address of the letter she had received from London. 'When you return to Berlin, if you find we've gone, please write and tell them so my babies will know I never forgot them.'

'Can Elsa have a star too?' Theresia held out her doll, dressed in finery far grander than she, made from remnants Rosa had collected in the workshop where she and Josef had once made fashionable suits and dresses.

Rosa couldn't help smiling. 'Of course she can. She's very special too.' And she'll have a very special star, she thought. A little scrap of yellow silk brocade, not this coarse cotton. She'll have the finest star of them all.

'And do Esther and Josef have to wear stars in England?' Theresia often asked about her baby brother and sister and Rosa tried to answer her questions honestly.

'No, not at all. Everyone in England is special. They don't need badges there.' *But will they one day?* she wondered. Everyone knew that Germany had invaded Holland and then France the year before. Britain was no distance from France, a short hop across the narrow channel of sea. *If the war goes well for Germany, if they continue advancing, will my youngest children still be safe in Britain?* Rosa knotted her final stitch on the hateful yellow star and bit the thread with a vicious tug.

SIXTY-SEVEN
ROSA
BERLIN, MARCH 1943

Dearest Mother,

I have no idea whether this letter is likely to reach you as I have no money for a stamp. I shall just trust that it might land in your hands one day.

Today our whole street has been ordered to gather in the synagogue in Levetsowstrasse in the Moabit district. We have been instructed to bring all our belongings with us, which means Theresia and I shall each carry only a very small bundle as that is all we now possess. All my furniture went long ago, sold or burned for firewood, and the mattress we have is torn and filled with vermin. I shall be glad to leave it behind for my German neighbours, who have shown us no sympathy despite being former customers of ours.

Liese is the only neighbour who was bravely loyal to us throughout, despite her own hardships. She left Berlin for the countryside nearly two years ago with her children. I miss her and she was often able to bring food, but she will be safer there if the bombing gets worse. We have not experienced much so far, but it is bound to increase as the war continues.

I have asked Liese to write to you if we do not return to Berlin when this war is over. I have also asked her to write to the address I received from London. I hope that Theresia and I will come back one day, but if we don't, I want my children to know that we never forgot them.

Tomorrow we have been told we have to walk all the way to Grunewald station. It will be a long tiring walk of more than two hours and I expect some in our large community will not have the strength for the journey.

I hope Theresia won't remember the last time she sat in a train and ask again why she couldn't go. I know now that I should have left her there. It was selfish of me to want to keep my child – I should have sent all my children away to safety.

There will be hundreds if not thousands of us at the station tomorrow and we have been told that trains will be waiting to take us east for work. I suppose that will be a journey of many hours too, so I have some bread in my pocket for Theresia. I like to think that work might mean money and food, but I doubt that in wartime Poland there will be much work for a skilled dressmaker.

In some ways I shall be sorry to leave Berlin, where we were happy for several years before life changed. Also, the train will take me further away from Josef, if he is still in Dachau. I pray that he is surviving, but we hear terrible reports about the camps and I fear the worst for both him and us.

But I must remain positive for Theresia. I cannot let her see how afraid I am, so I shall keep her close by my side and tell her we shall all be together again one day, speaking English with her brother and sister.

Your loving daughter,

Rosa

EPILOGUE

ESTHER, 2023

So, there you are. That's our story. Now you can see how Josef and I owe everything to Dora. Though I suppose we owe it to our mother too, for making that impulsive last-minute decision. She literally threw us into the arms of a stranger and that saved us.

We owe it to the children too, the ones who travelled with us on that train, for keeping quiet, and to Dora for keeping her nerve. It must have been terrifying when the train slowed and they thought they would be questioned by the guards who came aboard. They could all have been arrested if we'd been discovered and the children could have been sent back to their parents. When we were little we often asked Dora to tell us that part of the story again and we always laughed at the bit about the lipstick and the measles. Then Dora would dab some of her lipstick on our cheeks so we could look in the mirror and re-enact the whole scene on the train with lots of shrieking and laughter.

Dora wrote an account of that journey and how she received us into her arms. She told us the story many times and said that she was greatly relieved our compartment was not entered before the train reached Holland. What would have happened if the train had been searched, I dread to think. It's bad enough knowing how the children's luggage was searched, with dolls thrown out onto the tracks, but imagine if that had been real babies. They were quite capable of doing that, you know.

Our mother's letter means a lot to us. Dora kept it in the envelope that was in our basket. We have the photographs as well. On the back of one of them it says *Rosa and Josef Goldberg, 1930*, so we've assumed it was taken around the time of their marriage. It's important for us to be able to gaze at that picture and feel that we know something of our parents. The other photograph is of a chubby little girl with dark curls. She looks as if she is about a year old. A pencilled note on the back simply says *Theresia, 1932*.

It's nice to think we might once have had a larger family, but then that means our dear mother had another child to protect, who we assume couldn't be sent away. She'd have been about seven when we were born, so maybe our big sister was allowed to hold us for a while. But perhaps it would have been better if we didn't have other brothers or sisters. Can you imagine how dreadful it would have been for our mother, clutching the hands of older siblings as she walked into the gas chamber?

And Josef once said to me, 'I know our mother couldn't have known what went on in the camps, but I think it's a good thing she didn't keep us. You know what happened to twins in the hands of their Nazi doctors.' Well, I do know and I don't even like to think about it. While it would have meant we were saved for a time, it's horrific to even begin to ask what we might have suffered with those awful experiments. Thank goodness we were saved from such terrors.

We also have the tiny woollen bonnets we were wearing the day we were given to Dora. They are safely wrapped in tissue paper, to protect them from moths. I don't know how often Josef has looked at his, but I've held mine many times, thinking maybe our mother knitted them herself when she knew she was expecting us. It makes me feel close to her. I understand that yarn would have been in short supply by then, so perhaps she unravelled an old shawl or sweater to make sure we had something to keep us warm.

Dora's report recorded that she wrote to our mother at the address she had given on the letter, soon after we were safely in England. But she never received a reply, despite writing several more times. She always told us she hoped she had followed our mother's wishes and respected the trust our mother had placed in her.

I think the same was true for Ruth, who we grew up with thinking she was our big sister. She too was saved by Dora and Verity and lived with us until we were old enough to make our way in the world. Ruth has also had a happy life, although she never heard any more from her parents. Her elderly aunt and uncle in London never did come to claim her – I suppose they were too old and infirm to cope with a child. They left her their house in Hampstead in their wills though, so that was a great help to her.

When we were children, we were fascinated by the scar on Ruth's back. She was shy about it when she was young, but as she grew up she was willing to talk about how it happened and was prepared to talk openly about those terrible times as a warning to others. We were proud of her for doing that.

Dora often told us that we and Ruth were her family; she regarded us as her children. Maybe that is why she and Hugh never had children of their own, or maybe they felt the time had passed once the war was over.

But Verity had a family eventually. We didn't know all about her history until we were much older. We often returned to the big house in Yorkshire for summer holidays, where she lived with her husband, Rufus. They were very happy together and it was great fun for us children, playing with their two daughters. When we were old enough to understand, Verity told us about her first husband, Raven, and how she had eventually taken his ashes to Ireland. I thought it sounded very romantic.

Of course, we had happy memories of growing up in Yorkshire, even attending the village school for a time. Verity always said she had grown to love her family home because we were there. And when Rufus married her after his time away, she said she loved it even more.

We never got to hear exactly how he spent the rest of the war though and whenever we asked he'd always wink, tap his nose and say, 'I'm not allowed to tell, on pain of death.' That always made us squeal. He was no longer a diplomat or civil servant, but learnt to manage the family estate and opened the big house for visitors. Vee and Rufus are with us no longer now, of course, but their children have managed to make tourism profitable and the house and gardens receive thousands of visitors every year, like many other minor stately homes.

We also met Brenda Bradshaw, Dora's senior colleague, several times. Dora always said that Brenda's common sense and strength of mind were a great comfort to her on those journeys and the times when they were confronted with Nazi threats. We didn't get to know her very well, but I can remember our last visit to see her when she was quite frail, in her nineties. She was in a nursing home by then, but still very alert. She remembered us both and when I asked if there was anything I could get for her, she just smiled and said, 'Bring me glad tidings of great joy.' I like to think that our news about our thriving families was exactly that and brought her happiness as we showed her photos of our children and grandchildren. She must have taken great pleasure in knowing that the children she saved had gone on to produce families to replace those that were lost.

Years later, when Josef and I were older, we contacted the Association of Jewish Refugees to find out what had happened in the part of Berlin we had come from. We knew it wouldn't be good news, but we couldn't establish exactly what had gone on, although the first deportation from that area didn't happen until the autumn of 1941. Life must have been very difficult by then with people crammed together in terrible conditions, short of food. The largest deportation happened in the spring of 1943, when twelve thousand were horded together and then crammed on to trains that took them to ghettos in Poland. And we know what that meant in the end.

We'd like to think our mother may also have ended up in Dachau. It would be nice to think that she and our father were reunited and that's what we like to tell ourselves. But it's not very likely. By then the camp was packed with thousands of starving prisoners. The best we can hope for is that they saw each other again but didn't last long there.

But we do have reason to think that before our mother was forced to leave Berlin, Dora's first letter did reach her. And maybe, having received the good news that we were alive and well, she could leave with the hope that she would find us again one day. After the war was over, Dora received a letter from our mother's friend, Liese. She'd been given the address by our mother and she confirmed that we'd had a sister and that she and our mother were still alive at the end of 1942, according to letters she'd received.

Years later, Josef suggested we could look at the transport list of people who were made to leave Berlin. Funny, isn't it, how efficient the Germans always were? No covering their tracks there. We found several Goldbergs on the list and among them a Rosa and a Theresia. But the address given for them was not the one on the letter we have, so we can't be totally sure it's our mother and sister. However, we believe they probably had to leave Berlin in 1943, in that mass deportation, crowded onto trains destined for Poland, maybe for the Lodz ghetto, maybe directly to Auschwitz. We think that must be where they finally met their fate. You see, we feel sure that, if our mother had survived the war, she would have made contact with the Quakers in London and they would have been able to trace us.

Sometimes, Josef has asked me if I'd like to visit the camps, but I don't think I want to imagine the horrors in any more detail than I do already. I've heard of other Kinde, as we are known, whose family belongings have been discovered in Auschwitz. Suitcases that still contained photographs and letters. That might be comforting perhaps, to see pictures of our parents and maybe other relatives, to know something of our history. You see, Josef and I don't really know who we are.

But what we do know is that we are husband, wife, mother, father and grandparent. And we know that we were saved to make a good life. We thank our mother for having the courage to give us away and Dora for accepting us into her arms. We think that is a mark of true love and not a brand of evil.

A LETTER FROM SUZANNE

Thank you so much for choosing to read *The Twins on the Train*. If you enjoyed it, and want to keep up to date with all my latest novels, just sign up at the following link. Your email address will never be shared and you can unsubscribe at any time:

www.bookouture.com/suzanne-goldring

I hope you have enjoyed *The Twins on the Train* and if you did, I would be very grateful if you could write a review. I really appreciate hearing what readers think of my books and it makes such a difference helping new readers discover one of my novels for the first time. I love hearing from my readers and you can get in touch through my website or social media.

www.suzannegoldring.wordpress.com

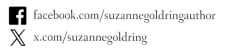

facebook.com/suzannegoldringauthor

x.com/suzannegoldring

AUTHOR'S NOTE

I find it hard to imagine the degree of fear that can prompt parents to send their children away with strangers, to a country where they can't speak the language. And how afraid of the future does a mother have to be to give away her newborn babies?

I was inspired to write this book when I discovered that British Quakers had been absolutely pivotal in making the famous Kindertransports happen. Despite having a Quaker stepmother, to whom this book is dedicated, I'm ashamed to say that I had been completely unaware of their important role, for which they won the Nobel Peace Prize in 1947. This was awarded jointly to the Friends Service Council of London and the American Friends Service Committee (AFSC) in Philadelphia, 'for their pioneering work in the international peace movement and compassionate effort to relieve human suffering, thereby promoting the fraternity between nations'.

Mindful of this important recognition, it seemed entirely appropriate to me to quote the words attributed to Edmund Burke at the start of this book: *It is necessary only for the good man to do nothing for evil to triumph*. I am aware that this attribution has often been questioned and I debated whether I should still use it, but I have great faith in The Oxford Dictionary of Quotations as an impeccable source. Furthermore, the words seemed particular applicable to the efforts of the Quakers. For if they had not been monitoring alarming developments in Germany and they had not lobbied the British Government, the Kindertransports would not have been mounted on such a tremendous scale with such enormous success.

When I began my research into the role the Quakers played in establishing the Kindertransports, I became fascinated by the depth of knowledge their representatives must have acquired through their extensive charitable works in Germany following the First World War. Their help for impoverished families and children meant they were widely respected in the country and were able to closely observe the changes being made by the Nazi Party when it came into power. In their party manifesto in 1920, the Nazi Party publicly declared their intention to segregate Jews from Aryan society. Then, during the first six years of Hitler's dictatorship, over four hundred decrees and regulations restricted all aspects of Jewish life. I have made only brief references to these restrictions in my novel, but Quaker volunteers, close to the affected communities, were clearly alarmed by developments. In daring to question the new regime they often met opposition and even imprisonment, but did not cease to work for peace and to help families escape oppression.

For that reason, I chose to begin my story in the years before the Kindertransports started. I feel it is important to understand the climate of the time and also to understand how the Nazis became so powerful. It was also interesting to discover that many in Britain approved developments in Germany and loved to visit its historic cities and countryside. But it was a shock to find that some visited and approved of Dachau, which was the model for the many concentration camps that followed.

All the most dramatic incidents I've covered in this story are based entirely on actual eyewitness accounts, although I have to admit that the basket thrust onto a departing train contained one baby in real life and not two. That account was covered in a couple of brief lines I discovered deep in material from the Quaker archives in London. There was no information on who the mother had been, nor on the girl who had received the basket, equipped with a baby's milk bottle and nappies.

In a similar way, I uncovered the incident of the mother who couldn't decide whether her daughter should undertake the journey to Britain and removed her three times. Also, the awful pain inflicted on the girl who was branded came to light in a report in the archives. These accounts illustrated to me how horrifying those times must have been, but there must have been many hundreds more unrecorded examples.

The more I learnt about the integrity of the Quakers, the more I appreciated that their work was absolutely crucial in making the Kindertransports actually happen. Their lobbying of British politicians and liaison with other refugee charities brought 10,000 children to the UK, to safety. They didn't have long to accomplish this enormous task, not even a whole year; they started in December 1938 and finished at the end of August 1939, just days before war was declared.

As I delved into the Quaker archives I became aware that, while the whole organisation was responsible for this huge achievement, individual stubborn and courageous women undertook lengthy trips to negotiate the transports. Bertha Bracey, the model for my Brenda, was involved in charitable work in Germany from 1921, when she was in her late twenties. Her detailed knowledge and tireless work helped to convince the British government that the evacuation and hosting of children could be accomplished. Florence Nankivell undertook the first transport from Berlin, in the centre of the Nazi world, despite being hassled by Nazi police.

At every stage, these indomitable women were belittled,

bullied, accused of smuggling and spying and sometimes briefly imprisoned. The incidents I have described where they confront Nazi officials in the Braunes Haus and have to deal with the arrogance and rudeness of Eichmann are based entirely on factual accounts. (The remarks made by Eichmann are taken almost verbatim from a report by the woman he insulted.) So is the incident involving the 'lucky stones' that turn out to be real diamonds, at a time when the state was confiscating all valuables from Jews.

And in contrast to these tireless workers, who knew they could eventually return to their homes, far from danger, I have included scenes showing the impact of the harsh Nuremberg restrictions on the Jewish people of Berlin. I chose to focus on a moderately comfortable Jewish couple, both born in Germany, who had established a successful business. Rosa and Josef had reason to think that they would continue to prosper, that these 'difficulties' would blow over and that they could stay in Berlin making fine suits and dresses. It seemed to me that with restrictions mounting, they were all sitting on a time bomb, which escalated after the horrors of Kristallnacht. One moment Rosa had a comfortable life and prospects, the next, without a husband, with Jewish businesses vandalised and forced to close, her life was shattered. Contemporary accounts of the terrible times they encountered helped me to imagine the horror of that dreadful night in November 1938 and subsequent events. But even so, I was continually shocked by the facts themselves, such as the ban on firemen actually doing the job they had been trained for.

I hope I have done justice to the stupendous efforts of the Quakers. They fed the children and then they saved the children. And I hope I have respected the memory of those who were not able to escape, but tried to keep hoping times would change.

REFERENCES

Travellers in the Third Reich – Julia Boyd

Germany 1945 – Richard Bessel

Endgame, 1945 – David Stafford

Auschwitz – Laurence Rees

Escaping the Nazis on the Kindertransport – Emma Carlson Berne

I Came Alone – Bertha Leverton and Shmuel Lowensohn

Flags in Berlin – Biddy Youngday

A Child Alone – Martha Blend

Pearls of Childhood – Vera Gissing

Failure of a Mission: Berlin 1937–1939 – Nevile Henderson

The Jewish Museum London – jewishmuseum.org.uk

World Jewish Relief – worldjewishrelief.org

United States Holocaust Memorial Museum – ushmm.org

ACKNOWLEDGEMENTS

I could not have fully understood the extent of the work undertaken by the Quakers without the guidance of Oliver Robertson and Lucy Saint-Smith from the library at Friends House in London, who directed me to their archive material. I am extremely grateful for their help, which gave me the context for the tremendous efforts undertaken in negotiating and facilitating the transports. And I must also thank a present-day Quaker, Loveday Craig-Wood, for that introduction.

During the long process of writing this novel I have been supported and encouraged by writer friends, particularly the Vesta girls, Carol McGrath, Denise Barnes and Gail Aldwin. Sharing regular extracts with the Elstead Writers Group has also ensured I did not lose sight of my intention to fully explore the climate of pre-war Germany.

And most importantly I greatly appreciate the insights of my editor Lydia Vassar-Smith, who always encourages me to take a step beyond what I thought was possible. I am so grateful for her support and also that of my former agent Heather Holden-Brown and her successor, Elly James. They all helped me to keep a sense of proportion when the task looked impossible.

Lastly, I must thank the entire talented and professional Bookouture team whose skill lifts my books off the page and into colourful reality. Many thanks for this, my eighth book with all of you.

PUBLISHING TEAM

Turning a manuscript into a book requires the efforts of many people. The publishing team at Bookouture would like to acknowledge everyone who contributed to this publication.

Audio
Alba Proko
Sinead O'Connor
Melissa Tran

Commercial
Lauren Morrissette
Hannah Richmond
Imogen Allport

Cover design
Eileen Carey

Data and analysis
Mark Alder
Mohamed Bussuri

Editorial
Lydia Vassar-Smith
Lizzie Brien

Copyeditor
Jacqui Lewis

Proofreader
Jane Donovan

Marketing
Alex Crow
Melanie Price
Occy Carr
Cíara Rosney
Martyna Młynarska

Operations and distribution
Marina Valles
Stephanie Straub
Joe Morris

Production
Hannah Snetsinger
Mandy Kullar
Jen Shannon
Ria Clare

Publicity
Kim Nash
Noelle Holten
Jess Readett
Sarah Hardy

Rights and contracts
Peta Nightingale
Richard King
Saidah Graham

Made in United States
North Haven, CT
02 December 2024

61528753R00214